I0778877

IN THE PALACE OF THE GREAT KING

a Catholic Novel

Julie Ash

Also by Julie Ash

Wild Grace: a pictorial pilgrimage to Clear Creek Abbey

Verbum Bonum Books
Locust Grove, Oklahoma
www.julieash.com

For my son, Daniel Troy Kipp, and for all the saints.

Through you, God showed me the truth among the lies

and taught me how to love as He loves:

with sacrifice, fidelity, patience, and devotion.

CONTENTS

Prologue: Catching the Bus ... 1

Chapter 1: "Behold the Heart" ... 5

Chapter 2: A Tale of Two Sisters ... 16

Chapter 3: "Bitter Sweet Symphony" ... 25

Chapter 4: A Secret in the Attic ... 29

Chapter 5: Boys and Babies ... 32

Chapter 6: Ten Thousand Souls in India ... 38

Chapter 7: Una Buena Chica ... 42

Chapter 8: No Shorts in Church ... 55

Chapter 9: La Imitación de Cristo ... 63

Chapter 10: False Alarm ... 72

Chapter 11: Doing the Best I Can, Part 1 ... 80

Chapter 12: No Deposit, No Return ... 89

Chapter 13: Doing the Best I Can, Part 2 ... 94

Chapter 14: All Hallows' Eve ... 100

Chapter 15: Visibilium et Invisibilium ... 117

Chapter 16: All Saints' Day ... 125

Chapter 17: Ecce Adsum ... 146

Chapter 18: Family Secrets ... 161

Chapter 19: Christ the King ... 174

Chapter 20: Advent ... 182

Chapter 21: Happy Indeed Is She ... 188

Chapter 22: Ecce Fiat ... 194

PART TWO: INTO THE NEW MILLENNIUM … 198

Chapter 23: Wait for Me … 199

Chapter 24: What Are You? … 206

Chapter 25: Pray for Me … 212

Chapter 26: The Nun's Story … 219

Chapter 27: "Drink at the Spring" … 225

Chapter 28: Nuns and Extraterrestrials … 232

Chapter 29: Bittersweet Symphony … 245

Chapter 30: Full of Grace … 251

Chapter 31: When Did We See You? … 254

Chapter 32: Treasure on Troy Hill … 258

Chapter 33: Help Wanted … 266

Chapter 34: I'll Be Home for Christmas … 272

Chapter 35: Time to Think … 278

Chapter 36: Green Bean Casserole … 288

Chapter 37: Converging … 292

Chapter 38: In the Churches … 299

Chapter 39: The Gates of Hell Shall Not Prevail … 307

Chapter 40: The Fire of His Love … 311

Chapter 41: Yours and All for You … 328

Postscript: Somewhere in Hell … 338

Acknowledgements … 343

For More Information … 344

About the Author … 344

Notes … 345

Prologue: Catching the Bus

*A*slan, a scarred old veteran of the alley-cat wars, sat calmly on the living room rug. With the peaceful dignity of age and the brainless apathy of a couch potato, voluminous folds of fat tucked comfortably beneath his furry legs, he was the picture of spoiled royalty.

Suddenly, a little black and white cannonball hurled itself from behind the sofa, leaped through the air, and trampolined off Aslan's back. Gleefully the little creature rebounded from her first assault, careening around the room like a hyperactive boomerang. Briefly stunned, Aslan lurched heavily at his attacker and hissed. Wookie rolled and jumped sideways, deftly avoiding his claws. She batted his old yellow head with a rapid combination of lightning sucker punches. Then, before her hapless victim could recover, she dashed left and in a split second vanished behind the television.

On the other side of the apartment, Linda Wallace was busy getting ready for work. She was an LPN—licensed practical nurse—in the pediatrics department at the world-renowned Cleveland Clinic. She had just finished tying her shoes when two loud thuds, followed by hissing snarls and the patter of running feet, brought her into the living room, where she caught the perpetrator red-handed...er, red-pawed.

"Oh no, not again!" she sighed. "Not again!"

Aslan was confused. He pounced after his assailant, but before he could catch her, Wookie sped around the room, dashed behind, up, and over the couch, and darted into the dining room. Down the hall she disappeared. Aslan gave chase, then stopped. He'd scared her off! Peace at last. Mission accomplished. Good riddance! He licked his shoulder in victory, curled up in a gelatinous yellow ball, and went to sleep.

"Oh my goodness! You two are somethin' else!" Linda laughed loudly at this latest fight contest between her new kitten, Wookie, and her big orange tabby cat, Aslan.

After a while, Wookie tiptoed back into the kitchen nonchalantly. She rubbed against the corner cabinet as though nothing had happened and then wandered over to nibble at her food dish. Aslan snored in peace.

"Wookie!" Linda said accusingly, "You ought to be ashamed of yourself!" She then walked over to console Aslan, scratching behind his ears. "Aslan, you poor baby!"

The chubby old tabby smiled happily in his sleep.

Glancing at the clock, Linda saw it was already time to go. She stood and buttoned her coat over her nurse's uniform, tied a nylon scarf under her chin, and reached for her purse. The bus would be here soon. Their driver was always on time. Checking to make sure the coffee pot was turned off, she grabbed her keys from the bottom of her purse and let herself out into the chilly, damp September dawn.

Fumbling, she clumsily dropped the keys in the doorway.

"Shoot!" She bent over stiffly to retrieve them.

Through the open door, Wookie darted out silently past her feet, unseen. Just as Linda was about to close and lock the door, the runaway kitten caught her eye. The black and white phantom curled herself around a pine tree, stealthily trying to hide.

"Hey, you." Linda stepped outside, bent down and picked Wookie up, and gently tossed her back into the apartment. "How many times are you gonna get locked out before you learn to stay home?" she scolded. "One of these days, a big ol' dog is gonna get you." She placed the key in the deadbolt and locked it, then hurried out to wait for the bus.

Undeterred, Wookie jumped up into the kitchen window and meowed in protest as she watched Linda walk towards the bus stop. Then, she stuck a wiry leg through a small crack in the screen and pushed as hard as she could.

As Linda waited, bus number 6 of the Cleveland Regional Transit Authority, known as the "RTA," rolled down Euclid Avenue with a soothing mechanical roar. Few passengers were out this early. Seeing the approaching coach, they reached for their wallets and clutched wrinkled dollar bills, grimy quarters, or bus passes. The long, white bus with the orange stripe, huge black tires, and dark-tinted Plexiglas windows glided rapidly towards them, coming so close you might think you were in danger of being run over. But the man behind the wheel was an expert driver. He had a dozen years of experience and could stop on a dime.

Hydraulic brakes screeching, the vehicle smoothly glided to a halt—forty-five to zero in three seconds flat, exactly three inches away from the curb. Cars behind cautiously processed around while the bus doors separated, elevator-style. Silently the glum-faced riders stepped up three steps, single file, into the long vehicle, carrying with them the pungent aroma of diesel engine exhaust.

The driver, a black man in his late sixties, was a veteran of many miles. While the engine efficiently hummed, he greeted them warmly as if they were special guests arriving at his party.

"Good morning!" his deep voice was gravelly, but full of good cheer.

"Transfer," muttered the first passenger, indicating he needed a free transfer to another bus to complete his journey.

"And how are you, sir?" The transfer card popped up from the fare box like toast from a toaster. The rider lifted it out and began walking to the back of the bus without answering.

"Good morning!" the driver said to Linda.

"Good morning!" she replied cheerfully.

"That cat of yours get out again?"

"She sure did," Linda said, sliding her bus pass through the machine. "If she don't stop, I'm gonna have to give her to my Aunt Bessie. Bessie never goes anywhere. And she lives on the tenth floor. No chance to get out from way up there!"

"Um-hmm! Cats and children—always runnin' away!" he replied.

Linda carefully made her way towards her favorite window seat close to the front. The driver repeated his hearty greeting eight more times until all the riders had entered, paid their fare, and slowly moved down the aisle to find seats. He watched over them from his rear view mirror, making sure all was in order as they seated themselves for the journey. Then, with a sideways glance towards the rear-coming traffic, he wrapped his strong arms around the steering wheel, and with a powerful roar of the diesel engine, they were on their way.

Steadily they rolled on. In just minutes, they passed old warehouses, apartment complexes, tall office buildings, and empty parking lots. As they reached the corner of 40th and Euclid Avenue, they passed a massive old stone church with towering Gothic spires and weathered cement steps. Deep inside, unknown and unseen, two cloistered Franciscan nuns were silently kneeling and praying in front of the Most Blessed Sacrament.

Chapter 1: "Behold the Heart"

A vowed patrol, in silent companies,
Life-long they keep before the living Christ.
In the dim church, their prayers and penances
Are fragrant incense to the Sacrificed.

– Ernest Dowson, "Nuns of the Perpetual Adoration"

Shrilly beeping, the ancient but determined electric Westclox instantly woke the sleeping abbess. Her dim eyes strained to see the numbers that glowed soft red from the clock perched apologetically on the small desk in the corner—the only furniture in the cell besides the small bed. It was ten minutes to four in the morning.

Willing herself awake, she raised herself to a sitting position and then in a single movement crossed the length of the cell to flick on the overhead bulb. Carefully so as not to splash, she bathed her face with cold water from the sink, slipped into the floor-length brown habit, and cinched the long white knotted Franciscan cord. The white guimpe and black veil lifted easily from their hook. After slipping on sturdy leather sandals, she stretched and yawned, then automatically reached for her gold-rimmed glasses. She was ready. Noiselessly stepping down the long hall into the forechoir, she glanced at her Timex watch. Four o'clock sharp. Sister Veronica's familiar footsteps gently padded close behind.

Two new prayer requests on the bulletin board caught her eye. John Dinsmore, an elderly parishioner and long-time friend of the monastery who was dying from complications of Parkinson's Disease had just taken a turn for the worse. The other was from an anonymous voicemail left by an unknown woman, frantic over her husband's firing the day before. With no money to pay the rent in two weeks, she feared they would be evicted and begged the prayers of the Sisters.

Reaching the door of the nuns' choir, Mother Mary Bonaventure blessed herself with holy water and quietly approached the two nuns kneeling before the altar. There, held in the nuns' gaze, the Sacred Host lay enthroned in an exquisite gold monstrance. A light was trained on the monstrance, making it glisten and shine. She and Sister Veronica made a profound genuflection, lyrical notes rising and falling in unison. Gracefully the two nuns whose places they were taking crossed themselves and did the same before returning to their cells. Mother Bonaventure and Sister Veronica knelt and together prayed the *Magnificat* and the Act of Adoration. Two divine encounters had ended; two more were about to begin.

A few cars passed on distant streets, muffled in the sleepy Cleveland darkness. Sister Veronica sighed. Deep within the choir, the atmosphere was peaceful. Walls of stained glass rose darkly all around them, the richly colored figures barely discernible in the weak moonlight. The honeyed scent of beeswax candles perfumed the air with a rich, smoky fragrance that was pungently intoxicating.

Gazing at the round white Host, an invigorating sense of warmth spread through Mother Bonaventure. Jesus Himself gazed back at her with the deepest, most profound love imaginable. Who could fathom it? It was a complete mystery to her why there weren't lines of young women pounding on the front door, begging to be let in. *If they only knew what it was like to be with Him, to belong to Him, she thought. If they only knew what they were missing...*

Reining in her wandering thoughts, she began to pray. First, prayers of love and praise. Then, heartfelt thanksgiving. So many blessings! Father Bradshaw's heart surgery had been a success! Their daughterhouse in India had finally raised the money to have their ancient water heater replaced. And the Ramirez child had been born healthy at full term, not prematurely as the doctors had feared. Finally, she offered prayers of petition—for their bene-factors, whose generous contributions enabled them to continue their way of life. Many people assumed that the nuns were supported by the Franciscan order or the local bishop. But that wasn't true. If it weren't for the generosity of ordinary people expressed in gifts large and small, they would have to take to the streets and beg like Saint Francis.

Next, she prayed for the man who had lost his job and for his family, and for all of the others who had asked the nuns for prayers—especially for dear old John Dinsmore. She begged God that he would die in the state of grace, that he would have a peaceful death—what used to be called a "happy" death—back when people prayed to Saint Joseph to be spared from an "unprovided" death. Back when people believed that to die suddenly, without time to call a priest, confess your sins, and receive absolution, meant the terrifying possibility of going to Hell.

Priests and bishops never talk about Hell anymore, she reflected. It didn't seem to fit with the modern idea of a loving, forgiving God. But many of the saints had had powerful, life-changing visions of Hell and Purgatory. Mother Bonaventure hadn't heard of any modern saints reporting visions of Jesus saying, "No, my child, you don't understand. When I said to fear the one who could send body and soul to Hell[1], I was only speaking metaphorically." Until then, she intended to go right on praying for God's mercy on the dying and the salvation—the saving—of souls. *No need for a Savior if there is nothing to be saved from,* she thought.

Forty years earlier, she had entered the monastery as a naïve nineteen-year-old. Raised in a happy, loving home, she'd had no idea of the vast extent of human suffering. After she became a religious, however, she soon learned. People from every walk of life—rich and poor, Catholics and non-Catholics alike—routinely begged the nuns' prayers.

---

[1] Gospel of Saint Matthew, 10:28.

The sisters heard it all. Sickness. Money worries. Lost jobs. Family fights. Childless couples longing for a baby. Crippling fears, deep depression, and crushing anxiety. Addictions, alcoholism, gambling, and infidelity. The list was practically endless. Quite often, they were asked to pray for family members serving in the military overseas. They were even asked to pray by college students afraid of failing their exams.

Years ago, these requests arrived in the mail in old-fashioned letters written in cursive, or conveyed in person in pleading whispers to the extern Sister at the nuns' turn, the big rotating cylinder where letters and packages were delivered just inside the front door. Today, they arrived in emails to the nuns' website or in voicemail messages left on the monastery phone. It didn't matter how they came—all were remembered, all were respected, all were prayed for. All were brought to the merciful Jesus with simple faith, great hope, and ardent love. The nuns were a silent but powerful presence in the city of Cleveland, night and day, since 1931. And yet, except for the few practicing Catholics in the neighborhood and the secular Franciscans who held their meetings in the monastery, no one really knew they were there or what they did all day.

The nuns believed it was their solemn duty and their special privilege to pray for the Church and the world. But there was more to being a nun—much more. There was something exciting and romantic to Mother Bonaventure about rising in the middle of the night to spend two precious hours with Jesus that made up for the perennial sacrifice of sleep. Sometimes, it was a real penance, and her eyes burned with exhaustion. But sometimes, like tonight, she felt like an eager young girl, secretly stealing away to meet her lover in the dark, quiet hours before dawn. Mother Bonaventure posed motionless on the wooden *prie-dieu*, her legs strong as steel from a lifetime spent on her knees. Despite the loss of sleep, she felt peaceful, rested, and refreshed. What would her meeting with the Lord bring tonight?

Prayers of reparation. Reparation—to repair. To fix. To make up for things stolen or lost, or for hurts inflicted. To kiss the wound and make it all better, as mothers often do. Anything could be offered in reparation. It was all in the intention. She could kneel all night and say all the right prayers, but if her intentions were wrong, if she did it out of a sense of pride or grudging duty, her actions would be less meaningful. She had to *intend* to make up for the sins and negligence of others, intend to make up to God for what was lacking, and atone for the appalling lack of love and obedience that were justly due to Jesus Christ as Lord of Heaven and Earth.

Jesus himself had asked for this back in 1675 in one of his appearances to Saint Marguerite-Marie Alacoque, a young French nun of the Visitation order. Opening her book of prayers, Mother Bonaventure meditated once again on the familiar, yet troubling, words:

"Behold the Heart which has so loved men that it has spared nothing, even to exhausting and consuming Itself, in order to testify Its love; and in return, I receive from the greater part only ingratitude, by their irreverence and sacrilege, and by the coldness and contempt they have for Me in this Sacrament of Love. But what I feel most keenly is that it is hearts which are consecrated to Me, that treat Me thus."

Ingratitude, coldness, and contempt—from priests and nuns? *May I never be cold to you, O Lord.*

She thought about the life-sized statue of the Sacred Heart of Jesus in the public side of Holy Angels Monastery. Surrounded by rows and rows of tall red glass candles, it was comforting to her just knowing it was there. If she looked out when she went to the Communion window, she could see the embracing arms of the statue stretched wide to welcome the whole world; but when she received Holy Communion, her eyes and her thoughts were firmly fixed on the Lord in the Most Blessed Sacrament. No need to gaze at statues then.

A few more silent minutes passed.

Dear Lord, please help the sick who are alone, all those who are abused—young children, the elderly.

Bless all those who are homeless and those who are unemployed. Help them find jobs, dear Lord. Help them find homes.

Help all those who are living in fear, those who suffer from mental illness and painful diseases. Help them get the help they need, dear Lord.

Bless our dear Holy Father and all bishops, priests, and religious. Help them to be faithful to their promises to You, and to their communities.

To their communities... She lowered her eyes and thought of her own community, a once-thriving holy sisterhood that had filled her heart and enclosed her body and soul for forty joyful years like a sturdy, beautiful beehive. But now, like dozens of other convents and monasteries around the world, the choir stalls were achingly, bewilderingly empty. As the older nuns passed on one by one, there were almost no young nuns there to take their places. She tried not to think about it because when she did, it broke her heart.

Tiny burning pinpricks stung the back of her eyelids.

Please, send us more vocations, dear Lord...

Since the tumultuous years following the Council, the number of young people entering the priesthood and religious life had dwindled to a mere trickle. The idea that God could be calling a young person to sacrifice his or her life in service to the Church solely for the love of God and one's fellow man seemed hopelessly sentimental, idealistic, and outdated. Modern life was all about finding yourself, being yourself, and enjoying yourself. Self-denial was a picture you took of yourself standing by a river in Africa, not a time-honored tool for attaining personal holiness and sanctification, whatever *that* was.

When Mother Bonaventure entered the Holy Angels Monastery on the Feast of the Presentation of Mary in 1962 as a nervous young postulant, she wasn't alone. Five prayerful, selfless young women had entered along with her. Back then, over thirty nuns had graced the smooth mahogany stalls, chanting the hymns, psalms, and antiphons of the Divine Office in Latin. With so many sisters, it had been fairly easy to always keep two nuns adoring Our Lord around the clock—keeping the "perpetual" in perpetual adoration.

But now, things were different. Years passed without a single letter addressed to *Reverend Mother Abbess* in a teenager's vaguely undisciplined cursive. No surprise visits at the grille from a nervous girl who had finally worked up the courage to tell Mother Abbess face-to-face her secret dream of being a nun. And it wasn't just her community that was suffering from a lack of vocations. It was like this everywhere.

After the radical upheaval that had barreled through the Church and society in the 1960s and 70s, a few of the nuns had asked for dispensations and left the order. Rewriting their constitutions, changing to shorter, simplified habits, and abandoning the timeless Latin prayers was too traumatic. The new Mass in English, where the priest faced the people instead of Jesus in the Tabernacle and the people received God's Precious Body standing up instead of kneeling at the Communion rail as had been the norm for hundreds of years, had seemed impossibly strange and unsettling. It was as though one morning everyone in America woke up and the president had ordered that from now on, to improve trade relations with our friends the Japanese, all street signs were to be in Japanese, and all drivers were to drive on the left side of the road rather than on the right. They wanted to obey, but somehow it seemed all wrong. What once had been second nature became awkward and confusing, and rules that had been in place for decades were suddenly tossed out like so much dirty bathwater.

When your superiors give you orders that seem wrong, what do you do? There were no easy answers. It was a difficult time. But somehow, many of the sisters made it through. They adapted, but the modernized Mass and religious garb mandated by Rome seemed to have had the opposite effect from what was supposedly intended. Rather than attracting young people with their campaign for modernization, it seemed to be repelling them. And now the stalwart, faithful nuns like Mother Bonaventure who had done as they were told and changed with the times were paying a hefty price.

Nuns like Mother Bonaventure who had steadfastly persevered were aging now. In January, they had buried their gentle long-time Sacristan, Sister Helena; their bespectacled, conservatory-trained organist, Sister Theodore Marie, had died of congestive heart failure the year before. Well into their seventies and eighties, there were only a handful left who could still handle the manual work required to keep their huge monastery running along with the ordinary day-to-day cooking and cleaning.

It was the same everywhere you looked. Mother Bonaventure had heard stories about the Dominican nuns in New Jersey and the Carmelites in New York who had been forced to leave their monasteries, monumental structures built in previous centuries, because they could no longer keep them up. Lack of vocations meant not only fewer sisters, but fewer donations as well. When young girls entered, their families could always be counted on to send gifts of money for their support. Young sisters were needed to keep the monastery running smoothly, doing the heavier work the elderly nuns could no longer perform. And young sisters always brought a liveliness, joy, and freshness to the monastery that made the burden of aging and the day-to-day monotony of cloistered life much easier to bear. Without them, it just wasn't the same. Knowing that other monasteries faced the same problems helped ease the sting, but it still didn't solve the problem.

And so they plodded on. In many communities, the elderly sisters couldn't be expected to navigate the long cloister halls and go up and down endless flights of stairs, so they prudently built smaller monasteries. Unfortunately, these new structures looked more like retirement homes, complete with handicap-accessible bathrooms and handrails, than monasteries where one wedded and worshipped the mysterious Triune God. These energy-efficient buildings were less costly to heat and easier to keep clean, but the old-world craftsmanship and materials so painstakingly worked in marble, glass, wood, and stone by immigrant Catholic craftsmen of the nineteenth century, and paid for by working-class Catholic families at great personal sacrifice, could never be replaced.

Priceless artistic depictions of the lives of Jesus, Mary, and the saints and the history of the Christian faith contained in those magnificent cloister chapels—the stained glass windows, lifelike statues, and artfully carved altars—had mostly been lost, and with it, the hopeful, calming presence of the Church in the inner city. Modernized parishes built in the suburbs in the 1980s and 90s looked more like motels than Catholic churches. They said it was because of changes in society that girls weren't becoming nuns anymore and the reason why Catholics were leaving the Church in droves, but she wondered.

To stay afloat, Mother Bonaventure had been forced in recent years to ask monasteries overseas for volunteer nuns to come to Cleveland and help out. And they came. These generous younger sisters hailed from Vietnam, India, Korea, and Bangladesh, where the people's faith had been sorely tried and proved in the fire of war and poverty. They were a welcome and much-needed addition to the monastery. These holy women sacrificed not only their secular lives, but their countries and families as well since most of their relatives were so poor that they could never afford to travel to the United States for a visit.

Although she was deeply grateful for their help, it seemed to Mother Bonaventure that this was only a temporary solution to their ongoing vocation problem. Perhaps they, too, one day would have to leave their beautiful home in favor of something smaller and more practical. The thought terrified her. Still, somehow she knew that God would provide. After all, it wasn't her job to figure out all the problems plaguing the Church. It was her job to keep praying, believing, and adoring. And that's exactly what she intended to do.

Mother Bonaventure looked at the exquisite beauty all around her and tried to imagine what it would be like to leave the place where she had lived, loved, and served God and the Church for forty years, but she couldn't fathom it. She trusted that He would provide, but as the years went by and no new vocations came, she found it hard at times to keep on trusting. Only God could give her that grace. So far, He had done so. What the future held wasn't so clear.

For a while, she simply rested in the Lord. Her second hour of Adoration was almost over. Time passed so quickly! She began to pray again, this time for the community of nuns under her care, her daughters in Christ. Ironically, many of her "daughters" were much older than she was. She was especially worried about Sister Marie Claire. At the age of a hundred and one, Sister Marie Claire still lived their life in community, determinedly pushing herself forward inch by inch on her aluminum walker with the tennis balls on the bottom so as not to scrape the hardwood floors, her rosary gently clacking on the metal bars.

But in March, Sister Marie Claire had caught a nasty virus that left her with a tired hacking cough for weeks. She seemed to rally around Easter, but for the past few days, she hadn't left the infirmary except for Mass, when Sister Agatha cheerfully wheeled her out in a wheelchair. She dozed through most of it, but at the Consecration and the Elevation, she watched Father Ambrose up at the altar with laser-like intensity until at last he brought her Holy Communion. Then, she would sink back, sighing against the blue woolen blanket which Sister Agatha had carefully folded over the back of the wheelchair, her frail body nearly disappearing, silently communing with her Jesus.

According to Sister Bernadette, the cheerful young Korean nun who faithfully brought Sister Marie Claire's meals to the Infirmary, Sister had hardly touched her food this past week, and although she displayed no other signs of illness than the lingering cough, it seemed to Mother Bonaventure as though Sister Marie Claire was preparing to cross the brave threshold to eternity any day now.

Chapter 2: A Tale of Two Sisters

You think you are at the center of things.
If you could only grasp that you are not ...

– Karol Wojtyla (Pope Saint John Paul II)
"Song of the Hidden God"

September 15, 1999
I was so miserable yesterday. I really felt like I was going to die! Everything has gotten pretty bad lately. My dumb sister Miss Perfect won't even talk to me anymore (not that I want her to.) She's too busy talking on the phone to even know if I exist. The only thing she says to me is "Tell Mom I'm going to Rachel's" or "Tell Mom me and Mercedes went to the mall." Or "If Eric calls" ... I hate her!!!!!!

Sept. 30

Halloween is just a month away, I can't wait!!! I can't decide if I want to be Queen Amidala or Sabrina the Teenage Witch! Kayla said she's too old to go trick or treating. How stuck up is that? She's only 13... She said her and her friends are going to have a Halloween party instead. I wish I had a nice big sister, instead of a little BRATTY one....

October 1, 1999

Today I got to go shopping with Krista. Krista's mom took us. I got some really cool Halloween makeup!!! Sparkly orange eye shadow and lip gloss. Fake long eyelashes and stick-on long fingernails. I already have the orange nail polish. I saved it from last year. Krista's mom is going to take us trick or treating. Then I can spend the night at Krista's house.

I wish Mom was more like Krista's mom.

Char Fisher closed and locked her secret journal and put it back in its hiding place under the mattress. It always made her feel better to write or to draw whenever she was upset about something.

Shutting the closet door, she got up and padded across the thick green carpet into the bathroom. Thoughtfully she planted herself in front of the full length mirror, gazing intently at her reflection. Large, clear blue eyes peered out of an almost pretty face that lately had started to break out. Her nose was rather pointed, and she had a bad habit of breathing through her mouth, which made her lips dry and chapped. Her hair was a pretty blonde color, but it was thin and limp, no matter how hard she tried to make it full. But her face had a delicate oval shape and an expression of kindness, sincerity, and intelligence.

Char was thin. But not the kind of thin that looked as if she had worked really hard to get that way. Char was too thin. She got so tired of listening to the other girls complain about being too fat, of not being able to lose weight, talking endlessly about diets. Nobody she knew actually wanted to gain weight—tried to gain weight—and couldn't. She felt like a freak. It wasn't fair!

Especially compared to her sister Kayla—beautiful, popular Kayla. Char burned with a familiar feeling of jealousy. They both had blonde hair and blue eyes, but any sisterly resemblance ended there. Kayla was a year younger, but looked at least a year older, due to feminine curves which Char did not possess. Kayla's hair was full and wavy, and her features were perfectly proportioned. She got good grades, danced in the River City Jazz Revue, and had a million friends. Everything about Kayla was attractive—including her dazzling smile. Char grimaced and stared disapprovingly at her own slightly crooked front teeth.

Even Kayla's name was pretty. Char. What a dumb name. She had always hated it. It wasn't even short for Charlotte, or Charmaine or Charlene. Just Char. Once, she had told her mother how much she disliked it.

"But it's a beautiful name! Don't you remember how we decided to name you after Lake Pontchartrain in New Orleans, Louisiana? Where Daddy and I had our honeymoon?"

How stupid! Named after a lake. *You're supposed to name lakes after people, not the other way around!* she wanted to yell. But it didn't matter why her mother had picked it. It was still an ugly name. It reminded her of the word "charred," and the other names she got called by the kids at school when she was younger, Charcoal and Charmin (like the toilet paper). One boy even called her "Shark-face" in third grade. Why did parents have to give their kids such stupid names?

Kayla. Now that's a pretty name.

Lately, every time the phone rang, it was for Kayla. Even worse, a couple of the boys at school had been asking Char to give messages to Kayla for them. That really hurt. She felt like Cinderella's ugly stepsister. Now, whenever the phone rang, she usually didn't bother to answer it. She pretended not to notice it was ringing. She acted like she didn't care, but the jealousy was burning away inside her like acid.

Leaving the bathroom, Char went down the hall to Kayla's room. She knew Kayla was at cheerleading practice, but she knocked on the door anyway, just in case. When no one responded, she opened the door a crack and peeked inside.

"Kay?" No answer. "Kayla?" Still no answer. It was safe. Char tiptoed into the pink princess-themed room, noticing all the photos pinned to the corkboard over her desk, the fluffy stuffed animals, the Backstreet Boys poster, the My Little Pony dolls, the Cabbage Patch dolls that Kayla no longer played with but kept on a high shelf. The autographed black and white photo of Chad Pritt, the famous actor Kayla had had a crush on since fourth grade.

Bright sunshine gleamed through the polished windows. Across the street, Craig and Josh Johnson were giddily racing their bikes down the sidewalk and into the street, oblivious to the danger. A few crinkled brown leaves softly drifted to the ground beneath Kayla's windows. Mesmerized, Char watched and wondered why even Kayla's bedroom seemed to hold a brighter light, a happier view, than her own.

For a few seconds, she forgot why she had come in. Then she remembered. She crept into Kayla's bathroom and was assaulted once again by her image in the mirror. She could hardly stand to look at herself. But this time, she had a plan. She turned on the faucet and dampened her hair, then selected a can of mousse from Kayla's collection of hair styling products. She globbed it on extra thick, ran it through with her fingers, and then washed the excess off her hands. Turning on the blow dryer, Char managed to fluff her hair into a wild-looking pouf.

Satisfied, she rearranged everything so Kayla wouldn't know she'd been there and went back to the kitchen to get a bag of chips and a Coke. She knew it was junk food and it was bad for her, but there wasn't anything else to eat except her mother's diet bars and carrot sticks, and she certainly didn't want or need those.

Returning to the great room with her snack, she pushed the power button on the remote, turning on their new big screen TV. She held down the channel button until she found the music videos. The pulsating music blaring in the background helped her not to feel so all alone.

Kayla was at cheerleading practice until four-thirty. She would probably go out to eat and hang out with her friends afterwards. Once she had tried to join them at Pizza Hut, but they just giggled and whispered when she came in and pretended not to notice her standing there. So she had bought herself a soda and gone home, vowing never to speak to any of them ever again.

Her parents, Paul and Barbara Fisher, were both successful lawyers. But that success came at a price. Chained to their desks and their phones, they were buried in mountains of paperwork until late in the evening. Many nights her father's new silver Audi didn't pull into their driveway until seven-thirty or eight—sometimes later if he was preparing for trial. Char was lucky if she got to spend an hour a week with him, and even then he often seemed distracted, as though he were thinking of something else. When the girls were younger, Mrs. Fisher had tried to be home by six in order to cook dinner for them. But now that Kayla was in middle school and often busy with after-school activities, a family dinner with all of them together was a rare thing. Sadly, it also meant that Char was usually all alone after school.

Now, she glanced up at the music video playing on the screen before taking out her social studies homework. A golden yellow wedding band was falling in slow motion from someone's finger. It hit the floor and bounced a few times before coming to rest. Then the pounding rap lyrics began. It was a song about being with another man's wife. Just then, the telephone rang. Char got up to answer it.

"Hello?"

"Hi, is Kayla there?" a deep voice asked.

"No. Who's this?" Char clutched the receiver nervously.

"Nobody. I'll call back later." Whoever it was hung up. Char's mouth turned down in annoyance. She shouldn't have answered the phone. It was never for her. Who were these guys, anyway? And why did they keep calling her sister?

"I'm just not going to answer it anymore," she said to herself, biting her fingernail. She glanced at the TV screen again. Everyone in the video was singing and dancing at a party. They looked so happy, beautiful, and energetic. A rapper clutched a whiskey bottle in his fist, taking a long drink. He gestured wildly at the camera and did a rap about partying. Char wondered for the first time where her parents kept the key to the alcohol cabinet by the bar.

But now the music was becoming annoying. This station always played rap music after school, and Char didn't really like rap. She grabbed the remote. Movies, cartoons, news. It was always the same. It was all boring. The shopping channel briefly grabbed her eye with a stunning blue sapphire bracelet, modeled by a young, attractive woman whose fingers were manicured with perfectly shaped French acrylic nails with white tips.

Only $300.00, or three convenient monthly payments of $115.00!

Staring at the expensive bauble, Char wondered when she would be old enough to have her own credit card and how much it would cost to get her nails done like that. Then they switched to a woman modeling an ugly black onyx ring, so Char kept channel surfing. Westerns, classic movies, sports, infomercials.

Then—wait. *What's that?* she thought. *Who's this?*

An old woman. *You never see old people on TV*, Char thought.

She was wearing glasses and was covered in a strange-looking outfit that looked like it came out of the Middle Ages. Sitting comfortably in an armchair directly facing the camera, the elderly woman spoke in a warm, kind, and friendly voice, as if chatting with a neighbor who had just dropped in for a cup of coffee. Her head was covered with a beautiful long black veil. Under the black veil was a white inner veil. A clean white headband covered her fore-head. On her lap, she cradled a large leather-bound book with the tender love and care of a mother caressing her little child. Her intelligent dark brown eyes sparkled intensely and saw everything. Everything.

Char watched, fascinated by the unusual gold medallion the old woman wore on a chain around her neck. She'd never seen one like it. Apparently, the woman had just made a joke, because the audience was laughing. The woman was laughing, too. It was a big, hearty, joyful laugh of total amusement that made Char feel delightfully happy inside, and she smiled in spite of herself. Why had she never seen this show before? Maybe it was some kind of a special program and wouldn't be on ever again. She decided to watch.

The laughter died down, and the veiled woman grew serious. She spoke slowly and deliberately, choosing her words with care.

"You and I must be concerned about the salvation of souls. About their welfare. Not only of your own—not only of your own soul, but the whole world! You can't look at a news program, you can't look at a magazine without looking at wars and the most terrible atrocities. And you know the sad thing to me? It's just news. I mean, people are murdered and slaughtered in fields and cities and all these places every day. Every day! We see buildings torn apart and children lying dead. And it's just news. Just news. Isn't that strange?"

Char stared intently at the brown-robed woman, who seemed at that moment to be looking directly into her soul.

"Do you ever cry?" the old woman asked. "Do you ever cry over those who starve? Those who are cold?"

Char knew that the only person she had ever cried about was herself. But here was someone who did care about others. Someone who cared very much. Char wasn't sure what she was listening to or why, but for the first time in her life, the person talking from the television screen wasn't trying to get her to act like someone else, or trying to get her to buy something, or trying to entertain her. The person talking from the television screen was simply being herself and was talking to Char as she was, her own self, asking her if she had ever cried. An old woman's raspy voice had pierced through the clouds of deception and illusions like the sound of a bell ringing from a tower. It sounded strangely like the truth.

The old woman kept talking, quietly yet firmly, smiling into the camera with a sweet, grandmotherly smile. "We don't seem to comprehend the awesomeness of the sin of murder. We somehow—have gotten so far from God. And so I ask you, in your prayers, to pray for conversion. For a change of life. A change of mind. A change of heart."[2]

---

[2] EWTN, "Mother Angelica Live," 1996.

A change of life? That sounded good. Was it possible? Could lives and hearts truly change? But wait—what prayers? She never said prayers. She didn't know any.

"You youth out there listening to me tonight—you have a lot of potential to go out and preach the good news that Jesus is Lord. But before you open your mouth, at least make the effort to live what you preach."

Oh. Religion. That's what this is all about, thought Char glumly.

At that moment the front door swung open, and Char's mother, Barbara Fisher, walked in. Thirty-four years old, tall and slender with short blonde hair, she juggled her keys, her briefcase, and a bag of groceries. She kicked off her high heels and yelled for Char.

"Hello! Got some groceries out in the car!"

Char bowed her head and without a word dutifully stepped toward the late model Toyota Camry. She didn't really like helping her mother. It made her feel like a household servant or something. *She didn't even ask me to help. She just assumes that I will.* Char paused and looked back at the television.

Mrs. Fisher hung up her keys on the key holder and padded into the great room, setting down her expensive leather briefcase, still clutching groceries. Following Char's gaze, she frowned at the image of the nun on the screen.

"What in the world are you watching? Give me that remote." Impatiently she strode to the couch, grabbed the remote and hit the power button.

"Mom!" Char cried in protest.

Mrs. Fisher eyed Char up and down. "What happened to your hair?"

"I—nothing." Char stared at the corner of the rug.

"Looks like you stuck your finger in an electrical outlet. Go get the rest of those groceries out of the car. And be careful of the eggs!" she ordered.

"Why do I always have to bring in the groceries? Just because Kayla's not here, I have to do all the work!"

"Because Kayla has a life, that's why. And for your information, Kayla helps out without having to be asked!" Mrs. Fisher snapped, and then immediately regretted it when she saw the flash of pain leap from her daughter's eyes.

But it was too late to take it back. Char ran all the way to the bathroom, tears streaming down her face, turned on the shower, and washed the sticky gel out of her hair.

Later, she calmly took out her journal and once again began to write.

I am SO BUMMED. Today Krista said her dad got a new job and they are moving to Denver after Christmas! They have to sell their house and move by January (unless Y2K blows everything up). She was pretty down about having to move again. I feel sorry for her. I think she was really happy here. But her dad couldn't find a job.

Now I won't have anybody to eat lunch with.

Char gnawed on the end of one fingernail, then chewed the ends of her hair.

Maybe it won't happen. Maybe they won't be able to sell their house right away and they'll have to stay for a while.

I'm going to miss her A LOT. It's so hard to find a friend that won't talk about you behind your back.

She paused for a while, rolling over on her back, and stared at the ceiling. Her mind felt strangely blank, but her heart felt like it was breaking. After a few minutes she turned back over and added one more sentence.

Mom loves Kayla more than me.

Chapter 3: "Bitter Sweet Symphony"

I have never been able to understand how it was that the schoolgirl who was so ultra-modern...who read anything she liked, was crazy about dancing, and up in all the 'pop' songs of the day, should have been suddenly literally called by her name one day.

– Dominican nun, in religion 20 years

℘t was the weekend. Barbara Fisher was at Studio Style in downtown Great Falls getting her monthly color and cut. Kayla was in her room, listening to the Back Street Boys and laughing on the phone. Char sat at the breakfast bar dangling her legs over the edge of the oak barstool, finishing the breakfast of juice, bagels, and cream cheese Paul Fisher had just prepared. Their firm had just won a big court case that had been dragging on for years, and he'd decided to celebrate. He'd spend the whole weekend at home, doing whatever he felt like. Oddly, he wasn't quite sure what that was. But he did know one thing—he needed to start spending more time with his family. Breakfast seemed a good place to begin.

The comforting aroma of toasted bagels and freshly ground coffee filled the spacious kitchen. Paul refilled his coffee mug and sat down across from his eldest daughter.

"You know what I've been thinking about?"

"What?" Char mumbled, her mouth full of bagel.

"I've been thinking about you always being home by yourself after school. Doesn't that get boring? Wouldn't you like to join the dance team or something with Kayla?"

"That's stupid," Char said, licking cream cheese off her fingers. "A bunch of girls in Styrofoam straw hats and short shorts, waving flags at halftime while everyone stares at you. No thank you."

"Okay. What about going down to the animal shelter and helping them out once a week? You could walk the dogs and pet the kitties. Stray cats need love, too." His brown eyes smiled encouragingly.

"And clean the cages and pick up poop. No way!" Char rolled her eyes, horrified.

Mr. Fisher raised his eyebrows, then frowned. "What about babysitting? You used to like watching Hunter and Jacob when they were little. Make some extra money?"

"Yeah, I guess. But they're too old for a babysitter. Hunter's playing football and Jacob is doing archery or soccer or something." She brushed the crumbs onto her plate and folded her napkin into a tiny rectangle, which she clutched tightly in her fist. For a few seconds, they sat in silence. Mr. Fisher picked up the *Wall Street Journal* and took a long sip of coffee from his mug.

"Daddy?" Char asked, staring at her plate.

"Yes?"

"Am I adopted?"

"What?" His eyes grew large, then narrowed. He stared intently at his eldest daughter. Setting his mug and the newspaper down, he stood up, walked over and gave Char a gentle hug. "What makes you ask that?"

"I don't know. I just feel like I don't fit in sometimes," she said glumly.

"I know the feeling." He was about to say more, but thought the better of it. Instead, he coughed and looked down thoughtfully at the tile floor. Then he thought of something.

"Say, are ya busy with anything right now?" He was about to call her "Pumpkin," but decided that would be going too far.

Char gazed at her father incredulously and shook her head. *This is something new!*

"No? Let's go up to the attic and look around. I'll bet we can find some neat stuff up there."

"Okay!" Char said, hiding her excitement.

* * *

Then we went upstairs to the attic and got out some old photo albums. It was cold up there and smelled funny. We looked at pictures for a long time. He showed me all my old baby pictures, and even one of Mom pregnant! She looked so funny! We even found some old baby clothes! I was really tiny back then!

Anyway, Daddy said I am definitely not adopted. He showed me a picture of him and Aunt Mary when they were kids, and her teeth looked just like mine (only not anymore since I got my braces off). He said if I was adopted, he and Mom would love me just as much. ☺

Char closed her journal and stared up at the ceiling, tapping her pink pen on her fingers.

"Char!" At the sound of her father's voice, Char jumped off the bed and ran down the hall to the kitchen, where Mrs. Fisher, newly coiffed, was eying the pile of dirty dishes left on the counter. Just then Kayla dashed in, still on the cordless phone, and grabbed half a bagel in a napkin. She slathered it with low-calorie margarine before skipping back out into the hallway and disappearing in a frothy wake of gossipy giggles. Char stared after her disdainfully. *How can anyone be so immature?*

"Char? Honey, do you think you could clean up the kitchen? Your sister seems to be otherwise occupied."

Paul walked over to the hall and for the millionth time flipped off the light switch Kayla had left on. Char's mother grabbed a Diet Coke out of the refrigerator, popped it open, and leaned against the counter as she listened to their exchange.

Char let loose with that little half-cough, half-vocalized sound full of shock and anguish that teenage girls give when they're dramatically upset about something.

"Waauhh!? Oh, Daaadd!"

Mr. Fisher was nonplussed. "Yes, Char?"

"I did the dishes last night!"

"Yes, and I'm asking you to do them again this morning. Does that seem like an imposition?"

"But I *always* have to do the dishes! Why can't Kayla do them?"

"Kayla isn't the topic of this conversation, Char. I'm asking you to do them. Will you please?"

"Oh, all right!" Fuming, Char grabbed the stoneware plates, glasses, and silverware and practically threw them into the sink.

Mrs. Fisher scolded her. "If those get chipped, you'll be paying for new ones out of your allowance!"

Without a word, Char threw the hot water spigot on full blast, opened the dishwasher, and pulled out both drawers. Her face turned fiery red, but she didn't cry. Two minutes later, she was done. She sulked back to her room and slammed the door. She picked up the wireless phone to call Krista, but Kayla was still on it.

"I'm talking!" she heard her sister's sing-song voice from the receiver.

"Hurry up, I need to make a call! You've been on there over an hour!"

"No, I haven't." Kayla and whoever she was talking to giggled.

"You're such a *baby!*" Char hissed, pushing the red power button. She resisted the furious urge to throw the phone at the wall.

Instead, she tossed it on the bed. Then, picking up a CD, she carefully removed it from its clamshell and set it in her boom box and pushed PLAY. "Bitter Sweet Symphony" always put her in a better mood. The lyrics were kind of depressing, but real. And the music was cool. It lifted her up. She watched as the silver disc began spinning around faster and faster. As the song played, she whirled around the room, waving her arms and singing along. *I can't change my mold, no, no, no...*

Chapter 4: A Secret in the Attic

Who has seen the wind?
Neither I nor you:
But when the leaves hang trembling
The wind is passing through.
Who has seen the wind?
Neither you nor I:
But when the trees bow down their heads
The wind is passing by.

— Christina Rossetti
"Who Has Seen the Wind?"

"I've got a surprise for you," Paul Fisher announced dramatically.

"How would you like to take a trip to Ohio?"

"Ohio? Really?" Char's face brightened with interest. "When?"

"I'm going to a conference at Case Western, and I thought, you know, we haven't had a vacation together since that one summer we went to Yellowstone Park. And that's been what—three years ago?"

"Yeah. I was eleven, I think."

"Well, I think we should all go and have a little vacation. We'll go see the Rock and Roll Hall of Fame and the Great Lakes Science Center. And they even have this huge shopping mall under an old train depot called Tower City. How does that sound?"

"Great! Is Kayla coming too?"

"Is Kayla coming too? Of course Kayla's coming. You didn't think we'd leave her home alone, did you?"

"No." Char felt guilty for asking.

* * *

October 6, 1999

I don't want to go to dumb Cleveland. I'm really mad cos now I'm going to miss trick or treating with Krista. But Daddy said me and Kayla are getting too old for that anyway.

Monday, October 25

Eric Mattson came up to me in the hall after History! I was so embarrassed, like I didn't even know what to say! So I stood there, with my mouth open, like //duhr ~ and he handed me this note and said: Would you give this to Mikayla? Yeah, I'm her delivery girl!! (Only I didn't say that.) I wanted to read it first, but I was afraid to ... So I didn't.

Wednesday, Oct. 27, Nineteen Ninety Nine!!!

Matthew smiled at me today in Science. I didn't know he liked me, I mean, maybe he doesn't really. What if he does like me??? He's so cute! He was just being nice. That's okay. I don't want a boyfriend anyway. Boys are stupid! All they care about is sports and cars and ....

And girls like my sister, Char thought.

Char shoved her journal back under the mattress. She was sick and tired of everything. She reached into the closet and dug out her sketchpad from underneath her shoes and winter boots. Thumbing through the pages, she had to admit to herself some of the drawings were pretty good. The first one she'd done was the tall old Chicago-Milwaukee-Saint Paul railway station tower in Great Falls. That was a year ago. Since then, she'd sketched the geese and ducks swimming at Gibson Park, and the Ninth Street Bridge spanning the Missouri River. She tried to draw the Charlie Russell statue in front of the Davidson Building, but she wasn't very good with human figures. Sometimes she drew pictures in her journal instead of writing. Sometimes a picture could say things she didn't know how to put into words.

When she was drawing just for fun, Char liked drawing buildings the best. But there weren't very many interesting buildings in Great

Falls. She wished she could go to a big city to draw the skyscrapers there. Then she remembered the trip to Cleveland. *Maybe there's some pretty buildings there, she thought.*

Char imagined smart, sophisticated city girls going to parties and football games, warmly bundled against the damp winter chill in layers of down and fur, laughing and talking with their boyfriends. She pictured brightly lit store windows featuring all the latest designer fashions. Maybe Cleveland wouldn't be a bad place to visit after all.

Just then, a noisy flock of Canada geese filled the sky in their classic V-formation, heading south. Winter was on the way. Char leaned in towards the window, pensively watching them fly over. It was only four-thirty, but already it was nearly dusk. Something about the natural world—the change of seasons, storms, the things man could not control—affected her deeply. A feeling of nostalgia washed over her. Outside, the ever-present Montana wind whooshed insistently, inciting a wild swarm of leaves that attacked the window like mad locusts. Char began pacing rapidly back and forth. Impulsively she decided to go back up to the attic.

Chapter 5: Boys and Babies

*You have not only a glorious history to remember and to recount,
but also a great history still to be accomplished.*

– Pope John Paul II, Vita Consecrata

"Kayla!"

"Mercedes!"

The two friends threw their arms around each other in a mock display of affection, giggling uncontrollably.

"Oh, *dahling,* did you miss me?" Kayla pretended in her best British accent. Mercedes laughed so hard she doubled up and couldn't answer.

"Oh! Stop it!" she gasped for air. "You're too funny!"

"Oh, you love it," Kayla teased, smiling happily at her friend.

Mercedes fell panting on the carpeted floor of the girls' gym dressing room. Kayla waited for her to catch her breath.

"Are you coming over later?"

"Yeah! If mom lets me." Mercedes pushed her headband back up and felt to make sure her ponytail was still in place.

"OK. You can help me pack."

"Pack for what?"

"We're going to Ohio for a week. My dad has to give a speech in Cleveland."

"Cleveland? Is Char going too?"

"Yeah."

Mercedes twirled her hair thoughtfully. "What's in Cleveland?"

"I don't know. The Rock and Roll Hall of Fame. Some other dumb stuff, I guess." Kayla stuffed her jacket and her book bag into a locker and changed into shorts and a t-shirt. It was almost time for cheerleading practice.

"Buy me something cool!" Mercedes retied the shoelaces on her Nikes.

"Okay." Kayla smiled.

Mercedes locked the locker containing her books, purse, and school clothes and turned to Kayla. "Ready?"

"Yup," Kayla replied. Quickly they exited the locker room and leaped up the steps into the brisk October afternoon.

The sky was clear, but it was getting dark. They half-walked, half-ran over to the football field where the boys were playing and stopped to watch. The boys in their class had grown taller and more muscled up this year, and with their heavy football pads on, they looked even older. Kayla and Mercedes tried to pick out who was who underneath the thick pads, face masks, and helmets.

"There's Jeff!" Mercedes cried and pointed to the center of the field where the players were in a huddle, planning the next play. Then, the huddle broke and lined up in formation, waiting for the hike. She glued her eyes to the number 50 jersey.

Suddenly, the quarterback fell back, searching for a receiver. Players broke and ran in every direction, and the defensive tackles pushed hard to reach the quarterback before he could pass. It was a maze of pushing, shoving and grunting players, yelling coaches and anxious parents. The quarterback saw an opening, but it wasn't going to happen. Buried under a pile of yellow jerseys, he fell to the ground, still clinging to the football. The intended receiver threw his hands on his hips and paced back and forth in frustration.

"Hi Jeff!!" Mercedes screamed, waving furiously. Number 50 looked at the two girls leaning on the chain link fence, but before he could react, the coach yelled.

"Johnson! Huddle!"

Number 50 jogged away. But Mercedes wasn't disappointed. She knew he had seen her.

"He's so cute!" she beamed happily.

"Yeah, but he's taken," Kayla warned.

"Oh, I don't care!" Mercedes retorted, but the smile had fallen from her face. Quickly she changed the subject and fished a pack of gum out of her coat pocket, ripping the wrapper. "So—what's going on with you and Eric?" she said, skillfully changing the subject.

"Eric." Kayla said coldly. "Eric can go jump off a cliff!"

"Oh, are we having a little spat?" Mercedes teased, offering Kayla a piece of gum.

"Spat? What spat? It's over!" Kayla hissed. "That stupid jerk! I hope I never see him again."

"You've got to be kidding."

"I am so serious!"

"He really ticked you off, didn't he?" Mercedes sympathized.

"Well yeah. ... wouldn't you be?" Kayla fumed, finally taking the proffered piece of gum.

"Oh, absolutely. That was so totally rude what he said to Jason about you, and in front of everybody? Like, he didn't know it was going to get back to you?" Mercedes blew a large bubble, which popped with a satisfyingly loud crack.

"Let's just forget about him. I really don't want to talk about it, okay?" Kayla said morosely.

"OK. I'm sorry, Kay."

"It's okay." Kayla thoughtfully unwrapped her gum and placed it in her mouth. "Hey! The Backstreet Boys are gonna be in Billings in March."

"Oh really?"

"Wanna see if your mom will take us?"

"Like, totally."

"'Tell me why-eee! Ain't nuthin' but a miss-stake! Tell me why-eee! Ain't nuthin' but a heart-break! I don't ever want to hear you say....I want it that way!!!'" Kayla sang dramatically.

"What way?" Mercedes asked philosophically.

"Oh, who knows," Kayla murmured, arms outstretched, spinning around and around like a crazed rock star ballerina in front of a screaming crowd of admiring fans. Then she fell down on the grass, panting. "I just love that song," she added wistfully. "Nick Carter is such a *doll*."

For a moment, they were silent. Then Kayla returned to reality.

"What time is it?"

"Almost three-thirty."

"We'd better go. Come on!"

They raced back to the grassy area in front of the gym just in time for cheerleading practice. Annie Johansen, Lisa Barnes, and Brittney Boland were already there, doing stretches and practicing drills.

"Hi Kayla! Hi Mercedes!" the girls said, smiling at them.

Annie looked at Kayla sympathetically. "I heard you and Eric broke up."

Kayla wondered how much was true sympathy and how much was trying to be nosy so she could have something to talk about.

"Yeah. It's no big deal." Kayla lied to the older girl, not wanting to show her true feelings.

"I'm sorry about that," said Annie.

Kayla liked Annie. She was always kind to the younger girls, not stuck up like some. "Thanks. We weren't really getting along. He's more interested in football than in me!" Kayla said.

"Give him a few years, he'll change!" laughed Brittney. All the girls laughed with her. Kayla was grateful for their friendship. It took some of the pain out of their breaking up. But she didn't dare let them know how much it hurt her.

Some of the girls at her school acted as if liking a boy too much meant there was something wrong with you. These girls said you didn't need a guy to be happy. Some girls even swore they would never have a boyfriend and made fun of those who did. They liked to put down guys and made jokes about them whenever they could, like "When God created man, She was only joking." And if a couple had an argument or broke up, these girls were quick with an "I told you so." Kayla could never explain to them how much Eric meant to her. So she didn't even try.

Kayla pulled her hair tighter through the scrunchie and wondered if Eric would ever love her more than he loved football. It was like there was this emptiness inside her heart, but when she was with Eric, the empty feeling went away and she felt happy inside. But being with the other girls and doing cheers soon took her mind off Eric.

Clumsily Brittney did a lopsided cartwheel and fell over sideways on the ground, laughing. Then, Annie and Lisa spotted Annie's mother, Mrs. Johansen, and Annie's new baby sister, Lily. They all ran over to say hello and take turns admiring the precious baby. Lily was just one month old and perfectly adorable. Her cheeks were plump and round, and her golden brown hair curled delicately around her tiny ears. She smelled delightfully sweet and clean. As the entranced girls watched, Lily stuffed her chubby fist into her toothless mouth and gazed spellbound at the world around her with round, trusting, shining eyes.

"Do you want to hold her?" Mrs. Johansen asked.

"Sure!" Kayla said excitedly. Sometimes when she was day-dreaming about Eric, she imagined a whole houseful of children, gathered around a tall green Christmas tree, opening gifts on Christmas Day, or seated around a big Thanksgiving table loaded with the delicious food she had prepared for them. She loved babies! But when their teacher talked to them in health class about birth control and family planning and overpopulation, she made it sound like babies were something to be avoided. Pregnancies had to be carefully planned. Children had to be carefully spaced. Children were, above all, time-consuming and expensive.

Kayla remembered when Annie had told them that her mother was pregnant. The girls had all giggled at this revelation—this unexpected, unplanned thing. But after Lily was born, everything changed. Annie beamed with joyful pride whenever she talked about her. Happily she told her friends about feeding and changing her and rocking her to sleep, singing little naptime songs from her own childhood that she had almost forgotten. And when Mrs. Johansen came to the school, newborn Lily snugly wrapped in stretchy soft cotton blankets, all of the girls—and many of the boys—flocked around her like groupies adoring their favorite rock star. They all marveled at the tiny, sleeping, precious new being that grasped their fingers so tightly, smelled so sweet, and looked so infinitely adorable just by yawning!

That's when Kayla decided she wanted a baby sister, too. Or maybe even a baby brother. She decided to bring it up on the way home.

That turned out to be a big mistake.

Chapter 6: Ten Thousand Souls in India

*The hunger for love is much more difficult to remove
than the hunger for bread.*

– Saint Teresa of Kolkata, M.C. (Mother Teresa)

rs. Fisher had laughed out loud. "What do you think I am, a baby factory?" she snorted. "Do you have any idea how hard it is to work while you're pregnant?"

Kayla had fidgeted with embarrassment. She hadn't really thought about it. She stared at the laces of her shoes, saying nothing.

"Morning sickness? Swollen breasts? Swollen ankles? Not to mention the *pain* of *childbirth?*" Mrs. Fisher nailed Kayla with her best courtroom voice, as if Kayla were a hardened criminal under cross-examination.

Kayla felt ashamed, even guilty. Did her mother regret having her? Was the pain of childbirth and the cost of raising a child too high a price to pay? She wanted to know the answers to those questions, but she was afraid to ask.

"It ruins your figure—you're never the same," she complained. "And then they keep you up all night feeding and changing them. You won't get a full night's sleep for the next twenty years!"

"But Mom, you're not fat!" Kayla said honestly.

Mrs. Fisher smiled half-heartedly. Then, seeing her daughter's crestfallen face, she quickly squeezed Kayla's hand after they pulled into the driveway.

Kayla hoped with all her heart that her mother didn't regret having her. But Kayla knew one thing. She wasn't anything like her mother. She wanted to have children.

Kayla grabbed a bag of groceries to carry in while her mother unlocked the front door. Setting them on the kitchen counter, she was headed towards her room when Char stopped her and held out a piece of paper.

"Here." Extending her hand, Char held out a folded piece of notebook paper by the very edges, as if it were something filthy and disgusting that she didn't want to touch.

"What's that?" Kayla asked suspiciously.

"Eric said to give it to you," she replied coldly.

"Eric?! What were you doing talking to *Eric?*" Kayla snapped and snatched the note out of Char's fingers, hot with jealousy.

"Nothing! I mean, we weren't, like, you know, *talking*. He just gave it to me and said 'Could you give this to Mikayla?' Don't have a cow."

"Char? Can you *please* get the rest of these groceries?" Mrs. Fisher asked, ignoring the drama.

"Mikayla?" Kayla smiled dreamily. "Does he always call me Mikayla?" Lost in dreams of romance, Kayla didn't notice the look of repressed rage on Char's face as she whirled around and ran to her room to read the precious missive. Char just stared after her with look of pure loathing.

"What a baby. You are such a baby!" Char shouted after her.

"Char! The groceries!"

"Okay! I'm going!" Char yelled, letting the front door slam on her way out to the car.

But Kayla didn't hear. She was too busy reading Eric's note of apology, complete with a little drawing of a stick-figure boy giving flowers to a little stick-figure girl.

* * *

Saturday, October 30, 1999

Halloween Eve! I am writing this on the airplane! There are like a hundred people on this plane. I can't believe there's so many people going to Cleveland.

Everything looks so tiny from up here! We won't get to our hotel until this afternoon. First we have to fly to Salt Lake City, which is NOT in the direction of Ohio. Then we have to fly east to

Minneapolis, which is in Minnesota. Daddy said Minneapolis is named after Minnie Mouse, but I knew he was only kidding. But dumb Kayla believed him! Ha ha!!! What a dork.

Mom said we can go shopping tomorrow and if we're good, she'll take us to see a movie at the Great Lakes Science Center Omnimax Theater, where the screen is all around you, 360 degrees!

We're so high up in the sky! If this plane crashed we'd all be dead just like that.

Sometimes I wonder what happens to people when they die. I believe in life after death, but what's it like? Do we float around on the clouds like angels? Or do we stay here on earth, like Halloween ghosts?

Char paused in her writing and looked out at the clouds, but she knew there weren't any angels out there. She wasn't so sure about the ghosts. Especially on Halloween night.

I don't think anybody really knows for sure. It's not something you can talk to people about. If you talk about death, they think you're weird. When I think about dying, I feel afraid. Maybe that's why nobody wants to talk about it. Because they're scared, too.

Tired of writing, Char shoved her journal into her book bag under the seat in front of her. She and Kayla shared one row of seats, their mother wedged strategically between them to keep them from arguing. Their father had taken the aisle seat directly to the right of them in the opposite row and was reading the paper. Kayla and Mrs. Fisher were both listening to music on their Sony Walkmans and paid no attention to Char. The flight attendant was carefully making her way down the aisle with her cart full of drinks and snacks.

Bored, Char peered across the aisle over her father's shoulder at the newspaper he was reading as their plane sped smoothly through the air.

Weather Watcher

Supercyclone Hits Eastern India, Thousands Dead
©*Associated News Service*

A supercyclone with winds in excess of 160 mph swept in from the Bay of Bengal to hit the eastern state of Orissa on Friday. This was the second tropical system to affect the region this month.

Up to 15 million people have been left homeless by the storm, with the death toll estimated as high as 10,000. Phone lines and power supplies throughout the state of Orissa were also wiped out. Media reports have compared this cyclone to a 1997 tidal surge which killed thousands in neighboring Andhra Pradesh, and claim this is the worst cyclone to have hit the Indian Bay of Bengal region in three decades.

For a long time, Char stared out the tiny oval window into the peaceful white clouds passing harmlessly beneath them. Then she leaned her head back, closed her eyes, and wondered what it would be like in Cleveland.

Chapter 7: Una Buena Chica

And you thought life would hide you
from the other life that overhangs the depths.

– Karol Wojtyla
"Song of the Hidden God"

Antonia Teresa Esperanza, "Tia" to her family and friends, sat at the kitchen table of her family's small two bedroom apartment in Cleveland, Ohio, reading her American History textbook. It was Friday, her day off, which meant an afternoon all to herself—more time to study. Mariah Carey was singing sweetly from the stereo. Tia kept it turned down so as not to disturb her mother, Gloria.

Aunt Delia always said Tia was tall and pretty enough to be a fashion model. But Tia had no illusions about her looks. She knew she looked nothing like the string-bean thin girls displayed in fashion magazines. Big boned, with wide hips and full, oval cheeks, she wasn't slender and petite like her mother or her mother's sister Delia. Her thick dark brown hair fell in long, spiral curls to her waist. She had taught herself how to make her face up with bright colors to complement her deep brown eyes and coffee-colored complexion. Her features were feminine and cute, but there was nothing weak about her. She carried herself with a dignity and purpose that made her appear much older than seventeen.

Gloria Esperanza hurried into the living room, nervously searching in her purse for a cigarette. Her reddish-brown hair, lately streaked with gray, was pulled back into a tight ponytail.

"Mama!" Troy, Tia's little brother, leaped up and ran to her side, jumping like an excited puppy. Gloria absentmindedly kissed the top of his head.

"We're almost out of toilet paper," sighed Tia.

"I'm going to work, Tia. You make sure you keep this door locked," Gloria called over her shoulder. Then she rushed out the door, shutting it behind her with a whoosh and a clunk.

"Bye," Tia answered softly, not knowing if her mother had even heard.

Troy walked back to the television and fell down cross-legged, resting his chin in his hands.

Tia loved her family, but she adored her little brother. He could make her laugh the way nobody else could. Even on her saddest days, when the gray Cleveland sky sank like an old blanket draped across Lake Erie and her spirits felt polluted like the thick mud at the bottom, Troy would make a crazy face, roll his big brown eyes, and giggle as if to say, *Hey! Can't you see this is world-class humor here?* And she would laugh in spite of herself.

Troy made Gloria laugh, too, when she was around. But he didn't see her very much during the week. Most nights, she worked downtown, cleaning up after the rich and powerful lawyers and accountants who worked in the skyscrapers during the day.

Tia knew what her mother's job was like. Against the rules, she had gone to work with her a couple of times when Tia was much younger and there had been nobody to babysit. Tia was amazed at how hard her mother worked. And yet, there was never enough money.

Now that she was older, Tia had a job, too. She'd been working after school at La Chic Boutique in Tower City for four months, and if she kept out of trouble, she might get a raise in two more months. Then she would be making $6.00 an hour! Tia loved her job. The customers treated her like she was an adult, not a kid the way most of her teachers did. It was fun looking at all the new clothes, and of course, making her own money.

Sometimes, Tia would find a little loose change on the dressing room floor where it had fallen out of their pockets while they were trying on new clothes to buy. She kept it up by the cash register until it was time to close up, and if no one claimed it, she took it home and gave it to Troy.

Since they'd moved to Cleveland that year, Tia did everything she could to make Troy's life a little easier. She often bought him a pack of gum or a comic book in Tower City to give him when she got off work. Then maybe he wouldn't have bad dreams, walking in his sleep, waking up in the bathroom and crying because he couldn't find his mother, and he couldn't wake up, and he couldn't find his bedroom. Then Tia would hold him, gently calling his name and stroking his cheek until he finally awoke, clinging to her and crying, "Mommy!! Where's Mommy?"

After Gloria left for work, Tia walked over to the refrigerator to see what to fix for dinner. Inside were a half a package of hot dogs, buns, a jar of pickles, three cans of Diet Coke, a jar of salsa, and a not quite a half gallon of milk. She checked the cupboard next. A box of cereal, a can of refried beans, two cans of tomato soup, some rice, ground coffee, and a brown paper bag. Some apples, maybe? She opened the bag gingerly and scowled. Just a couple of packs of cigarettes Gloria had stashed for safekeeping.

Tia sighed and rolled the sack back down again and placed it back in the refrigerator. She was tempted to smoke one herself, but she didn't want to smoke with Troy around. It was bad enough their mother did without her setting a bad example, too. Besides, her mother would be furious if she got into her stash. She tried to forget about them.

"Tia?" she jumped at the sound of Troy's voice.

"What?"

"What's for dinner?"

"How about a hot dog?"

"I want tacos! I'm starving!!" he answered. "Can I watch TV?"

"Okay, but no noise! I'm trying to study," she said, placing the hotdog and a bun on a paper plate in the microwave. Troy jumped to the TV and turned it on in one swift motion. A cartoon blasted into the apartment.

"Turn it down!" she commanded.

"Okay, Tia!" he grinned at her, turning the volume down a tiny bit.

"Come on! I said turn it down. If you can't mind, you'll have to go to bed."

"Okay! I said okay, didn't I?" he whined.

"Oh, you little twerp!" she walked over to him and pretended to punch him. He giggled and rolled over on his side, tickled that he had gotten his sister so wound up.

She laughed and picked him up by his heels, shaking him gently. He grabbed at the air and shrieked with delight.

"Are you gonna behave?" she said in mock anger.

"Yes! I mean, No!! I mean, Yes!!!" he screamed.

"What?" she shook him some more.

He was laughing so hard he couldn't speak. Tia carefully set him down again, smiling at his happiness. He panted for air until he finally caught his breath, then sat up and said, "Hey, look! It's on!"

One of Troy's favorite shows was on. Troy laughed at the actors' antics, and Tia smiled. When Troy was happy, she was happy. Engrossed in the show, he forgot about their game. Quietly Tia smoothed her shirt, stood up and went back into the kitchen. Just as the microwave bell dinged, the phone rang.

"Hello?" Tia answered.

"Hey, you." It was Kanisha from Biology class—Tia's only friend in Cleveland.

"Hey!" Tia smiled.

"What's up, girl?" Kanisha sang into the phone.

"Not much, what's going on with you?"

"Not a thing, not a thing. Just kissed my sweetie good-bye and sent him on his way. Hey, what are you doing on Friday at noon?"

"Just eating my lunch," Tia replied.

"Well, why don't you come downtown with me and Jake? We could use another opinion."

"Another opinion about what?"

"My engagement ring!"

"Your what? Did Jake ask you to marry him?" Tia gasped.

"No, not yet. But he'll get around to it. He just doesn't know it!" Peals of laughter burst from the phone.

"Ya'll are crazy," Tia scolded.

"Crazy for ice, homegirl!" Kanisha laughed so hard, Tia laughed too.

"I know that's right! But I can't leave school at lunch time. I've got Spanish at twelve-thirty."

"Oh, come on, Tia!" Kanisha urged. "You can skip that la-la-la class just once. You're not going to flunk if you miss just once!"

"Well..."

"Wait for me down by the flag, and we'll go catch the bus together, okay?" Kanisha cajoled.

"I don't know," Tia hesitated. "Maybe."

"What do you mean, 'maybe'?"

It would be so nice to go out and have fun for a change. But she wanted to go to college even more. She'd never be able to afford tuition. The only way she'd be able to go to college is if she were awarded a scholarship. She just couldn't afford to let her grades slip.

"I can't, Kanisha. I'm sorry!"

"All right. Well, I gotta go. Eugene's got to use the phone. I'll catch you later," Kanisha said flatly.

"Okay. Bye." Tia sighed. She liked this girl, but sometimes she wondered about the things Kanisha tried to talk her into. Besides, who wanted to hang out with a couple? That would just make her feel lonely.

So now that she didn't do what she wanted, Kanisha was going to be mad. She just didn't understand how Tia felt about her grades and why she tried so hard to keep them up.

You couldn't get a scholarship from babysitting.

She glanced over at Troy, who was totally focused on "Pinky and the Brain." Too bad he couldn't get into his schoolwork the way he could get into TV shows. Maybe if they played videos of teachers teaching, like on public television. Jazz it up a little with music and graphics, like *Sesame Street*. Then it would at least seem like more fun, she thought. Maybe then he could pay attention.

Tia put Troy's hotdog on a paper plate, added a couple of pickles and some chips, poured a glass of milk, and set it on the table. "Here's your food," she said.

"I wanted a taco!" he whined.

"I know, but we don't have any lettuce or cheese."

"Can I eat it in front of the TV?"

"No way José, you know Mom won't let you eat on the floor like that."

"Okay," he said glumly. For a split second, he was torn between the TV and the food. But hunger finally won out, and he dashed to the table and wolfed down his food. He swallowed half a glass of milk in two gulps, set it back on the table, then quickly dashed back to his spot on the floor in front of the TV.

"Aren't you gonna finish your milk?" Tia asked.

Troy was so wrapped up in the show that he didn't even hear her.

"Troy!" she said, louder. He looked up.

"Huh?"

"I said, aren't you going to finish your milk?"

"In a minute."

She gave up. "Oh, all right." She wondered how long it would be before he was hungry again and wished there were more food in the house. Opening one of the Diet Cokes, Tia dutifully went back to her history homework.

When she looked up, it was eight-thirty. Past time for Troy's bath. Ignoring his cries of protest, Tia turned off the TV and patiently ran a tub for him while he peeled off his clothes. As usual, he took about a half an hour to get the job done. He seemed to lose all track of time playing in the water with his toy boats and rubber ducks. But by nine, he was clean and sweet-smelling and ready for bed.

Now, it was story time. Tia helped Troy pull the covers back, and he climbed into bed.

"Darkwing Duck or Uncle Scrooge?" Tia asked, holding up two children's books.

"Uhhhhh, Darkwing—no! Scrooge! I mean, DARKWING DUCK!"

"Okay." Troy got settled, and Tia launched into cartoon mode.

"I am the terror that flaps in the night!" she began dramatically in her best cartoon duck voice. Troy giggled hysterically.

After the story was over, Troy thought of something important.

"Tia, I had to eat lunch with Miss Lewis today!"

"How come?" Tia asked, putting the book down.

"She made me go to the principal's office *again*." Troy rolled his eyes with annoyance. "I didn't even *do* anything! She just *said* I did. She is so mean! But she's nice to the girls! She's just mean to us *boys*."

Tia's heart sank. She wished she could think of something she could do or say so that he would never get in trouble again and he could learn to sit still, be quiet, finish his work, and just generally behave himself, but she couldn't. So she just did her best to listen, to comfort him, and to understand why her baby brother was such a ball of disorganized dynamite.

* * *

But it was getting late. He needed to be asleep. That, at least, she could manage.

"Okay, let me hear you say your prayers. In the name of the Father, and of the Son, and of the Holy Spirit," she helped him start.

"Amen!" Troy proclaimed loudly, crossing himself. "Dear Jesus, bless my Mama, and my Tia, and my friend Ethan, and Miss Lewis, and God bless all the kids at school, and God bless Mama..."

"You said that already."

"...and God bless Auntie Delia, and Robbie, and Bobby, and Abuelita Isabel in Heaven. Amen!" Troy said firmly with the faith of a child who knows God hears all prayers.

"Amen," she said softly.

When she heard the name of their beloved grandma Isabel, who had died just a few months earlier, Tia's eyes stung with tears, but she hid her sadness from Troy. Bending to kiss him goodnight, she felt his little arms wrap tightly around her neck and shoulders. After a few seconds, she tried to disengage herself from his grip and stand up, but he would not let go. He loved his sister. With her, he was safe. Without her, the world was a big, scary place. Finally he dropped his arms, and she stood up and smiled.

"Good night, I love you, hasta mañana!" she said.

"Good night, I love you, hasta mañana!" he echoed.

Walking to the doorway, she turned and flipped the light switch off.

"Tia?" he asked.

"¿Que?" she answered.

"Are you going to take me trick-or-treating tomorrow?"

"Yes, but only if you're good!" she said emphatically.

"Can I have another hug and kiss goodnight?"

"No, you just had one, that's enough. Now go to sleep!"

"But I'm scared!"

"Scared? Of what?"

"Of monsters!!"

"Monsters? There aren't any monsters. Go to sleep! Good night!" she said firmly, and walked out into the hall, shutting his door not quite all the way. She left it open just a crack so she could hear him if he needed her.

It was really hard for Troy to settle down at night. She could hear him humming and talking to himself quietly, repeating scenes from TV shows and from books she read to him. It was as if he had a perfect memory for things he heard on TV or from story books. *Too bad he doesn't have a perfect memory at school,* she thought.

It was almost nine-thirty, and she still hadn't eaten any dinner. There was plenty of milk left, so she poured herself a bowl of cereal. Thoughtfully debating whether to work on her algebra or indulge in a little TV, she decided what she really wanted was to take a hot shower. It would refresh her, and maybe the sound of the running water would help Troy relax and fall asleep. Even when it came to something as simple as what time she took a shower, she thought of Troy, not realizing the way in which almost every single aspect of her life related in some way to her family. If someone had pointed it out to her, she wouldn't have believed it. It just came naturally to her to make sacrifices out of the love and caring she felt for them.

All of a sudden she felt exhausted. She laid her head down on the table, too numb to move. After dozing for a few minutes, she finally dragged herself to her feet and trudged into her bedroom, where fully clothed, she collapsed on the bed and fell into a deep, dreamless slumber.

* * *

The next morning, rapper MC Hammer shocked her back into reality, blasting from her clock radio. Rolling over, she turned the sound down so as not to wake Gloria, who had only been home and asleep for a few hours. She listened to the music for a while and then pulled herself upright. Getting up in the morning was a real chore. She was definitely not a "morning person." If she had the chance, she'd sleep until noon.

But not today. Time to get Troy up and get them both ready for school.

Groggily she took a short version of the hot shower she'd planned to take the night before and then went in to wake her brother. He wasn't a morning person either.

"Mmmmmm!!!!" Troy groaned angrily.

"Wake up, sweetie!" Tia gently shook Troy's shoulder.

"No!" he moaned.

"Come on! It's time to get up!"

He lay motionless.

"Tee-Roy the Boy!" she shook his shoulder again, a little harder this time.

"Aw, leave me alone!!" he grumbled, eyes still shut tight.

"Come on, now!" Tia cajoled, lifting him into an upright position. At last, the big dark eyes flew open. Rubbing them with his fists, he yawned, dropped his head to his chest, and slumped backwards.

"Troy! You wake up, right now, you hear me? Or I won't fix your cereal. You get UP RIGHT NOW!" Tia shouted in spite of herself.

"OKAY! I'm gettin', I'm gettin'!" Troy seemed offended at the whole idea.

Satisfied that he was finally awake, Tia went back into her bedroom and began to dress. Returning to the hallway, she peeked into Troy's room. Just as she had feared, he was still in bed. She was all business now. No more coddling, no more "sweetie." She grabbed the blankets and sheet and pulled them off of him, chilling him with a blast of cold air.

"Nooo!" he protested.

"Shhh! You'll wake Mama!" Tia hissed.

Tia grabbed his arm firmly and gently hoisted him up.

"Up! Now! *¡Ándale!*" she propelled him onto his unsteady feet and purposefully guided him towards the bathroom. He was up now. Heaving a sigh of relief, Tia was glad the first obstacle of the day had been surmounted.

Now it was time to make breakfast. She opened the refrigerator and got out the milk and a Diet Coke. Then she got out the cereal and fixed Troy a bowl. Next, she popped the top on the Coke and took a drink. She put a piece of bread in the toaster, walked over to the table, and sat down to drink her not-so-healthy breakfast.

Troy came down the hall dressed in his school uniform, barefoot. He came over to Tia, and she gave him an affectionate hug and kiss.

"Good morning!" she said brightly.

"Mor-ning!" he sang. He skipped over to his chair where the bowl of cereal was waiting.

"The Father, the Son and the Holy Spirit, Amen," he whispered, hitting himself in the forehead and the stomach in a half-hearted attempt to make the Sign of the Cross. Tia frowned.

"Blessus oh Lord and these Thy giffs, which we're about to receive," he blurted, rolling his eyes heavenward, "from Thy bounty, through Christ Our Lord, Amen. In the name of the Father, and the Son, and the Holy Spirit. Amen!" he rushed through the blessing and began shoveling cereal into his mouth.

"Slow down! You'll get milk all over your shirt!" Tia warned. He gave her a big smile in return, dimpled cheeks stuffed like a chipmunk, bouncing his head from side to side. Tia rolled her eyes and began gathering up her homework books and papers, placing them inside her book bag. She glanced at the clock on the VCR. It was already a quarter to seven—almost time to go.

"I gotta go get ready, okay? When you finish your cereal, put the bowl in the sink," she reminded him.

He nodded his head, chewing busily.

Tia hurried to the bathroom to finish getting ready. It seemed like there was never enough time. She was always having to rush, and she hated it. Sometimes, she felt like she was trapped in a race with no finish, like a mouse in an exercise wheel, spinning around and around. She was always running and running, but never getting anywhere.

Her grades were good, but she wasn't happy. Kanisha told her that what she needed was a boyfriend, but she wasn't interested in having a boyfriend. She wasn't really sure what she wanted. Deep down she knew she wanted something—needed something or somebody—but she couldn't put a name to it.

Then she thought of James. James Demars sat in the row ahead of her in keyboarding class. He had a huge smile that made her feel happy inside, and he took care with his appearance when most boys her age didn't really care how they looked. His short black hair was shiny and smooth, and he always looked clean and neat. He had good manners and a fine attitude. She hadn't told anyone—not even Kanisha—but she'd had a crush on him all that year. She watched him in class and wrote their names together in her notebook, "James and Tia Demars," and "Mr. and Mrs. James Demars," over and over as if writing it could somehow make it come true.

One day, he had caught her staring at him, and she actually felt her heart stop beating in her chest. Then, it began pounding so hard that she was sure everyone, including James, could hear it. Embarrassed to death, she had looked down, her face hot. When she dared to look up again, he was smiling at her—right into her eyes—and she had felt like she was going to explode. But then the teacher had stopped by his desk to ask him a question, and James had turned away. She had fought to catch her breath, praying no one would notice.

By the time the bell rang, she was under control again, but she couldn't forget the crazy way he had made her feel. She fantasized about him that night, imagining they were alone together after school, alone in the hallway, and he would walk over and without a word take her in his strong arms and kiss her. But something told her that wasn't going to happen.

Finished with his cereal, Troy turned on the TV, and Tia was jolted out of her fantasy. Seven-fifteen! Late again! Running to her room, she quickly stuffed her books in her backpack, grabbed her purse and jacket, and rushed back into the living room, switching off the TV as she ran.

"Tia!" Troy complained loudly.

"SSSHHH!! Don't wake up Mama! Come on, we've got to go!" Grabbing Troy's book bag and coat, she managed to get him into his coat and out the door while holding both of their book bags. How many mornings had played out exactly the same way? Why were they always late? Why couldn't she get more organized? *How do mothers of young children manage? I can barely handle just one,* she thought as the apartment door closed behind them with a metallic click.

Chapter 8: No Shorts in Church

I was about eleven years of age when...suddenly I felt the presence of our Lord in me. I 'recognized' him immediately. I remember very clearly saying to myself; 'It is Jesus.'

– Trappistine, aged 42, in religion 19 years

The Cleveland RTA redline train, also known as "the Rapid," whooshed into the station with the screeching squeal of steel wheels on steel rails. Everyone boarded quickly, the automatic doors closed, and the train screeched away towards downtown, all in under thirty seconds.

Tia enjoyed her time on the train. It was one of the few times she had to herself. She always listened to her Sony Walkman while riding to her after-school job at Tower City, the high-end mall built underneath the old Terminal Tower building where the underground train ran.

Now that the year 1999 had actually arrived, an old song by Prince had become popular again. The song's catchy lyrics bounced out of Tia's stereo: "Life is just a party and parties weren't meant to last." Was that really true? Was life just a party? A place for having a rocking good time, dancing as fast as you can until you die? It sounded like fun, but Tia's life was no party. But listening to the driving beat, she tapped her foot and forgot about all of that. She imagined she was on her way to a phat club where she would dance with James for hours under a glittering, spinning ball covered with tiny mirrors. Then the song ended, and took out her homework.

It was for her favorite class—Psychology. The assignment was to write a 3-page essay entitled, "Belonging and Identity: The Story of Myself." She had thought it would be an easy "A." What could be easier than talking about yourself? But she found it was harder than she had expected. She didn't even know what to put for her name. It took three entire sentences to explain.

"My name is Antonia Teresa Esperanza. But nobody calls me that, except my grandmother. Everyone else calls me Tia, because that's what my brother called me when he was little since he couldn't say 'Antonia.' I am half African American and half Mexican American."

She reread what she had just written and crossed out the last sentence. Sometimes, her mixed racial heritage was no big deal, but here, it was hard to deal with. In Texas everyone assumed she was a Latina because of her last name since Hispanics were the majority ethnic group in San Antonio.

But in Ohio, it was different. Living in Willie Pearl's house on Cleveland's East Side where blacks were in the majority, she felt everyone assumed she was black. Tia had always identified with her Hispanic heritage. After all, her mother's family was Hispanic, and her dad was nowhere in sight. Now she wasn't so sure.

She wished she knew more about her dad's side of the family. She had hoped to get to know her grandma Willie Pearl, but the old lady was hard of hearing and didn't seem interested in getting to know her new-found grandchildren. She decided not to write anything about that, though. Too much pain and confusion. Mostly, she just wanted to be herself and to be accepted for who she was. Was that even possible?

"I am seventeen years old and a senior at Jefferson High School. I have one brother named Troy, who is eight. I was born and raised in San Antonio, Texas, to Gloria and William Jackson."

Her parents' names looked strange placed next to each other, but she liked the way it looked. She wanted people to think that her mother and father had been married. In her eyes, they *had* been married. Then she realized that wouldn't work because her last name wasn't Jackson, too. So she changed it to say, "Gloria Esperanza and William Jackson."

William Jackson.

Tia missed her father in a way that no one could understand, not even her mother—especially not her mother. It wasn't like she thought about him all the time. It was just that there was an empty space in her heart where memories of his loving presence should have been. It gnawed at her and robbed her of strength and the freedom to enjoy life the way she was certain other girls did.

At school, there were girls with eyes full of light and life. They laughed their way through the halls and didn't worry about their grades, didn't worry about their looks. They seemed to dance from one exciting moment to the next like there was nothing in life but Hollywood heroes and cartoon parties, and every day was created just for them.

Tia caught these girls looking at her sometimes. When she walked by, they would pause mid-giggle, and when they saw her, they and she both understood that she was different somehow. She watched them look at her as if they were deer in the forest who had spotted a mountain lion and they weren't sure whether to stand their ground or run. But she kept her dignity and her distance. They usually decided she was harmless and left her alone, not like some of the other girls who were constantly teased and harassed because they were different, because their clothes or their hair or their personalities didn't measure up to the popular ones.

When they left San Antonio and moved to Cleveland, she had thought everything was going to work out between her parents. Her mother had believed that, too—believed it enough to sell all their furniture, leave behind their family and friends, and trek fifteen hundred miles north. Maybe her dad had believed it as well. *But believing something doesn't always make it true,* Tia thought sadly.

How she missed sunny San Antonio! The fiestas, the Battle of Flowers parade with the flashy floats and traditional Mexican dancers twirling their colorful, long full skirts. The national festivals of Diez y Seis—Mexican Independence Day—and Cinco de Mayo, when the soulful mariachi bands in their big straw sombreros proudly played their trumpets. Luscious food, lifelong friends, and sizzling hot summer days. All of it gone, just like that.

Cleveland was so different. The people weren't rude, but they weren't exactly sociable, either. They were just sort of serious and hard-working all the time, not warm and fun-loving like the people of South Texas. The skies were always low and gray, never that high, bright turquoise blue she'd known since youth. She never realized how much she loved it until it was gone.

In the end, it wasn't leaving her friends and material possessions behind that hurt Tia the most. What hurt the most was leaving the house where she had spent so much time with her grandma—her Abuelita Isabel. Abuelita Isabel had died the year before. Memories of Saturday afternoons spent sitting on the porch of the little white frame house with red amaryllis growing in the front flower beds, the spicy aroma of her grandmother's tamales warming on the stove, while bouncy Tex-Mex tunes danced across the hot street from the stereo of their neighbor's 1957 Chevy truck. Smiling, she remembered her twin cousins, Robbie and Bobby, playfully scream and chase each other through the sprinkler in the little yard, loving the long summer days.

No matter how hot and noisy the San Antonio summers got, it always seemed dark, cool, and peaceful in her grandmother's house. She especially remembered the big picture of the Sacred Heart of Jesus on the living room wall and the huge rosary with the hand-cut black onyx beads and sterling silver crucifix draped gracefully around it. A red glass candle flickered gently in front of it, carrying Isabel's prayers to the Lord Jesus, *el Señor*, while she was busy with her housework.

The little house was always spotless, and her grandmother was always there—to listen, to smile, and to feed her the wonderful Mexican cooking that Gloria never made. Fluffy homemade flour tortillas; cool, smooth guacamole; refreshing ceviche; spicy Spanish rice and chili relleños; and crunchy chicken flautas. Abuelita Isabel didn't speak English very well and Tia didn't know much Spanish, but it didn't seem to matter. They could always communicate from the heart.

One day when Tia was about nine or ten, it had been too hot to play outside, so she sat on the living room floor of her grandma's house, watching TV. Suddenly, volleys of rapid-fire Spanish shot back and forth—first from Gloria, then from Isabel. Pots and pans banged dangerously in the kitchen. Tia had caught a few words here and there, but mostly she didn't know what was being said. Did she hear her own name tossed between them like a ball in a game? She had cringed to think her mother and grandma were arguing over her. Was it something she had done? Fighting back tears, she had sat quiet as a statue, wishing she could sink into the floor.

Finally, Gloria stormed out the back door, letting it slam. Abuelita Isabel burst purposefully into the living room, purse in hand, a dark blue shawl tossed over her shoulders. What was happening? And why was Abuelita carrying her shawl when it was ninety-eight degrees outside?

"Come, Antonia. *¡Vámonos!*" Gently but firmly, Isabel grasped her arm, lifted her to her feet with one gnarled hand, and punched the TV's "off" button with the other. Tia didn't dare ask where they were going. Following along obediently, she hurried along beside her as Abuelita stepped out the door into the stifling August heat.

It was late in the afternoon, but the sticky air was hot as fire. Together they began down the shimmering sidewalk. Grandma Isabel couldn't walk very fast, but despite the heat she seemed to be walking faster than usual. Ten minutes later, just as Tia had bravely worked up the courage to ask where they were going, they were there: Our Lady of Guadalupe Catholic Church. Dozens of people were already there, slowly climbing the front steps. As they reached the entry, the bells of the church began to ring, calling the faithful to the Saturday Vigil Mass. Smiling, Abuelita Isabel removed the shawl from her shoulders and tied it around Tia's waist.

"Why do I have to wear this?" Tia complained.

"*Es muy malo mi nieta*. No shorts in Church!" Grandma Isabel explained firmly, her black eyes flashing with determination.

"But, Grandma!" Tia cried, embarrassed to have this shawl around her waist, through which her short pink play shorts could still be seen.

"Shhh! *¡Cállate!*" her grandmother shushed her and led her up the stairs to the door of the old Spanish mission-style building.

Inside, it was refreshingly cool and dark. An usher smiled and greeted them, speaking in Spanish to her grandmother, and in English to Tia. How did he know Tia spoke only English? But before she could wonder at this, Tia had to adjust her eyes from the blinding summer light outside to the dim, candle-lit interior. She could barely see where she was going. She didn't mind her grandmother's hand firmly grasping her own.

As they walked in, Isabel dipped her fingers into a white marble holy water font and blessed herself, and then Tia. She didn't know how to explain to her granddaughter what to do, so she just did it for her. The holy water felt cool and strangely comforting. Tia noticed everyone using it as they came into the Church from the vestibule.

They were just in time. All of the pews in back were full, so they had to walk all the way to the front to find a place to sit. Tia cringed with embarrassment as she imagined everyone staring at her and her makeshift "shawl skirt." As they reached the second pew from the front, her grandmother did a strange thing. Holding the pew with one hand to steady herself, she bent down with her right knee touching the floor, slowly bowing towards the altar. Then she indicated for Tia to do the same.

What was she supposed to do? She felt petrified, certain that everyone was looking at them and her funny shawl skirt. What to do next? Grandma Isabel motioned with her hands again, jabbing towards the floor. Tia stared at her, uncomprehending. Then, another family came in, and all five of them took turns genuflecting the way Abuelita had. Tia finally figured it out and mimicked what they had done, satisfying Abuelita Isabel. Thankfully they finally sat down. Automatically her grandmother knelt on the kneeler in front of them to pray. Tia gawked at the colorful stained glass windows full of things she had never seen before and wondered what would happen next.

Mass was about to begin. Two altar boys, the lector and the priest slowly processed up from the rear of the church where Tia and her grandmother had first entered. Singing softly, they slowly walked up the aisle until they reached the front, accompanied by sweetly dignified sounds coming from an old organ in the choir loft blending with the voices of the people in the pews. When they reached the front of the church, they genuflected towards the altar before walking up the steps of the Sanctuary.

Tia had no idea what was going on. She forgot all about the argument earlier. The Mass was in Spanish, and while her grandmother had no trouble following along and making the responses, Tia was lost. She stared at the colorful statues. They seemed to tell a story all their own. The yellow lighted candles on the altar held her gaze, and as she watched the actions of the priest and altar boys, she was surprised by the intense desire she felt to know what was happening.

When it came time to receive Holy Communion, Abuelita Isabel motioned for her to stay seated in the pew. Tia was scared. Why was everyone getting up and going up to the priest in front of the altar? What was happening? Why was the priest giving them all little white wafers on their tongues? Why couldn't she go, too?

She watched her grandmother intently. After receiving Holy Communion, Isabel came back to their pew and knelt down. She closed her eyes, covered her face with her hands, and silently prayed. Tia didn't know what to do, so she crawled into a half-kneeling, half-sitting position and clasped her hands in front of her face like Abuelita Isabel, peeking from behind her fingers at the priest purifying the sacred chalices and listening to the beautiful organ music.

As the Mass ended, the organist began playing a different hymn, and the priest and servers processed back out towards the front door. The people all sang. Tia could still remember her grandmother's face at that moment, so full of peace and happiness and light. Abuelita Isabel had beamed at her and patted her on the shoulder.

"Muy bien, mija! You want some ice cream? ¡Feliz Fiesta de la Asunción!"

Tia didn't know what it all meant, but it didn't matter. All she knew was that she loved Abuelita Isabel more than anyone in the whole world.

Chapter 9: La Imitación de Cristo

*I pardon you from the heart; very soon we will
see each other before the divine tribunal;
the same judge that is going to judge me will be your judge;
then you will have, in me, an intercessor with God.*

– Blessed Anacleto González Flores
Martyr of the Cristero War, 1927

When she looked back on that year, Tia tried to remember if Abuelita Isabel had seemed more tired than usual. If she had, maybe Tia had tried to explain it away by thinking her grandmother was just getting old. They went to Church every Saturday night, just like always. They cooked their Saturday night dinner together, just like always. Maybe Abuelita Isabel didn't eat quite as much as she used to, but Tia couldn't remember her ever complaining.

One night, Tia had overheard her mother talking to Aunt Delia on the phone. After she hung up, Gloria had said Abuelita Isabel wasn't going to be able to take her to Mass on Saturday. No explanation. No offer to take Tia herself. Nothing. Tia's heart sank and she had the strange feeling that something was very wrong. Had she done something to upset her grandmother? She wracked her brain, but she couldn't think of anything. Tia had known better than to ask questions, so she said nothing.

The following Wednesday, Aunt Delia came to take her to religion class in her shiny white Olds Cutlass Supreme.

"Where's Abuelita?" Tia asked timidly.

"Get in, mija," Delia held the door open for her niece and she slid into the passenger seat. Robbie and Bobby were in the back seat, munching on Doritos and drinking from juice boxes. They grinned at her between crunches, kicking their feet and playing and talking happily to each other.

Delia spoke softly over the idling engine so they couldn't hear. "Your Abuelita is sick, Tia."

Tia drew her breath in sharply. "What's wrong?"

Delia glanced at the twins in the rear view mirror and then looked at Tia gravely. "She has cancer, Tia. She is seriously ill."

For a while, Tia could not speak. Delia's words simply did not register in her brain.

"Can't they do an operation or something?" she finally blurted out.

"They said it's inoperable. Dr. Garcia said she only has a few months to live." Pressing her lips together, Delia put the car in gear and eased the car out of the parking lot.

Tia gasped, clapping her hand over her mouth. *It's not true! She doesn't look sick! It has to be some kind of a mistake!* Terror filled her heart with sadness and cold dread. Death was something that happened to other people. She couldn't live without her sweet Abuelita! Hot tears stung her eyelids. Turning away so Delia wouldn't see, she stifled a sob.

* * *

As they drove in silence to the church, Tia remembered something her Aunt Delia had once said. Thinking of it now, she felt a tiny whisper of hope. It had been at the funeral for her Aunt Carmen, her mother's youngest sister. She had died when Tia was only twelve. Beautiful Carmen Esperanza had turned down many proposals of marriage before accepting Ross Benson, a wealthy man who lived in a sprawling ranch-style house with a sparkling blue swimming pool north of San Antonio. Traveling all over the world on their private plane attending horse shows and auctions, they were rarely home. Tia hadn't known her very well. But when Troy was born, Aunt Carmen and Uncle Ross had agreed to be his godparents.

Tia remembered the beautiful white baptismal gown they had bought for Troy to wear and the pretty card with a savings bond as a baptismal gift. Afterwards, Tia remembered marveling at this strikingly beautiful woman with the stylish gold James Avery jewelry, who had given her such a powerful hug before leaving that she smelled like Halston perfume for hours.

After Carmen's funeral, Aunt Delia had told her that Carmen had wanted her to have her antique dresser and that she, Tia, must take very good care of it because it had come from with Abuelita Isabel from Mexico when she and her family had moved to the United States in 1927. Tia was surprised. "Your Aunt Carmen really loved you, Tia," Delia had said.

"But I hardly ever even saw her!" Tia replied.

"That doesn't really matter. You were her niece. You were family. Carmencita would have wanted a daughter like you, Tia."

Tia felt a surge of love mingled with sadness. This woman she hardly knew had loved her, and now she was gone. She felt happy and devastated all at the same time.

"Auntie Delia?" she had asked. "What happened to Auntie Carmen?"

"Your Aunt Carmen fell and hit her head when she was out riding one of their new horses. Didn't your mother tell you that?" Delia frowned.

"Yeah, she did. I know how she died. I mean, what happened to her soul?"

"Her soul!" Delia was caught off guard. "Why are you asking me such a thing?"

Tia didn't know what to say. It was just a question that popped into her mind without thinking. "I'm sorry," she said automatically.

Then a funny thing happened. Aunt Delia began to sob. Tia had patted her arm anxiously. Delia had finally sighed and wiped her eyes.

"No, mija," Delia had dabbed carefully at the mascara running under her eyes. "It's okay. I'm the one who should apologize." Tia relaxed. Aunt Delia wasn't mad after all.

Just then Gloria had returned from the ladies' room and was motioning for Tia to come along. Gloria had walked up stoically,

wearing her usual jeans and t-shirt and sunglasses. Casting a
sideways glance of suspicion at Delia, she had grabbed Tia's arm.
"Come on Tia! Let's go!" she had said, pulling Tia towards the car.

Tia looked at Aunt Delia expectantly.

"Carmen is in Heaven, mija," she said firmly. "She is with Our
Lord Jesus! I promise! *¡Con el Señor Jesús!*"

And Tia had immediately felt better. "Bye, Auntie!" Tia had
called over her shoulder as she followed her mother to the car. Delia
had smiled bravely and waved in farewell, clutching her Kleenex,
still too choked up to speak.

If Aunt Delia was right and Aunt Carmen was in Heaven with the
Lord Jesus, then Tia was certain that when Abuelita Isabel died, she
would go to Heaven and be with the Lord Jesus also. And that made
her feel a little bit better. Even so, Tia started going to daily Mass,
praying fervently for her grandmother's recovery. She even stayed
to pray the holy Rosary after the early Sunday Mass with the old
ladies of the parish, surprised to see a teenager in church at that
hour. Tia believed with all her heart that if she just prayed hard
enough, faithfully enough, Abuelita would be cured. But after a
month, Isabel had only grown worse. By then, Tia was afraid to visit
her in the hospital—afraid of what she might see. But she continued
to pray, lighting candles in front of the statues of Saint Anthony and
Saint Therese at Our Lady of Guadalupe.

One day after school, Tia had finally taken the bus to sprawling,
bustling Santa Rosa Hospital in downtown San Antonio. The white
floors gleamed, shrouded in the sharp odor of antiseptic. An elderly
volunteer at the information desk solemnly informed her that her
grandmother's room was on the fourth floor. The dinging elevator
efficiently whisked her up the four levels to the cancer ward. As the
steel elevator doors whirred open, Tia's heart began to pound
deafeningly. Smiling kindly, a young nurse at the nurses' station
glanced at a chart, then pointed. Room 407B. Tia moved on wooden
feet and rubbery legs along the shiny corridor, peeking gingerly at

each room number, until at last she saw the familiar figure lying caught beneath a spider's web of tubing. And she knew. As soon as Tia saw her there, lying in the narrow white hospital bed with the chrome rails next to the lighted monitors, she knew.

For the breadth of a heartbeat, Abuelita remained still. Then, her eyes flickered open.

"Antonia!" she whispered. Thin arms, bruised and taped with tubes, lifted to hug her. Tia bent down gently and fought to hold back the tears burning the back of her eyelids.

"Abuelita!" Tia breathed quietly into her neck.

"I wan....chyou.... be... a good girl," she struggled to speak. Her deep brown eyes gazed deeply into Tia's. *"¡Una buena chica!"*

"Si, Abuelita," Tia saw the truth shining out from the depths of her grandmother's dark brown eyes, once so joyful and loving, now tired and full of pain. Tia trembled with fear mixed with sadness. "I'll be good, I promise. ¡Yo seré buena!"

Abuelita Isabel closed her eyes for a moment and then opened them just a little. She tried to say more, but the effort was too much for her, and she convulsed in a fit of coughing. Tia bent over her, watching helplessly. A nurse walked in to check her vital signs and the I.V. that was slowly dripping fluids into Isabel's arm. She spoke rapidly in Spanish to Tia's grandmother, who smiled quietly in response, trying hard not to cough. Turning and smiling at Tia, she made some quick notations on the chart and walked out of the room just as quickly as she had entered, thoughtfully closing the door behind her.

Isabel's eyes were closed now, and she breathed unevenly. Tia looked lovingly at her, trying to memorize her face. The soft gray hair, still black in places, the kind face, the tiny frame made even tinier now beneath all the tubes and monitors. Tia noticed the little dangling silver and turquoise earrings she usually wore were missing. She looked around the room and wondered what they had done with them. The gold Miraculous Medal that Isabel always wore on a tiny gold chain was still around her neck. Seeing it, Tia sighed with relief.

Tia turned toward the small window and looked out. Outside in the parking lot, people were coming and going. Giant white clouds floated gaily in the hot blue summer sky. She stared at them in disbelief. This wasn't really happening. It couldn't be.

When Gloria arrived a half hour later, Tia was sitting on the edge of the chair by the window, silently clutching her rosary. Gloria walked into the room, and Isabel woke up. She smiled weakly at her daughter and tried to raise herself up to talk. For a split second, Tia felt a flash of jealousy. She wanted her grandmother all to herself. She didn't like it when she had to share her with anyone else, especially her mother. In the past, whenever her mother and grandmother spoke to each other, they often ended up arguing. She prayed they wouldn't argue now.

Tia walked over to the bed and stood protectively over her Abuelita. Isabel turned and smiled at her, and then focused her attention back on her daughter and began speaking in Spanish, very slowly. As Tia watched, she strained with all her mind to understand what was being said. But Gloria had chosen not to speak Spanish to her and Troy when they were little. Gloria had wanted them to learn English, and to be accepted as Americans. She didn't want them to be called that horribly humiliating name—"wetbacks." Tia knew nothing of this. She only knew that Gloria and Isabel shared a special kind of bond in the Spanish language that she did not. She felt as if she had been deprived of something very special that should have belonged to her. She felt excluded. She shot an angry look at her mother and walked back to the window.

The afternoon shadows were lengthening. The second shift nurses coming on duty were parking their shiny cars and walking in, talking and smiling. Glumly Tia turned back towards the bed. Gloria was holding Isabel's hand. They smiled at each other with deep devotion. Tia just stared at them. What kind of change had taken place that the two of them were now on such good terms? What had her grandma said to her mother? She would never know. It wouldn't help to ask; she knew her mother wouldn't tell her even if she did.

A soft knock sounded at the door, and the oncologist, Dr. Garcia, walked in. Tia felt a momentary sense of comfort, but it was quickly poisoned by a roaring surge of panic. *Do something to make her get well!* a voice inside her screamed. But she could only stand mute, powerlessly watching and waiting to see what would happen next.

Dr. Garcia smiled, walked over to Gloria, and patted her gently on the shoulder. He spoke warmly to Isabel while reading her chart. Gloria besieged him with questions, first in English, then in Spanish. He answered so softly that Tia could barely hear him. She stood motionless at the window. It was as if none of them even knew she was there.

Why was Jesus allowing her grandmother to die? Why hadn't He answered her prayers? In the courtyard below surrounded by flowers stood a tall white statue of Jesus. Was it supposed to be comforting? Tia stared at it accusingly. Inside she felt empty and cold. Who was this Jesus who allowed so much suffering in the world? How could it be that her sweet grandma, who always went to Church and always said her prayers and always worked hard taking care of her family, was wasting away in a hospital bed, hooked up to tubes?

Tia turned quickly, and ignoring her mother and the doctor, ran out of the hospital room. She sped past the gossiping group of nurse's aides who stared at her in surprise as she rushed through the hall past the steel-doored elevators, down the three flights of stairs, and out into the parking lot. Panting hard, she kept running all the way to the bus stop, where she doubled over and sobbed like a little child, oblivious to onlookers. She knew. She knew she was losing her very best friend. She knew she would never see Abuelita Isabel ever again.

* * *

Isabel's daughters, Gloria, Aunt Delia, and the youngest, Margie, Tia's other aunt who lived in Houston, sat in the cool living room of their mother's little house. Around them were several opened boxes—plastic containers full of sewing supplies, yarn, old recipes, and costume jewelry. Layers and layers of clothing still on hangers were piled on the sofa. The three sisters spoke quietly as they wrapped the precious items one by one in newspaper and placed them in trunks and cardboard boxes, some to sell at a garage sale Delia was planning, others to be divided among them. They were packing up Abuelita's things, getting the house ready to put on the market.

There was the large collection of Avon perfume bottles that Isabel had kept over the years. Even though they were empty, they still retained a trace of a scent that made it seem like Isabel was still there. Each of the sisters chose two or three, and then Tia was allowed to choose one for herself. The rest were placed in the box to sell. There was the silver-rimmed china, and the old crystal glasses from Mexico City, where Isabel and Jorge Esperanza had spent their twenty-fifth wedding anniversary, the "second" honeymoon, Isabel said, never having had a real honeymoon when they first got married, so young and so poor. There was the big black onyx rosary, which Margie immediately claimed.

"Nobody prays the Rosary anymore," Gloria said disparagingly.

"I don't care. I want it anyway." Margie wrapped it lovingly in tissue paper. "Mama loved it."

Delia glared at Gloria. "God knows she prayed it for you."

Gloria rolled her eyes and stood up. "I'm going out for a smoke."

"Can ya'll please not argue?" Margie looked from one to the other pleadingly.

Delia picked up an old book and thumbed through it. "This old one is in Spanish," she said. "Does anyone want it?"

"Not me," said Gloria as she grabbed her lighter and closed the door behind her.

"Why does she have to be like that?" Delia said.

Margie looked at the book in Delia's hand. "Does it say anything on the inside? Where did she get it?"

Delia flicked the first few pages. "Nothing. I don't know where it came from." Then Delia looked at Tia and smiled. "I guess we can sell it?" she asked.

"No wait, I'll take it!" Tia said.

"But it's in Spanish, mija."

"I know. I don't care. I still want it."

"What's the title?" Margie asked.

"Let's see. *La Imitación de Cristo*," Aunt Delia read aloud. "The Imitation of Christ. Here you go, Tia." Delia smiled and handed the worn leather book to her niece. Tia held it gently. She didn't care if it she couldn't read it. It had been Abuelita's; that was all that mattered.

* * *

Suddenly, the RTA train jerked on the rails and screeched to a slow crawl, and Tia was jolted out of her memories. Coming to a complete stop, the automatic doors swished open. For a moment, Tia stared dumbly out the window. Passengers were quickly embarking and disembarking. They had arrived at Tower City. Just in time, Tia grabbed her things, rushed out the double doors before they rumbled shut, and headed for La Chic Boutique. Then, the train reversed direction and headed back towards the other side of town.

Chapter 10: False Alarm

Why should a man be scorned, if, finding himself in prison,
he tries to get out and go home?

– J.R.R. Tolkien, On Fairy-Stories

While the other students worked quietly on their geography assignments, Troy gripped his pencil and stared at the book in front of him. The lines marched neatly across the page. He saw the big red letters at the beginning of the chapter. He began reading the assignment. At first it was interesting. But after about ten minutes, he grew bored. He folded the corner of the book's page inward in the shape of a perfect triangle. He unfolded it and noticed that the crease was still there, even after he pushed down on it and tried to smooth it out again. He scratched the glossy paper and noticed the scratch marks his fingernail left. He scratched some more and made designs on the paper like the branches of a tree.

Like any boy, his body yearned to push itself to the limits—to explore, to compete, and to take risks. His muscles ached to run, climb, and throw. His heart longed for a man's guidance and example to teach him the secrets of life. Instead, he was forced to sit quietly for hours, reading and writing words on a page about things that weren't real to him, taught by a woman who didn't understand him and who criticized nearly everything he did. He looked up towards the front of the room, but there was nothing to look at except the blackboard and the little African violet on Miss Lewis' desk. The only way to change the view was to go to the pencil sharpener. He raised his hand and waited.

Mary Beth Lewis was twenty-two years old and fresh out of college. This was her first teaching assignment. Like so many days before it, today had been a very long day. She'd been on her feet all day, and her new shoes pinched.

"Yes?" she said irritably.

Troy's large, brown eyes fixed on his teacher's face, and he lowered his hand.

"May I sharpen my pencil?"

"No. You're supposed to sharpen your pencil *before* class, remember?"

"But I've used it up already, see?"

She stepped over to his desk. "Let me see your notebook. You haven't written a single sentence, Troy. And your pencil is perfectly sharp. Please get to work. The period is almost over."

"Please??"

"I said no, Troy."

"Pleeeeaaase? I'll do it really quick!"

"SSHHHH!!! One more sound from you, and you'll be in the office!" she barked. Whirling, she stalked to the front of the classroom.

Obediently Troy gripped the edge of his desk and hunkered over his book. A few minutes later, he flashed a fun-loving smile at his best friend, Ethan. He bounced his head from side to side, dancing to music no one else could hear. Ethan stole a sideways glance at Troy and smiled sadly. He hoped his friend wasn't about to get in trouble once again.

Miss Lewis glared. Sighing, she continued the lesson.

"Let's review what we studied last week. Which state borders California to the north?" Her eyes darted around the room. A slim Puerto Rican girl seated in the front row shot her hand high into the air. Lisa Mendoza was a whiz at geography, and everything else.

"Lisa?"

"Oregon?" Lisa replied, pretending not to be sure of her answer.

"That's right! Very good!" Miss Lewis smiled broadly. She was pleased when her students knew the answers and behaved. If they didn't, word quickly got out among the parents and through the grapevine back to Father Sanders, the pastor. She'd heard stories of what happened when Father Sanders called you into his office in the Rectory for a little "chat." She imagined the tall, black-haired priest with the powerful voice towering angrily over her.

"None of our parents pays their hard-earned money to send his or her child to our school, only to have them subjected to the antics of some ill-mannered, rebellious clown! They send their children here to *learn,* Miss Lewis! If you can't control your class, I'm sure we can find someone else who can!"

Miss Lewis cringed. She suspected Troy Jackson had a learning disability, but there was no money for special education teachers in parochial school budgets. She wished she had the time to give him the extra help he needed, but it just wasn't possible. She had to keep the class on track, and she had to keep Father Sanders happy. She needed her job, as little as it paid. She considered her options.

Troy tried to read his Social Studies textbook. He wasn't sure what page they were on. He wasn't really all that certain what chapter they were on, either, but he looked hard at all the pages. He looked over at the open book on Ethan's desk. He saw a picture of the missions of California. He strained to see the page number but couldn't quite make it out. He looked at the pages of his own book. Kansas wheat fields. Nope. That wasn't it. Go back a few pages.

What's this? Indians dancing in their traditional costumes in South Dakota? That looked really interesting. He stifled the impulse to show the picture to Ethan. He knew he'd get in trouble for talking. Just then, a fly buzzed onto his desk. He tapped at it gently with his pencil, smiling as it flew back and forth. Entranced by the sound, he tapped some more. Pretty soon, he was tapping out a dance rhythm, playing the drums, softly mouthing the words to a popular rap song he liked. Just then, Lisa Mendoza turned and frowned at him.

"Shhhhh!" she hissed loudly, just like Miss Lewis. Troy stuck his tongue out at her and crossed his eyes. Following the sound of the hiss, Miss Lewis turned from the board just in time to see a tongue stuck out at her favorite pupil.

"That's it! You're finished here!" she shouted, turning red in the face.

"What did I do?" he cried.

"What did you do? What did you do?!! You know very well what you did. Now get yourself down to the office!" She paced to her desk and wrote out a referral slip.

"Here!" she shouted, thrusting it under his nose.

"I didn't *do anything!*" he insisted, looking mournfully at the slip of paper.

"Go!" she pointed to the dusty classroom door. Slowly, muttering under his breath, he made his way towards the hall.

"I didn't DO anything!" he protested again, glaring at Lisa.

Muffled snickering erupted behind his back as the other students watched him finally leave. As the door closed behind him, he heard Lisa. "What a relief!"

He knew Lisa hated him. He hated her, too. He hated school, period. But he wasn't unhappy to go to the office. At least he could get away from their teasing and taunting, away from Miss Lewis' frowning disapproval, away from the boring, *so boring*, lessons. Why didn't anybody else get in trouble all the time like he did? He tried his best, but it didn't seem to matter. He got sent to the office at least once a week.

He shuffled into the principal's office and handed Mrs. Palinski, the school secretary, the note from Miss Lewis. A colorful bowl of Jolly Rancher candies sat enticingly on her desk.

"Can I have a piece?"

"Sure, honey," Mrs. Palinski said kindly. "But you'd better wait to eat it until after you talk to Mr. Ortega."

Mrs. Palinski got up from her desk and went in to give Mr. Ortega the note. Troy instantly grabbed three pieces of candy, unwrapped one and stuck it in his mouth, holding the other two tightly in his fist. Plopping down in a chair to await his fate, he noticed Goldie and Finny, the goldfish, and jumped up again to take a closer look. He pressed a sticky finger against the smooth aquarium glass and bent down to look at them eyeball to eyeball.

"Hi Goldie! Hi Finny!" he said, grinning.

Mrs. Palinski came back to her desk and sat down again.

"How old are they?"

"I don't really know, Troy. They were full-grown when I started working here three years ago."

"How old are they gonna get?"

"I think goldfish can live to be fifteen or twenty years old, if they're cared for properly."

"What do you have to do to take care of them?"

"Oh, feed them, but not too much! Make sure the water is clean. It doesn't take much to keep a fish alive."

"It doesn't take much to keep a fish alive," Troy repeated, looking at the aquarium. "I bet you're going to live to be fifty years old!" Turning again to the secretary, he asked, "Do you have any pets?" Just then, the door to Mr. Ortega's office opened.

"Troy Jackson. We meet again. Please come into my office." The tall, thin principal waved him in.

Troy's heart fell to his feet, followed by his stomach. But once he was in Mr. Ortega's office, he started feeling better again. Far from being a punishment, it was more like a reward. Finally out of that stupid classroom! This was interesting. This was what a man's work world looked like. A man with power. A man with authority. The man in charge.

Piles of books, files and papers lay all over the desk and spilled into more piles on the floor, where a brown briefcase sat open, filled with even more papers. A colorful stack of "Be a Saint for All Saints Day" posters were propped up against the wall. An apple, a half-eaten sandwich, and a bottle of water were on his desk next to a brown paper bag. Not at all neat and tidy the way his mother and his teachers always said things ought to be.

Birds were singing outside the open window of Mr. Ortega's office. Miss Lewis insisted the windows stay shut in her classroom, so the breeze wouldn't blow their worksheets on the floor, or so she said. Troy decided that when it came to being neat and tidy, his mother and teachers didn't know what they were talking about. And if they didn't know what they were talking about when it came to being neat and tidy, they probably didn't know what they were talking about when it came to most things.

A small figurine sitting on the edge of the desk caught Troy's eye. It was of a bearded man in a brown robe, with tiny birds circling above his outstretched arms. He wanted to ask who it was, but he was a little scared of the principal and decided it would be best to keep his mouth shut. It was the second time this week he'd been sent to the principal's office. He didn't know what Mr. Ortega might do to him. Or worse, what his mom might do to him when he got home.

"Troy, sit down," Mr. Ortega gestured to a wooden chair in his office. Troy plopped down and began swinging his legs.

"Troy, this is the third time you've been in my office this week. I thought the last time we talked, we had arrived at an understanding," the principal began thoughtfully. He gazed into Troy's eyes. Troy gazed back. The swinging legs stopped.

"I've called your mother to come pick you up. Until your behavior improves, I'm afraid I have no choice but to send you home for the rest of the day. You'll be responsible for completing your assignments at home, of course."

Troy big brown eyes focused on the worn, muddy tips of his shoes. He pressed his feet into the bottom of the principal's desk in front of him and listened to the birds chirping outside. Big leafy sycamore trees towered outside the school window. Had anyone ever climbed them? He envied the robins that flew from treetop to telephone pole and back again, swooping and diving freely. He watched the cars passing by outside and wondered who was driving them, where they were going, and what they were going to do when they got there. He gazed at the houses that sat silently across the street and wondered who lived there, how many children they had, what kind of pets they had. He wondered if they were haunted with ghosts of their dead occupants. He wondered if he would ever make it out of school alive.

"Troy? Are you listening to me?" Mr. Ortega said sternly.

"Yes. I have to go home for the rest of the day," he repeated.

"Troy, I must tell you—if you don't learn to be quiet in class and do the work Miss Lewis gives you, it is very possible that you will no longer be allowed to attend school here." Mr. Ortega studied Troy's face for a reaction, but there was none. *If only I could reach him,* he thought. *He's an intelligent child. What is going on inside of him? Does his mother spoil him? Is the father involved at all?*

"I can't go to school here?" Troy's eyes widened. "Why not?"

Mr. Ortega sighed. "We have to see some improvement, Troy. If you can't be quiet in class, it disturbs the others who are working. Can't you understand that?"

"Yes," Troy said. He would try his hardest.

"Now go outside and wait for your mother. I will speak with her when she comes, and then you may go home."

Troy slid out of the chair, relieved that the scolding was over.

"You are a bright young man, Troy," Mr. Ortega placed his hand on Troy's shoulder as he opened the door. "I know you will do the right thing. Mrs. Palinski, please let me know as soon as Mrs. Esperanza is here."

"Yes, sir," she answered as he retreated back into his office.

Troy sat down dejectedly in one of the waiting room chairs. Not even Goldie and Finny could cheer him up this time. He knew he was in for it when he got home.

"Better go get your backpack, Troy," Mrs. Palinski said. "That way you'll be all ready to go when your mom gets here."

"Okay."

Walking to his locker, he passed the red fire alarm on the wall.

Pull in case of emergency. Troy didn't know what an emergency was, but it looked like an interesting object, so he reached up, grabbed ahold, and pulled.

Within seconds, the hallway was full of panicked teachers and grinning students, evacuating. Another alarm was ringing at Cleveland Fire Station 17, and soon a big red fire truck and shrieking ambulance were speeding up East Fifty-Fifth Street to the rescue.

Troy didn't bother to grab his backpack. He simply followed the other children outside to the parking lot, just like they practiced during fire drills. In the hallway the children processed out of their classrooms, heady with excitement. As she watched the line of students exiting the building, Miss Lewis looked strangely at him out of the corner of her eye. He couldn't be sure what she was thinking, but he knew it wasn't good.

Chapter 11: Doing the Best I Can, Part 1

Per mysterium sanctæ incarnationis tuae,
Libera nos, Jesu.

                – Litany of the Most Holy Name of Jesus

Gloria Esperanza sat on the edge of her bed, trying to wake up. It was one o'clock in the afternoon. She had just gotten a phone call from Troy's school, shocking her out of a deep sleep. For her, it wasn't lunchtime. Like many janitors, nurses, and service personnel, she worked at night and slept during the day.

Gloria was worn out, but she'd never admit it. She worked hard for a janitorial service, where she and her fellow workers cleaned office buildings in downtown Cleveland after the lawyers and accountants and their secretaries and staff had gone home for the day. Night after night, they vacuumed miles of hallways, emptied hundreds of black plastic trash cans, and cleaned endless rows of restrooms. She polished brass-handled glass doorways and hauled huge bags of garbage down the service elevator. She washed their shiny new coffee pots. She carefully brushed eraser crumbs off of heavy walnut desks and threw out half-eaten bagels and Styrofoam cups of herbal tea with the little tags still dangling over the edge.

Gloria was grateful for her job, but working at the Pace Picante salsa factory in San Antonio had been way more fun. She'd had that job for seven years, until the day Campbell's Soup bought them out and moved the factory to Paris, Texas, four hundred miles away. She was given a generous severance package, but with so many bills to pay, and friends and relatives to pay back money she had borrowed, the money ran out fast.

Despite the fact that Gloria was a hard worker, there was never enough money. Sometimes she was tempted by the nickels, dimes, and quarters carelessly tossed into partly opened desk drawers in the offices she cleaned, but she ignored them, even though it would have paid for an extra loaf of bread. She felt envious as she vacuumed around the piles of high-heeled shoes the secretaries kept tucked away under their desks. She herself had only two pair. But she didn't dare touch them. If anything were reported missing, even an old pair of shoes, she could lose her job.

Gloria dreamed of a better life. When her mother, Isabel, passed away the year before, her property had been divided between Gloria and her brothers and sisters. Gloria thought she would finally be able to buy her own home. But her credit was ruined from too many years of being behind in her bills, and no one would give a single working mother a loan for a new house. So she paid off her credit cards, bought Troy a Nintendo and Tia some new clothes, and put the rest in savings. She hoped that when Tia was ready for college, she would be able to pay for her tuition. She knew that she had to keep some for herself, too, for when she was too old or sick to work.

Gloria was sure Tia would make it into college. She was such a serious girl, a good student. Top in her class, they told her every year on parent-teacher conference day. Unlike Troy, Tia was never in trouble. Never skipped school. Always did her homework. But since they'd left San Antonio and moved to Cleveland, Tia had changed. The light in her eyes wasn't as bright. She seemed a little sad and sort of distant, like her spirit had traveled somewhere far away.

But it was Troy she was really worried about. She didn't understand him. She'd tried everything she could think of to get him to behave, but he just wouldn't. Or maybe, he couldn't. Maybe she should put him on those pills like the doctor said.

It hadn't been any better when they lived in San Antonio. At first, in Kindergarten, they didn't seem to expect too much of him. After all, he was only five. In first grade, they began to call her. Troy didn't do his homework, they said. *Homework for a first grader?*

If Troy did do his homework, he forgot to turn it in, or he lost it. He wouldn't sit still, couldn't be quiet. She was scared for him. If she couldn't find a way to get him under control, he would end up in prison, or worse. And now, she had gotten another phone call from the school asking her to come get her son. *What has he done now?*

On another night six months before, after yet another phone call from the school, she had decided to try to find Troy's father. Maybe Troy could stay with him for a while. Maybe what he needed was a father to look up to. She didn't know where William was living, so she had called his mother, Willie Pearl, who lived up north in faraway Cleveland.

"Hello." The deep voice that answered the phone had sounded hauntingly familiar.

"Hello, is ... May I speak to Willie Pearl?"

"Who's this?"

"Gloria. Gloria Esperanza. Who is this?"

"Gloria? Texas Gloria?" the man on the phone seemed delighted.

"Yes," she smiled hesitantly. Was something good finally going to happen?

"River Walk Gloria?"

"Yes! William? Is that you?" she said excitedly. She couldn't believe he actually remembered the first time they met.

"Yeah, it's me. Where you at?"

"Still in S.A."

"San Antone? Well I'll be. How's it going?"

"Good—good, I mean—well, all right I guess. I'm good. Tia is fine."

"Alright! Good news! So what you been up to?"

Gloria thought she heard Willie Pearl shouting in the background.

"It's nobody, Mama, I got it!" he shouted back.

Nobody. Is that how it is?

"I just need to ask you a favor," she began.

"Now hold on, I asked you a question!" he responded. She could hear Willie Pearl's voice fading away as if he were moving into another room. Maybe it was okay after all.

"Oh, well, I'm okay," Gloria lied.

"You always did know how to take care of yourself, didn't you?" he teased. "You always were a good woman!"

Gloria felt herself flush with pleasure. But then she remembered the reason she was calling.

"William, I need to talk to you about Troy."

"Troy? What's up with Troy?" he asked.

"He's really been getting into a lot of trouble at school. I've tried spanking him, taking away his Nintendo, I even promised to take him to a Spurs game if he would just behave for one whole week. I've tried everything! He's always in trouble, he's failing his classes, and I don't know what to do with him."

"Hmm."

"I was thinking maybe if he spent some time with you, maybe you could get him to behave."

"Well, jeez, Gloria, I don't know."

"I'm telling you William, I can't take no more of this. Calls from the school two and three times a week, the doctor's telling me to put him on pills. I don't have the money for pills! I'm scared, William! What if he don't learn to behave himself, what then? I don't want him growing up to be like some criminal, you know? Like those boys in Columbine who went and shot up their high school." Tears came to her eyes and she wiped them away impatiently. She hadn't realized how upset she was until she started talking. "Ever since my mom died, it's like, everything is just getting to me."

"Isabel died? When?" William asked softly.

"In January, last year. She had the lung cancer. None of us kids knew about it. She never told anybody until she was almost gone," Gloria sobbed.

"Hey, Gloria, that's too bad," William tried to forget that he and Isabel had never really gotten along. "I'm sorry, sweetie."

"Thank you. I appreciate it," Gloria sniffed.

"Hey, why don't you pack up those kids and come up here for a while?" William said.

"Really? But—I don't have a lot of cash right now," she said truthfully. Her mind raced ahead, trying to think what it would to be like living in Cleveland.

"No? Didn't your mother leave you anything when she passed?" William asked cautiously.

"Oh, well, yeah," Gloria admitted. "But most of that is for Tia's college. I put it in savings."

"Oh, that's cool," William said. His mind was spinning cartwheels. "That ain't no problem. I can send you the money for gas. I got me a little something saved up. How much you think you'd need?"

Gloria couldn't believe her ears. This was the man who abandoned her when she was pregnant, cheated on her, left her stranded with two hungry mouths to feed, and skipped out on his child support payments. This was the man who never once sent a Christmas or birthday card, who never once picked up the phone and called his own flesh and blood for ten years. How much did she need? Oh, maybe ten grand. But why he was being so generous all of a sudden?

"You guys can stay here if you want. I'm living with Mama now. She's got a big place here. Plenty of room. How about I sent you a thousand, that be enough?"

A thousand dollars? Gloria was stunned.

"Oh, yes! You—oh my goodness! That would be fantastic!" she exclaimed.

"What's your address now?" he asked. She gave it to him breathlessly. She couldn't wait to tell Delia about her good fortune. Everything was going to be all right now!

* * *

They had left in their old brown Mercury Sable station wagon, pulling a U-Haul trailer jammed to the top with all their belongings. Tia's antique dresser, which she had inherited from her Aunt

Carmen. Gloria's old piñata collection, Troy's stuffed animals, toy cars, and videos. Mattresses, blankets, shoes, and coats. It would get cold in Cleveland, Aunt Delia had sniffed sadly into her Kleenex, making sure her older sister packed winter coats, hats, and gloves. A tortilla press, and Tia's Panasonic stereo with all her Ricky Martin, Gloria Estefan, Selena and Mariah Carey albums and CDs.

The plan had been for them to move in with William, his mother, Willie Pearl, and his younger sister, Gina. They lived in a big old three-story, five-bedroom house that would have been considered almost elegant when it was built back in the 1920s. But the years had not been kind to the neighborhood. The residents couldn't afford to keep their property up, and many homes had fallen into disrepair. Those who could afford to had moved to the suburbs. But Willie Pearl liked where she was and refused to move to a smaller place.

At first, things seemed to go well. William seemed genuinely happy to see them. When he took them for rides along the Lake Erie Shoreway in his old black Lincoln Continental, he wrapped his arm around Gloria, turned up the stereo, and sang old Motown tunes with gusto. Gloria seemed happy and relaxed, and for the first time, Tia felt like she had a real father. Troy followed him around like a puppy.

But William Jackson had other things on his mind besides fatherhood. He had never known Troy. He loved his children, but he wasn't quite sure how to be a dad. His own father had abandoned them when he was born, and though he tried to do his best, he just didn't know how it was done, and it scared him and made him feel unsure of himself. The money he'd gotten when he hurt his back on that construction job six months ago was almost gone. His back was still bothering him, and he didn't know if he could find another job. He was afraid of the future. But he didn't tell Gloria that. Nor did he tell her the real reason he'd invited them all to move to Ohio.

Two months later, when his good buddy Bulldog Jenkins called him up, asking him to come down and shoot some pool at Ace's Tavern, he threw on his leather jacket, got in the Lincoln and told himself he'd be home in time for dinner. No need to tell Gloria where he was going. When he finally crawled home at two a.m., reeking of alcohol, she screamed at him in Spanish, damp, crumpled wads of Kleenex in her hands and all over the kitchen table. Witnessing the chaos, Tia's stomach had knotted in fear and anguish, and she prayed that Troy stayed fast asleep.

The next afternoon, William had come home bearing a bouquet of flowers and presented it to Gloria with a card. Tia watched as her mother's face lit up in a way she had never seen before. Light danced in her eyes as she opened the card, then threw her arms around William's neck and kissed his check. *"¡Mi querido!"* she had exclaimed, hugging him tightly. Tia wasn't sure what was happening, but she had a nagging feeling in the pit of her stomach that something still wasn't right.

After dinner, William opened a beer and handed it to Gloria, then opened one for himself and began telling Gloria about his dream of owning a liquor store. Tia washed the dishes, listening.

"I've already got the spot picked out. There's an empty store over on Seventy-first. Perfect location. Already got shelves and everything. I just need to get a license, get the inventory, hire a couple of clerks, and we be in business! I'll give you half! You don't have to work or nothing. Just maybe help me with the books, the numbers stuff, you know. I'll do the rest. What do ya say? Are you with me?" William was so excited it was hard not to get caught up.

"Yeah! Sure, why not?" Gloria took a swig from her beer and eyed William. He'd never been so talkative before, and she wasn't quite sure what to think.

"All's we got to do is meet the realtor, you know, the agent? Who's renting the place out. Until we get enough to buy the building, we got to rent. So they maybe give us a twelve month lease?

Twenty-four month? I have to find that out. But being as how you've got all the cash, you can be the one to make that decision. I'll let you handle all that!" William beamed.

Gloria was amazed that William trusted her to make such an important decision, all by herself.

"We'll go down there tomorrow, okay?" he cajoled.

"Okay!" Gloria smiled, then grew serious. "Wait a minute," she said, setting her bottle down on the lamp table. "What do you mean, 'I've got all the cash?' What cash?"

"The cash! You know, the money for the rent," William's eyes grew wide.

"I don't have money for no rent," she said, frowning.

Tia stole a furtive glance at her scheming parents.

"Oh! Wait!" William wiped his hand across his forehead, feigning confusion. "I thought ... didn't you say you had some money in savings, baby girl?"

"Yes." Gloria loved it when he called her his baby girl.

"Well, okay then. Whew! You sure had me going there for a minute! I was like, whoa man! Do we have the money for our store or not!" He laughed with relief. "So, it's gonna be great, baby girl. We'll have our own business. I was thinking we could call it "G.W.'s", for Gloria and William!" his eyes pleaded with her as if this was the most important part of all.

Gloria snickered. "G.W.'s? G.W.'s Liquor Store?" That sounded corny! Then she stopped to think. Maybe if the store did good, there would be enough money coming in to help pay for other things besides Tia's college. Maybe this was a good opportunity. William was a good man. She could tell this was something that was really important to him. And maybe, if the store did good, maybe William would settle down and ask her to marry him. It was a risk, she knew, but it was common knowledge that people who were afraid to take risks in business never got anywhere. You had to spend money to make money. Nothing ventured, nothing gained.

She stubbed her cigarette out in the overflowing ashtray and stood up. She walked over to the window and looked past the grimy curtain out into the gray Cleveland sky, then turned to face him.

"Let's do it!" she said enthusiastically.

"Aw, that's my girl!" William smiled a huge pearly white smile, got up and opened his arms wide. Gloria hugged him and laughed as he lifted her up and swung her around in a crazy dance, unaware that Tia was watching thoughtfully from the kitchen.

Chapter 12: No Deposit, No Return

They should put a warning label on you
the way they do diet soda.
The sweetness is artificial
and has been known to cause heartbreak.
No deposit, no return.

— Nora Angeline Page

The next day, they drove to an abandoned storefront on East Seventy-First Street. A little red Chevette with faded paint was parked in front, freshly washed. A man Gloria had never seen before got out of the car, sidled over to the Lincoln and gave William's hand a strong shake. William got out of the car and lit a cigarette, cupping his hand into the breeze. Then he and the man walked over to the empty building.

Gloria wasn't sure what to do, so she sat and waited. As the men talked in low voices, she looked over at the storefront. It was a decent building, but the glass was covered in dust and dirt from years of sitting vacant. A big "FOR LEASE OR SALE" sign in blue letters was taped to the front with a phone number to call Fred Gorman Realty for more information.

William and the realtor walked over and peered through the glass, trying to see into the empty store. Gloria got out and tried to act like a businesswoman so the realtor would know that they were legit.

"Gloria Esperanza," she said, sticking out her right hand.

"Gloria! I've heard so much about you," the realtor smiled warmly and shook Gloria's hand.

"And you are?" Gloria asked.

"Oh, I'm sorry, ma'am. Reese. Reese Myers. Pleased to meet you, Mrs. Esperanza!"

Gloria frowned. "You're not Fred Gorman?"

"Who?" Reese turned to look questioningly at William. Gloria waited for an answer.

There was an awkward pause.

"Fred Gorman. The realtor?" Gloria pointed at the sign.

"Oh, Fred!" Reese laughed a little too hard. "Fred. Uh, Mr. Gorman couldn't make it today, so he sent me instead," he explained in a jovial tone. "I'm sure you understand, sometimes we businessmen can't be two places at the same time! Mr. Gorman had another commitment—my associate—I mean, we work *together* on some of our more important transactions."

Gloria glanced over at William, who was busily putting change into the parking meter. Jingling his car keys, he walked over and wrapped his arm around Gloria.

"This here girl is *my* most important transaction, Mr. Myers!" William teased. "Now what can you tell us about this beautiful piece of property?"

Reese Myers cleared his throat. "Yes. Well, it is a beautiful property, Mr. Jackson. You are quite right about that. I would have to say that this is one of my most *promising* and *underappreciated* properties that we—uh, Mr. Gorman and myself, have currently available at this time."

William nodded, listening carefully. "Um-hmm." Then, to Gloria, he whispered, "See! What'd I tell you?"

Gloria's earlier fears began to subside as William clasped his hand on her shoulder. Reese Myers walked them around the other side of the building and they followed.

"....this corner lot, as you can see, is strategically placed on Euclid Avenue, one of the busiest streets in the City of Cleveland. And over here," he gestured towards the dumpster in the alley, "as you can see, you have a full access to the alley, including the private and exclusive use of the City of Cleveland's waste disposal service. For a small monthly fee, of course." William squeezed Gloria's shoulder reassuringly.

Reese Myers looked up towards the upper stories of the building. "And should you be so inclined, Mr. and Mrs. Jackson—uh, oh, I mean, Mrs. Esperanza—my mistake, ma'am, you two sure do make a cute couple—if you should be so inclined, we also have available a two bedroom apartment for rent, right above the store. Which can be negotiated into the contract, of course."

Gloria thought it might not be a bad idea to rent an apartment too. If she and William ever got on Willie Pearl's bad side, at least they'd have a place to go.

"We could rent out the apartment, too," Gloria said. "That would be more money coming in!" She was proud of herself for thinking of it.

"Sure, honey, whatever you say," William gave her a quick kiss and a wink.

"So, what do you say, is it a deal?" Reese asked, looking at them, palms together.

"What do you think?" William asked, smiling.

Gloria felt a flush of confusion overtake her happy feeling. It was all so good! She couldn't quite believe her luck. Then something occurred to her.

"Wait! What about the inside?" she asked. "We haven't seen the inside!"

Reese Myers shifted on his feet and darted a glance at William and back again to Gloria.

"Yeah, Mr. Myers, we want to see the inside, too!" William exclaimed.

Reese smiled. "Of course! I mean, uh, of course you would want to see inside! Unfortunately, I am afraid that Mr. Gorman, uh, Fred, my partner, has the only set of keys to this particular property, and I, uh...." He looked anxiously at William.

"You get your Mr. Fred Gorman on the phone then and tell him we ain't signin' *nothin'* until we've seen the inside, Mr. Myers!" William glared.

"Oh I understand, Mr. Jackson, believe me, I do understand and I appreciate where you're comin' from on this because I myself, I would *never* rent a property sight unseen, I would never expect a businessman such as yourself and Mrs. Esperanza..."

"Gloria!" she corrected him.

"Gloria! My apologies, Gloria. Truly, I understand where ya'll is comin' from. However, as I said, Mr. Gorman—he has the only set of keys, and I—well, I am afraid that he is unavailable for any foreseeable length of time this afternoon. However," he brightened with a helpful idea, "however, if you would like to come back tomorrow, I am sure that Mr. Gorman would be able to conduct you on a tour of the interior of the property," he clasped his hands over his chest.

"No, we don't want to come back tomorrow, Mr. Myers," William said firmly. "We want to sign this lease *today!*"

"Oh, yes, Mr. Jackson, I do understand, and I applaud your fine sense of the business end of things. Why as a matter of fact, I believe Mr. Gorman has another party of interest in these—in this particular property, which I believe he may be showing early tomorrow morning, around seven a.m., to be exact. Which—well, I guess you might say that this is a *once in a lifetime opportunity* ya'll have right now." Mr. Myers looked at them imploringly.

Gloria looked up at William, but his face was inscrutable. He seemed to be thinking over Mr. Myers' statement about a "once in a lifetime opportunity." He licked his lips and then turned and smiled at Gloria.

Gloria was in a hard spot. She didn't want to lose what might be her only chance at being a respectable business owner. And she didn't want to disappoint William or lose his love. She looked again at the "FOR LEASE OR SALE" sign. It all looked legitimate. She looked at William questioningly.

"I don't think we should sign a lease until we see inside!" she whispered.

"You're right, honey," he said, giving her another quick kiss. Then, to Myers, "We can't sign a lease today. You show us inside, and then we'll think about it."

Reese looked disappointed, shrugging his shoulders. "Okay. I just would hate to see you two lose out here. But I can't say as how I blame you." Gloria's heart sank. It was all going to fall apart, and it was her fault. The inside was probably just fine. They should sign a lease and get this store before somebody else snatched it up.

Then Reese Myers snapped his fingers. "I got it!" he exclaimed, looking first at William and then at Gloria. "A deposit! You give me a deposit, to hold it, until you see inside—just 'til tomorrow. Mr. Gorman can show it to you tomorrow. All I need is a small deposit, and that way he can't lease it to somebody else!" he declared.

William smiled his biggest smile. "You'd do that for us?" he said gratefully. "That's really great. Isn't that great, Gloria?" he squeezed her shoulder again.

A deposit? Why hadn't she thought of that.

"Sure! How much do you need?" she had asked. And Mr. Myers just smiled as she pulled out her savings account checkbook.

* * *

They had celebrated into the night and the wee hours of the morning, and Gloria had finally fallen asleep on the couch. The next morning, groggy and hung over, she woke to a cold, empty room. William was gone.

A note with her name on it was on the kitchen counter. She never told them what it said. She lit a cigarette and read it twice. Bursting into tears, she ripped it into a thousand pieces. Then, she got on the phone to Delia, slamming the bedroom door behind her.

Tia didn't know what had just happened, but she knew it was bad. The dream she had of being close to her father was over.

Chapter 13: Doing the Best I Can, Part 2

When I was thirteen, we visited Lourdes…
Who was the man hanging on the Cross?
'A malefactor of long ago.'
Ah, they did well to punish him…I replied.

– Carmelite nun, aged 53 years

William never came home after that, and he never called. Willie Pearl had blamed it all on Gloria. Gloria went back and forth between blaming herself and blaming William. She knew he'd never be back. It had all been a big mistake. He hadn't really loved her. It had all been a scam. But Gloria was tough. She was a survivor. And she had her family to think of. She packed them up and moved them out into a low rent apartment in Midtown.

Gloria was glad to be out of Willie's house, but Troy was unhappy. He really missed his dad. It made him angry that one minute he was there, and the next minute he was gone. Tia knew that Troy was hurt, and it made her mad that Gloria just didn't seem to understand the pain that had been inflicted on them. She wished they had never left San Antonio. It was the only home they'd ever known. And now, the only father they'd ever known was gone, too.

After a while, they had settled into their new apartment, and things seemed better. Tia and Troy grew even closer. They knew that they could only depend on each other. But Tia was tired of always having to babysit, on top of all the homework and her job at La Chic Boutique. She wanted to enjoy her last year of high school. She wanted to go to a few parties—not that anyone ever invited her. It was hard going to a new school in a new city, where she didn't know anybody and people weren't very friendly to begin with. She wanted to go to a football game, a dance—anything to get out and enjoy herself for once. But it just wasn't possible. They couldn't afford to pay a babysitter, and he wasn't old enough to stay home alone. For a while, Troy still went to Willie Pearl's after school, but he hated it. The old lady was hard of hearing, and she tried to make him eat soggy egg salad sandwiches when all he wanted was one of Grandma Isabel's bean and cheese tacos.

Gloria tried her best to support them. She had gone to an employment agency and quickly found the cleaning job. It was a union job, too, so wages were a little better, but money was still tight. Sometimes, Gloria had to choose between paying the phone bill or buying food. Once, she hadn't paid the phone bill, and they turned the phone off. Then, when she had the money to pay her bill, she tried to get it turned back on, but the phone company demanded a huge deposit on top of the money she owed them from before. She didn't have the money for the deposit, so they didn't have a phone for six months.

Gloria had yelled and cried and cursed them. She hated the rich phone company executives with their big fancy houses, their shiny new cars, and their easy living. She resented these people with money who didn't give a second thought to people like her and her kids. The wealthy didn't care if people like them lived or died. Just pay your phone bill every month. Just empty my trash for me at night. Don't speak to me on the street. Don't mess around with us. We're the phone company, we're powerful, and you are nothing. You are nobody.

When payday came around, Gloria would take her check down to the grocery store to cash, for which they charged her a small fee. Then she would buy money orders to pay the utilities, the rent, and the bill at the hospital from when she had pneumonia the winter before. The money orders cost her small fees as well. Afterwards, she would walk over to the RTA and buy a monthly bus pass, which was cheaper than paying full fare every day. Longingly, she would look at all the food she could buy, anything she wanted, but she knew she had to wait until she got her food stamps for that.

Then she would take what little cash was left and buy cleaning supplies, which food stamps didn't pay for: soap, toilet paper, shampoo. And, of course, cigarettes, and maybe some nail polish or new earrings at Woolworth's. But usually nothing for herself. This month, she got a birthday card for her sister Delia. That set her back $2.50, plus 33 cents for the stamp to mail it. She would have to cut back on her smokes a little bit to pay for it.

Gloria tried not to think of Troy's school shoes, getting tighter every week, and the worn shoelaces that had been tied and retied in knots to hold them together a few more weeks. If worst came to worst, she would have to ask Tia for money. She hated to do that. She didn't want to take away the one good thing her daughter had earned for herself: her own money.

Too many nights had been spent worrying about money. Too many days had been spent burying her anxiety over Troy with too many cigarettes. She missed her friends and family in San Antonio. And she missed her mother, Isabel, who had just passed away the previous spring from lung cancer. She knew she should hate him, but she even missed William Jackson and the way he used to sing to her in the front seat of his fancy Lincoln and call her "baby girl." So when the school called and woke her up to inform her of Troy's latest crisis, she was truly at the end of her rope.

* * *

When Gloria arrived, the entire student body, teachers and staff, were standing in the parking lot. Curious people stood on the sidewalk across the street, staring. A fire truck was positioned in front of the school, lights spinning and flashing, but to her immense relief, no water sprayed and no smoke billowed from the school building. A firefighter wearing full protective gear stood talking to Mr. Ortega and writing notes on a clipboard. A news team from the local network was standing around, watching and waiting for something to happen. The cameraman stood ready, camera in hand, but there was nothing to film.

Quickly Gloria spotted Troy in the row of third graders. Striding purposefully, she grasped him by the hand, like he was a little kid or something. He was totally embarrassed and kept trying to pull away.

"Troy!" she fumed. "What happened?"

"Nothing," he said truthfully.

"What do you mean, nothing? There's fire trucks here, something must have happened! Anyway, I don't care about that. You are in big trouble for a little boy! I'm sick and tired of getting calls from this school waking me up to come and pick you up because you can't behave!" she nearly shouted, causing the others to look.

"Mrs. Esperanza!" Mr. Ortega excused himself from talking with the fireman and quickly stepped over to where Troy and Gloria were. Gloria stopped reluctantly. She had no desire to hear once again what a bad job she had done as a mother raising this child.

"Mrs. Esperanza. Thank you for coming," Mr. Ortega began. "I'm sorry about this—this situation we seem to be having today. I wanted to speak with you, but unfortunately," he gestured with both arms, "I must attend to this. Would you be available to meet with me tomorrow at four?"

"Sure," Gloria lied. She would agree to anything to get away from there.

"Fine. I'll see you tomorrow, then. Thank you, Mrs. Esperanza. Troy, remember what I said, now."

Mr. Ortega walked back to where the firemen were gathered by their vehicle. Two other firefighters walked out of the building, having carefully searched for smoke or fire and finding none. The all-clear was given, and the teachers and students calmly filed back into the school building.

All except Troy. Gloria had him by the arm. The school counselor had recommended that Gloria take Troy to a psychologist and have him tested for learning disabilities. The counselor had said something about "attentional difficulties" and "impulsivity," whatever that meant. She tried to remember the name of the medicine that the doctor might put him on, ritta-something. Ritta-when?

Ritta-then? But Gloria had no money to take Troy to some strange doctor. After all, he wasn't sick. He was just an active boy, that's all. *Those teachers are full of frijoles,* Gloria thought. Still, she wished he could behave so they would quit calling her all the time.

She knew an education was important, and she wanted her son to have a good life. She had to get tough. All the way home from school, Gloria yelled at Troy. It was a long, enraged lecture in Spanish mixed with English that terrified him and left him feeling lost and confused and afraid.

"What you need is a good spanking! Don't you know how to be good?" she yelled. Troy proudly fought back the tears for as long as he could.

* * *

"Why'd you do that?" she asked him later, after things had calmed down. "Don't you know you'll get in trouble for talking back to the teacher?"

"They always blame me for everything," Troy tried to explain. "Josh and Michael talk all the time, but they never get in trouble!"

"I don't care about the other kids, it's you I'm worried about," she said, and banished him to his bedroom. "You are grounded for a week! No Nintendo, no movies!"

"Mom!" he cried, "I'm doing the best I can!"

Later, she knocked softly on the door, tiptoed in and told him good-bye before leaving for work. He was laying on his bed, talking to Deano, his green stuffed dinosaur.

"I love you, mijo." She kissed him gently on the forehead, stroking his cheek with her hand. Be a good boy for me? Please?" she asked.

"Yes, Mama," he whispered. He wanted so much to please her.

"Okay, you say your prayers before time to sleep, okay?"

"Okay."

"You be good for Tia, okay?"

"Okay."

"You do your school work, okay?

"Okay. Bye, Mama!" He hugged her tight.

"Adiós, baby," she said, kissing the top of his head. Like always, she told herself that everything was going to be all right.

Chapter 14: All Hallows' Eve

He sits in ambush with the rich, in private places,
that he may kill the innocent.

– Ps. 9:30 (10:8)

*P*aul Fisher lay awake in the dim morning light. "Just two more months," he murmured to his wife.

"Um-hmm."

A heavy silence followed.

"Our IT guy is going to drive us crazy before it's all over with. He's got us copying all our documents onto backup diskettes. My secretary's working overtime all this week trying to get it all done," Paul whispered so as not to wake Char and Kayla.

"Well, it's a good thing you took off this week. It'll give her a chance to get finished before the end of the year."

"Yeah. Before the end of the century!"

"Do you think we'd better take out some extra cash just in case? I heard they're saying the ATM's might go haywire."

"Yeah," he paused.

"I think you'd better take out a couple of thousand. And take the car in and have them check it out."

"Okay."

Barbara Fisher rolled on her back and stared up at the ceiling. "I heard a caller on Larry King last week say he thinks Iraq is going to try to attack us while we're all living it up on New Year's Eve."

"Never happen. They're too far away. By the time they got half-way here, our missiles would totally blow them away."

"Yeah, but Saddam Hussein's not a sane man. And he hates our guts."

Paul reached out to squeeze his wife's waist. "You worry too much!" he said, burrowing his head into her shoulder.

"You just wait!" she raised her voice. "New Year's Day in the year 2000, you're going to turn on the news and ..."

"Mom ... Dad .... it's seven in the morning!" Char moaned sleepily. "Can't we sleep late?"

"It's not seven o'clock here, sweetie." Paul reluctantly stood up and stretched. "It's nine. Cleveland's on Eastern time! So get up! We've got a busy day ahead!" He reached for his glasses and pulled on his bathrobe.

A muffled groan came from the other queen sized bed. "Get up girls!" Barbara Fisher called out cheerfully. Kayla obediently opened her eyes and stared up at the ceiling, threw off the covers and stuck her feet into her old pink slippers. She slowly stood up and shuffled off to the bathroom.

Char lay motionless, pillow bunched up under her elbow. She didn't move a muscle. Mrs. Fisher narrowed her eyes. "Char!" she warned.

"I'll get up when she gets out of the bathroom," Char mumbled.

Mr. Fisher was already dressed and busy with his cordless shaver. He grabbed the remote with his free hand and flipped on the news channel.

" ...These refugee children are finally returning to their homes in Kosovo after spending the past five months in safe havens here in Australia," said the reporter. "But in the wake of all the fighting, no one knows for sure what they'll find when they get there. Michael Plante, reporting from Sydney." The screen switched to the anchor's desk.

"Thank you, Michael, for that report. That's really a hard thing to comprehend. How are those children going to survive without homes, without their parents?" asked the perky young news anchor. "When we come back, the amazing story from Russia—the first fully-preserved woolly mammoth has been dug up after being frozen in ice for more than twenty-three thousand years! Stay with us!"

"They're probably going to clone it," Mr. Fisher muttered, clicking off his shaver and rubbing his chin.

"So what if they do?" Mrs. Fisher retorted. "Wouldn't it be great to see a real live mammoth?"

"You're talking *Jurassic Park*, now, hon. I don't think I want to go there," he replied, shaking his head. "I'm going to go find a paper. Be right back." He swung into a tweed jacket and headed out toward the hotel lobby in search of the *Wall Street Journal*.

"Still killing trees!" she tossed after him, pulling out her laptop to check her e-mail.

Kayla emerged from the bathroom and looked tentatively at her sister, still buried in the bed. Barbara Fisher glanced up.

"Get up, Char," she ordered. Char stretched, yawned regretfully and sat up, looking like the living dead.

"It's freezing in here!" she complained. "Why can't we turn up the heat?"

"Well there's your robe. Put it on," her mother pointed.

Char wrapped her thin arms around herself and mumbled, "No, that's okay." Hugging herself tightly, she stumbled around Kayla and headed towards the bath. Kayla stared and rolled her eyes.

"Suit yourself." The bathroom door closed with a clacking thud.

Kayla sighed and wondered why her sister was so grouchy. She picked up the remote where her father had laid it and played with the buttons until she found MTV. Her mother ignored her, typing instructions to her stockbroker back in Great Falls. Kayla stared at the nearly naked dancers on the screen, tapping the remote on her leg in time to an old hit song by Madonna that had nothing virginal about it.

"Better get dressed so we can go have breakfast," Mrs. Fisher said.

Just then Mr. Fisher returned with his newspaper. "Ready?" he asked to no one in particular. He glanced at the television and did a double-take. "What kind of garbage is that?" he said rather loudly. He shot a look at Kayla and then glared at the screen.

Kayla jumped up and turned off the TV, throwing her arms around his neck. "Nothing, Daddy," she said brightly.

"Nothing, huh? You know I don't like you to watch that kind of stuff."

"I know! It's nothing, really, Dad. It's just a song!" Kayla brushed it off.

Barbara Fisher looked up from her e-mail and peered at them over her bifocals.

"Never mind that," he replied sternly. "You girls need to get ready. I'm going to go down to the restaurant and get us a table." Picking up the newspaper, Mr. Fisher quickly left the hotel room. He didn't want to get entangled in an argument with his teenage daughter so early in the morning.

"Why won't Daddy let us watch MTV? Everybody else does."

"I don't know, Mikayla. Your father has some strange ideas at times." Mrs. Fisher sighed. "He worries about you and your sister, that's all. All fathers do. Now why don't you get ready now, all right?" Mrs. Fisher walked gracefully to the bathroom door and knocked. "Hurry up, Char, other people have to use the bathroom, too."

Kayla smirked and turned the TV back on, flipping to another channel.

"It has been two years since Mother Teresa died, and her order, the Missionaries of Charity sisters, continues to grow worldwide, serving the poor and destitute, orphans, the dying and the abandoned. Now, two years after her death, thousands of people continue to journey to Calcutta to visit the tomb of this saintly nun and to volunteer in the homes she founded.

"But Mother Teresa's influence extends far beyond the streets of Calcutta. In 1994, she filed a brief with the United States Supreme Court on behalf of the plaintiff in the appeal of Alexander Loce, a father who tried to stop his girlfriend from having an abortion."

The TV screen flashed a picture of Mother Teresa as the announcer read from the court document.

"Human rights are not a privilege conferred by government. They are every human being's entitlement by virtue of his humanity. The right to life does not depend, and must not be contingent, on the pleasure of anyone else, not even a parent or sovereign." Kayla watched as the station showed video clips of the tiny, wrinkled Albanian nun in the blue and white sari.

"Give yourself fully to God. He will use you to accomplish great things on the condition that you believe much more in His love than in your own weakness."

Kayla stared at the screen, wondering. She didn't think of herself as being weak. She thought she was pretty invincible. *What is she talking about? She looks kind of weak to me,* Kayla thought. *She must be talking about herself.*

"What are you doing? Get ready!" her mother ordered.

"Okay, Mom." And she turned off the television.

* * *

After breakfast, they decided to begin their first day in Cleveland at the Great Lakes Science Center.

"What time do they open?" Barbara Fisher asked, checking her Hamilton watch.

"Nine-thirty." Paul answered.

"Do you think we can walk it?"

"I think so," he replied. "It's only about seven or eight blocks."

"I'm ready if you are. Come on, girls!" she smiled, and the four of them set out. The wide sidewalks were teeming with more people than Char and Kayla had ever seen in one place before. Homeless, shaggy-haired men in greasy rags stood on the corners while Black women proudly sporting huge hairdos and long acrylic nails slowly pushed baby strollers covered in blankets. Arab women draped modestly in head scarves went about their errands. Teenagers joked around, obviously cutting class. Gawking tourists with cameras around their necks peered at maps, stared up at skyscrapers, and tried to figure out where they were. The Fishers did likewise.

"It's yucky out here!" Char complained after just one block. "It's too hot and sticky!"

"First you were too cold, now you're too hot. Make up your mind!" Mr. Fisher remarked.

"Oh, come on. Would you rather be back home? It's twenty degrees and snowing in Great Falls," said Mrs. Fisher, herding the girls towards the street. She glanced about nervously.

"Let's just enjoy our trip. Do you think we could do that?" said Mr. Fisher.

"Okay! Forget I said anything," Char groaned. Kayla gathered her hair into a ponytail and ignored them.

"I think we need to head this way." Mr. Fisher gestured towards Ontario Street, and together they forged toward the intersection to cross at the light, staring at the throngs of people all around them. The streets were filled with buses, cars, and taxicabs. At the green light, the huge mob raced *en masse* across Ontario Street like horses out of the gate at the Kentucky Derby. Everyone had to walk quickly to keep from being left behind, or run over. Except for the homeless people. They had nowhere to go, so they weren't in any hurry. Taxis honked as they pushed past, and people with something to live for jumped out of the way.

Kayla and Char craned their necks, trying to get their bearings. There was a huge baseball stadium just south of them. A very long line of RTA buses was parked bumper-to-bumper at the east curb, where throngs of office workers and students waited to board. Drivers stood talking and laughing, enjoying their brief break at this main transfer hub. Some drivers were getting off their shift while others were just beginning. Kayla tried to imagine what it would be like to drive a bus all day, the same route, the same streets, over and over for eight hours, day after day after day.

The light changed again, and they raced across Euclid Avenue, their parents huffing and puffing to keep up.

"Wow! Look at that! Can we go in there?" Char exclaimed. They were standing in front of the BP Building, a modern 45-story office building built back in the 1980s when Cleveland was emerging from its polluted past as a dirty industrial city on the verge of bankruptcy into the bright new future of urban renewal.

"Sure! Let's check it out," Mr. Fisher said enthusiastically.

A wonderfully modern creation in glass and marble welcomed them into a light-filled atrium full of airy trees and cool, sparkling fountains. Paul, Barbara, and Kayla followed Char as she skipped through the revolving brass-handled glass doors, marveling at the beauty inside.

"This is sooo cooool!" Char breathed, staring up into the great open hall full of light.

"It is beautiful," her mother agreed.

The atrium was built like stair-steps, with the ceiling at the front entrance gradually expanding upwards the farther inside you went, until you could see all the way up into the glass-walled offices eight stories up. The walls of the atrium were tinted glass and brass, and the floors were a pale rust-colored marble. Well-dressed business-men and women in black or gray wool trench coats hurried quickly past, full of importance. They carried leather briefcases and folded umbrellas as if they were signs of superiority, membership cards issued only to members of an elite club.

Lined with shops, the center of the atrium was filled with large planters full of huge rhododendrons, palm trees, schefflera and ficus trees mingled with white French-style cafe tables with patio umbrellas. In the center of the atrium was a lovely cascading fountain. It was a soothing, beautiful place—so different from the steel-gray city streets just outside.

"Let's get some coffee," Paul suggested, spotting a coffee bar.

The girls ran ahead and looked at the menu.

"Can I get a muffin?" Kayla asked.

"But you just had breakfast!" Mrs. Fisher cried.

"I'm still hungry!" Kayla said vehemently.

"So am I," said Char.

"Sure, get whatever you want. This is our vacation!" Paul said.

After they got their coffee and muffins, they sat at a cafe table and admired the building's interior while Char snapped picture after picture on her digital camera.

"Boy, wouldn't you love to work in here," Paul said in amazement.

"I'll bet the rent is outrageous," Barbara answered. "But it is gorgeous!"

"I'd love to see the offices up there!" he added.

"Well, maybe someday we'll open a branch office here in Cleveland," she joked.

"Yeah, right, just as soon as we win that big antitrust suit against Microsoft!" Paul quipped.

After finishing their coffee and muffins, they slowly went back out through the front doors. Char didn't want to leave and had to be physically pulled out the door, still snapping pictures.

Crossing Superior Avenue, they made their way to the shiny new Key Tower building rising majestically into the sky. At fifty-seven stories, it was the tallest building between Chicago and New York and had a huge interior with six banks of elevators. But unlike the BP Building, the interior of Key Tower was cold and businesslike. No plants and fountains greeted them, just a lighted rectangular directory of names and office numbers. A husky security guard wearing a dark suit and tie and a headset stood nearby, eyes fixed on five security screens.

The Fishers stopped and looked around, trying to take it all in. Finally, Mr. Fisher walked up to the security guard and smiled. The guard glanced up, then lowered his head back down to watch the screens.

"Excuse me. We're from out of town. Can you tell me if there is an observation deck on the upper floors?"

"No observation deck."

Mr. Fisher turned and shrugged apologetically.

"What's the point of having the tallest building if you can't go up to the top floor?" Mrs. Fisher muttered critically, but the guard ignored them.

"No kidding. I think the Terminal Tower has one. It's not as tall, but it'll be fun."

"I wanted to ride the elevator, Dad," Kayla pouted. Char rolled her eyes.

"I know, hon, but the man said it's not open to the public."

"Come on! Let's go to the Science Center!" Kayla ran to the heavy revolving glass doors and began to push as hard as she could, barely budging it. "I can't get this stupid door open!" she laughed.

Char ran up next to her and helped push, and together they got the huge doors to turn, allowing them to walk through.

"Man, they don't want people just dropping in here, do they?" Paul Fisher muttered as he shoved.

"It's because of the bank," Mrs. Fisher said.

"Huh?"

"This building houses a bank, see?" she pointed to the old Society for Savings Building, built in the 1880s, which was attached like a barnacle to the massive skyscraper.

"Oh, yeah. I think you're on to something."

"They don't want people in here unless you've got business here."

"Well then, we'll just take our business elsewhere!" Paul Fisher joked.

They finally made it through the huge revolving doors. Kayla stuck her tongue out at the security guard on the way out.

"Kayla!" her mother scolded. Char snickered.

"Sorry, mom," Kayla giggled, glancing at Char. The family headed east up the street.

"Hey, that's nice," Mrs. Fisher admired the graceful statue of a man in the middle of a fountain in the wide plaza east of the tower.

The fountain was turned off for the winter, but they read the inscription on the plaque affixed to the black marble surrounding the pool.

"It says this is a Peace Memorial, in honor of all those who gave their lives in the military," their father read. But the warm, sticky wind blowing off Lake Erie pushed them away from the Memorial. They hurried across the empty plaza towards St. Clair and Lakeside Avenues.

"Daddy, I'm tired!" Char cried, her hair clinging to her cheeks in damp yellow strings.

"Oh, you're always complaining!" Kayla accused. Char made a face at her and stuck out her tongue.

"We're just about there!" Paul tried to sound cheerful, but it was oppressively warm and humid, and they were all suffering from jet lag. He decided he'd better get them a cab for the trip back. "Hey hon, what's the weather supposed to be like tomorrow?"

Ignoring her husband, Mrs. Fisher pointed to the silver dome-like structure on the lakeshore to their left. "There it is!" she exclaimed.

"Thank goodness," Char mumbled to herself.

"Mom, is this where you said they have the theater with the 360-degree screen?" Kayla panted, walking faster.

"Yes! The Omnimax. I think they're showing a movie on the space shuttle today." Barbara smiled. "Look at all those school buses!" Ten yellow school buses were parked in front of the Great Lakes Science Center.

They finally made it inside and drank in the cool, dry air-conditioned air. The big silver building was full of fun interactive science exhibits. Groups of school children on field trips raced excitedly through the large rooms full of displays, while parents and teachers chatted in corners and tried the exhibits themselves.

Char immediately spotted the lighted interactive tornado display and jogged towards it. Kayla followed. Incredibly, by directing warm white steam inside a three-foot high box with open sides, the scientists had designed a real miniature tornado that you could touch. Char placed her hand gingerly inside the swirling white vortex and smiled with delight. As her hand blocked the warm air swelling up from the base, the tornado disappeared. Startled by a strange feeling of dread, Char jerked her hand away, and the innocent wisps of white began swaying and swirling up once again.

"Cool beans!" exclaimed Kayla, placing her hand inside and drawing it out again and again. Happily she flashed a smile at Char.

But Char no longer wanted to play with the hypnotically spiraling column. She just wanted to leave.

"Come on!" Kayla cried. She wasn't going to let Char's bad mood ruin the fun. Grabbing her sister's arm, she pulled and dragged Char away to the next exhibit.

There were so many interactive displays that they couldn't decide which one to try next. Pulling on a twenty-foot-long lever, they lifted a huge car engine weighing hundreds of pounds. They jumped against photosensitive screens as flashing lights went off, and their shadows stayed on the screens for a minute or two after. They drew designs using a compound pendulum swinging from the ceiling (the designs looked just like the ones he used to make on his old Spirograph, Paul said.) Touching an electrically charged globe made their hair stand on end and they giggled at each other's crazy hairdos. They were having so much fun that they didn't even notice their mother standing a few feet away, happily taking pictures.

Soon it was time for the first movie showing in the Omnimax Theater. The seats in the theater weren't like normal movie seats. These seats tilted backwards so that you were facing the ceiling! The Fishers leaned back and stared upwards, laughing like little kids, wondering what was next. When the movie started, video and sound surrounded them, all around the walls and on the ceiling. It was like you were really there. Real life, only bigger.

When the movie ended, Char and Kayla dashed down the steps of the escalator to the ground floor, where a small hot air balloon was rising and falling. At the push of a button, a blast of hot air shot the balloon fifty feet into the air, then floated down again after the air was cut off. Barbara snapped photo after photo, amazed that her daughters were getting along so well. This vacation idea of Paul's had definitely been a good thing. It was great fun, and before they knew it, the morning was gone. When Paul reminded them it was time to go see the Rock Hall, they didn't want to leave. Meanwhile, the red low-battery light on Barbara's camera was flashing. She dug through her bag, persistently searching for more.

"Darn it! I left my extra batteries back at the hotel," she said, frowning.

"I'm sure they have some in the gift shop," Paul replied.

"I don't want to buy them here. Their prices are way too high."

"Why don't we walk around and find a store? There's got to be a drugstore around here, I would imagine."

They stopped at the information desk for directions, and after walking several blocks finally found a discount drug store, where they stocked up on water, gum, magazines, candy, a map of the city of Cleveland, batteries, and postcards. Back on the street, they headed to the Rock Hall again so Barbara could take some more pictures. Char and Kayla hammed for the camera, pretending to be fashion models on a photo shoot. Barbara laughed and Paul felt more relaxed than he had in years. They were finally having a good time together as a family.

* * *

Char saw him first.

He kept his eyes on the sidewalk in front of him as he walked. He had learned the hard way that if he looked into the eyes of the people he passed, he would have to endure their shock, sadness, anger, and revulsion. So he kept his eyes firmly focused on the pavement.

"Pig!" one woman called out from across the street.

He could always tell the ones who had had them. Their reactions were the most violent. He knew the pain of their loss and their guilt was what made them so angry and that they blamed him for showing them the consequences of their actions. He tried not to take it personally, but the whirling vortex of painful emotion that swirled around him was like the eye of a hurricane when he passed. So he prayed as he walked.

Hail Mary, full of grace, the Lord is with thee ...

The Rosary was his lifeline, his umbilical cord to the Blessed Mother. He clutched it tightly wrapped around his knuckles and silently tried to show the world the work of Satan. But the world did not want to see. Shocked mothers shielded their children's eyes or quickly tried to distract them. Sometimes he heard them hissing indignantly as he passed by.

"Oh, how disgusting!"

"Sick!"

"Why do they let people show things like that?"

"Children shouldn't have to see things like that!"

Even those who were sympathetic to his cause sometimes muttered things like, "He shouldn't be doing that, it just makes people more upset," or "Why do they have to show things like that to get their point across? Nobody needs to see something like that."

Things. Things like that. But that was the whole point. They weren't just things. They were people. Tiny, little, helpless people who had the misfortune to be conceived in America after 1973 by women who, for whatever reason, didn't want them.

Char tried to nudge Kayla quietly so their parents wouldn't notice, keeping her eyes glued to the poster-size picture the man carried. As Kayla looked up, Char pointed, and Kayla's eyes grew wide with open-mouthed horror.

People around them were reacting. You could feel it in the air. *Please God, don't let her see!* Char silently prayed with all her soul that their mother wouldn't look up. But it was too late.

For a second, Char and Kayla thought their mother hadn't noticed, because she made no sound. But as he passed carrying the poster, Kayla stole a glance at her mother's face. Barbara Fisher's eyes blazed hot and cold as anger mixed with shock, grief, and disbelief all at the same time. At first she couldn't speak, her mouth contorting strangely. Then the dam broke.

"How dare you!" she shouted. "How dare you! Who do you think you are that you have the right to go around forcing people to look at something like that? Don't you have any human decency? Don't walk away from me, you coward! You can't face the truth, can you? That's right! Just walk away, you @#$*&!" she snarled and cursed.

People were starting to stare. Kayla and Char wanted to crawl into a hole and die from embarrassment. They looked helplessly at each other and cringed at the ugly language that erupted from their mother's mouth.

"Barb," Paul tried to soothe his raging wife. "Sweetheart... Come on, let's not make a scene," he said quietly, trying to guide her away.

"Make a scene?! He's the one making the scene, not me," she shouted, pulling away from his hand. "Honestly! I can't believe this! Leave me alone!" and she raced ahead of them like a nervous gazelle.

"Oh, my gosh," Kayla breathed in total shock.

"I cannot believe that just happened," Char mumbled.

"Me neither," said Kayla, glancing nervously at their father.

"Barbara!" Paul cried out. "Wait! Come on girls, we've got to catch up to her. We don't want to get separated." And they hurried up the sidewalk after her.

When they reached her, Barbara's face was twisted with grief and rage. She began rummaging wildly through her purse, avoiding their shocked stares. "I'm sorry. I...I have to go back to the hotel," she said in a shaky voice. Looking up, she quickly scanned the street next to them and then went back to rummaging through her purse. "Can't we get a cab or something? I don't want to walk all the way back there. My feet are killing me!"

No one spoke. For the first time in her life, Char saw tears welling up in her mother's eyes.

"Sure," Paul finally answered with a forced cheerfulness that made Kayla's stomach tie up in knots. "There's one up ahead. Taxi!" he shouted too loudly.

A brand new green Chevrolet Impala taxi was parked at the curb. When Paul shouted, the driver jumped out and held the doors open for them.

"Where you folks from?" the taxi driver asked in a friendly voice.

"Montana," Paul answered glumly.

"Montana! You're sure a long way from home! Is it true, do they still have buffalo and grizzly bears out there?" he asked.

At first no one answered.

"There are lots of bears in Glacier Park," Paul finally offered.

"We just have the Dawg Pound here!" the cabby answered brightly.

"What?" Paul frowned. He was in no mood for conversation with this stranger. But the taxi driver seemed undeterred, and his friendliness was contagious.

"The Browns' mascot. You know, the Cleveland Browns? Our football team? They're building a new stadium a few blocks from here. The real hard-core fans are called the Dawg Pound. Then, of course, we've got the Indians," he chatted on cheerfully.

"Indians? What kind of Indians?" Char asked, thinking about all the Native American kids she went to school with back home.

"The Cleveland Indians! American League Champions of 1995! We almost made it to the Series, but those danged Yankees get us every time!" he laughed and shook his head. "Just like they got Atlanta last week. But that's okay. One of these days, we'll have the World Series at Jacobs Field," he predicted confidently.

"I thought he meant real Indians!" Kayla whispered. Char snickered quietly.

"So that's what that big red smiley face is I keep seeing every-where," Mr. Fisher said. Barbara just stared out the window, gazing at the darkening shadows. It was the five o'clock rush hour, and the traffic downtown was starting to get heavy.

"Yeah, that's our mascot! Chief Wahoo!" smiled the cabby, pulling up to the curb by the Renaissance.

"My name's Ray. Here's my card," he said, handing his business card to Paul. "If you guys need a ride while you're in town, just give me a call on my pager and dial in this code, and I'll call you right back and pick you guys up," he grinned broadly at them.

"OK, thanks, I'll do that. Thank you." Paul paid the fare and gave the cabby a generous tip.

"Thanks a lot! You guys have a good time," Ray waved and closed the cab doors behind them as they left.

"Man, what a nice guy. And what a clean cab! Must be brand new," Paul said to Barbara, but she didn't answer.

When they arrived back at the hotel, she headed for the bar without a word. Paul tried not to watch her walking away and instead steered Char and Kayla to the elevators.

Back in their hotel room, Paul tried to lift their spirits by making plans for the evening. He paged through the *Plain Dealer* to see what was showing in the Tower City Cinema.

"*The Insider* looks pretty good. It says 'Russell Crowe gives the performance of his career as a tobacco company scientist who learns his employers have been chemically enhancing the addictive properties of nicotine in the cigarettes they sell. Al Pacino plays the *60 Minutes* producer who tries to get the story on the air.'" Paul laughed. "It says 'any movie where Al Pacino gets to tell somebody off is by definition a good movie.' What do you guys think?"

"That sounds okay," Kayla said numbly. She didn't care what movie they watched. Anything would be better than just sitting there after what had just happened. She wanted to cry, but she didn't want to ruin their vacation any more than it already was.

"Char?" he asked.

"Yeah, sure. Sounds great."

"Okay, *The Insider* it is." Paul's face was pale and hard but he tried to sound upbeat. "I'm gonna hit the showers. You two be okay out here?"

"Sure, Dad," Char said quietly. Kayla didn't bother to answer.

Paul disappeared into the bathroom. Kayla turned on the TV, mindlessly flipping through channels. Char just sat on the bed, staring at the carpet. They tried to block it out, but neither one of them could erase the image of that man and the picture he had been carrying. It might have helped had they been able to talk about it, but it was too horrific to even discuss. At least, not yet.

They had never seen a photograph of an aborted fetus before. Not in any of their science books. Not in any of the movies they watched or the magazines they picked up, and certainly not on TV. They knew about abortion, of course, but this was different. They hadn't really thought about a fetus as looking like a baby. They had always pictured it as sort of a fishlike creature with gills or something, or just a blob of cells. Not a human being.

Now they understood, just a little bit, what all the arguing and all the protest marches were about. But what they couldn't understand, and what worried them the most, was why their mother had gotten so upset.

Chapter 15: Visibilium et Invisibilium

Sancte Michael Archangele, defende nos in praelio.

– Prayer to Saint Michael the Archangel

$\mathcal{I}$t was finally Halloween. Tia had promised to take Troy trick-or-treating after she got off work. She didn't mind doing it because she knew how much fun it would be for him. She wanted to give him all the happy, fun times she possibly could.

Some of the families at Troy's school were having All Saints Day parties instead of trick-or-treating. They said Halloween and all the emphasis on witches and ghosts was of the devil, and it was better to dress up as one of the saints instead. After all, that's how Halloween got its name—from the Catholic feast of All Hallow's Eve, the night before the big feast of All Saints Day. But to Tia, it didn't really matter. Some kids would get out of control and egg houses, but then some kids always got out of control, no matter what you did. Halloween just gave them an excuse to prowl the neighborhoods and cause trouble.

To Troy, it was a fun day to dress up as one of his favorite characters. This year, he was going to be Darth Maul from *Star Wars*. Many of the boys wore Darth Maul masks. Tia thought Darth Maul looked a little like the devil, with his orange-and-black-streaked face, the evil smile, and, of course, the horns. She wondered if Troy should be dressing up like the enemy of God. Then she overheard a middle-aged couple talking on the Rapid one Sunday afternoon.

"Wasn't that interesting? I didn't know peasants used to dress up as witches and evil spirits at Halloween to mock them and hide from them."

"Yeah, what did Father Lawrence say? Everybody stripped off their scary costumes at midnight, when it was officially All Saints Day, and had a big bonfire to burn up all the witches and ghosts? Kind of like a group exorcism or something!" They laughed together.

What a great holiday, Tia thought. Too bad more people didn't understand the spiritual origins of Halloween. They kept the candy and the goblins and threw out the saints. No wonder things got out of control.

Troy already had his mask and costume on and was begging to go out.

"Just a minute—I just got home!" Tia protested.

"Hurry up! I don't want to miss trick or treating!" Troy begged.

Tia went to turn off the television. Troy's cartoons were over, and the national news was just starting. She paused for a moment to listen.

"The death toll from today's crash of Egyptair Flight 990 now stands at 217 confirmed dead. The Boeing 767 aircraft crashed today into the ocean off Massachusetts, less than an hour after taking off from New York for Cairo, killing all 217 people on board."

How awful! May they rest in peace... Tia prayed silently. She tried to imagine what it would be like crashing into the ocean from so high up in the air, but it was too awful even to think about.

"Come on, Tia!" Troy demanded.

"Okay, okay. Let's go." Tia murmured, grabbing a flashlight.

They started trick-or-treating in their own apartment building. At the first door they knocked on, a radio blared from behind the door, but no one answered.

"Probably still at work," Tia said. They moved on to the next apartment. Tia knocked gently and an elderly woman opened the door just a crack. When she saw Tia and Troy, she unchained the door and Troy called out, "Trick or treat!"

"Oh my goodness!" the woman pretended fright at the sight of the Darth Maul mask.

"What are you?"

"Darth Maul!" Troy exclaimed proudly.

"Well, Darth Maul gets a Tootsie Roll!" She offered Troy a bowl full of candy. He took one gingerly and examined it before dropping it happily into his plastic pumpkin candy carrier.

"What do you say?" Tia reminded him.

"Thank you!" Troy sang out.

"Thank you," Tia smiled at the old woman, who was already shutting and chaining the door.

They went on to four more apartments. One was a young mother with a baby in her arms and a toddler in diapers clinging to her legs. Tia wondered for the hundredth time how women took care of more than one young child at a time.

They continued up the street into the warm night air. It was just starting to get dark.

"Hold on to my hand!" she reminded Troy.

"No! I can go by myself!" he shouted, trying to pull away.

Tia held on to him tightly. "You want to go home?" she threatened.

"No! No! I'll be good! I don't wanna go home!"

After walking about a block, they reached a row of homes with brightly lit porches. Some had Halloween pumpkins, black cats, or cartoon-faced witches on display. They walked up the steps together. Troy knocked on the door of the first house.

"Trick or treat!" Troy said quietly. Tia could never understand why he was so bold around her and their mother, but when it came to strangers, Troy was almost shy at first.

The door opened.

"Happy Halloween!" the man said, offering a dish of candy corn to Troy.

"Thank you!" Troy remembered without being told this time.

They went on to three more houses. Then Troy begged, "Can I go up to the next house by myself?"

"No, we'd better go together."

"Pleeeeez?" Troy whined loudly.

"I said no! We don't know who lives in that house!"

"PLEEEEEEEZZZZUH!" Troy was a consummate beggar, and he pulled hard on Tia's hand.

Tia looked at the last house and sized it up. There were two bright porch lights and a big friendly orange Halloween pumpkin sitting on the porch rail. The living room curtains were drawn back and revealed a normal looking living room and ruffled lace curtains on the window.

"Okay, but you come right back when you're done," she warned.

Troy raced up the sidewalk and bounded up the steps to the house. He knocked on the door, not seeing the doorbell. He waited, but no one came. He knocked again and then, seeing the doorbell, he pushed it.

Just then, Tia spotted a group of older boys coming up the street, all dressed in black. There were five of them, and they were much bigger than Troy. Wearing gory, blood-covered masks, they carried what looked like real swords and knives. Tia sucked in her breath. Trying to keep the fear from her voice, she shouted.

"Troy!" She didn't want to scare or embarrass him, but she had a bad feeling. The boys were drawing closer. Like quicksilver she made a beeline between them and her brother.

The owner of the house had opened the door and was speaking to Troy, who was slowly choosing some candy off a plate. As the owner shut the door, Troy gleefully spun around towards Tia. At that moment, the four big kids reached the sidewalk in front of the house. Troy took a step down, then froze at the sight of their hideously ugly masks. He stepped sideways as if to run, but there was nowhere to go and no way to avoid them. They boldly paced up the steps, and one of the kids bumped Troy, knocking him down.

"Hey! What do you think you're doing?" Tia yelled loudly. The kids jerked around to look at her and took off running, jumping down the stairs. At the sound of her voice, Troy leaped up and ran towards her.

"Tia!" he yelled.

Her heart pounded with indignation mingled with fear. "Are you okay?" she asked him.

"My knee hurts."

"Those were mean kids," she said.

"Those were very mean kids!" Troy said.

"Come on, let's go home!" Tia said.

"Okay," Troy replied. "I don't want to go trick or treating anymore."

Tia seethed with anger at them for ruining her brother's Halloween. What made them act like that? She just didn't understand it.

After they got home, Tia looked at Troy's knee. It was red, but not skinned. Luckily, he was wearing his jeans under his costume.

"Why were they wearing those scary masks?" Troy asked gravely.

"I guess they wanted to look really scary," Tia answered.

"They did look really scary," Troy declared.

"Come on, let's see what candy you got!" Tia changed the subject.

Troy was eager to check out his loot. After making sure all the packages were safe, Tia let Troy have two pieces and then took the rest and put it away for later. He begged for more, but she was firm and told him she would read him two bedtime stories if he got in the tub right away. The bribe worked, and soon he was clean and tucked in.

Later, Tia was just about to fall asleep when she woke with a start. Troy was crying! She threw off the covers, ran to his room, and flicked the light switch. He was sitting upright in his bed, his face full of terror. Tia wrapped her arms around him and he dissolved into tears and sobs.

"What's the matter, sweetie? I'm here now, it's okay!" she soothed and comforted him.

Still he sobbed until finally he could speak. "I had a bad dream!" he wailed.

"Oh, that's okay. It was just a dream! It's all over now!"

"There was monsters and they were chasing me!" he cried, more quietly now.

"Oh, I'm sorry. Here, blow your nose," she said, handing him a tissue.

Troy blew and wiped his nose. "Can I come sleep in your bed?" he whimpered.

"There's no monsters, see?" Tia gestured around the room. Trying to calm him, she dutifully checked beneath the bed. "No monsters under the bed!" Next, she opened the closet door. "No monsters in the closet. No monsters!" she declared cheerfully.

Troy sniffled, still uncertain. He clutched a stuffed elephant to his chest and tried to catch his breath. "Look! Over there!" He pointed to the corner.

"Oh, that's just your Halloween mask. See?" she held it up for him to see it was just an empty rubber mask. Troy was unconvinced.

"I'll take this in my room, okay?" she offered.

"Okay," Troy agreed. "Tia?" he called to her before she had even made it into the hallway.

"Huh?"

"Don't leave me!"

Her heart melted. Tossing the mask down, she hurried back and threw her arms around him again, kissing him on top of his curly brown hair.

"Don't worry, sweetie, I'll never leave you!"

"Promise?"

"I promise!"

"Tia?" he asked.

"What?"

"I'm scared," he whispered.

Tia couldn't understand why her brother was still so terrified. She didn't know what to do. He was too old for her to rock in the rocking chair, and it was too late to watch TV. What did her mother do when she had woken up with bad dreams as a child? She couldn't remember. Then all of a sudden it came to her.

"¡Un momento, hermanito!" Tia opened the top drawer, then the middle drawer. She didn't like to go through her mother's things, but this was an emergency. Closing them, she whispered a silent prayer and opened the bottom drawer. There it was! A little brown glass bottle that had once held vanilla flavoring sat in the corner of the drawer. Tia examined it. It was still half full. She took it from the drawer, closed the drawer, and stood up. Turning, she walked into Troy's room, trying to remember what to do.

"Look what I've got!" she smiled.

"What?" Troy asked, curious.

"Holy water!"

"Holy water? What's that?"

"It's water that's been blessed by a priest! You use it to bless yourself in church. And it's extra good at getting rid of monsters!" Tia said encouragingly.

"Really? Even big mean monsters?" Troy asked.

"Even big mean monsters," Tia answered, unscrewing the lid.

"Okay, here we go," she said. Tia wasn't quite sure what the proper words of blessing were, but as long as it helped Troy to go to sleep, she didn't think it mattered too much, and so she made up a prayer as she went along.

"With this holy water, I bless this room," she prayed, tossing a few drops on the bed and in the corners of the room. Then, for effect, she added loudly, "And all monsters have to leave right now!" Smiling, she moistened her index finger with the water and lightly traced the Sign of the Cross on Troy's forehead. "With this holy water, may God bless you and keep you safe. Amen."

"Amen!" Troy said, grinning. Then, hugging his elephant, he snuggled into his pillow. "Tuck me in!"

Tia smoothed his covers and tucked them up tightly under the mattress so he felt snug and secure. "Good night!" she said, and gave him a kiss on the forehead.

"Good night, Tia!" Troy yawned a big yawn. Tia patted his hair and turned to leave.

"I love you, Tia!" Troy said.

"Love you too, baby," she answered, turning out the light.

Tia went to replace the holy water in her mother's drawer, marveling at how easily it had calmed her brother down. Suddenly, she decided to bless herself with it, as well. "If it works for him, maybe it'll work for me," she thought. And with that, she replaced the bottle, got back in her own bed, and before she knew it was fast asleep.

Back in Troy's room, two small—nearly invisible—transparent crab-like creatures silently scuttled into the closet and hid themselves, afraid for their miserable lives. A mysteriously powerful force, which they did not understand and which they were powerless to resist, had just knocked them off of Troy's bed and hurled them against the far wall.

Chapter 16: All Saints Day

God, you are so near:
Transform our closed eyes into eyes open wide,
Encircle the soul's frail breeze
Rose petals trembling in mighty wind from every side.

– Karol Wojtyla
"Song of the Hidden God"

Char and Kayla woke early. Although it was 10:00 a.m. in Cleveland, it was only 8:00 a.m. back home, and their parents still weren't up.

When their mother hadn't returned from the hotel bar by eleven the night before, after leaving strict instructions not to open the door, Paul went down and brought her back, red-eyed and weaving and slumping. He'd helped her into bed and she'd gone to sleep peacefully, but the room reeked of alcohol even now. The last thing they wanted was to be around when Barbara Fisher woke up with a severe hangover.

"You know what I want?" Kayla whispered.

"What?" Char mouthed silently.

"I want to go shopping at Tower City!"

"Right now?"

"Yeah! Why not?" Char nodded in agreement, and Kayla smiled.

Char slid into her jeans and a blue jean blazer while Kayla tip-toed to the bathroom to brush her teeth and fix her hair. Char joined her in front of the huge wall-length mirrors and double sinks, unscrewed the top of one of the hotel's lotion bottles, and sniffed.

"Umm! This smells good!"

"Hmm...sweet! Let me try some."

The bottle slipped between them and fell to the floor.

"Oh, snap!" Kayla giggled.

"Shh!" Char cautioned.

Kayla clapped her hands over her mouth. "Let's get out of here," she whispered nervously.

Quiet as mice, the pair crept out of the hotel room and took the whirring elevator down to the main floor. Just outside the lobby in the adjoining mall known as Tower City, two gigantic statues of the Tasmanian Devil and Bugs Bunny beckoned at the entrance of the Warner Brothers store. Cartoon-themed products lined the shelves, hung from racks, and performed on screens. They took turns posing for each other's pictures in front of Taz and Bugs, and then skipped inside to shop.

"I love this place! Where else can you buy Scooby Doo underwear?" Kayla giggled.

"Or Roadrunner earrings?" Char laughed out loud. She was happy, but it felt weird. She couldn't remember when the two of them had gotten along so well. It was almost embarrassing. But they were having too much fun to worry about how they were supposed to act, and so they just enjoyed themselves, forgetting their former arguments and their mother's atomic meltdown.

After spending over an hour going through racks and racks of clothes and fun displays, Char bought a cute Dot Warner key chain and a soft Snow White sleep tee with pink edging around the sleeves. Then she picked out a bracelet for Krista. Kayla found a yellow cotton Tweety Bird nightgown with matching fuzzy slippers and a Taz zippered coin purse for Mercedes. Afterwards, they stood around in front of the store's big screen TV and watched cartoons, cracking up at "Tom and Jerry" and casting sideways looks at each other.

"What do you want to do now? You wanna go for a walk?" Kayla asked, swinging her bag full of loot.

"I'm hungry," Char replied.

"Me too. Let's go find some food!" They wandered out of the store and looked around at all the shops.

"Caribou Coffee! That sounds cool." Char pointed to the coffee stand with the big reindeer logo, and they hurried to get in line. A short wait later and they took their banana bread muffins and vanilla lattes and plopped down at one of the white metal café tables. Soft music played over the PA system while people strolled slowly by, enjoying their day. Char and Kayla sipped their steaming lattes and nibbled their muffins.

A young woman who looked to be about eight months pregnant walked by, pushing a stroller barely containing a kicking toddler. Thinking of their mother, Char and Kayla exchanged looks. Finally Kayla broke the silence.

"You know what? I want to have a big family someday."

Char picked at the muffin crumbs that had fallen onto her napkin, putting them into her mouth one by one. Her leg bounced up and down nervously beneath the table.

"I want three boys and three girls." Kayla stated. "Do you think that's weird?"

Char just shrugged.

"Oh! Did you see that picture of Madonna and her daughter Lourdes on the cover of that magazine at the Rock Hall yesterday?" Kayla piped up.

"I don't remember."

"She just turned three last week. She is so cute! I'll bet she's gonna be a huge star someday just like Madonna!"

"Yeah, probably," Char said. "Having babies isn't so bad. I mean, if you want them and can take care of them."

"But...what about the ones no one wants?" Kayla thought of the man with the sign they'd seen the day before. She believed in women's rights, but it was totally inconceivable to her that any mother could kill her unborn child.

"I guess they can be adopted by someone who does want them," Char reasoned.

"Yeah! Like the Robertsons adopted those kids from India and China? They have like six kids now, and three of them are adopted!" Kayla leaned forward excitedly.

"Yeah and they're really good in school. Amaya is always on the Honor Roll," Char answered, slowly sipping her latte.

"So..." Kayla wanted to bring up the pro-life protester and how upset their mother had been, but she didn't know how.

Char looked around at all the shiny storefronts and waited. It wasn't like Kayla to confide in her. It also wasn't like Kayla to be at a loss for words.

"So, why did Mom get all freaked out yesterday? I mean, it was a really gross picture and everything, but..." her voice trailed off.

Char looked down and stared at the designs on her paper napkin. She had a pretty good idea what the reason was, but she was afraid to say it. She tried to look Kayla in the eye, but she just couldn't.

Suddenly, Kayla's face went pale. "You don't think she had one, do you? I mean, that would be so—like, that would mean we had—could have had—a brother, or another sister! Wouldn't it?" Kayla's eyes grew wide with shock.

"Yeah. I guess it would," Char said quietly.

Kayla made a strange strangled sound, looking off into the distance. Then she slammed her palms down on the table.

"Oh my gosh! I can't believe Mom was pregnant before and never told us!"

"I can," Char replied morosely.

There were probably lots of things their mother hadn't told them, and probably never would tell them. When you're little, you look up to your parents like superheroes, but the day comes when you realize they don't always have all the answers. They may not even be asking the right questions. It was true: their mother could have aborted a child. But it was too horrible to think about. All Char knew was that she couldn't stand to talk about it anymore, and if

they didn't leave that very second, she might start screaming and
not be able to stop.

"Come on, let's get out of here!" she said suddenly, abruptly
getting to her feet.

"Okay," Kayla answered sadly. They were having so much fun,
and now it felt like everything was ruined.

Char wadded her napkin into a ball and pushed it into the empty
paper coffee cup before shoving it forcefully into the nearby trashcan.

They didn't say a word. They didn't have to. They both knew they
just couldn't go back to the hotel room and face their mother's
selfish secrets. Gathering up their shopping bags, they quickly
walked back to the entrance of Tower City and headed for Public
Square.

* * *

Rushing to be on time, Tia arrived for her shift at La Chic Boutique
that afternoon with a pounding headache. The penetrating miasma
of expensive perfumes reeking from the pricey department store
across the walkway made her feel nauseated. She tried her best to
smile at the customers, but she was drained from being up late with
Troy the night before. He got so hyper from eating Halloween
candy—even just the two pieces she allowed him to have—that he
had bounced up and down on his bed, singing crazily, for what
seemed like hours. Even holy water couldn't solve that problem.

"Excuse me, is this on sale?" a thin thirty-something woman
held up a red knit pullover.

"Yes, everything with the orange dot is fifty percent off," Tia
answered politely. She jerked the drawer beneath the cash register
open, futilely searching for a painkiller amidst the pencils and pens
and extra rolls of cash register tape. Overhead, the speakers blared
edgy pop tunes. She glanced furtively at the clock. Three twenty-
five. She always called Troy at three-thirty to make sure he'd gotten

home from school okay. Sometimes the bus dropped him off at three-fifteen, but sometimes it took a little longer. Tia debated waiting a few more minutes. She wanted to give him plenty of time to get inside and get his coat off. But if she didn't call soon, the high school crowd would arrive, and then things would get really busy.

Quickly Tia punched in the number to Grandma Willie's. No answer. She tried again. It rang a dozen times.

"Hello?" Finally a creaky voice answered.

"Grandma, it's me. Is Troy home yet?"

"Why, didn't you call just a minute ago?" Grandma Willie sounded confused.

"I called, but you didn't answer. Is Troy there?" Tia snapped.

"Don't sass me, child. Yes, I believe I hear him upstairs. What's the fuss?"

"I'm sorry, Grandma. Just—please don't let him eat too much candy before dinner."

The thin woman came up to the cash register, ready to buy the pullover. She frowned.

"I've gotta go. I'll be there around nine-thirty. Thanks, Grandma!" Tia hurriedly hung up.

"Hi, how are you?" she asked in a friendly voice. The thin woman didn't answer.

Some of them were more talkative than others. Most would make small talk with her, and some would talk half the night if she let them. Shopping was like therapy for some people, Tia decided. They came in every week and bought something, often returning it the next day, just to have something to do. Just to have a friendly, familiar person to talk to. She expertly folded the new sweater before placing it in the plastic bag with the receipt.

"Have a nice night!" she said, handing it to the woman, who nodded and quickly walked away.

A couple of girls from her school were over at the clearance rack by the entrance to the mall. She knew they had spending money even though they lived in a low income neighborhood, like she did. Tia wondered where all that cash came from. Then, she felt a little pull in her stomach. She was being envious and judgmental. To ignore it she started straightening the credit card applications in the drawer, trying to look busy. The supervisors watched the sales associates on the security camera.

Tia checked the dressing room and hung up some clothing a customer had tried on but left behind. She picked up several hangers someone had left on the floor. How could people be so sloppy and careless? Back on the sales floor, she rang up a customer's purchase and waved at her one of her classmates from biology, Chad, and his girlfriend, Emilee.

The little pull in the stomach again. *What's up with that?*

She paused, looking around the store. Nothing seemed out of place. She looked at her watch. Four o'clock. She checked the time on the cash register. It was the same. Nervously she checked to make sure her purse was in its place and it was, securely locked in the bottom drawer. Her wallet, keys, and all her money was there.

Still, something was wrong.

Tia peered up at the ceiling, at the security camera, and out at the shoppers casually strolling by. Maybe she was just tired. Maybe she just needed to slow down and relax a little, spend some time with friends. Friends. Kanisha! That was it. She'd given in and told Kanisha she'd meet her and Jacob at the flagpole to cut class, but later changed her mind. When she didn't show up, Kanisha would have been mad. She'd give her a call later and apologize.

A couple of jocks came in, looking for a birthday present for a girlfriend. She guided them to the jewelry display and helped them pick out a pair of earrings that were on sale. She gift-wrapped the earrings and tucked them with a gift receipt into a bag. She handed it to the young men and thanked them for shopping at La Chic Boutique.

Then it hit her, hard. A feeling in the pit of her stomach. Something was wrong. Troy was in danger. She didn't know how she knew, but she had never been so certain of anything in her life. Shaking, she dialed the number for Grandma Willie. It rang fourteen times before Grandma Willie finally picked up.

"Grandma! It's Tia! Where's Troy?"

"What are you all in a tizzy about? Didn't I just tell you he is upstairs?"

"Please, Grandma!" Tia begged.

"Oh, all right. Just a minute, I'll check on him." The old black phone thudded loudly where Grandma set it down on the table. Tia panicked at the thought of her ninety-year-old grandmother inching forward with her walker, trying to work herself up to shouting over the television so Troy could hear her calling his name. This could take forever!

Tia gripped the phone and tried to remain calm. Five minutes went by. She couldn't wait! She had to find Troy. She knew he needed her, and he needed her now. She disconnected the call and speed-dialed the store manager, Leah Watson. Leah had given Tia strict orders to call her in case of an emergency.

"Ms. Watson? This is Tia," she said breathlessly.

"Tia! Is everything all right?"

"Yes, I mean, no, not exactly. I mean..." she took a deep breath. "I just have a terrible feeling something's happened to my brother. I have to go home! Can you come down right now?" she pleaded.

Tia hadn't been working at La Chic Boutique for very long, but Leah Watson knew a good girl when she saw one. She knew Tia wouldn't make up an excuse just to take off work.

"You lock up the store and put up the break sign, and I'll be right down. You be careful, Tia." Leah cautioned.

"Thank you Ms. Watson! I'm sorry!" Tia stammered.

"It's all right! You go take care of your baby brother, and you call me if you need anything, okay?"

"Yes, ma'am. I'm going right now!" Tia hung up, grabbed the sign, her purse and her keys, locked the store, and ran for the bus.

* * *

The Warner Brothers Store was close to the Public Square entrance, so Kayla and Char were out on the sidewalk in no time. They peered with uncertainty at the row of buses parked in front of them. Dozens of people milled around, waiting for their bus or their ride. It was the middle of the afternoon and warm for late October. They walked on towards the corner and wondered where to go next.

"Got any change?" A scary looking man in ragged clothes asked, and they froze in fear. Nervously Kayla gave him a quarter. He smiled a mouthful of greenish yellow teeth, said "God bless you!" and hobbled away while the poisonous odor of his unwashed clothing lingered in the humid air.

"PEW!" Kayla fanned her face in disgust.

"Be nice! He can't help being poor!" Char chided her.

"I know, but he could at least *bathe!*"

"Well maybe he can't afford to buy soap!"

"Soap doesn't cost much!" Kayla argued obnoxiously.

"Duh! Maybe he doesn't have a place to shower. Did you ever think of that?"

"Duh! Maybe I don't care!" Kayla pouted angrily.

Suddenly, Kayla cried out and pointed excitedly. "Look! It's Chad Pritt!"

"What? Where?" Char demanded skeptically, her eyes scanning the crowd.

"Over there! Getting on that bus!" Kayla squealed and pointed again. There were so many people, Char couldn't see. Besides, she was certain that Chad Pritt, the very famous and very handsome actor, wasn't in Cleveland, and even if he was, he certainly wouldn't be riding around in a smelly city bus. But Kayla wasn't so easily deterred.

"Come on!" she insisted, grabbing Char by the wrist and pulling her towards the bus.

"Wait a minute! Mom and Dad don't know where we're at!" Char pragmatically tried to reason with her boy-crazy, star-struck sister.

"They don't care! I don't care! Char! It's CHAD PRITT!" she shouted right in Char's face as though she were deaf. A couple of high school students looked at her and started laughing.

Char examined the sea of heads once again. Black heads, beaded and braided heads, scarved heads, hat-covered heads, all huddled tightly together, straining to be the next in line to get on board a cool air-conditioned bus. Yes! Maybe there *was* a blond man in his twenties getting on the Number 6! He stood out from the crowd.

"I see him!" she said brightly.

"Come on! Let's go!" Kayla exclaimed, pulling her arm. "Maybe we can take his picture!"

Maybe it would be fun. Maybe it would be okay. Maybe this would take their minds off abortion, their mother's drinking binge, and scary homeless people.

She knew it was silly. She knew it wasn't really Chad Pritt. But they just couldn't go back to their hotel room—not yet. Char let herself be dragged along.

Towering dark clouds had gathered, and it smelled ominously like thunder. Large icy raindrops touched their flushed faces as together they ran expectantly towards the waiting bus.

* * *

Troy slowly dragged his book bag behind him as he made his way to Grandma Willie's house after school. So what if it got dirty? He was sick of school and tired of always being in trouble. He wasn't sure if he liked this new city, either. He missed Abuelita Isabel, Auntie Delia, and his fun-loving cousins, Robbie and Bobby.

He spotted a crumpled Coke can on the grass and kicked it. He laughed a little as it landed on a nearby bush, startling the birds hidden there. They flew away to a nearby tree to discuss this frightening development.

Troy saw a stick on the ground and picked it up. He scraped it along the side of the bricks as he slowly made his way to Grandma Willie's. He didn't like the idea of spending another lonely afternoon cooped up with that old lady. He'd never seen her before until just a few months ago, and he was now supposed to love and respect her as his grandmother. Abuelita Isabel used to make him *sopapillas* after school. Grandma Willie just sat in her rocking chair and grumbled and complained. She was so different from Abuelita Isabel that he had trouble believing they were actually related.

He quickly learned that if he ran upstairs and turned on the TV as soon as he got home, he'd be too far away to hear Grandma Willie's grumbling voice. Pretty soon, Grandma Willie would doze off, and he could sneak downstairs and see if there was anything in the fridge. Later, Tia would call and make sure he got there safely. He would do his homework and play his Nintendo until she came to get him and take him home.

Suddenly, something moved in the shrubs. He blinked his eyes and stood motionless, watching. He thought he heard a tiny whisper of leaves. A flurry of birds flew out of the branches and there, hot on their trail, leaped a black and white bundle of hunting energy. Troy's mouth fell open with surprise, then turned up in a huge grin. A kitten!

The novice hunter was obviously disappointed that her prey had escaped. Then she saw Troy. She froze in her tracks and studied this new, large creature. It wasn't as big as some that passed by, but you couldn't be too careful. Best not to be too friendly just yet.

"Hey, kitty!" Troy made the first move.

The kitten looked mournfully at Troy as if to say, "Don't you feel sorry for me? Did you see all those birds get away just when I finally had them cornered in the bush?"

"Here, kitty!" Troy crouched down and held out his hand to the brave little feline. Forgetting all about the hunting mishap, the small furry animal took a few small steps forward and sat down. It was as close as she dared to get.

Taking this as a sign of friendship, Troy stood up and walked towards her. But no self-respecting kitten was going to let herself get captured so easily by a third grader. In the flick of an eye, she dashed up the sidewalk and around the side of a fenced lot.

"Wait! Kitty!" Troy called out cheerily, trying to lure her back. She paused at the sound of his voice and turned to eye her pursuer, then cleverly trotted off, enchanted by this new game. She darted across the street. Troy followed, not bothering to look to see if any cars were coming.

He wandered after the little cat for several minutes without any luck. Then, he looked around. There! Thinking her pursuer had given up the chase, the kitten sat down to give herself a quick bath of victory. She was so busy licking her shoulder that she didn't notice Troy sneak up and grab her. Frightened, she let out a high-pitched "meow," but Troy petted her gently. Sensing she was safe, she snuggled down into his arms, purring quietly.

But now—how to get to Grandma Willie's?

It had been warm and muggy all afternoon, with dark clouds. Little misty drops that he didn't even notice at first began falling from the sky. But as the rain came down harder and faster, and the wind began to blow in big gusts that kicked up twisters of dust in the street and blew paper and empty plastic pop bottles in his face, he began to feel afraid. A weird feeling overcame him as he realized he didn't know where he was.

Confused, he stopped. Tia had taught Troy that if he ever got lost, he mustn't talk to strangers, but call 9-1-1. Troy looked around. Where was a phone? Then he remembered something else Tia had taught him. A prayer. How did it go? *Remember, O most greatest Virgin Mary...* No, that wasn't it. *Remember, O most gracious Virgin Mary...* The rest of the prayer escaped him. Rain pelted his face, and tears began to stream down his cheeks. Determinedly, he shoved the tears from his eyes with the heel of his palm. Troy was a big boy. He could take care of himself. Then why did he have this strange sinking feeling in the pit of his stomach? He decided he'd better turn around and go back the way he came. But which way was that?

"Come on, kitty. It's all right," he murmured in the purring kitten's ear.

Cars and taxis whizzed past. There! A big black Lincoln! Was it his dad's car? He couldn't tell for sure. He started to call out, but it was too late. It had already gone by, and he didn't recognize the lady behind the wheel. It must have been somebody else. Troy buried his face in the kitten's soft fur. Was Daddy ever coming home again?

Just then, a loud crack of thunder made him jump. Instinctively, he turned around and started running for Grandma Willie's, clutching the kitten to his chest. But all the streets looked unfamiliar, and he didn't know which way to go. A little twisting knot clutched at his insides and he felt tears welling up again. All of a sudden, a bearded man in a beat-up brown Toyota Corolla pulled up to the curb next to him, skidding on the gravel.

"Hey, kid!" the man shouted. Troy turned to look, but his sister's warning words rang out in his memory like a clear bell: *Don't talk to anybody you don't know!* Terrified, he bolted and ran.

But now the sky had turned a dark greenish black. He had never seen the sky that color before, and it frightened him even more. The streets looked strange and unfriendly. And worst of all, the bearded man had gotten out of the brown car and was chasing him down the street!

* * *

By the time Char and Kayla boarded the bus, it was standing room only. They tried to see where the Chad Pritt look-alike had gone, but there were too many people in the way. Now the driver was staring at them, waiting for them to pay their fare.

"How much?" Kayla asked, a little nervously.

"One dollar," the driver answered.

Another passenger raced towards the bus while Kayla clumsily fished a wrinkled dollar bill out of her purse. The latecomer pounded on the closed doors; the driver opened them. A tall girl with long brown hair stepped up, flashed the driver her bus pass, and grabbed an overhead rail just behind them.

"Transfer?" the driver asked Kayla.

"Huh?"

The driver could see that they were from out of town. He spoke slowly and more loudly this time. "Do-you-want-a-transfer!" It was an order to be obeyed, not a question to be pondered.

Kayla's mouth hung open. The bus drivers in Great Falls were not like this. "What's that?" she asked, her face flushed with embarrassment.

"Are you going to transfer to another bus?" the driver explained, as patiently as it was possible for him to be at the seventh hour of his shift with a hundred people anxiously waiting to be someplace in a hurry, and he was the one responsible for getting them there.

"I don't think so," Kayla said uncertainly.

"No." Char shook her head. "Thank you."

"Then find yourselves a seat, and hang on!" the driver boomed.

A couple of old ladies in the front chuckled at the rich white girls who didn't know how to ride the bus. And headed for the east side of town, at that.

"But there are no seats!" Kayla whispered loudly to Char.

It was true. All of the seats were taken. They were packed in like sweaty sardines. The driver gave it the gas as the light turned green at Ontario, and the girls almost hit the floor once again as the bus lurched forward, slowly grinding through the thick afternoon traffic. Clutching the silver chrome handrails, they hung on for dear life. If they lost their balance now, they'd end up lying in someone's lap.

The rain was coming harder now, blowing sideways, so the driver flicked on the big wipers. He expertly maneuvered the bus in and out of the lanes, pulling swiftly up to the curb every couple of blocks, letting some folks off while still more got on. The air conditioner blasted cold air on them, and Char soon found herself shivering from the damp raindrops now turned to ice water on her skin.

In the front seats reserved for the disabled, an elderly woman wearing a ratty looking wig covered with a torn nylon scarf and clutching a metal walker sat cursing and swearing loudly. Her aged voice was hoarse from yelling at her invisible enemies. Char and Kayla exchanged terrified looks. Finally the driver, who had driven this woman many times, took control.

"That's enough, now!" he ordered, and miraculously, the shouting woman fell silent.

Kayla looked at Char and exhaled a sigh of relief.

At the next stop, a seat opened up, and Char sank down next to a college student. Kayla gripped the seat handle behind her and tried to peer out the window. Was it just the tinted bus windows, or was it getting really black outside? Where were they? The bright lights of downtown were a mile behind them now. Finally, it dawned on them. It was getting dark, it was pouring rain, and they were two inexperienced girls in a strange big city on a bus full of people they didn't know. They didn't have a clue where they were, where they were headed, or how they were going to get back.

* * *

Tia raced all the way from La Chic Boutique to the Tower City escalators only to find them frozen at a standstill, broken down. A repairman was busy working on the mechanism, but there was no way to get around him. So she sprinted past dozens of shoppers, flew up the stairs two at a time, and dashed out the Euclid side doors to the bus stop, her heart pounding. She had to find Troy.

Panting heavily, she forced down a growing sense of panic as she saw the doors of the Number 6 bus flip shut just as she got there. She slapped on the doors, and the driver promptly opened them for her. She jumped on, flashed her bus pass, and grabbed a handrail just as he pulled away from the curb. She wondered where she should get off, where to start looking. Her conscience nagged her for leaving work for no good reason, but if there was even the smallest chance that something had happened to her little brother...

"Cleveland State," the driver announced the first stop.

Char and Kayla watched as several students got off the bus, including their ersatz Chad Pritt look-alike, who clearly wasn't who they thought he was. Kayla felt ashamed and disappointed. But Char had other worries on her mind, like how they were going to get back to the hotel.

The doors slammed shut, and they were on their way once again, to somewhere. But where? They strained to see through the darkened windows at the dirty, unfamiliar city streets. A couple of sleazy looking bars were just opening for business, neon lights blinking erratically. Anemic street lights dotted the sidewalks, giving off a pinkish-yellow glow.

"We need to get off this bus," Char murmured darkly to Kayla.

"I know!" Kayla's voice quavered.

At the next stop, in front of a dilapidated apartment building, an elderly Black gentleman in a stylish fedora hat and dark suit stood patiently in the rain, waiting for the bus to pull over. His cane steadied him as he slowly took the steps up into the bus.

"Hello, Mr. Kendall. How are you this fine afternoon?" the driver greeted him warmly.

Maybe this is an okay neighborhood, Char thought. But then she heard rap music blasting violently from a passing car, and her stomach sank.

"You want to get off here?" Kayla whispered, eyes wide with fear.

Char shot her a panicked look. This was no place to wait for a return bus to take them back downtown. And besides, it was pouring rain. But she was the oldest. She was responsible for both of them. She had to make a decision, and make it fast.

"No! Not yet." Char strained to see ahead through the wet darkness. But she could see nothing except old apartments and big empty looking warehouses. Nothing looked safe, nothing looked like home. Her heart began pounding, and she started to feel dizzy.

Tia stared out the bus window, watching for signs of Troy. She tried to remember if he was wearing his coat when he left for school that morning, but she couldn't be sure. She decided to get off at their usual stop and start searching around their apartment. But then something made her ask the bus driver. If Troy had been on Euclid, maybe the driver had seen him! Carefully she eased up to the front of the bus.

"Excuse me, I was wondering—did you see a little boy, eight years old?"

"Honey, I see lots of people. There's people all over this city," he said gruffly. Then, in a kinder voice, he asked, "What's your little boy's name?"

"Troy. He's my little brother."

"Little brother. Ah, I see." As the driver paused to think, Char watched and strained to listen, hoping to glean some useful information as to their location.

"He's supposed to go to our grandma's after school, but he never made it. I don't know where he is!"

"Well," the driver paused again. Tia bit her lip and hoped. It wasn't likely Troy would have been noticed by a driver who passed thousands of people all day long.

"Yes. I do remember seeing a child, where was it? Okay. I remember. It was about five blocks from here, maybe up around Forty-Fifth."

"Which way was he heading?"

"Headin' west. And I didn't see him yet this time around. So maybe you better get off at the next stop," he advised.

"Thank you! I appreciate it," she said. She scribbled her phone number on a piece of paper. "Please call me if you see him. His name's Troy."

"I will do that."

Seeing Tia was about to get off, Char jumped to her feet. Here was another girl who was about their age. Maybe she could help.

"Come on!" Char jerked her head at Kayla, who followed close behind. Together they walked towards Tia, who was standing at the top of the steps, holding the handrail by the front exit.

The driver signaled his intention to pull over. Suddenly, Char felt a powerful urge to grab on to the nearest handrail. Just as she did, a huge empty cardboard box tumbled into the street driven by a mighty gust of wind. The driver hit the brakes hard, and Char felt the full weight of Kayla's body falling into her. She gripped the bar with all her strength while Kayla grabbed Char's arm to keep from falling flat onto the floor. Then the bus stopped, and everything was all right.

"Sorry, ladies," the driver said warmly. "Everybody okay?"

Char and Kayla nodded numbly, hearts pounding. The sisters clung together, shaken. The box rolled over heavily as another fierce gust pushed it out of the street and onto the sidewalk. The driver eased the bus up to the corner, the air brakes hissed, and the doors swung open. Tia jumped off first, and Char and Kayla followed right behind her.

That was when they heard it. It was a long, loud, mournful wailing sound that gave them chills.

"What's that?" Kayla cried out in terror.

"Looks like there's a bad storm comin'!" the driver said, scanning the sky. "You girls get inside someplace safe!" With that, the bus pulled away and slowly shrank in the distance. Their last shred of security was gone.

"That's the tornado warning siren! We've gotta get out of here!" Tia shouted, jogging off down Euclid Avenue.

"Tornado?!" Char moaned.

A loud clap of thunder made them shriek. They swirled around to the northwest and searched the sky for signs of a twister, but all they could see was a huge canopy of heavy, menacing blackness.

"Oh my God! Let's get out of here!" Kayla cried, then stupidly realized they had nowhere to go. Directly in front of them was a huge old stone church, and diagonally across Euclid Avenue was an empty parking lot. A government office was on their left, but it was after business hours, and the workers had all gone home. The place looked dead.

The pounding rainstorm was much worse than it had looked from the safety of the bus. It was an evil, unnatural rain, bent on destruction. The reliable sound of the bus engine as it pulled away from the curb was drowned out now by the screaming of the storm warning siren, rising and falling, rising and falling. A vicious roaring wind hurled leaves, trash, and small branches towards them, stinging their skin and blinding their eyes with spitting needles of rain. The sky was a strange, dark mix of green and black. Slashes of pointed lightning bolted across the western sky and lit up the clouds like massive living creatures bearing down on them to rip them apart.

Searching for shelter, Char's eyes darted over the huge stone church on the corner. But it looked more like an eerie gothic castle than a welcoming sanctuary. The old stones of the church were blackish gray from ancient steel mill smoke. The steps to the entrance were worn with age, and the massive wooden doors looked as if they hadn't been unlocked in centuries. Turning away, Char instinctively raced after Tia, and Kayla followed.

"Wait!" Char cried. "Can we come with you? We're lost!"

"I've got to find my little brother!" Tia shouted over the wind, barely stopping to look at them. Char and Kayla ran after her, hands clasped, struggling to keep up with the older girl.

"Troy!" Tia yelled loudly.

"Where is he?" Kayla gasped.

"I don't know! He was supposed to be at our grandmother's house. Troy!!!" Tia screamed even louder, hoping he would hear and answer her.

It was almost completely dark now. The dim street lights cast a sickly yellowish glow beyond their steel bases. Tia fought down the urge to cry. The rain had plastered her hair to her face. In vain she tried to wipe the raindrops out of her eyes. Where had he gone? Maybe he had gone to Grandma Willie's. Maybe she should go there, too, and get out of the storm.

Finally she stopped fighting the hot sting of tears welling up in her eyes, and a prayer of agony poured out of her heart. "Oh Jesus, please!" she cried aloud. "Where is he?"

As if to mock her, the wind suddenly pummeled them with a roaring blast that would have knocked Char down were it not for the fact that she was tightly grasping Kayla's hand. The pouring rain blinded them, gritty blowing sand burned their faces, and they were forced to turn their backs and let the wind push them back across the street.

They had no choice now. The wind was blowing so hard they could barely stand, and it was too dark to see if a tornado was bearing down on them. They had to take shelter. As they made their way back up Euclid, the wind tried to force them back. Fighting to stay on their feet, they finally made it to the west door of the church. They gripped the rails and struggled up the steps, but when they tried the doors, they were locked up tight.

Determinedly they stumbled back down the steps and around to the north entrance. As they climbed to the top of the steps, the heavy wooden door on the right side swung open. Just then, Tia's foot slipped on the wet concrete and she lost her balance. Arms flailing, she fell sideways, landing hard on her right arm.

"Owwww!!!"

"Are you okay?" Kayla reached out towards her.

"Yeah! I — I think so," she winced at the pain shooting through her arm.

"Can you get up?" Char shouted over the roaring wind.

Tia bravely struggled to her feet, and the others followed. The door of the church was still wide open, so they quickly climbed into the entry leading to the dark vestibule.

Once inside, they looked around to thank whoever had opened the door for them. But no one was there.

"That's weird," Kayla panted nervously. "That door just opened all by itself!"

"It was probably just the wind," Char answered breathlessly, her voice echoing weirdly in the empty entryway.

The big door closed easily behind them with the onslaught of wind pushing it from the outside. They leaned against it panting, wiped the rain from their faces, and tried to catch their breath.

Inside, it was pitch dark but much quieter. Then, another flash of lightning and a cannon blast of thunder shook them.

"Come on!" Char shot a desperate look at Kayla. "Let's go find a phone and call mom and dad!"

Tia nodded, still holding her arm. Maybe these girls' parents would help her find Troy.

They were almost deaf from the pounding thunder. The storm was right above them now. Clinging together, they tiptoed slowly towards the left, guided by the constant flashes of lightning that slashed through the arched windows flowing with rivers of rain.

The entryway opened up into a large gathering room with tables and chairs and an old piano in the corner. As they inched their way into the empty gathering room and away from the windows, they saw a dimly-lit parlor that extended into the hidden interior of the building.

Kayla tiptoed into the parlor first, and screamed. There, surrounded by flickering candles and colorful flowers, was a dead body lying in a casket.

Chapter 17: Ecce Adsum

This divine choice dumbfounds me...I could weep for gratitude, more especially when I think how much more perfectly others would have corresponded with his graces.

– Poor Clare nun, aged 82, in religion 61 years

The small nun who had faithfully been keeping vigil by the casket jumped up.

"What? Who's there? Oh my goodness!" she gasped, looking from one soaking wet girl to the other. "What are you doing here?"

"The storm—we came in to get out of the storm! The door was wide open!" Tia panted, holding her arm.

"What door? Show me," the nun said nervously. "All the doors should have been locked after Mass today!"

An older nun approached quickly from the back of the parlor. She was dressed exactly like the first nun, wearing a simple brown habit tied at the waist with a white rope-like cord. A round white collar encircled her neck, and a long black veil covered her hair and fell to her waist in neat, generous folds.

"Sister, is everything all right?" she asked gravely. "I thought I heard screaming."

"Yes, Mother. These children just came in from the storm. We were just about to go check the doors."

"Yes, Sister. Please make sure the doors are locked." Turning to the girls, she smiled warmly. "And who are our lovely guests?"

"I'm Ti — Antonia Esperanza," Tia said politely. Then, looking apologetically at Char and Kayla, "And I guess I don't know your names."

"I'm Kayla Fisher." Kayla smiled nervously, still eyeing the casket.

"And I'm Char. Char Fisher," Char said shyly. She wasn't sure how to act. She had never met a real nun before. Suddenly, a picture flashed into her mind of the kindly old nun she had seen on TV, and she wondered if that nun lived here, too.

"I am very pleased to meet you girls, even in this weather! I am Mother Bonaventure." She gestured towards the first nun who had just finished checking the doors. "This is Sister Angela, and this—" she nodded respectfully towards the coffin, gently touching the gold monstrance that hung from a cord around her neck, "This is our dear Sister Marie Claire, who passed away early this morning. Sister Marie Claire was a hundred and one years old."

"A hundred and one?!" For a moment, Kayla's amazement was stronger than her fear.

"Sister was born in 1898 and entered our community in 1922. Seventy-seven years given to God," Mother Bonaventure added wistfully. The girls stared in awe at Sister Marie Claire's serene, peaceful face.

"She doesn't look that old," Kayla whispered in Char's ear.

"What happened? Was she sick?" Char asked.

Mother Bonaventure smiled. "Sister Marie Claire has gone to be with Our Lord. Now, can you please show me the door that was unlocked?"

Sister Angela bowed to Mother Bonaventure as Tia led the way out of the parlor, and together they all walked back into the vestibule.

"This is where we came in," Tia explained.

"I see," Mother Bonaventure pulled tightly on the door handle to make sure it was closed firmly, then wound a strong metal chain around the two handles and padlocked it.

"Why do you chain the doors like that?" Kayla asked, setting down her drenched shopping bags on the heavy black entryway mat.

"Not everyone who walks these streets has respect for God's house and God's people," the old nun said with a touch of sadness.

"We're searching for my little brother, Troy. Have you seen him?" Tia asked anxiously, still cradling her arm.

"No, I don't think so. Oh, my dear, are you hurt?" Mother Bonaventure's bright hazel eyes glowed warm and full of concern.

"I fell on the steps." Gently placing her hand on Tia's shoulder, Mother gestured towards the parlor. "But I'm okay."

"Let's go into the kitchen and take a look."

Kayla glanced at Char nervously and hesitated. She wasn't sure she wanted to walk back by the casket again. Tia, however, seemed confident and relaxed.

"Don't worry," Mother Bonaventure said reassuringly. "The kitchen is just around the corner."

Kayla smiled uncertainly, but obediently followed the others back to the monastery kitchen. It was pitch dark except for an ancient glass oil lamp glowing on the table. Outside, the storm still raged and thunder bellowed furiously. Char cringed at every flash of lightning, but Mother Bonaventure simply smiled again and said, "Don't worry. Everything's all right now. You're very safe here. But let's get the three of you dried off. You're soaking wet!"

Over by the big gas stove, another nun was busy heating hot water and pouring it into steaming cups. She was dressed just like the other two, except she wore a white veil. Her pearl-white smile contrasted beautifully with her dark brown skin.

"Children, this is Sister Beatrice."

Sister Beatrice flashed a bright smile and bowed slightly, handing them steaming cups of hot chocolate.

"Sister Beatrice is from India," Mother explained. "Could you get us some towels, please, Sister?"

"It's a terrible storm we're having today!" Sister Beatrice said cheerfully as she headed over to the clean linens closet.

"Oh, it's so bad out there! The wind is blowing like ninety miles an hour!" Kayla said, sipping her cocoa.

"At least!" Char agreed. "Even worse than Montana!"

"May I take a look?" Mother Bonaventure said to Tia. Tia let go of her arm, slowly removed her jacket, and rolled up the sleeve of her blouse, wincing.

"I'm afraid your nice jacket is torn," Mother Bonaventure noted matter-of-factly. A red lump was forming where she had hit the steps, but the skin wasn't broken. "That's too bad. Can you move your fingers, dear?"

"Yes. I think so." Tia wiggled her fingers and moved her arm back and forth.

"Good. It doesn't seem to be broken. Now, you must tell me— where are your parents? What were you doing out in this bad weather?"

Unexpectedly, a man's voice called out loudly from the gathering room.

"Mother Bonaventure!"

Eyes flashing, the abbess excused herself and walked quickly out of the kitchen, through the parlor, and into the Guild Room.

"Yes, Brother Alan? What is it?"

"I've got a little lost soul here who needs your help, Mother!"

Standing next to the drenched brown-robed Franciscan friar was an eight-year-old boy, soaking wet, cradling a black and white kitten in his arms, and desperately trying not to cry.

"Well hello, there!" Mother said cheerfully. "What a cute little kitten! Where did you find him, Brother?"

"I was just coming back from the hospital when all of a sudden this *storm* blew in. And when I was coming up Fortieth, I saw these two!" He patted Troy's shoulder.

Turning to Troy, she asked, "What is your name, my dear?"

"Troy," he mumbled and sniffed, trembling with cold and fear.

"Hello, Troy," Mother said kindly. "I'm Mother Bonaventure."

"By the way," Brother Alan said, "the phones are dead over at the rectory. Have you tried yours yet?"

"No, but if yours are out, ours probably are too." Mother sighed. "Oh well. *Deus providebit!*"

"Huh?" the little boy wrinkled his nose at the nun.

"DAY-oos pro-vee-DAY-bit. It means, in Latin, God will provide!" Mother Bonaventure explained with a smile.

"God will provide?" he repeated.

"Troy!!!" At the sound of her brother's voice, Tia raced joyfully into the parlor, threw her arms around him, and covered him with kisses.

Troy squirmed with embarrassment mingled with relief. The kitten, however, being squished between the two, mewed loudly and stuck her tiny, razor-sharp claws into the nearest object, which happened to be Tia's injured arm.

"Ow!!!" she cried, then laughed. "Who's this?"

"I'm going to name him Thunder!" Troy declared solemnly.

"Thunder! That's a great name!" Tia smiled, petting the kitten on the head.

"Well, we've certainly had a lot of that today, haven't we?" Mother said, and they nodded in agreement. "Let's get you dried off now," she said, guiding Troy towards the kitchen, then turned to thank the bedraggled Capuchin brother. "Thank you, Brother Alan."

"Not at all, Mother," the friar nodded, smiling. Then, turning to Troy, he added kindly, "You be careful now, okay? Next time, no more running after stray kittens."

Troy gazed up at him gratefully. "Okay."

"Maybe I'll see you around some time," Brother Alan raised his hand in farewell.

"See you around," Troy echoed.

Brother Alan turned to go, and then stopped.

"You know," he said thoughtfully, "there's an after-school program over at Immaculate Conception, not too far from here. Maybe Troy might like to go there after school?" he looked inquiringly at Tia.

Troy's eyes lit up. Anything would be better than Grandma Willie's.

Tia looked at Troy, gauging his reaction. "Would you like to maybe give it a try?" she asked.

"Yes," Troy said.

"What is it?" Tia asked.

"They have time for studying, and they do arts and crafts and games and stuff."

"Do they have Nintendo?" Troy asked.

Tia smiled. "That's his favorite thing," she explained. "He'd play all day if we let him!"

Troy made some battle sounds and energetically squeezed an imaginary game controller. Char and Kayla tried hard not to burst into giggles.

"I don't know about that." Brother Alan replied, grinning. "But even if they don't have Nintendo, I'll bet they've got a lot of other fun stuff. How about basketball? Do you like to play basketball?"

"Sure!" Troy nodded.

"Well, I know for a fact there's a basketball court there. Maybe you and me could shoot hoops together someday."

"Okay," Troy nodded some more, then pressed his face into Tia's leg, overwhelmed with shyness at all the attention and relief at being reunited with his sister.

"Okay! It's a deal." Brother Alan smiled again and turned to go.

"Thank you!" Tia called out after him gratefully.

"You're welcome!" Brother Alan waved good-bye before heading down the long hallway into another wing of the building, leaving large wet sandal prints on the tile floor.

"Where is he going?" Troy asked. He already missed his new friend.

"Brother Alan lives in the rectory next door," Mother explained.

"What's a rectory?" Troy asked.

"A rectory is a house where priests live." Mother was patient with her young questioner.

"Oh," Troy said. "Is Brother Alan a priest?"

"No, he's a religious, like me," she explained. "Oh, that reminds me. Brother Alan?"

"Yes?"

"Would you please tell Father I think we may have taken a direct hit tonight? I'm afraid there may be some damage to the roof."

"I'll tell him tomorrow as soon as he gets back from Cincinnati," Brother Alan promised.

"What's a religious?" Troy asked.

"A religious is a man or woman who makes special promises to Jesus to serve Him in the Church, in a religious community. Like a big family," Mother answered.

Just then, Sister Beatrice arrived, carrying four large bath towels. She handed one to Tia, and two to Char and Kayla, who had followed Tia after she ran out of the kitchen. She then proceeded to dry Troy's face and hair with the fourth one. Troy did his part, grasping one end of the towel and rubbing Thunder's head.

"You dry him, and I'll dry you!" Sister Beatrice laughed, and Thunder mewed.

"I think he's hungry," Troy said. "Are you hungry, Thunder?"

Thunder mewed again.

"All done!" said Sister Beatrice. "Maybe we can find him some milk, okay?"

Char tried to imagine what her mother would have said if she had tried to dry off a stray cat with one of their bath towels. She decided Sister Beatrice's approach was much kinder.

"All done!" said Troy, smiling for the first time. "Are you a religious?" he asked, drawing a huge smile from the Indian nun.

"Yes, I am!" she laughed, glancing at Mother Bonaventure. "And hopefully a good one!"

"Yes, I think you're a very good one," Troy said emphatically, watching Thunder lap up the milk Sister Beatrice had put out for him.

"And you're lucky you have such a good sister! Did you know she was out looking for you in this weather?"

Troy hugged Tia tightly, not knowing what to say.

"I was so worried about you, mijo!" Tia said, stroking his hair.

"I'm sorry, Tia!"

"I'm afraid we can't call your parents just yet," Mother Bonaventure informed the girls. "The storm has taken out our telephones. You'll have to stay here until they're working again." Char and Kayla looked at each other and then at Tia, wondering how long that would be.

Another rumble of thunder rolled out of the sky and echoed through the building, seeming to shake the very foundation with its force. Troy clung tightly to his sister's unhurt arm, and Thunder dashed under the piano, trying to hide. Sister Beatrice was too quick for him, though, and handed the would-be escape artist back to her new owner.

Mother was decisive. "Let's go into the church."

The children wanted to stay with Sister Beatrice in the cozy warmth of the kitchen, but they had no choice but to follow their hostess back into the parlor. Pausing briefly next to Sister Marie Claire's coffin, they stood motionless while Mother Bonaventure spoke quietly to Sister Angela. Respectfully they gazed at the peaceful face of Sister Marie Claire lying in the simple coffin, surrounded by flowers and a tall rack of candles.

"It feels like there's angels all around!" Kayla whispered incredulously. Tia and Char nodded in agreement. For the first time that afternoon, none of them felt afraid.

As Mother Bonaventure guided them back into the vestibule, lightning flashed in the windows, followed by distant thunder, but the wind wasn't howling like before.

Peering through the windows, Tia saw large tree branches lying in the middle of the wet street. There were no cars out, and it was still raining, but not as hard. The vicious storm was finally coming to an end.

They approached the double wooden doors that led into the church, where Troy spotted a large, life-sized statue. It was an older man with white hair and a long white beard, wearing an ankle-length red robe and sandals. In his left hand was a large book, and a long silver sword was at his side.

"Who is that?" Troy asked excitedly.

"That is the glorious apostle Saint Paul," said Mother Bonaventure.

"Saint Paul? Why does he have that sword?" Troy asked.

"Do you see that book in his hand?" Mother replied.

"Yeah," Troy replied.

"That is the Holy Word of God—the Bible, or Sacred Scripture. And Saint Paul teaches us that the Word of God is the sword of the Spirit," she explained.

"Cool!" Troy gazed at the statue, open-mouthed. Then he reached out and gently ran his fingers along the silver blade.

Mother Bonaventure smiled and pulled on one of the heavy double wooden doors to their left that led to the church, holding it open for them.

"And this," she said simply, "is Holy Angels Monastery." What they saw next took their breath away.

"Wow!" Kayla gasped and stared.

"Oh, my...goodness." Char mouthed the words, but hardly any sound came out. It was as if they had suddenly been transported into another place and time. The ugly black and gray bricks outside were just a disguise. For inside the rough, dark exterior of the old church lay majestic beauty of celestial proportions.

The western wall was lined with tall magnificently colorful stained glass windows. Graceful columns painted with beautiful designs were strategically placed to support the high arched ceiling. Rising behind the long white marble altar was a dark screen of intricately carved mahogany woodwork and behind that, a curved, vaulted apse. The smoky, sweet scent of candles mingled with the lingering fragrance of old incense, cloaking them in a soft blanket of mystery. Kayla inexplicably found herself wondering what it would be like to stand at that altar, wearing a beautiful white dress with Eric by her side.

Tia, however, didn't say a word. This was unlike anything she had ever seen before, even at Our Lady of Guadalupe back in San Antonio. Painted flourishes of wheat and tendrils of green ivy decorated the high arches, and tall rows of carved wooden angels watched over them from the grille that separated the public church from the nuns' choir. Six large white marble statues of angels, three on each side, knelt in wordless adoration beside the altar. And two beautiful golden doors were poised gracefully at the center of the sanctuary just behind it.

Char was speechless. All her life she had loved beautiful buildings, mostly just in pictures. But this—this was something far beyond her wildest imaginings.

Strangely, it wasn't just the beauty of the place that captivated them. There was an atmosphere of safety—a feeling of peace and security that enfolded them like a warm, comforting blanket. It was as if ten thousand prayers had worked their way into the very bricks and mortar, as if the entire edifice was built of faith and prayer rather than wood and glass and stone. All the pain of their mother's meltdown, the terror of the bus ride, and being lost and alone in the storm, was forgotten. For a long time, no one spoke.

Then Troy broke the spell, running full speed up the center aisle, feet nimbly skimming the terrazzo marble floor, clutching his hapless kitten to his chest.

"Wait! Troy!" Tia started after him, but it was too late. He ran up the steps into the sanctuary and rolled behind a large flower arrangement under the long marble altar, giggling.

"Troy!" Tia hissed. "Come out of there!"

"You can't make me!" he laughed.

Tia was so embarrassed she wanted to sink through the floor all the way to China. Reaching under the altar, she tried to grab him, but he deftly rolled away. Thunder meowed loudly in protest and struggled to escape from Troy's grip. Watching the show, Kayla giggled nervously. Char was too busy admiring the chapel to notice.

"It's all right." Mother Bonaventure said lightly. "Troy, would you like to light a candle for Sister Marie Claire?"

"Yeah! Can I?" Troy quickly crawled out from beneath the altar, jumped down the sanctuary steps and followed Mother Bonaventure over to a towering statue of the Sacred Heart.

Tia, Char, and Kayla joined them, taking in the beauty all around. Rows and rows of flickering votive candles in big red glass holders glowed warmly on a black wrought iron candle rack.

"All right. But first, we need to say a prayer for Sister Marie Claire," Mother said.

Troy shut his eyes tightly for a few moments, crossed himself, and then opened them wide again. "Okay, I prayed. Can I light it now?" he asked hopefully.

"Eternal rest grant unto her, O Lord, and may perpetual light shine upon her," Mother Bonaventure slowly recited the traditional prayer for the dead. "May her soul, and the souls of all the faithful departed, through the mercy of God rest in peace. Amen. In the name of the Father, and of the Son, and of the Holy Spirit."

"Amen!" Troy knew that part.

"Now, you may." Mother Bonaventure handed Troy a long thin taper. He placed the tip at the flame of one of the dozens of other candles. Once the taper caught fire, he selected one of the candles that hadn't yet been lit and touched the burning tip to the wick. As soon as it caught, he plunged the burning taper into a bowl of sand.

"Very good!" Mother said approvingly.

Troy tilted his head back and stared up at the statue of Jesus, arms outstretched. "That's a big statue!"

"Yes, it is."

"It's so beautiful," Tia breathed. "Thank you, Mother Bonaventure."

"You're most welcome, Tia. And thank you, young man, for praying for our dear Sister. If you will excuse me, it's time for evening prayer now. Will you be all right here for a few minutes?"

The girls nodded. Troy was still busy watching the flickering candles.

"I'll be back in twenty minutes," she smiled and quickly disappeared through a hidden doorway in the intricately carved grille.

* * *

Making their way to the other side of the church, Char and Kayla stood quietly by one of the front pews, staring at the sanctuary. They had never been in a Catholic Church before. Behind the long marble altar, surrounded on either side by rows of carved wooden angels on top of the latticework grille, were two golden doors, about three feet tall. The golden doors were closed, and a crucifix hung over them.

Tia walked over to Char and Kayla. Her eyes were transfixed by those doors. It seemed as if she ought to know what lay behind them, but she wasn't sure. She tried to remember if she had ever seen doors like that in any of the other churches she had been in, but she couldn't. It was a total mystery.

Tia whispered to Char, "So, where were you guys going?

Char shrugged and stared into the distance. "We weren't going anywhere. I mean, we thought we saw…" Her voice trailed away and she looked over at Kayla.

"We thought we saw Chad Pritt. But it wasn't him." Kayla said simply.

"Chad Pritt? On the East Cleveland bus?" Tia was incredulous. "Where are you from?"

"Great Falls." Char smiled with embarrassment, then shot a sideways glance at Kayla.

"Great Falls? Where's that?"

"Montana," Kayla replied, staring at her pink fingernails.

"Oh, that explains it. Weren't you afraid you'd get lost?" Tia whispered.

"I was just following *her.*" Char tilted her head towards Kayla.

"You might wanna think about that next time. You could've got yourself into all kinds of trouble."

Char swung her arms from side to side and then wrapped them protectively around her waist. "Yeah, no kidding."

Kayla tapped her foot against the tiled floor, then walked a few steps up the main aisle and slumped into one of the pews.

Tia shook her head and sighed. Slowly walking up the aisle, she finally sank down into the second pew from the front to wait for Mother Bonaventure. Troy soon scooted over from the rows of candles and plopped next to her, leaning his head on her shoulder.

"He's so lucky to have her," Kayla whispered. "She's a good sister."

Char nodded.

Kayla looked away, studying the white marble angels in the sanctuary. "You're a good sister, too, Char. I'm sorry I've been such a pain!"

Char turned to Kayla in surprise, then smiled. "It's okay."

Kayla smiled in return and squeezed Char's arm.

Just then, lamps flickered on behind the wooden grille, revealing a beautiful dome behind it. It was curved like the inside of a Fabergé egg, decorated with delicate colors and intricate floral designs. Before they had a chance to wonder what was going on, a small bell rang in the distance, and the sweet sound of angelic singing floated towards them from the other side of the grille. It was unlike anything they had ever heard before—a soft, almost dream-like sound.

Kayla and Char clung together, utterly silent. As the nuns chanted Vespers, Char drank in the intricately painted walls and elaborate stained glass windows. Kayla sat quietly, eyes closed, thinking of Eric and what an incredible story she would have to tell him when they got home.

Suddenly, something she'd seen on TV the day before popped into her head. They had been interviewing Mother Teresa of Calcutta on the news, and she had said, *"Give yourself fully to God. He will use you to accomplish great things on the condition that you believe much more in His love than in your own weakness."* Maybe that's why these women were here in this monastery, she thought. To her surprise, she started to cry. Char reached in her pocket, pulled out a tissue and handed it to her. Kayla smiled gratefully and wiped her eyes.

As the nuns prayed and sang, Troy and Thunder slept peacefully, leaning on Tia's shoulder, lulled to sleep by the nuns' sweet, soft chanting. But Tia was still hypnotized by the golden doors above the sanctuary. She stared at them, compelled by them, yearned for them. The time passed without their knowing it.

As the singing ended, the lights went out in the cloister chapel, and the vaulted rose-colored ceiling on the other side of the chancel went dark. All too soon, Mother Bonaventure came back to fetch them.

"I believe our phones are working again," she began. "Would you like to try to call your parents now?" she asked.

Char and Kayla exchanged looks.

"We're staying at the Ren—I mean, the Rinna...something." Kayla struggled to remember the name of their hotel and looked anxiously at Char.

"The Renaissance Hotel at the Tower City mall," said Char.

"Alright, we'll call them right away," Mother Bonaventure said, hands folded at her waist. "And what about you, Tia?" she looked at Tia gently. "How can we get ahold of your family?" Hearing Tia's name, Troy woke up and rubbed his sleepy eyes.

"My mother's at work," Tia said, lowering her eyes. *My parents aren't staying at a fancy hotel. My mother is a cleaning lady.*

"Is there some way you can reach her?"

Tia looked off into the far corner of the nave. "No, there aren't any phones where she works."

Mother Bonaventure pondered this for a moment. What kind of job would a woman have at night that had no telephones close by? And what mother would leave her children at home fending for themselves?

"But we just live a few blocks from here. We can walk the rest of the way." Tia began inching towards the dark double doors, Troy's hand tightly gripping hers.

"Oh, no," Mother said firmly. "We can't allow you to walk home in the dark, especially with that arm," she added. "We'll find a way to get you there."

Turning to Char and Kayla, she added, "Girls, come with me, and let's call your parents now. Then we'll call a cab for Tia and Troy."

Kayla and Char stood up, tired yet refreshed, and followed Mother Bonaventure down the hallway.

"We'll be right back!" Mother called over her shoulder to Tia, whose face visibly blossomed with relief.

Chapter 18: Family Secrets

Angels surround the faithful with the most tender care and love.

– Saint Bernard of Clairvaux

Less than half an hour later, Barbara and Paul Fisher were in the Guild Room, hugging their daughters tightly.

"You have no idea how worried we were!" Mrs. Fisher cried. "There's power outages all over the city and trees down everywhere!" Then her voice grew cold. "You could have been killed!" Her eyes were bloodshot, and her breath reeked of alcohol. Her voice sounded unnaturally harsh in the quiet church.

"Thank you, Sister Bonaventure, for helping them out," Mr. Fisher said respectfully.

"It's *Mother* Bonaventure," Char corrected him.

"That's quite all right," Mother Bonaventure said cheerfully. "I'm just thankful that we forgot to lock the front door this afternoon! We had a larger than usual crowd here today for the holy day."

"Oh, that's right, I forgot. Today is All Saints' Day," Tia said thoughtfully.

"Yes, thanks so much," Mrs. Fisher said archly. "But it's late, and we've troubled you enough. Are you girls ready to go?"

"What about Tia?" Kayla asked.

"Tia?" Mrs. Fisher echoed, glancing around at the tall teenager with the long brown-black hair. "Who's Tia?"

"This is Tia. She was with them when they got caught in the storm," Mother Bonaventure gestured to Tia, who stood patiently waiting for Mrs. Fisher to acknowledge her presence.

"Oh, hello. Are you okay?" Mrs. Fisher asked, noticing the way she was cradling her arm.

"Yes, I think so," Tia smiled.

"Her brother got lost, and she was looking for him. That's how we met," Char explained.

"He was chasing this cutest little kitten!" Kayla chimed in.

"Well, that's interesting, isn't it. You'll have to tell us all about it on the way back. But we've got to go now." Mrs. Fisher smiled stiffly. "It's been a very long day."

"Yeah, I'm sure Mother Bonaventure has better things to do than babysit a couple of lost teenagers!" Mr. Fisher joked.

"You should see the inside, Mom! Please?" Char exclaimed, holding her mother's arm beseechingly.

"Maybe some other time," Mrs. Fisher objected. "Our cab is waiting. We must go."

"Mr. Fisher, could I ask one favor? " Mother Bonaventure interjected. "Would you ask your driver if he would come back after he drops you off? Tia and Troy need a ride home, and I don't think there are many cabs out tonight."

"Absolutely. I'd be happy to," Mr. Fisher said, smiling at the stranded children. "Girls? Are you ready?"

"Yes," they answered dutifully.

"Well, thanks again." Mr. Fisher shook hands with Mother Bonaventure, then looked at his bedraggled daughters. "When we get home, you two are getting cell phones. This is not going to happen again!"

"Yes, Daddy!" Char's eyes were solemn and thoughtful. She felt bad for worrying her parents.

"Yes, Daddy." Kayla stared at the floor by the doorway. She wasn't used to getting in trouble. But getting *cell phones?* That wasn't a punishment at all. That was more like a reward!

"Goodbye, girls!" Mother Bonaventure said brightly. "Come visit us again someday!"

"We will!" Char said. "Thank you!"

"Bye!" Kayla said, smiling brightly.

Mother Bonaventure smiled back, then opened her arms for a good-bye hug. Following her example, Tia did the same. Then she and Troy went back into the church to wait for their cab ride.

Mr. Fisher led Char and Kayla down the steps to the waiting cab. Mrs. Fisher followed. The girls waved at Mother Bonaventure standing just inside the entrance and then stepped into Ray Brolick's cab, "The Cleanest Cab in Cleveland." Ray gave a thumbs-up sign to Mother Bonaventure, letting her know he'd be back for Tia and Troy. Then he made a big U-turn and headed back towards downtown. Turning to face Char and Kayla in the back seat, he grinned widely.

"So! You girls got a taste of Cleveland weather, huh?" Char and Kayla glanced sheepishly at the cab driver.

But Barbara Fisher gave them no chance to answer.

"What happened to you?" she nearly shouted.

"Mom! You won't believe." Kayla exclaimed, launching into all the details of their great adventure: seeing the guy they thought was Chad Pritt, the bus crammed full of passengers, the terrible storm, the dead nun, the fabulous, beautiful church that looked like something out of a European travel magazine, and the generous, kind-hearted nuns who lived there.

"Mom, it was so cool inside!" Char breathed when Kayla had finished.

"Yeah, like a castle out of the Middle Ages or something!" Kayla's eyes widened.

"It was more like a palace!"

"And the nuns! Dad, you should have heard them singing, behind the grille, it was like totally unreal."

Mrs. Fisher frowned at her daughters, mouth hanging open with disbelief. Mr. Fisher smiled nervously and braced himself for what was surely coming.

"There were like fifty carved wooden angels on this dark wall thing in between the Church and where the nuns stay!" Char rapidly tried to explain the grille that separated the cloister from the public Church. "And in between the wood carving was this ruby red background and there was this hidden door where you can go inside and *it was so cool!!"*

"Well! I'm glad you both had such a wonderful time!" Mrs. Fisher said archly, turning to face them. "Did you ever stop to think, even for a minute, what you were doing?" She glared at them accusingly. "This isn't Great Falls. This is *Cleveland!* Do you have any idea what kind of people walk the streets looking for girls to kidnap? Do you have any idea what happens to them? They end up in the morgue, or worse. Do you have any idea what you've just put your father and I through?" she ranted.

Char and Kayla sat uncomfortably, staring alternately out the spotless windows of the taxi at the sidewalks piled high with soggy, mangled tree branches that had been ripped off by the high winds and then down again at their cold, wet feet. Char was used to her mother's vitriolic lectures, but Kayla was not. She bit her lower lip and bravely tried to stop the tears that were beginning to flow. Charitably, Char pretended not to notice. She seemed to listen gravely to her mother's every biting word as though she hadn't realized the danger into which she, the oldest, had placed them. But the truth was, she had known, and she had gone anyway. Recklessly she had let Kayla's excitement sweep her onto the bus against her wiser instincts. *Never again,* she vowed silently.

"You know, really, Cleveland is pretty safe! Compared to a lot of places," Ray Brolick tried in vain to intercede for his young passengers.

"I'm sorry. Did I ask for your opinion? There is no need for you to get involved here!" Mrs. Fisher said coldly.

"Sorry! I was just trying to help!" Ray rolled his eyes and then glanced sympathetically into the rear mirror at Kayla and Char.

Paul Fisher reasoned with his wife. "Okay, I think we all need to just calm down a little bit. The girls are fine—everything is fine—and I think they learned a valuable lesson, haven't you, girls?"

Char and Kayla nodded briskly.

"Calm? I am very calm, thank you! My daughters—my *teenage daughters*—have been missing in a strange city for two hours in a violent storm, and they tell me they've been locked up inside some throwback monastery with a bunch of Catholic *nuns?* And I'm supposed to be happy about this?"

"We weren't locked up, Mom!" Kayla argued, sniffling. "We were safe!"

"Well maybe you weren't, but *they* certainly are! Do you know why they don't ever go outside that place? Because they can't, that's why. They're not allowed to. And that's not all they're not able to do! The Catholic Church—which is run by men, by the way—has been oppressing women for two thousand years. So don't ask me to buy into this crazy fairy tale of yours! *And don't ask me to calm down!"* Mrs. Fisher shouted, clenching her fists and pressing her lips together in a desperate attempt to stay in control of herself.

Char stared intently at the digital fare meter on the center of the dashboard counting the miles while Kayla pretended to study the approaching downtown skyline.

"Aunt Mary was a nun." Char said simply.

Mrs. Fisher's head swung to the left, shooting a lightning-bolt glance at Ray as it swiveled on around accusingly towards Paul, her mouth slightly ajar. Coldly she laughed, then stopped, turning back to face the front. "Someone's been snooping around where they shouldn't have. Or did your father decide to blab all the family secrets?"

A chilling cold settled over the cab and all its passengers. Mr. Fisher kept his calm. "She's fourteen, Barb. She has a right to know where she comes from."

"I'm not disputing that, Paul. It's just a case of really bad timing, that's all."

"And for the record, I didn't tell her. She was asking questions, and I showed her some old family pictures. She must have gone back through the rest and figured it out for herself." He smiled a little half smile at Char, who smiled wanly in return.

"Aunt Mary was a nun? Like the nuns here?" Kayla asked incredulously.

"No, honey. Aunt Mary was a teaching sister. But that was all a very long time ago." Paul replied, looking abstractedly into the distance.

"But I thought Aunt Mary lived in Milwaukee with Nana," Kayla continued.

"Yes, but that was later. She left her community after all the things that happened in the Church in the seventies."

"What things?" Char asked.

"Can we *please* talk about this some other time? I have such a splitting headache," Mrs. Fisher pressed her hand to her forehead.

"Yes, I think your mother has had enough Catholicism for one day. We'll talk about this later, if we make it back to Great Falls alive."

* * *

Char and Kayla knew their mother was wrong about the nuns. They weren't oppressed in the slightest. If anyone was oppressed, they were, for having to listen to their mother's vitriolic outbursts. But they didn't dare tell her so.

They rode in painful silence the rest of the way back to the hotel. Smoothly Ray eased the cab past the BP Building to a very slow stop in front of the Renaissance, and Paul jumped out to pay the fare. He grabbed a fat wad of bills out of his wallet.

"Thanks a lot, Ray," he said. Then, *sotto voce*, "Sorry about all the trouble." He shoved the tip into Mr. Brolick's thick fingers.

"No problem! I know how it is. Being a parent isn't easy!" Then, whispering, "Being married ain't a piece of cake either, buddy," and slapped him on the arm.

Mrs. Fisher slowly got out and began walking unsteadily towards the hotel entrance. Char quickly dug in her purse and whispered something to Kayla, who nodded. Scribbling on a piece of paper, and checking to make sure their mother wasn't watching, Char handed it to Ray while Kayla pretended to go through their Warner

Brothers shopping bags. Strangely, the Tweety Bird bedroom slippers with the fuzzy yellow trim she had been so excited about a few hours before now looked like a silly child's toy. Why had she bought them?

"Give this to Tia, please!" Char whispered urgently to the cabby.

"You got it, kiddo!" Ray whispered back with a conspiratorial grin. He quickly tucked the note up under his sun visor. "Hope to see you guys next time you're in town!" he said loudly as he swung into the cab to go back for Tia.

"Thanks, Ray!" The girls smiled gratefully and waved good-bye.

"Would you two *please* hurry up!" Mrs. Fisher scowled. "It's bad enough that you've worried us half the day. Do we have to wait half the night now?"

"Mom," Kayla tried to explain. "We weren't trying to worry you, we just…" She gave up when she saw the stony look on her mother's face.

"We'll discuss your punishment tomorrow night when we get home," she snapped.

Char and Kayla exchanged looks of dismay as they followed their parents back into the Renaissance. Punishment? They were sorry they had worried their parents. They hadn't meant to cause trouble. But no punishment, however severe, could ever take away the memory of what had been given to them that night. They would never, ever forget that very special place and the very special people they had met.

* * *

Mother Bonaventure locked the door and sighed with relief. The Fishers were safely on their way back to the hotel. She walked back into the parlor and spoke briefly with Sister Agatha, who had taken Sister Angela's place in the vigil with Sister Marie Claire, and then made her way back into the church to check on their other two visitors. Tia was still sitting in the front pew, but Troy was fast asleep, his head on Tia's lap. Thunder the kitten purred content-edly, curled up on Troy's shoulder.

Tia didn't notice Mother Bonaventure had returned and was standing next to them. She had been captivated by the golden doors, the white marble altar, and the six angels kneeling in silent adoration.

"Would you like to come back into the parlor to wait for the cab? Or would you like to stay here?" Mother Bonaventure asked.

"I think I'll stay here," Tia said, nodding towards Troy. "I don't want to wake him."

"I understand. You're a good sister, Tia. How is your arm?"

"It hurts, but I'm okay. Thank you." Tia smiled, hiding her embarrassment. No one had ever told her she was a good sister before. It was just something that came naturally to her. It wasn't something she had to try to do, it was just an expression of the love she felt for him. But still, it was nice to receive a compliment, especially from someone as important as Mother Bonaventure.

"Mother, can I ask you something?" Tia whispered urgently. Mother Bonaventure nodded.

"What's behind those doors?" she gazed again at the golden doors she had been staring at all evening. Mother Bonaventure smiled knowingly. With a voice full of love and understanding, Mother nodded her head ever so slightly, and to Tia's amazement, spoke the name of Jesus.

"It's beautiful, isn't it?" Mother Bonaventure asked. "Would you like to see?"

Wordlessly wide-eyed, Tia nodded expectantly. Being careful not to wake Troy, she slid out from under him and knelt on the padded kneeler in front of her. Mother Bonaventure genuflected before ascending the sanctuary steps. Tia remembered the time her grandmother had taken her to Church and done the exact same movement, a little more stiffly perhaps, but the same. And she remembered how embarrassed she was because she didn't know how to genuflect, too, and how clumsy she felt dropping to one knee and then standing back up again without losing her balance.

Mother Bonaventure moved silently behind the main altar and carefully reached up and removed the golden crucifix from the curved door panels. Then, ever so slowly, she opened first the left door, and then the right, to reveal the most beautiful gold monstrance Tia had ever seen in her life. At the center of the monstrance was a fiery ring of diamonds, and in the center of the ring was a consecrated Host.

Tia knew what a consecrated Host was. It was what the priest gave the people when they received Holy Communion. It was the Body and Blood of Jesus Christ. It looked like a round wafer of bread, and it tasted like a round wafer of bread, but during the Mass, the priest changed the host by the power of the Holy Spirit into the Body and Blood of Jesus Christ. It was an awesome thing and a holy thing, and only a Catholic priest could do it.

It was done for the first time by Jesus Himself at the Last Supper, on the last night he spent on earth before he was arrested and condemned to die. He said, "This is my Body, which is given for you. Do this for a commemoration of me."[3] And the priests and the people of the Catholic Church had been doing that ever since, for two thousand years.

Consecrated Hosts that were left over after Mass were kept in a special place, to be taken to the sick for Holy Communion, or saved for the next Mass. But what Tia didn't know was that there were special communities of nuns whose entire reason for being was to adore Christ in the Most Blessed Sacrament—Jesus Himself—day and night. At that very moment—in fact, every day and every night, twenty-four hours a day, there were one or two nuns kneeling on the other side of the golden doors, adoring the Eucharistic Lord and praying to Him for the needs of others. And not only there, but in

---

3 Gospel of Saint Luke, 22:19.

dozens of other monasteries around the world. Every two hours, two more nuns would take their place, so that at every hour, throughout the years, prayers of praise, adoration, and petition were continually being offered to Jesus Christ by these heroic women, virtually unknown to the rest of the world.

Tia knew none of this. All she knew was that her heart felt as though it were about to burst. She stared at the Host, feeling as if Christ Himself had somehow arranged for her to be there with Him in this incredibly beautiful place on the holy feast of All Saints.

Sensing that Tia needed to spend time alone with the Lord, Mother Bonaventure genuflected, then quietly returned to the cloister. As she left the Chapel, she said a quiet prayer for Tia, for Troy, and for the Fishers.

* * *

Tia stared at the Host, entranced. Her soul was filled with a feeling she couldn't describe. She tried to pray like she usually did, but when she tried to put her feelings into words to say to God, nothing came out. Her brain felt numb in the presence of something she couldn't comprehend. After a while, she was able to think again, but found herself filled with questions she couldn't answer, questions which had never occurred to her before.

How can this be real? How can a little piece of bread be changed into God, but still look and taste just like a little piece of bread?

Tia had been taught and had believed this dogma of the Catholic faith since childhood, and yet it still seemed unbelievable to her at times. She was almost afraid to think about it, for fear that her doubt might be displeasing to God. Then she remembered something her religion teacher had taught them when they were preparing for their first Holy Communion. She was only six years old at the time, but she still remembered it.

"Some of Jesus' first followers couldn't believe it when He told them that He was the Bread of Life. A lot of them said, 'This is too much!' and left. Then Jesus asked the other disciples if they were going to leave too. But Saint Peter didn't leave. He stayed. He said, 'Lord, to whom would we go? You have the words of eternal life.'"[4]

Tia understood why those other disciples had left. It *was* a hard thing to believe. On the other hand, she couldn't understand how anyone could know Jesus in person the way those disciples had and still leave Him. It made no sense. Jesus—who had healed the sick, cast out demons, changed water into wine—and given them all so much love and understanding, given them everything He had to give, down to the very last drop of His blood, and still, they walked away?

Her faith wasn't really something that she could explain. It was just there. It was like a sixth sense almost. She knew Jesus was there, because she could feel it. She could sense it in the depths of her soul, every time she set foot into a Catholic Church. There was something there. "No, that's wrong," she thought to herself. "Not something. *Someone.*"

* * *

"Tia," Mother Bonaventure suddenly tapped her on the shoulder. "Your cab is here. I took the liberty of paying him for you. I'm sure you didn't plan on paying for a cab fare tonight," she added kindly.

"Thank you so much, Mother." Tia gazed into Mother Bonaventure's compassionate brown eyes. She wanted to stay longer and tell her about all of her questions, but she was exhausted from the day's events, and her arm ached. What she really needed more than anything else was to get safely home with Troy, take a long, hot shower, and go to sleep. As always, Mother Bonaventure genuinely seemed to understand.

---

4 Gospel of Saint John, 6:69.

"We're always here if you need us, Tia," she said reassuringly.

Tia gently raised Troy to a sitting position to help him wake up. He was just too big to carry, especially with his book bag and Thunder.

"Troy!" she said softly. "Wake up!"

Troy opened his eyes gradually, blinking, unsure of where he was.

"We've got to go home now. Come on, get up!" Tia helped him to his feet, and he yawned. Then, remembering the storm, he huddled against Tia and pressed his face into her hip.

"It's okay, the storm is over now. We don't have to walk, we can take a cab. Okay?"

"Okay," Troy mumbled.

Mother Bonaventure slowly walked with them to the front doors.

"We'll be praying for you, dear," she said, giving them both a warm hug. "Take care of your sister, Troy."

"Okay, I will," he promised, yawning hugely.

* * *

"Oh, hey! Wouldja look at this guy! What a cute little kitten!" Ray Brolick grinned at Troy and Thunder as Tia helped them into the cab. Tia smiled, but Troy was too sleepy to respond. He climbed into the back seat, curled up and fell asleep almost immediately, his head in Tia's lap.

"Where to?" Ray asked.

"3019 Bingham. The Richmond Apartments," Tia answered.

"Bingham. That's just a few blocks from here. We'll have you home in ten minutes!" Ray said, glancing into the mirror. "Man, it's been a wild night tonight. Tornado siren went off, but I don't know if one touched down or not. Trees are down all over town. Power's out in Lakewood and downtown, too. Gonna have to wash my cab tomorrow! Got pretty dirty in all that wind!"

Tia was too tired to answer. But she smiled at this friendly cabby who was so worried about keeping his green taxi shining and spotless.

As the new Chevy Impala sped them quietly and smoothly down Euclid, Tia felt rich. Riding in this fancy new cab was nothing like being crammed into a noisy, dirty city bus. She imagined what it must be like to be a movie star riding everywhere in the back of a fancy limo.

"Hey look!" Ray pointed to the northwest. "A rainbow!" Tia followed his gaze. The storm clouds were dissolving into thin patches of gray, and there in the arc of blue sky was a brilliantly colorful rainbow. The sun was beginning to go down, and the whole Western sky was aglow with a soft yellow light.

"Wow!" she said. "That's beautiful!"

"See, not only do you have the cleanest cab in Cleveland, we ordered up a rainbow just for you!" Ray joked. Tia laughed and caressed the back of Troy's head.

As the cab pulled up to Tia's apartment, she wondered if she would be able to wake him up. He was a notoriously hard sleeper.

"Wake up mijo," she said softly. Troy was out cold. "Troy!" She shook him and he blinked his eyes, and then fell back asleep.

"Wake up little man!" Ray said loudly. "I gotta get home myself!"

Troy looked around, unsure of where he was, and whined. "Mama?"

"We're home." she reassured him. Smiling gratefully at the cabbie, Tia reached for the door.

"Oh wait! I almost forgot." Ray reached up and pulled Char's note from the visor. "One of the girls said to give this to you. Man, I woulda felt bad if I forgot to give you this." Shaking his head at his forgetfulness, Ray handed the note to Tia with Char and Kayla's address.

Chapter 19: Christ the King

– Sister Mary Madaleva Wolff, C.S.C.
"I Visit Carmel"

*L*ater that night, safely at home in her own bed, Tia awoke with a start. She'd managed to sleep well for several hours, but now her arm throbbed painfully. Hovering between sleep and wakefulness, a strangely urgent sense of mystery filled her heart and gave her no rest. A memory surrounded her, the hazy memory of a powerful dream.

Two white hinds, a male and female. Great, graceful creatures with tall, reindeer-like antlers were leaping side by side in perfect unison, the way you saw figure skaters sometimes, so close as to be one creature. The white hinds leaped together across the fields of her imagination and away in some mystic dance of meaning which she did not yet understand.

She fell back asleep and continued to dream.

She was back with Mother Bonaventure and the other nuns at the monastery. Invisibly she listened as they sang and prayed their beautiful, ancient prayers, but they couldn't see her. She tried to sing along with them, but when she opened her mouth, no sounds came out. As she looked at the nuns, she thought one of them looked familiar. Abuelita Isabel! She was smiling at Tia and singing, and it seemed the most natural thing in the world. Tia's heart filled with emotion, and she felt her grandmother's love enfolding her like a soft blanket.

Then the dream shifted. It was her grandmother's funeral. The priest was standing at the cemetery with his holy water, ready to bless the casket before they slowly lowered it into the grave. But she wasn't there! The casket was empty! Abuelita Isabel was alive! Where was she?

Once again, the dream shifted. Tia was back in Abuelita Isabel's little house. There her beloved grandma was, standing at the stove, cooking dinner. The food smelled mouth-wateringly wonderful. Char and Kayla were there, too. Tia wanted to run up and hug Abuelita, but she couldn't move. She wanted to cry out, but she couldn't speak. Slowly Abuelita Isabel turned around and saw her standing there, lost and afraid. When she smiled comfortingly, Tia never felt so happy and relieved.

Then she woke up.

Her room was still dark with the solemn darkness of November. Thoughts of the events of the previous night forcefully crowded into her mind, and her heart began to pound. The bad feeling she had had at work, her panic over Troy's safety. Running for the bus, the storm overpowering them so quickly, falling on the steps, and reeling from the terrible, shrieking, demonic tempest—and all of it fading away in the grace-filled monastery.

Pulling the comforter over her shoulders, she tried to go back to sleep, but it was impossible. Her mind was a tangled web of emotions. How different from the calm, peaceful quiet of the monastery church. Gradually, soothing images from her dreams gently replaced her fears. She had felt so happy to see Abuelita Isabel in her dream. Her grandmother's house had been home—the place where she had felt safe, the place where she knew she was loved.

She had felt safe at the monastery, too, and so comfortable talking with Mother Bonaventure. How sweet and friendly Sister Beatrice had been! Tia felt like she belonged there, but that didn't make any sense either. It must have just been the effect of the storm, and falling down, and all the excitement. And yet...

A deep sense of longing filled her. Something—someone—was trying to communicate with her. Something new had come into her life. Or perhaps it was something that had always been there, but she hadn't been ready for it until now. Straining to see in the darkness, she sensed a presence, but saw nothing, heard nothing. Tears overflowed as she struggled to make sense of it all.

"Oh, God!" she whispered, pleading for an answer. Nothing but the sound of distant traffic echoed from the window. She lay on her back for a long time and stared into the darkness, not knowing who or what she expected to see. So she simply listened and waited. The room stayed black as night, and she lost track of time.

Suddenly, she remembered her Confirmation back at Saint Matthew's in San Antonio two years before. The solemn ceremony of the bishop's anointing with chrism in front of all her friends and relatives had left her dazzled, yet full of questions. There had been a great sense of anticipation of something important approaching, but that hadn't yet arrived. Tia had chosen Therese as her Confirmation name. Her mother had disapproved, saying she already was named Teresa, her middle name, and that she should have picked something else. But Teresa of Avila wasn't the same as Therese of Lisieux, Tia had argued, even though people often got the two mixed up.

They were both Carmelite nuns, but they were two entirely different people. Teresa was Spanish and Therese was French, and their approach to prayer was different, too. Although Tia admired Saint Teresa, the great Spanish mystic who with Saint John of the Cross was responsible for reforming the Carmelite Order in the sixteenth century, she felt a special bond with Saint Therese, the one lovingly called the "Little Flower." Heroically Saint Therese had died of tuberculosis when she was only twenty-four years old, but not before promising, "I shall spend my Heaven doing good upon Earth."

So Tia offered a tearful prayer to her young Carmelite patroness. "Help me, Saint Therese! Little Flower ... please help me!" she begged, struggling for words. "Please help me find...whatever it is I'm looking for! Help me understand what's happening to me!"

After a while, a peaceful quiet slowly entered her heart. She made the Sign of the Cross, and then gently eased into a restful sleep. Not far away, the familiar roaring of a passing bus could be heard.

Hours later, just before the alarm clock shocked her awake, it seemed as though she saw the face of the Little Flower, smiling at her from her convent garden. Sweetly perfumed rose petals were softly falling ... falling ... right on the place where she had hurt her arm.

* * *

"It's not broken," the nurse said cheerfully to Tia and Gloria. "The doctor wants to order x-rays just to be sure, though. It's gonna hurt for a few days, but you should be okay with some Ibuprofen. We'll get you a prescription." She examined the scratches Thunder had left on Tia's arm. "Those scratches look like they came from a cat's claws."

"Just a scared kitten," Tia laughed.

"Kittens' claws are the sharpest! I had a kitten myself until two days ago, but she ran away. I sure miss that little critter. She was a pistol," the nurse added.

Tia frowned for a moment and then asked, "What did your kitten look like?"

"She was black with a white chin, white belly, and white sock feet. Why? Did you find a stray kitten?"

"No, but I think maybe my brother did!" Tia exclaimed. "Wait here! I'll be right back!" She dashed into the waiting room where Troy sat with his new companion, Thunder.

"Troy, come here!" Tia motioned.

"Why do I have to see the doctor? I'm not sick!" he protested.

"You don't have to see the doctor, just come on." Tia urged.

"Okay." Troy grumbled yet complied, and walked back into the examining room where Gloria and the nurse were chatting about the terrible storm the night before. The nurse looked up at Troy and Thunder as they walked in.

"Wookie!" the nurse exclaimed.

"He's Thunder!" Troy pouted, sticking out his lower lip. Was this lady going to take his kitty away?

"Thunder? Let me take a look. Yep, here's where Aslan scratched her on her ear day before yesterday. This is Wookie, all right."

"Mommy! You said I could keep Thunder!" Troy wailed.

"Sshhh!" Gloria waved her finger at Troy. "This lady lost her cat yesterday. If it belongs to her, we have to give it back!"

Troy pulled Wookie/Thunder away, and his face darkened with anger. "No! He's mine! I found him!"

"It's a 'she,' not a 'he,' honey," Linda Wallace said gently, then tilted her head. "You know, Mrs. Esperanza, I already have a big spoiled tabby cat. I don't really need this one, too. Besides, Wookie was beating up on my old Aslan like you would not believe!"

Little by little, Troy's frown eased as he listened.

"And run away, out the door, every morning! I had to watch that little cat like a hawk!" Linda laughed and then shook her head with finality. "No, I think he—I mean she," she said chuckling, "belongs to you now. Miss Thunder, you've got a new family!"

"Oh, no, we couldn't do that," Gloria said. "She's your kitty!" Troy held onto Thunder, gravely looking from one woman to the other.

"No, no. I made up my mind." she said. Then, turning to Troy, "You can keep her. You just take real good care of her, now, you hear?"

"I will!" Troy said solemnly. "I'll feed her and brush her and clean her kitty box every day!"

"And you watch and make sure she don't run out the door every time you open it. She's a wild one!"

"Yay! I get to keep you!" Troy sang and jumped, and Thunder held on for dear life. "Why did you name her Wookie?"

"Thank you, Ms. Wallace!" Gloria smiled with gratitude as she shook Linda's hand.

"If you'll give me your address, I'll come over tonight after I get off work and bring you her food dish and some kitten chow." Linda added. Then, replying to Troy's question, "When I first got her, she chewed on everything in sight. I was going to call her "Chewie," which reminded me of that big brown shaggy thing in *Star Wars*."

"Chewbacca the Wookie!" Troy smiled.

"That's right! Only, I figured 'Wookie' was a better name than 'Chewie.' But you can call her whatever you want, honey."

"Thank you," Tia beamed. Finally something good was happening.

"Thank you!" Troy mimicked his sister.

"Don't thank me, thank yourself!" Linda said to Troy. "You're the one who rescued her!"

"I rescued Thunder, and Brother Alan rescued me!" Troy shouted happily.

"Who's Brother Alan?" Linda asked, looking from Tia to Gloria and back to Troy.

"It's a long story," Tia laughed.

* * *

Tia wondered for a long time about the events of that day. How amazing it was that they had been led to the monastery in the first place. Troy would have been all right, even if she hadn't gone looking for him. Brother Alan had seen to that. But what about Char and Kayla? Who knows what would have happened to them if they hadn't gotten off the bus with her that night? The thought frightened her a little.

When Ray Brolick came back to get her after dropping the Fishers off at their hotel, he'd told her about the way Mrs. Fisher had yelled at Char and Kayla.

"I just don't get it," he said gravely. "She shoulda been happy her kids were safe, instead of gettin' all mad at them."

"Yeah, my mom gets mad at us too, sometimes," Tia confided. But the words were no sooner out of her mouth than she realized that it wasn't just sometimes. Gloria was always angry about something. If she wasn't mad at Troy, she was mad at the school, or at one of the other women at work, or the phone company, or one of her sisters. Although she'd never really thought about it before, it was true. Tia had assumed everyone's mother was like that—stressed out, angry, and blaming everyone else. And though they were different in every other possible respect, Gloria and Barbara seemed to be exactly the same when it came to their emotions.

Tia didn't really know how other mothers acted. On those rare occasions when she went to a friend's house, their mothers were always at work, or driving home from work, or shopping at the supermarket after work. Only the grandmothers were at home: Abuelita Isabel and Willie Pearl.

Tia reread Char's note for the third time. It wasn't really a note; it was just their address.

Char and Kayla Fisher
4160 North River Glen Drive
Great Falls, Montana 59407

Tia folded it up again and put it in her purse. She was glad they wanted to be friends. They had been through an incredible experience together, something no one else could possibly understand. She wrote to them the very next day.

When they wrote back, Kayla sent a picture of herself in her cheerleading uniform, and Char sent her a pencil sketch of Holy Angels Monastery. Tia admired the precise way she had drawn the fine lines and details of the church, all from memory. Seeing it, she felt a little catch in her throat. Strangely, it made her want to go back to the monastery all over again.

But what Tia wondered about most of all was her own reaction to the events of that day. Praying with and hearing the nuns singing from their chapel on the other side of the grille had been unforgettable. She felt it had affected her somehow. Something was different. A new desire had been awakened in her, and she knew her life was forever changed. But how it had changed, and exactly what she was supposed to do about it, were unclear to her. It nagged at her for weeks.

When the answer finally came, it didn't come all at once. It came in bits and pieces, like clues on a treasure hunt where finding one clue leads you to the next one, and the next, and on and on, until at last the treasure is found. She didn't know the whole answer yet, but at last she knew what she had to do.

* * *

The phone rang and rang. Finally an answering machine clicked on.

"Hello. You have reached Holy Angels Monastery. The Sisters are at prayer or are otherwise occupied. Please leave your intentions after the tone, and we will bring them before the Lord. Thank you for calling, and may God bless you."

BEEP!

"Hello, Mother Bonaventure? This is Tia—I mean, Antonia Esperanza... I was wondering, could I come by and talk to you?"

Chapter 20: Advent

Drop down dew from Heaven
and rain down the Just One.

— "Rorate Cœli" Hymn for Advent

Tia agonized in the days leading up to her appointment with Mother Bonaventure. Pleasant memories of meeting the kind, motherly nun were overrun with anxieties over what Mother Bonaventure might ask her. But between school and her job and caring for Troy, there wasn't much time to think about it.

Gloria's eyes were sharp. When it came to her children, her intuition was even sharper. Tia had kept the appointment with Mother Bonaventure a secret from everyone, but just as she was about to leave for their meeting, her mother stopped her.

"Where are you going?"

"I ... to Mass." Tia buttoned her blue jean jacket and wrapped her striped wool scarf around her head and neck.

"Where to Mass?"

"Holy Angels."

"That place with the nuns?"

"Yes, mama."

"Why don't you take Troy with you?"

Tia thought fast. Gloria must suspect something, or she would never have made that suggestion. He was usually way too fidgety, tapping his feet on the kneelers and humming little songs to himself. She had offered to take him with her a couple of times before, but he always wanted to stay home with Gloria on the weekends since he hardly ever saw her during the week.

"I can't. It's almost time for...the bus." She almost said "my appointment," but she caught herself in time.

Gloria sensed something was up, but she couldn't be sure.

"All right. Get going then."

"Bye, Mama." She reached out to give her mother a hug, which Gloria barely returned.

"When you get home, I want you to watch your brother so I can go to the store."

"Sure, Mama. Bye, Troy!"

"Bye, Tia!" Troy barely looked at her, totally engrossed in *Star Wars*.

* * *

The colorful wooden sign in front of the monastery with the scenic picture of the Virgin Mary holding the baby Jesus said, "Keep Christ in Christmas." Tia knocked on the door with a strange mixture of excitement, anticipation, and dread.

"Please come in." Sister Angela, the portress, kindly welcomed Tia and guided her into the monastery parlor, or "speak room." It was sparsely furnished with chairs and a small table. "I'll let Mother know you're here."

"Thank you." Tia spoke politely, but her heart was pounding. What would Mother Bonaventure want to talk to her about? Would she be allowed to join them? What if she said something foolish and made a complete and total fool of herself?

Traditionally, monastery speak rooms were divided in two sections: the enclosure side and the public side. The nuns could speak with their visitors through a large window, hence the name, "speak room." For over a thousand years, cloister speak room windows were barred with a heavy metal grille and a thick curtain between the two sections to protect the nuns' solemn vow of enclosure. Now, in most monasteries the grille and curtains had been removed. Only the wide counter remained, leaving the large window-like opening. A large oil painting of Saint Clare, ensconced in a carved antique wood frame, graced the far wall in the enclosure side. The colors were rich and dark, and she held a golden ciborium.

Unaccustomed to being alone, Tia unbuttoned her jacket and slowly removed her gloves and scarf, carefully placing them on the chair beside her as she waited. She folded her hands in her lap and stared at the painting of Saint Clare, too nervous to pray. On impulse, she took the gum out of her mouth and wadded it up in a piece of paper. After what seemed like hours, the enclosure side door opened, and Mother Bonaventure entered the sparsely furnished room and closed the door quietly behind her. Tia perched expectantly on the edge of her seat as Mother Bonaventure sat down in a chair on the other side of the window.

"Hello, Tia. How is your arm, dear?"

"Oh, it's fine now. We had it x-rayed, and it wasn't broken or anything. Just a bad bruise."

"I'm glad you had it checked. I broke my arm once, way back when I was a child of thirteen. I'd been up on a ladder, helping pick apples, and my little brother George threw an apple at me! I lost my balance and fell. My parents didn't take me to the doctor until the next day after it started turning purple!"

Tia's eyes widened. "That must have hurt!"

"Yes, but people didn't go to doctors back then as much as we do now. We were expected to take care of things by ourselves. Have you had to take care of things for yourself very often, Tia?"

"Yes," Tia answered. It was amazing. After just one meeting and one phone call, this woman could read her like a book.

"And that has made you grow up a little bit faster than some of your friends, hasn't it." It wasn't a question, it was a statement.

Tia just nodded. It felt weird talking about herself.

Mother Bonaventure waited.

"I guess so," Tia finally said.

"Well that can be a good thing, having responsibilities. It teaches you and others what you're capable of. I think you've taken good care of your little brother, Tia. He needed you, and he was very fortunate to have a sister like you. That was very brave of you, going after him in the storm the way you did."

Tia smiled and tried not to feel embarrassed. She wasn't used to compliments. Why was Mother Bonaventure talking like this? She thought they were going to talk about God, or about what she would have to do as a nun.

"But growing up so fast can be challenging. Do you ever feel that maybe you missed out on some things that the others girls had that you didn't have?"

In a way, it was true—sometimes she wished she'd had more time for herself, time to go to friends' houses and hang out at the mall. Time to just be herself, time to do nothing at all if she felt like it.

"I guess so. Sometimes. But not really."

"Did you miss growing up with your father?"

At that, a cold fist clutched Tia's tender heart. She hadn't thought of that. She thought Mother Bonaventure was talking about missing material things, not people she loved.

"Yes." Tia's voice was barely audible. She stared glumly at the droplets of ice water clinging to the tips of her snow boots.

"I'm sorry. Is that too hard for you to talk about?" Mother Bonaventure said gently.

Tia drew a steadying breath. "No, thank you. I'm okay."

"Good." Mother Bonaventure smiled what she hoped was a reassuring smile. This was new territory. She had never had an aspirant from a broken home before—if one could say there had been a real home in the first place.

Tia looked up at the large oil painting of Saint Clare on the wall behind Mother Bonaventure. The saint's face radiated peaceful love and serene beauty, and Tia felt calmer just by looking at it.

"When we spoke on the phone, you said that you were doing well in school." Mother Bonaventure said encouragingly.

Tia nodded and smiled.

"What is your favorite subject?"

"Psychology," Tia replied.

"Psychology. That's interesting. They didn't teach Psychology in high school when I was a girl. What else are you taking?"

"Spanish, History, Biology, Algebra, and Speech. Oh, and P.E. I wanted to take Art," Tia added, glancing up at the painting, "but they didn't have room. So they gave me P.E. instead."

"I see. And what about your spiritual life? Do you make it to Mass every Sunday?"

"Yes."

"And on holy days? You know Tuesday is the Feast of the Immaculate Conception."

"Yes."

"And do you say other prayers?"

"I pray the Rosary most every day," Tia said. "And I pray to Saint Therese."

"The Little Flower?"

"Yes."

"What about Saint Clare? You see we have her painting here," Mother Bonaventure turned towards the wall and gestured.

"I don't really know anything about her," Tia admitted.

"Chiara Offreduccio—that was her name in Italian—was born to a wealthy family in Assisi in 1194."

"Oh, wow. That's a long time ago! Chiara is a beautiful name."

"I brought you a little book about her life I thought you might like to read." Mother Bonaventure drew a small worn book from beneath her scapular and handed it through the window. "When she was eighteen, she met a man who changed her life forever— Francesco Bernardone. Do you know who that is?"

Tia thought for a moment. "No. Oh, wait! Is it Saint Francis?"

Mother Bonaventure beamed. "Yes, that's right! And there are a couple of holy cards in there too. Those are for you to keep. The book I need back, when you're finished. There's no rush. Take your time."

"Thank you, Mother! I promise I'll take care of it."

"That would be wonderful. Now, tell me what your own dear mother has to say about all of this. Have you discussed your desire for religious life with her yet?"

Tia's face clouded over. "No, I haven't."

"Oh? Why not?"

Tia shook her head and stared at a spot under the window. "I'm pretty sure she won't like it. As a matter of fact, I know she won't."

"Ah. Parents often don't, at first." Mother Bonaventure smiled understandingly, and Tia brightened a little. "But we will pray. And you must pray as well."

"Oh, I will. I mean, I've *been* praying. I've been praying a lot!"

"When do you plan to discuss it with her?"

Tia paused. She hadn't really made any plans. But she didn't want to sound immature.

"I plan to discuss it with her this weekend," she said boldly.

"This weekend. Let's see." Mother Bonaventure looked to one side and squinted. "Next Saturday is the vigil of Our Lady of Guadalupe. I believe that is the parish you told me you were baptized in, wasn't it? I think that is *most* providential, Tia. Most providential."

Chapter 21: Happy Indeed Is She

A vocation is so mysterious a gift, a thing so locked in the inner court of the soul, where God alone speaks His wishes, that no one can properly describe or explain it.

– Mother Mary Francis, P.C.C.

Tia's apartment building didn't allow real Christmas trees. A fire hazard, they said. The only sign that it was Advent in the Esperanza household was the little reindeer decoration Troy had bought at the Santa Shoppe at the after school program he went to. He'd bought it for two dollars as a Christmas gift for Gloria, but he couldn't resist giving it to her early. So it hung ridiculously on the front of the refrigerator, its jingle-bell nose ringing every time the fridge was opened.

"Mama?" Tia asked.

"What?"

"I need to talk to you. About something important."

Gloria looked at Tia, and her face paled. "Are you pregnant?"

Tia suppressed a rising rush of anger. Her mother really didn't understand her at all.

"No, Mama." Tia was resolved to be patient.

Gloria exhaled. "Oh, thank you Jesus." Then more gently, "Okay. Troy? Troy!"

Troy ran in from the living room.

"Mijo, go outside and play for a while. I need to vacuum."

"Okay, Mama. Can I go to Dillon's house?"

"Sí, I mean, yes! You may. Be careful outside and no talking to strangers, okay?"

"Sí, I mean yes, Mama!! Excuse me, Wookie!" Troy moved Wookie, who had been napping, off his jacket, pulled it on, zipped it up, and ran to the closet. After pulling on his mittens, cap, and boots, in seconds he was out the door.

Then, he ran back in and gave his sister a quick hug. "Bye Tia!!"
And again he dashed happily out the door. Wookie stretched and
stepped over to her water bowl for a long drink.

Gloria pulled a cigarette out of the worn leatherette case and
held it between her fingers, playing nervously with the lighter.

"What's wrong, Tia? she said finally, lighting up. "Are you in
trouble at school?"

"Nothing's wrong, Mama. I'm sorry. I didn't mean to worry you,"
Tia began.

Gloria sucked in a big draw of smoke, and blew it out again,
fixing Tia with her eye.

Bravely Tia took a deep breath and blurted, "Mama, I want to
become a nun."

Gloria exhaled as though she'd been punched in the gut, smoke
billowing up from her face like a volcano. She shoved her cigarette
into the ashtray, and taking a sharp breath, jumped to her feet.

"Over my dead body!"

Tia's face collapsed into a cauldron of emotions. Grief,
disappointment, and rage played over her smooth features as she
steeled herself for her mother's blowup. Stoically she stifled the
urge to run to her room and slam the door. She was going to be
mature about it, even if her mother couldn't. She set her face in firm
resolve, looked at Gloria, and waited. And waited. And waited. A
thick, palpable silence hung in the air between them. It was almost
more than Tia could bear.

"Tia," Gloria's face softened unexpectedly. "Why do you wanna
do that? You can have anything you want. You can go to college.
You can get your own place. Maybe, someday, even get married and
have a family. Look at you!"

Tia didn't know how to answer. This wasn't what she had
expected.

"You're so smart! And you're not even out of high school yet!
You have your whole life ahead of you! Why you wanna throw it all

away? I know it's been hard moving up here, going to a new school and everything."

"That's not it, Mama. I don't want to go to college. I don't want to get married. I want to be married to Jesus."

Gloria's eyebrows shot up. "Married to Jesus? Who's been filling your head with that crazy talk? Jesus is God, Tia. You can't marry God."

"Saint Clare says you can. And I believe her! And Saint Therese, too!"

"Saint Therese? That was like a hundred years ago. This is now! You! Your life, your future, Tia. Don't just throw it all away on some crazy dream! Nuns are very lonely people, Tia. They spend all their life not talking to anybody, not even each other. They never have fun, they never get to go out or see their family or anything. Is that the life you want?"

"You don't understand! It's not like that!"

"How do you know? You won't know what it's like until you get there, and then it'll be too late! They'll lock you up, and your life will be over."

"No it won't! Stop—just please stop trying to talk me out of it. I made up my mind, and there's nothing you can do to stop me!"

Like lightning, Gloria's hand struck her hard across the face. Tia gasped.

"Let me tell you something! You think you know it all." Gloria ranted. *"¡Niña estúpida!* I know more about it than you. There were nuns at my school when I was a girl. I know about nuns. You ever had one hit you? Or smack your hand with a ruler? Married to Jesus. Those women were married to the devil!"

Tia spun around and rushed to her room. Grabbing her coat and purse, scarf and gloves, she bolted out the door before Gloria could finish relighting her cigarette.

"Hey! I told you I need you to watch Troy! Hey! Wait! Come back here!" Gloria shouted after her, but the words hit the closing door like clenched fists on an ivy-covered wall.

* * *

It was too cold to walk far, so Tia caught the first bus she could find. She had to get away. Once safely aboard, she plugged in her headphones, letting the music wash away the sound of her mother's voice and the stinging welt on her face. She stared out the windows at the bare trees, the snow-covered yards, and the Christmas lights hanging from the roofs of the houses. What was it like to live in your own house, not a rented apartment or someone else's house, she wondered. They all looked so cozy and happy and safe. Lush, green Christmas trees, decorated and alight in the windows. Gloria hadn't gotten around to putting up their spindly artificial one yet. Tia had intended to put it up after she got home from Mass on Sunday, but now...

Tears rolled down Tia's face. Her mother had ruined everything. What would she say to Mother Bonaventure? As Tia reached in her purse for a tissue, she noticed the book the abbess had given her. Pulling it out, she read again with joy from the fourth letter of Saint Clare to Agnes, the former Princess of Bohemia. Agnes, who one day would be known as Saint Agnes of Prague, had, like Clare, given up a luxurious life to wed the poor, chaste Christ.

> *You have been marvelously espoused to the spotless Lamb*
> *who takes away the sins of the world (1 Pt 1:19; Jn 1:29).*
> *Happy, indeed, is she*
> *to whom it is given to share this sacred banquet,*
> *to cling with all her heart to Him*
> *whose beauty all the heavenly hosts admire unceasingly,*
> *whose love inflames our love,*
> *whose contemplation is our refreshment,*
> *whose graciousness is our joy,*

whose gentleness fills us to overflowing,
whose remembrance brings a gentle light,
whose fragrance will revive the dead,
whose glorious vision will be the happiness
of all the citizens of the heavenly Jerusalem…

Tia wiped the tears from her eyes and read and re-read the beautiful words, and after a while she felt calmer. She still dreaded having to tell Mother Bonaventure what had just happened. But she had no choice, unless she wanted to lie, and she wasn't about to do that.

Monday night after she'd fed Troy his supper and Gloria was miles away at work, Tia picked up the phone. Gripping the receiver, she waited for the answering machine, but to her surprise the sweet-voiced Sister Secretary answered. Soon Tia was pouring out her aching heart to Mother Bonaventure.

"She wouldn't even listen! I didn't get a chance to tell her anything. She just went off on me like I was a criminal and she was the judge, the jury, and the executioner."

"She must love you very much, Tia. Otherwise she wouldn't be trying so hard to protect you," Mother Bonaventure tried to console the distraught girl.

"Protect me? She doesn't care about protecting me. She just wants to control me. She doesn't care one bit about what I think or what I want."

"Well, there may be some of that, too, but I think her motives are sincere. She is judging by the world's standards, but she means well, Tia. You must try to see things from her point of view. To her, you're getting ready to turn your back on everything she values— everything she has tried to obtain for herself and couldn't: marriage, money, and independence."

Tia shook her head. It didn't make any sense. Why was Mother Bonaventure taking Gloria's side in this? What about her vocation? What about what *she* wanted? What about *her* dreams?

"Yeah, I suppose. But that doesn't give her the right to hit me."

A shocked silence thrummed through the telephone line.

"Oh, Tia. She hit you?"

"Slapped me right across the face. And not some little tap. She hit me hard. My mom is strong."

"Oh. I am so sorry." Mother Bonaventure said quietly, thinking how to respond. "It was wrong of her, Tia. Has...she ever hit you before?"

"No. This was the first time." Tia bit her lip, trying to keep the jagged misery out of her voice. She didn't want Mother Bonaventure to know how messed up her family was. If she knew, they'd never accept her. There was a pause on the other end of the line, and fresh tears stung the back of her eyelids. It was hopeless. Tia knew that her dream of being a bride of Christ was over.

"Would you like to come in on Saturday? Then we could talk some more," Mother Bonaventure asked.

"Oh yes, please!" Tia's heart pounded with excitement.

"After Mass. Then, we'll talk. You'll see, everything will be all right. And we'll be praying for you and for your mother, that she will see things clearly and treat you fairly."

"Thank you so much!" And she breathed a huge sigh of relief. Maybe she had a chance. Maybe it wasn't hopeless after all.

Chapter 22: Ecce Fiat

*My dearest daughter, make a particular effort to practice
sweetness and submission to the will of God, not only in
extraordinary matters, but even in the little things that occur
daily. Make these acts not only in the morning but also during
the day and in the evening, with a tranquil and joyful spirit.
And if you should fail in this, humble yourself, make a new
proposition, get up and continue on your way.*

— Saint Padre Pio, Letters III

It had snowed the week before Tia came to see Mother
Bonaventure for their next appointment. Someone had cleared
off the steps, but snow clung beautifully to the wrought iron fence
and handrails and covered the shrubbery like dollops of Cool Whip
on gingerbread cakes. Inside the public chapel, the nuns had
erected a traditional Nativity crèche with lifelike statues of Mary
and Joseph waiting near an empty crib, watching in anticipation of
the long-awaited arrival of the Christ Child in just a few more days.

During Mass, the readings for the Fourth Sunday of Advent
echoing the Virgin's *Magnificat* seemed to pierce her heart with
sweet joy. *My soul proclaims the greatness of the Lord...The
Almighty has done great things for me, and holy is His name.* She
tried to catch a glimpse of the nuns when they went up to Holy
Communion from the enclosure side, but she could only see a few
veiled heads here and there at the Communion window as they
received Our Lord from the hands of the priest. And soon she would
be one of them! *Behold the handmaid of the Lord. Let it be done to
me according to thy word.*[5] When Tia returned to her pew after
receiving Holy Communion, it seemed as though she were floating
above the kneeler, so great was her happiness.

[5] Gospel of Saint Luke, 1:48.

Afterwards, Sister Angela whisked her right in to the speak room, and Mother Bonaventure was soon seated in the same small chair as before under the portrait of the lovely Saint Clare.

"How are you, Tia? I hope this week hasn't been too awful for you after what happened with your mother. Were you able to patch things up?"

Tia lowered her gaze and thought. "Well, not exactly," she said uncertainly.

Gloria had kept pretty much to herself all week, but she seemed to be trying to show Tia she was sorry, even if she didn't say it. She had done some of the chores that Tia ordinarily was expected to do, like taking out the trash, wiping down the kitchen stove and counters before leaving for work in the afternoon, and making sure Troy had done his homework before he started watching TV. But she hadn't apologized, and they still weren't speaking.

"Did you try to discuss your plans with her again?" Mother Bonaventure questioned.

"Oh, no. I don't think she'll ever change her mind. Once my mother makes her mind up, that's it. There is no changing it. And besides, I don't want to make her mad again!"

"Of course. I only meant that sometimes after a cooling-off period, people can discuss their differences more rationally."

"My mother isn't rational," Tia said bluntly. "At least when it comes to other people's opinions."

"I see." Mother Bonaventure considered this carefully. "At least there have been no more arguments. What about the rest of your family?"

"I haven't told anyone else," Tia said.

"Do you think they would be more supportive?"

"I think my Aunt Delia might."

"Is she your mother's sister, or your father's?"

"My mom's. But she and her are totally different. My Aunt Delia is a very understanding person. And, she's a Catholic. Like, I mean, she goes to church every Sunday."

"That's good. And your father?"

Tia swallowed and took a deep breath. "No. I mean, I haven't told him."

"Do you ever get to talk to him?"

"No." Tia was mortified. She didn't understand what this had to do with her wanting to become a nun. What difference did it make whether or not she got to talk to her father? She didn't even know where he was. He wasn't part of her life. Was that her fault?

"That is most unfortunate." Mother Bonaventure said. "Did you get a chance to read the book I gave you?"

"Yes, it was really good." Tia relaxed, thankful that Mother had changed the subject. "Here, you can have it back."

"Which part did you like best?" Mother Bonaventure reached out to take the book from Tia's hand.

"I liked the part where she ran away in the night to meet Saint Francis, and he cut her long hair and gave her a plain dress to wear so she could become a nun. And her brothers tried to stop her, but they couldn't get through the door."

Mother smiled at the old familiar story. "Yes, sometimes we have to overcome great obstacles to our vocations, Tia. And sometimes the greatest obstacles are from those we love the most, and those who love us the most."

Tia nodded, but she didn't understand why Mother Bonaventure was talking about obstacles. An unwelcome feeling of frustration began to knot up in her stomach. Mother Bonaventure didn't understand. She would be graduating in just six months. She needed to get her plans firmly in place.

"I have discussed your situation with the novice mistress and the rest of the council, and we feel that it would be best for you to wait a few more years to enter. Of course, you must finish high school, but then you will only be eighteen. Two more years of school or work would be good for you and help you more fully discern God's call in your life. We will, of course, keep in touch, and we can continue to meet periodically."

Tia's heart plummeted. *Two and a half years?* How could she ever wait that long?

Not waiting for Tia to answer, Mother Bonaventure continued. "Will you be coming to Midnight Mass with Troy?"

Midnight Mass? How could she think about Christmas when she'd just had the one thing she wanted in life taken away from her?

"I— yes." She refused to yield to the temptation to cry.

"Good. We will see you then." Mother Bonaventure stood to leave. The meeting was over. Tia stood up as well, quickly grabbing her scarf and gloves so the abbess couldn't see her face.

"Don't be discouraged, dear. We will be praying for you, and I will be in touch. This is only the beginning." Mother reached up and lightly traced the Sign of the Cross on Tia's forehead. "God be with you."

Tia bravely managed a smile, too overwhelmed to speak, and slowly walked back to the bus stop.

Part Two – Into the New Millennium

Contrary to everyone's fears, the world did not end on December 31, 1999. After all of the hype about "Y2K," the end of the millennium turned out to be something of a non-event. Computer systems did not malfunction, ATM machines worked just fine, and inter-continental ballistic missiles didn't accidentally shoot up into the sky in a doomsday scene of death and destruction. Life went on much as before, at least for a while. But other worlds had ended, or were soon to end.

On New Year's Day 2000, in Columbine, Colorado, life was still anything but normal. The following year, the World Trade Center's iconic Twin Towers would come crashing down in New York City. Two months prior to that, in July 2001, Marty Baron took over as editor at the *Boston Globe*, changing the paper's focus to local investigative journalism, a move that would ultimately have profound repercussions for Catholics in Boston and throughout the world. A deadly enemy had attacked the Church, but not with planes or guns.

But for every heartbreaking tragedy that man creates, God has a magnificent response. Because it isn't always the events that make the news and the talk shows that count so much, sad though they may be; rather, it is the radical choices made by quiet, ordinary people of faith that cumulatively shape history and are, in the end, the ones that ultimately prevail, pushing back, by the grace of God, the ghastly gates of hell.

Chapter 23: Wait for Me

Either die or conquer.

– Saint Margaret Mary Alacoque, V.H.M.

For three long years, Tia applied herself to her schoolwork, worked part time at Tower City, and volunteered as a patient concierge at the Cleveland Clinic, helping to guide patients to their appointments. She went to Mass every Sunday at the monastery and visited with Mother Bonaventure about once a month, either in person or by phone. In June 2002, she graduated from high school with honors and was accepted into the General Studies program at Cleveland State University, where she made the honor roll twice. And she waited.

Six weeks after graduating high school, she was invited to Jacob and Kanisha's wedding. Kanisha looked radiantly happy and stunningly beautiful, and Tia had been envious. The bride's white satiny sheath with the pale mauve ribbons fit her perfectly, and the lily-of-the-valley braided into her up-do had made Kanisha look like a goddess. Jacob looked like a totally different person in his black tuxedo. Everyone had plenty to eat and too much to drink, and the music blared at the reception until the park closed at ten. After Kanisha and Jacob left in a rented limo for their honeymoon at Geauga Lake, Tia had taken the bus home, painfully self-conscious even though she had exchanged the high heels for Nikes. She wrapped up tightly in a raincoat so no one would look at her standing on the street in her blue dress.

But a year later, Kanisha was back home with her parents. Jacob had started "dating" a girl from their old school, and Kanisha found out. Kanisha had called her up every night for a week, weeping and nearly hysterical, letting her grief out in huge waves that seemed to Tia as though it would drown them both under the weight of it. *How could this have happened?* Tia wondered. They had seemed like the perfect couple. What had gone wrong? Jacob filed for divorce a few weeks later. It was over before it ever began. Maybe having a boyfriend and getting married wasn't the wonderful fantasy life she had imagined it to be, Tia thought. And she stopped feeling envious of other people's lives.

After that, she tried to spend as much time as she could in adoration at the monastery. Her prayer time was like that of Saint John Vianney—the great Curé of Ars, France, who when asked what he was doing so often in front of the Blessed Sacrament simply replied, "Nothing. I look at Him, and He looks at me." Somehow, it helped. Little by little, she found herself calmer, more peaceful, and more focused on her vocation.

Mother Bonaventure had said she could apply to enter after she turned twenty in October, but she was resolved to wait as long as it took. And if these nuns wouldn't take her, there were other monasteries that might—there was a beautiful Poor Clare Colettine monastery on Cleveland's far west side in the suburb of Rocky River, or maybe Mother Angelica's community, the Poor Clares of Perpetual Adoration in Hanceville, Alabama. But her heart was at home at Holy Angels.

At the end of their last visit, Mother Bonaventure had given her a well-worn copy of *A Right to be Merry*, the light-hearted true story of the founding of the Poor Clare monastery in Roswell, New Mexico. Written by the Abbess, Mother Mary Francis, it revealed details of religious life and of a religious vocation in a way that spoke directly to her heart.

There! Tia thought. *There is someone who truly understands how I feel!*

"A true vocation is a call so compelling that a soul must loosen its hold on the dearest and even the holiest of its loves to rise up and follow the summons."

Well, she had answered the call. She had followed the summons. Now, it was just a matter of time.

Gloria didn't notice when Tia got home from Cleveland State that night. Gloria had sprained her ankle at work and had the week off, doctor's orders. She was sitting in the brown armchair in the living room, leg propped up on a pillow. Wearing new black bifocals and holding a sheaf of papers, she was talking animatedly to somebody on the phone.

Ignoring her, Tia grabbed a Diet Coke out of the refrigerator and the tuna salad sandwich and apple slices Gloria had made for her. It was strange having her mother home at night, Tia thought. Strange, but nice. Just as she was about to head back to her bedroom, she spied a letter addressed to her lying on the table. She picked it up and glanced at it as she started down the hall. Oddly, the return address was in Great Falls, but the postmark read "Pittsburgh, PA."

In the hallway, heavy metal music pounded from inside Troy's bedroom. Tia wondered that the neighbors hadn't called the cops. Tentatively at first, then harder, she knocked on the door. No response. Carefully she opened the door just a crack. She didn't want to intrude on his privacy. Troy was sitting on his bed, playing the air drums and bobbing up and down. As Tia opened the door further, Wookie dashed out in a desperate attempt to locate a quieter spot.

"Troy!" Tia called out.

No response. He couldn't hear over the noise of the boombox.

"Troy!!"

Finally he whirled around and grinned, pounding the air with imaginary drumsticks.

"Turn it down!" she ordered.

Annoyingly, he pretended not to hear, squeezing his eyes shut and lip-syncing with the band.

Tia strode over to the CD player and hit the power button, but Troy just kept right on playing. After all, he knew the tune by heart.

"Troy, that's too loud! We don't want to bother the neighbors."

"Hey Tia! Guess what?"

"What?"

"I met Mike downstairs, and he was really nice. He let me wear his hat."

"Who's Mike?"

"He's the guy that lives downstairs. The guy with the motor-cycle."

"Oh. Okay."

"He's really cool. He's got an autographed Metallica poster and some other cool stuff. He works as a security guard. Did you know that?"

"Nope. I sure didn't. So'd you do your homework?"

"Uh-huh."

"For real? Or for pretend?"

"For real." Air drumming commenced once again.

Tia was skeptical. "Let me see."

Air drumming continued.

"Troy!" Tia shouted. Why couldn't he pay attention? He seemed to be off in his own little world, having a great time.

"What?"

"I said, show me your homework!"

"Okay." Hopping off the bed, he unzipped his book bag and rummaged through it, removing crumpled papers. "Here!" he said at last. "I got a "B" on my History test!"

"Oh, that's cool. Awesome job, bro. But where's that home-work?"

Troy dug some more. "Ewww!!!" He held up a smashed peanut butter sandwich that had been there since August and tried to hand it to Tia.

"I don't want that! Go throw it away."

Troy set it on the floor and kept rummaging.

"Oh, here. I was supposed to give this to Mama."

Tia looked at the school office memo. It was marked, "Notice of In-School Suspension."

"She's supposed to sign that."

"This is from last week!" Tia examined it closely. A box had been checked next to "Non-compliance with school policy on weapons." Then a handwritten note: "Troy pretended his pencil was a spear and threw it at the ceiling." Tia rolled her eyes. Some of these teachers were out of control.

"Here! Here's my homework."

Tia looked at the sloppily written essay on the exports of Hawaii. It looked presentable enough.

"Okay. Thank you," she said, handing it back to him. "I'm going to take this ISS form to Mama. She's gonna be mad you didn't give it to her last week, mijo."

"I couldn't! She wasn't here, and then I forgot."

"I don't want to argue with you. Just remember next time to give Mama anything you get from the school! If she's not here, leave it on the table and she'll see it when she gets home. Okay?"

"Okay." Then he pulled the black hood from his hoodie over the top of his head, striking a threatening gangster pose. "'Sup, homie?"

"I'm serious! Now go throw that sandwich away before some-body steps in it!"

Troy picked up the dried up, moldy lump of bread and peanut butter and slam-dunked it into the trash can in the corner, where it hit the edge and bounced out onto the floor again.

"Not in there, in the kitchen!"

"Would you throw it away for me?" Troy begged.

"No. You do it. And use your headphones! No more loud music!"

"Okay." Troy leaned over and gave her a hug and then ran to the kitchen to dispose of the dead sandwich.

Tia sighed and shook her head. What a mess. So who was this Mike person? No wonder he didn't mind the loud music coming from their apartment. He probably liked it. Dropping her book bag by her bedroom door, Tia walked back into the living room with the

ISS notice. Grinning, Troy sped by her on the way back to his room and shut the door.

Gloria was finally off the phone.

"Mama?"

"Hey. How was school?"

"School was good. Mama?" she began gingerly, "Troy got ISS again." Tia handed the form to her mother, who pursed her lips in anger.

"What's wrong with this kid? Dios mío, I swear he is going to be the death of me!" Gloria struggled to stand up and hobble back to Troy's bedroom on her one good leg. She banged forcefully on the door a warning and then opened it.

"Troy!" she yelled, and then shut the door behind her.

Tia cringed. So much drama over a pencil—a pencil! It was hard to believe. Still, she was worried. Troy had been getting in trouble at school more and more these past few months. He had been diagnosed as special needs and had an IEP,[6] but all their efforts seemed to have no effect on his grades or his behavior. The school psychologist suggested they try medication, but Gloria had refused. "I'm not going to put my boy on drugs!"

If school is like this now, Tia wondered, *what will it be like when he gets into high school?* Tia pushed the thought from her mind. It was too scary to think about.

The knock at the door jolted her out of her thoughts. She peered through the peephole. It was Mike, their downstairs neighbor. He was staring apologetically at the peephole and holding Troy's red and blue Cleveland Indians baseball cap in both hands.

Tia cautiously opened the door.

"Hey. Sorry to bother you, but your little brother left this in my apartment today."

"Oh, I'm so sorry. Thanks for bringing it back."

---

[6] individualized education program

"No, it's okay. He's a great little dude. I'm Mike, by the way."
Shifting the hat to his left hand, he offered Tia his right, and they
shook.

"I'm Tia. Nice to meet you."

"Hi Tia. Here you go." He handed her the hat, and for a minute
he just stood there, as though he wanted to say more.

Tia stared at his wiry arms covered with tattoos and felt slightly
repelled. He was a small man, not as big in person as he seemed to
be when she saw him riding around on his Harley. He smelled
faintly of cigarette smoke—that homey smell she'd grown up with.
He also smelled of beer, which vaguely reminded her of her father.
Suddenly something clicked in the back of her head, and she almost
felt, rather than heard, a buzzing sound in her ears. Something
wasn't quite right about him, but at the same time—

"I don't know how to say this," he began slowly, tilting his head
to one side, "but would you maybe like to go out with me
sometime?"

Immediately Tia's face flushed, and the buzzing noise increased.
Who was this man standing two feet away from her? She swallowed
hard and took a deep breath.

"Um, yeah. I would."

"You would?" Mike said incredulously.

"Yeah! I mean, yes. I would." *What am I doing? What am I
saying?*

"Alright! Well, how about tonight?" he grinned smoothly. "What
about right now?"

Tia's heart began pounding just as she heard Gloria come out of
Troy's room and start hobbling up the hallway. And just like that,
she stepped out into the stairwell next to him and quickly shut the
metal door behind her.

Chapter 24: What Are You?

Do not be satisfied with less than the fullness of God's love and life.
You know it is within your reach, and He wants it for you.

— Mother Aloysius of the Blessed Sacrament, O.C.D.

Two hours later, Tia dashed up the stairs back to their apartment. She hoped and prayed that Gloria wouldn't still be up. But the light was on, and since it wasn't like Tia to just leave like that without telling anyone, she was probably in for a solid thirty minutes of questioning as soon as she walked through the door. And she didn't want to deal with it.

She stopped at the top of the stairwell just long enough to catch her breath. Furtively she pressed her ear to the door before inserting the key in the lock, but the apartment was quiet. Maybe she had a chance to get in. Turning the key as slowly as possible, she opened the door a tiny bit. Still no Gloria. Stealthily she tiptoed inside the doorway and shut it without making a sound. Gloria was peacefully asleep, covered with an afghan and stretched out on the couch. Seeing her, Tia realized for the first time the sacrifice their mother had made in letting her and Troy have their own rooms. They couldn't afford a three-bedroom apartment, so Gloria slept on the couch each day while they were at school.

Tia crept silently back to her room, holding her breath. Safe! Closing the door behind her, she breathed out a heartfelt prayer of thanksgiving. She'd escaped her mother, and she'd escaped Mike. Kicking off her shoes, she spied the unopened letter on her dresser and opened it.

June 12, 2002

Dear Tia,

> *How are you? It's been so long since I've written, but last week, I started thinking about you and just had to write.*

A lot has happened... Kayla was in a terrible accident about a year ago. She was on top of a pyramid for cheerleading, and something happened and she fell. She broke her collarbone and her wrist, and had a mild concussion and was unconscious for five minutes. We were so afraid! When they took her to the hospital, they found out she was pregnant! I couldn't believe it. I thought they'd made some mistake! Mom totally freaked, and things were pretty bad for a while. Dad wanted her and Eric to get married, but Eric couldn't handle it, and they broke up. It was awful! Kayla was so messed up, she almost quit school. But she didn't, thank goodness!

Mikel Paul was born on August 10th. He is so cute!!! He weighed 7 pounds 2 ounces. He has fluffy black hair and blue eyes. I am enclosing a photo of him. I'm an auntie!!!

So what have you been doing (besides going to school)? Are you still working at Tower City? Are you still planning on joining the nuns? I think that is so awesome.

I hope you get this. Maybe you've already joined...??

I can't believe I'm going to be starting college in two more months! I've been accepted to Carnegie Mellon in Pittsburgh. We're here today and tomorrow for summer orientation. All the new freshmen come with their parents and tour the campus and the dorms and meet the other kids and their parents. I'm going to major in Fine Arts with a concentration in Architecture.

Pittsburgh is a really cool place, very friendly people. <u>Lots</u> of bridges! It's a really good school, and I'm lucky I got accepted, but sometimes I wonder if this is where I belong. It's so different from Montana. I don't want to ruin my life going to the wrong school...

How is Troy? He must be 11 or 12 now? Tell him I said "hi."

So things were really bad for a while, but it's better now that Mikel is here. Everything is different now. I help Kayla with him after school so she can do her homework. Mom takes care of him while Kayla is at school half days, and then when she gets home, Mom goes into the office. Mom works at home too, and so far it's going pretty good. I babysit Mikel at night at least once a week so Kay can get out of the house.

I feel bad for her. Britney and Annie still come over sometimes, but most of her so-called friends have dumped her. Please pray for her! She didn't get to do any cheerleading all last year. She still gets a little dizzy sometimes from the accident. She is still kind of depressed. She really misses Eric. She adores Mikel, but she says she doesn't know what to do if Eric doesn't marry her. She doesn't want to live with Mom and Dad forever. But I think she is afraid to live on her own.

I feel bad having to leave her and Mikel when I start college in September. I almost want to wait a year so I could stay home and help, but Mom and Dad said no. I have to live my own life now.

Write back soon! Call me!

Your friend always,

Love, Char

Poor Kayla! Tia thought as she folded the letter and put it back in the envelope. She could have lost the baby, or worse—she could have been killed. It was a miracle she hadn't been. A mother at sixteen! She thought that kind of thing only happened to poor girls like her mother, not rich white girls like the Fishers. Kayla was lucky Char was there to help.

It was hard to imagine Kayla with a little baby. Tia studied the photo of the littlest Fisher and smiled. What would the world be like when Mikel was all grown up? What would he become? Would Eric do the right thing and marry her? Or would Mikel grow up fatherless like she and Troy had? She had to remember to pray for the Fishers the next time she went to Adoration, especially Kayla and baby Mikel... Mikel... Mikel... *Mike.*

Then she remembered what she'd been doing the past two hours.

She thought she felt the pounding vibration of a stereo under her feet. It unnerved her to think that Mike's bedroom was right under hers. It had been a strange evening, starting with the way she had felt compelled to sneak out without telling her mother where she was going. It wasn't like her at all. But she'd felt so confused, and rebellious, and excited, and she hadn't been able to resist.

They had gone down to the parking lot. He'd asked her if she wanted to go for a ride on the bike or just stay in and watch a movie. The thought of being alone with Mike in his apartment frightened her; she'd wisely opted for the bike ride instead. He'd seemed relieved in a way, like he'd been a little bit scared, too.

He straddled the black leather seat and long chrome pipes. "Hop on," he said, throwing his weight on the starter. As the Harley came to life, they took off from the parking lot smoothly, easing out into the light traffic and up to Euclid Avenue, riding without helmets towards downtown and then out the Shoreway past the calm blue-gray waters of Lake Erie. They'd cruised around for an hour, enjoying the cool night air. The wind blowing in her face made her feel free and alive, and the rumbling roar of the Harley made her heart pound. Everyone seemed to be watching them, or so it seemed.

They'd stopped at a little hoagie stand on the near West Side. Kids were riding around on their bicycles, eating popsicles. He'd parked the bike next to some picnic tables under a dusty locust tree strung with little white lights and bought them meatball sandwiches with pickles, chips, and Cokes. *He even remembered the napkins,* Tia noticed happily.

After they finished eating, he smoked and talked about his mechanic shop he'd had since high school in Spokane, how his mother had gotten cancer and had to go to Seattle for chemo, had to quit her job at the JC Penney store at the mall, and the only way he could cover her rent and utilities was to sell the shop and go to work at the Greyhound bus depot. In the end, after six months his mother had died, and after the funeral and the estate sale, and after the lawyers had filed the probate papers he'd signed as executor of her estate, sold her Chevy Impala and paid her bills, leaving him a grand total of $1,548.76 after legal fees, he'd taken off on his Harley in search of a new life. And here it was, in Cuyahoga County, and weren't those Indians having a great year? And did she like baseball?

Tia smiled and nodded and listened even though baseball was the last thing she ever thought about. It didn't matter. Mike was different from anyone she'd ever known. He was twenty-six, never married. *Almost married once,* he had said, stubbing out his cigarette in the empty hoagie tray. *But I escaped,* he added with a wry smile. Tia wondered what he meant by that, but didn't think it would be polite to ask.

"How about you? You got a boyfriend?"

Tia shook her head shyly. "No."

"Well today's my lucky day." He grinned, looked at her pointedly and then stood and stretched. "It's hot out, even at night. Doesn't get hot like this in Washington."

"This isn't hot," Tia said matter-of-factly.

"Oh no? Where are you from, with that southern drawl of yours?"

"San Antonio," Tia said smiling.

"Texas, okay. Yeah I guess it does get hot down there, doesn't it?"

"Yup. Sure does," Tia agreed. "And it stays hot until October."

To her consternation, he looked at her appraisingly again.

"Can I ask you something personal?"

"Sure."

"How old are you?"

"Twenty-one," she lied, surprised at herself.

"Twenty-one, eh. Are you sure? You look about eighteen to me."

Tia just shrugged and sipped her Coke.

"Can I ask you something else?"

"I guess."

"You're from San Antonio, you said. What are you? Are you black? Latino? Or what? You kind of look like a Cuban girl I dated a long time ago, back in Tacoma."

Tia stiffened. Here it was again, this questioning of her racial background. She resisted the urge to say, *None of your business!*

"Why does it matter what I am?" she retorted.

"Naw, I just wondered, that's all. Don't get all bent out of joint. I didn't mean nothin' by it."

Tia pressed her lips together, biting her lower lip. She looked down, then looked up and fixed him with a darkly luminous gaze. "I am a *person*. Okay? A person. That's all."

"Okay. A *person*. Well, I guess I blew that one, didn't I? Never mind. And excuse the hell out of me. You ready to head back?"

Was she ever! She was ready to go back, and she was ready to resist being put into categories, and she was ready to stop catering to the curiosity of other people so she could be placed into further categories in order to suit their idea of who she was and who she ought to be.

"I'm ready when you are." She tried to keep her voice light, but the annoyance crept in like a shadow.

He got up then without saying a word, threw their trash in the barrel, strode over to the bike, and climbed on without looking back. Within seconds, they were jetting back to the East side.

Chapter 25: Pray for Me

One feels so clearly that it would take no more than an orange peel to precipitate one into an abyss. One first deliberate infidelity, consented to and not made good, and one may become an "unfrocked" nun even as a jubilarian, as we hear happened to a Trappistine extern sister. Anyone who would cast the stone at her and say: 'That could never happen to me!' would show how little she knows herself and would be evincing more stupidity than pride.

– Benedictine nun, aged 63, in religion 42 years

The long hot shower she took when she got home couldn't quite get rid of the uncomfortable feeling that clung to her skin like a stain. Tia resolved to push the whole thing out of her memory. Grateful for something to take her mind off her misery, she re-read Char's letter. *She'll be starting college right about the time I enter the monastery,* Tia mused.

Gently her thoughts drifted towards the future, and she began asking herself the same question she'd been asking herself for the past three years: *What will it be like being a nun?* It seemed to her as though it would be truly wonderful, but what would it be like never to have children or grandchildren, never to marry? Would she regret her choice? What would it be like living behind closed doors in the same place for the rest of her life? It all seemed so drastic and difficult. And yet, in the deepest core of her truest self, she knew that God was asking her to do exactly that.

Then the memory of her date and the uncomfortable feeling returned. *Why did I do it? Why did I go out with that man?* Tia tried to reassure herself, telling herself she was home, and she was safe, and that nothing bad had happened, but she had the distinctly unpleasant feeling that she had barely escaped from a death trap, like a frightened deer dodging away from the sights of the hunter's gun.

Hugging herself, she looked up at the picture of the Sacred Heart on her wall, the one that had graced her grandmother's living room for so many years. Was it only her imagination, or did He look perturbed? She rubbed her eyes and looked away. There on her dresser was the other book Mother Bonaventure had lent her, *The Story of a Soul, the Autobiography of Saint Thèrése of Lisieux*. She went over to it and opened it up, lying on her bed to read.

Now we suffer and are in the midst of our struggles, and yet we can feel such delight in thinking that God has withdrawn us from the world, so what shall we feel in heaven when, surrounded by eternal glory and endless peace, we can realize how incomparable was the favor He did us in choosing us to dwell in this convent, His house and the gateway to heaven?

She read and re-read the lines, then looked back to the picture of Jesus, hanging inscrutably on the wall. *You chose me? I thought I was the one who chose You*, she thought. Painful tears of regret stung her eyes and streamed down her face. *The only one on this earth who really loves me for me... I am so sorry, Jesus! Please forgive me!*

And it all washed away in a torrent of tears. When she finally stopped crying a few minutes later, her eyes fell on the door of her closet. Suddenly inspired, she jumped up, wiped her face, and threw the door open. Stacks of shoes, sandals, and boots and boxes of belts, leggings, and skirts covered every square inch of the closet floor. Stylish blouses and sweaters and jackets hung from metal and plastic hangers, and half a dozen pairs of mostly too-tight jeans were folded and draped neatly over still more hangers. She began ripping them out two or three at a time, throwing them on the floor until a huge pile quickly formed.

Energized, she turned to her antique dresser from Aunt Carmen. Except for a couple of pieces that had been gifts from family, out went the costume jewelry, the perfume, the hair ties and clips, the purses and bags and the makeup. Intensely relieved, she zipped into the kitchen and procured a large green garbage bag and returning to her bedroom stuffed it full. Tying it up, she wrote a note and taped it to the bag. It said very simply the name of a famous and beloved French priest who cherished and helped the poor in the name of Christ and whose name even today remains affixed to hospitals, clinics, and thrift stores all over the world: *Saint Vincent de Paul.*

There. That's better, she thought approvingly as she viewed her newly cleaned closet. When she went to La Chic Boutique this weekend, she would buy a plain knee-length skirt and some looser jeans or dress slacks. No more would she dress to impress anyone. *Except You,* she said to the picture of Our Lord. *I'll wear the clothes You would want me to wear.*

Tia sighed. It was almost midnight. In Montana, though, it was only ten o'clock. She picked up the phone and dialed Char.

"Hello?"

"Hi, may I speak to Char, please?

"Who's calling?"

"Tia Esperanza."

"Oh, hi Tia! It's Kayla."

"Hi Kayla! I hope I'm not calling too late."

"Nope! I'll go get her for you. Hang on. How's it going?"

"Fine. I hear you're a mama now."

"Yep. Little rascal keeps me pretty busy!"

Tia laughed. "Mikel is a beautiful name. And he's a beautiful baby. Char sent me a picture of him."

"Oh, yeah. He is a pretty cute little guy. I'll keep him! *Char! It's Tia Esperanza!*"

Tia heard muffled sounds and the patter of feet.

"Here you go. Bye, Tia! Take care!"

"Bye, Kayla!"

"Hello, Tia? Is it really you? How's it going?" Char said excitedly.

"I'm just fine! How are you?"

"Good! We just got back from Pittsburgh a couple of days ago. Did you get my letter?"

"Yeah! I just got it tonight. That's awesome about Kayla having a baby."

"Yeah, we think he's pretty awesome too! So tell me how's the nun thing going? Did they say they'll take you?"

"No, not exactly. Mother Bonaventure said I could enter when I turn twenty, and that's not for four more months."

"Oh, wow. Well, that's not too far off."

"Yeah. It's just hard to wait."

"Yeah, I'll bet. So how's your mom with that?"

Tia hesitated. "Actually, we haven't talked about it lately."

"Seriously?"

"I know it sounds crazy, but you should have seen her the first time. She flipped *out!* After that, we didn't talk about it. But she knows. Because when I graduated, my aunt and uncle had a party for me, and my uncle's mom was there, she's real nice, and she asked me what I was going to do now that I had graduated. And my mom was right there, and I said, 'I'm gonna go to Cleveland State.' And that's all I was gonna say, but then she said—my mom said—'And then what?' Like she was asking me if I was still wanting to go off and become a nun. Almost like she wanted to know, but she was afraid to ask me. And I was like, 'And then when I turn twenty, I'm going to join the Adoration nuns!'"

"No kidding! Then what happened?"

"It got real quiet. Nobody knew what I was talking about, except my Aunt Delia. And my mother, of course. I could tell she was shocked that I'd said it, and she was really disappointed, too. I think she thought I was going through a weird phase or something, like she didn't believe me. And that was it. She never brought it up after that and I didn't either. I know she doesn't like it, but I was like, I am not a child anymore. I have to make my own decisions now."

"Wow. So you're really gonna go through with it?"

"Yes, I am. With God's help, yes I am."

"That's like the most amazing thing, Tia. I'm so happy for you."

"Well, don't be too happy for me just yet. They haven't officially said I can enter."

"Oh, but why wouldn't they? They need new members, don't they?"

"I don't know. I mean, Mother Bonaventure said they would accept me. So I am pretty sure they will say yes, but until they actually do say yes, you can come, it's not a for sure thing."

"Tell them you need it in writing."

Tia laughed. "Yeah I was thinking that same thing, you know? I want that acceptance letter like I got from Cleveland State."

"And signed by the pope!" Char giggled.

"Yeah!" Tia laughed. "Only I'll probably just get a phone call. But that's okay. I don't mind. Just so long as they take me, that's all I care about."

"I'm sure they'll take you, Tia. There's no reason for them not to."

"Thanks Char. I hope you're right." Tia sighed.

"I wish you could come out to Montana and visit. It's really nice out here in the summertime."

"I'd like that too. But right now, I have to keep working. I'm helping my mom with the rent so she can get a car and maybe start her own business and quit working for that cleaning company."

"What kind of a business?"

"She wants to open her own restaurant. Which is weird because she never cooks at home, right?"

"Really?" Char laughed.

"I'm serious! But it's been hard on her working at nights, and Troy bein' by himself all the time after school. It's not good for him.

There's all kinds of strange people around here at night." She thought of Mike and shuddered. "Pittsburgh's not that far from here. Maybe you can come visit."

"Yeah! Maybe next summer I can stop off on my way home."

"That would be nice, Char. I'd really love to see you again."

"Me too! It's great to finally talk."

"So how is Kayla doing?"

Char paused. "She's doing okay. She has some bad days, but I think she's handling it. She kind of has to, you know?"

"Yes, I do know!"

"So, I mean, it's kind of hard at times, trying to go to school and take care of Mikel, and keep mom happy, and everything, but it's weird. It's like our family is closer now than it was before all this started. Does that make sense?"

"I think so."

"I'm just worried about what's gonna happen when I'm gone."

"Me too! I worry about that a lot. Troy has been getting into trouble more and more."

"My parents are going to have to pay for a babysitter so Kay can get out and get a job or something. I mean, Eric's not working, so he can't pay child support. At least not yet anyway."

"It takes money to raise a child," Tia agreed.

"It takes a ton of money. I mean, just diapers? Come on. We spent like a hundred dollars a month on diapers and wipes when he was first born, I kid you not. It was unreal."

"Wow. That is a lot. I never realized."

"But, I mean Mom and Dad can afford to. It's not like we're destitute or something."

"You're lucky," Tia said.

"Yeah," Char replied.

"No, I don't mean it that way. I mean you're lucky you have both your parents."

For a moment, Char was silent. "Yeah. I guess I am."

"Both of you. All of you."

For a minute, neither of them said a word.

"Can I ask you a favor?" Tia said.

"Sure, anything."

"Will you pray for me?"

Once again, Char didn't know how to respond. No one had ever asked her that before. It presupposed that she did, in fact, pray, which wasn't true, although she had sent up a desperate plea for divine help after Kayla had her accident, and again when her sister went into hard labor with Mikel. That was about as prayerful as she got. But how could she say no?

"Um, sure."

"Thanks, Char. And I promise I will be praying too. For you, and for your family," Tia assured her solemnly.

Chapter 26: The Nun's Story

For beautiful eyes, look for the good in others;
for beautiful lips, speak only words of kindness;
and for poise, walk with the knowledge
that you are never alone.

– Audrey Hepburn

Walking back to her apartment, Char took the stairs two at a time to the third-floor studio she'd been living in ever since the dorm caught fire the first week of class. She'd been living in Pittsburgh going to Carnegie Mellon for a month now and was finally starting to adjust.

Aaron Kepner, her boyfriend of two weeks, waited expectantly on the mud-brown polyester couch, casually clasping his hands in his lap. Although the black wool pea coat he wore wasn't new, it was clean and it kept him warm in Char's chilly apartment. An engineering major attending Carnegie Mellon on a scholarship, Aaron devoted his free time to memorizing chess moves, videotaping silent films on VHS, and lately, hanging out with Char.

"Want some tea?" Char quickly strode across the tiny living room.

"Uh, no thanks. Well, I mean, sure."

Aaron stood up and shoved his hands in his coat pockets as Char filled the silver teapot with water.

"Lemon or chamomile?"

"Whatever you're having," he replied amiably. He walked over to the five-by-ten foot galley that served as Char's kitchenette. Char glanced at him and smiled a contented half-smile.

"Did you get your paper done?" she asked.

"Yeah, finally."

"That's good. I've got one due in history, but it's not for another couple of weeks."

Aaron stared at the curlicues of steam rising from the teapot's spout. As Char was getting honey out of the cabinet and spoons out of a drawer, placing them next to two stone-colored mugs containing tea bags, he suddenly reached over and grabbed her arm, startling her.

"What?" she stared at him intently. Slowly, he pulled her toward him and kissed her.

"What was that for?" she blurted.

Just then, the teapot began to whistle shrilly. Aaron didn't answer. He stared at her intensely. Char laughed nervously, swirling away to turn off the gas burner, and poured the boiling water into the mugs. Aaron walked up behind her, carefully placing his hands on her shoulders. Gently turning her around, he pulled Char very close and stared into her eyes.

"I love you." And he kissed her again, only longer.

Finally Char pulled away. She looked at the floor, then out the foggy window, glanced uncertainly into his eyes, then back at the floor again.

"What?" Aaron's eyebrows rose in disbelief and he threw his arms out in frustration. This had been happening a lot lately; whenever he tried to be romantic with Char, she pulled away. It was driving him crazy.

"I just—I feel like we're moving too fast," Char explained.

"Too fast? We've been seeing each other for almost a month!"

"I know! I just don't want things to be…" Char searched for the right words.

"To be what? Tell me, okay?" Aaron struggled for patience. He didn't want to scare her away, but she was being too standoffish. He took off his coat and threw it on the kitchenette table, folded his arms across his chest, and leaned back against the counter, waiting.

Char paced across the worn green rug towards the couch and back again. Shaking her head, she frowned and spread her fingers wide, combing the air with them decisively. "You make me want to be with you, Aaron."

"So?" Aaron couldn't believe he was having this conversation. "What's wrong with that?"

"Nothing!" Char declared. "Except we're not married!"

"What!?"

Char hadn't meant to say "married." What she had meant to say was, "we haven't been together long enough to know each other well enough for that," but what came out was "we're not married." It sounded surprisingly good, and it was too late to take it back, so she decided to run with it.

"Yeah! We're not married, Aaron—we're not even engaged."

"I hate to break it to you, Char, but people who aren't married get together all the time. This isn't the 1950s!"

"I know that!" Char countered. "And look what happens to them! Girls get pregnant, or they get STDs, or they get dumped, and then what? What happens then?"

Aaron threw his head back and stared into the distance. "Oh, I know what this is. This is all about your sister, isn't it?"

"This is *not* about my sister!"

"Oh, yes it is. You're afraid you're going to get pregnant and I'm going to leave you." Aaron's face softened. "Well, that is not going to happen." Walking towards Char, he reached up and gently touched her hair. "I would never do that to you. And if something happened..."

Char folded her arms across her chest.

"Look, if you want me to go, fine. I'm going."

Char's face fell. "I didn't say that. I just don't like feeling pressured, okay?"

"Okay!" Aaron smiled a twisted little half-smile and shrugged, walking towards the door and slipping into his coat. "No pressure."

Char refolded her arms across her stomach and rocked back and forth on the balls of her feet, staring bleakly at the cracks in the faded linoleum. She bit her lower lip self-consciously.

"I'm a virgin, Aaron."

Aaron paused and silently gazed at the floor. "I know." Looking up again, he tiptoed to where she still stood immobile. Kissing her hair, he patted her shoulder and briskly walked to the door. "I'll call you," he said to the mute ceiling. The door closed inevitably behind him, and he was gone.

Quivering like a leaf, Char sank to the floor in a heap of misery. Hot tears of frustration and anger streamed down her reddened cheeks, leaving big wet blotches on her shirt. She wasn't good enough, she thought wildly. She wasn't pretty enough. That was the problem. If only she looked more beautiful, he would have stayed. He wouldn't have cared that she wanted to wait. He would have respected her wishes and admired her resolve.

Aaron had been her first boyfriend, her only boyfriend. She knew deep down that he wouldn't call again, wouldn't come by and invite her out for sandwiches at Steeltown Subs, where they would sit and talk for hours about everything from Pittsburgh's four hundred and forty-six bridges to Pittsburgh Steeler Troy Palomalu's impossibly long, curly hair. He wouldn't be waiting for her after Economics, ready to walk to the campus mall.

Finally, the storm of tears ended. Drawing her knees up to her chest and rising to her feet in one smooth upward movement, she stepped into the kitchen and poured the cold cups of tea down the drain, turned the gas burner on again, and put fresh water in the teapot. Calmly, she rummaged in her purse for a wad of Kleenex, blew her nose, and patiently waited for the water to boil. Soon the hissing steam whistled in the spout, and Char poured herself a cup of lemon tea with extra honey.

As she sipped the soothing brew, she looked for a spot in the window that wasn't covered with dusty grime, but there wasn't one. The sky was a dull gray, and the shadow of the persimmon tree growing up from the cracked sidewalk was as black as the wrought iron fence surrounding it. She stared at the faded red Formica that covered the tiny kitchen table next to the window. She thought of calling Kayla, but decided to wait. Kayla would just tell her to find another guy to hang out with, and then she would start complaining again about the high cost of diapers.

Revived by the tea, Char tried to think of something to do to take her mind off of Aaron. The table by the television was piled high with textbooks and notebooks, but she didn't feel like studying. She didn't feel like reading, either. She'd already done her laundry. And it was too cold to go for a walk. The big beige IBM computer Aaron had brought over for her to use for school sat dully in the corner. He hadn't hooked it up for her yet, and she didn't feel like trying to figure out where all the cords and plugs went or how to connect the modem.

I've got to get out of here, she thought. Her eyes landed on the *Pittsburgh Post-Gazette* folded on the coffee table. She grabbed it and began whisking through the pages, looking for something—anything. Then she saw it.

The Second Annual

Audrey Hepburn FilmFest

sponsored by the William T. Clements Foundation and the Pittsburgh FILM FANatics Society, presents

Funny Face,

Breakfast at Tiffany's &

The Nun's Story

Saturday, September 28, 2002

Roxy Theater, 8911 Gilchrist Avenue

The first film, *Funny Face*, had already started. She had just enough time to catch the bus to Oakland before *Breakfast at Tiffany's* began. Quickly, she rushed into the bathroom to rinse her tear-streaked face.

Chapter 27: "Drink at the Spring"

*"I do not promise to make you happy in this world,
but in the next."*

– The Blessed Virgin Mary, Our Lady of Lourdes
to Saint Bernadette Soubirous

As Char locked the deadbolt to the apartment on her way to the bus stop, she heard the door open and close to the apartment two doors down. She'd wondered who lived there, wondered whose violin she heard faintly, the circling notes like birds singing behind the walls. Glancing over her shoulder, she glimpsed a young woman about her age, taller and maybe a year older. Walking past, their eyes met briefly. Then, the other girl smiled and spoke.

"Hi."

"Hi."

The strange girl looked at her sharply. "Are you in Dr. Miller's class? Philosophy?"

Char vaguely remembered seeing her before and nodded. "Yeah. Have you started on the mid-term yet?"

The girl rolled her eyes. "No! You?"

Char smiled wanly. "No. I was going to today, but..." She didn't want to talk about the fight with Aaron.

"I know. Who wants to write about David Hume, right?" the girl stuck out her hand in introduction. "Celia Cerase. I was just going out to get some coffee. Want to come?"

Char paused and thought. "Well, I was thinking about going to the Roxy for the Audrey Hepburn FilmFest."

"Do you have a car?"

"No."

"Oh. The buses don't run very often on Saturday. It'll take you an hour to get there. Why don't you come with me and I can drive us?"

Char smiled. "Yeah, that'd be great! Thanks!"

Celia slung her bag over her shoulder and zipped down the stairs. Char followed. They burst through the steel and glass entrance and out to Celia's faded maroon 1980 Chrysler Cordoba.

"You're so lucky. You've got a car!" Char exclaimed.

"This old thing? Pffft! It gets me around." She unlocked the passenger side for Char, who hopped in gratefully. She noticed a string of beads hanging from a long silver chain wrapped around the big rearview mirror.

"I wanted to buy a car, but my dad said not for my first year," Char said.

"First year? I thought freshmen had to live in the dorm." Celia looked at her probingly.

"Yeah, well, I did, until some idiot left a candle burning and set the place on fire."

"Oh, I remember now. Pratt Hall. So'd you lose all your stuff?" Celia was sympathetic.

"Not everything. I got out with my book bag, my CD player, and my coat."

"Bummer."

"Actually, my room didn't burn. It just had smoke and water damage. Still. Everything pretty much got toasted." Char had loved the photo of Kayla and their parents she'd taken in front of the BP Building in Cleveland. They'd all looked so happy that day! The frame survived the fire, but the glass had broken and the photo had been ruined. She wondered if she'd saved the negative, if it was still in her things back home.

"Where are you from?" Celia asked.

"Montana. How about you?"

"Montana? Wow. I'm from Ashtabula. That's in Ohio."

"Oh, really? Is that anywhere near Cleveland? I have a friend in Cleveland."

"It's about an hour from there. What does your friend do?"

"Do? Um, actually, she's a nun. Or, she's gonna be, pretty soon. She just entered six months ago."

"Wow, really? My aunt is a nun. I mean, a sister. She's with the Holy Trinity Sisters in Euclid."

Char's mouth dropped open. "I—my aunt was a sister, too!"

"Oh, wow. Really?" Celia seemed surprised but not shocked.

"Yes!"

"That's cool. Which order is she with?"

"I don't know."

Celia threw a curious glance at Char, who was blushing with confusion.

She probably thinks I'm lying, Char thought. "I wasn't really raised around her. All I know is she was a nun, and then she left."

"Oh, that's too bad." Celia nodded. "That happened a lot, actually, back in the sixties and seventies."

"Really?" Char replied hopefully. Maybe it wasn't so weird. Coming from Celia, it sounded very normal.

"So we'll have to go out to my aunt's community sometime. They have the Lourdes Shrine. Have you ever been there?"

"No. I haven't been anywhere, really."

"Oh, we'll have to go there someday. It's really beautiful."

"Sounds nice!"

"It's only about an hour from here. So you're Catholic?"

"No."

"You're not?" Celia's eyes widened. "I just assumed—when you said your friend was a nun and your aunt was a nun..."

"Yeah, no, it's okay. I'd still like to go."

"You would?"

"Sure! What's the name of that place again?"

"It's the National Shrine of Our Lady of Lourdes in Euclid, Ohio."

"Oh. Who is Our Lady of Lourdes?"

"You never heard of Our Lady of Lourdes?" Celia was incredulous.

"Uh-huh." Char shook her head.

Celia straightened and took a deep breath. "Lourdes is a city in France where the Blessed Mother appeared to Saint Bernadette in 1858. People from all over the world go there on pilgrimage. Only some people can't afford to go to France, so they go to the Shrine there in Ohio. They have a piece of rock from Lourdes under a spring of water, just like the real one."

"Oh. But why?"

"Why what?"

"Why do they go there?"

"Because the water is miraculous! People get healed there all the time. There have been like sixty medically confirmed miraculous healings—and those are just the ones submitted for medical certification."

"What's in it?"

Celia laughed. "What's in it? Grace! The love of God and the blessing of Our Lady. That's what's in it!"

Okay, this is getting really weird, Char thought.

"So if you're not Catholic, what church do you go to?" Celia asked.

"We—I don't really go to church." Char shifted uncomfortably.

"Oh," Celia said politely. "Sorry. I didn't mean to ask a bunch of personal questions."

Char stared out the window and fidgeted with the end of her seat belt. They rode along in silence while Celia threaded her way through the light Saturday traffic. A few minutes later, Celia parked the big Chrysler in front of Daria's Bakery, right across the street from Kangaroo Koffee.

"No drive-up here. We have to go in," Celia explained as she shoved the car into park.

"No problem." Char released her seat belt and climbed out, fishing in her purse for cash, grateful to be out from under the microscope.

Checking each way for traffic, they rushed across the middle of the street. Despite the cold, college students sipped steaming drinks at tables set up outside. Some were energetically engaged in political debate, while others sat alone or chatted casually. Char and Celia ignored them and made a beeline for the coffee shop.

"Oh jeez, look at the line," Celia grumbled. Char glanced at her watch and wondered for the third time whether or not they'd make it in time for *Breakfast at Tiffany's*.

Celia folded her arms thoughtfully and began studying the art posters on the wall. "So what are you majoring in?"

"Architecture," Char replied. "Actually, I'm kind of between Art and Architecture."

"Architecture! That's cool. My brother Tony was an architecture major for a while. Then he switched to art history. Then he changed to something else—I think it was European history? I don't know. I never could keep up with that guy."

"Does he go to Carnegie?"

"No, he started out at Kent State, and then he went to France for a year on a foreign exchange program."

"Oh," Char said. "That sounds interesting. Where is he now?"

Celia studied the posters as though she herself was an art major, analyzing every colorful detail. "Not sure. He dropped out of school and started working for a magazine in Paris last year, last time we got a letter from him. But we haven't heard from him for a while now."

"Oh. I'm sorry," Char said kindly.

"No, it's okay." Celia shrugged and then smiled sadly. "I do miss him. But, sometimes you have to let go, I guess."

The line finally moved up to the barista. Afterwards they rushed with their lattes back across the street. There was a tiny break in the traffic, and Celia pointed the Cordoba towards Forbes Avenue, hit the gas and headed north. Char checked her watch once again.

"We're gonna make it!" she exclaimed.

"Do you like old movies?" Celia asked.

"I *love* old movies. I think it's cool to see how people lived in the past," Char replied between sips of coffee.

"Movies are so different now than they used to be. People were so different. They talked differently, they dressed differently—everything was different."

"My dad always says, 'nothing is permanent except change.'"

Celia glanced at her and paused to take a long drink. "Change is good, if it's for something better. If it's for the right reasons."

"Change can be scary, though. Like coming out here!"

"But if you aren't willing to change, you can't grow."

"That's true. I think." Char wrinkled her nose and took another sip of hot coffee. The vanilla latte tasted wonderful, and she felt herself relaxing as soothing warmth slowly spread through her lanky frame. It was nice to have someone to talk to.

Celia laughed. "I remember when my aunt was telling me... Oh *crud!* What's this?"

A train of cars had formed a long line down the street, stopped behind a huge yellow dump truck; city workers with orange safety vests were busily performing some kind of maintenance or repairs in the middle of Forbes Avenue.

"Great," Char said. "There goes our movie."

Celia's eyes darted around and behind them. For a moment it looked like she was going to make a giant U-turn and head back the other way, but there was too much traffic. Char sighed and squinted her eyes across the street full of shops and small businesses as if she could find a way out. They were stuck.

The city was full of all kinds of people going about their business. *A person could sit for hours just watching them*, Char thought. A middle-aged woman carrying a big grocery bag walked by with her small white poodle on a leash. A black teenager in a brown ski cap strode thoughtfully past her, heading in the opposite direction. Then, a wildly wailing siren somewhere in the background interrupted her daydreaming. *Someone is sick or dying; someone is in trouble,* she thought.

"Maybe it won't take too long," Celia craned her neck optimistically, looking up the street. A man in an orange vest was slowly waving a few cars at a time around the big truck, surrounded by bright orange safety cones. Celia drummed her fingers on the steering wheel, eyes darting from the rearview mirror to the side view mirror, up the street, and back again. After what seemed like hours, they finally made it past the bottleneck and sped to the Roxy Theater.

Chapter 28: Nuns and Extraterrestrials

Place your mind before the mirror of Eternity.

– Chiara Offreducio (Saint Clare of Assisi)

The afternoon shoppers on Gilchrist Avenue were giving way to Saturday night daters and partiers: a younger, edgier crowd. Kids with nose rings, spiky hair and tattoos flew by on skateboards or congregated outside the convenience store across the street, smoking, talking, laughing, and drinking beer.

The Roxy Theater was located in a shabbier part of Pittsburgh, but it continued to draw patrons because it ran full-length classic films. Once or twice a year, they showcased silent movies and brought in a professional organist for accompaniment. This time, though, was all about Audrey—Audrey Hepburn—the classy actress from the 1950's with the teeny, tiny waistline and the huge brown eyes.

"'All proceeds from the Audrey Hepburn FilmFest to support the Audrey Hepburn Children's Fund,'" Celia read aloud from the movie poster as they bought their tickets. "I didn't know she was a UNICEF Ambassador, did you?"

"No. What's UNICEF?"

"The United Nations International Children's Fund, or something like that."

"Oh. Cool!"

They stepped inside the once-glamorous Roxy and looked around.

"It looks like *Breakfast at Tiffany's* is almost over. Do you want to go in now or wait for *The Nun's Story*?" Celia asked.

"Hey, look!" Char's face lit up. "*E.T.!*" Among the wall posters showcasing upcoming attractions was the familiar image of a boy on his bike flying across the moon, a hooded figure mysteriously perched in the basket attached to the bike's handlebars.

"Wow! Twenty years!" Celia said. "I can't believe it's been that long since it came out."

"I love that movie! I had the video. I used to watch it over and over until the tape finally cracked. Remember VHS?"

"Yeah. My mom still has some of those," Celia chuckled.

"'E.T., phone home! E.T., phone home!'" Char mimicked the alien's famous line, and they doubled over laughing.

"That is hilarious! We have to come see it," Char exclaimed.

"Absolutely!" Celia agreed. Suddenly, her face grew serious, her voice secretive. "That's a *Christian* movie, you know."

"Huh?" Char shot her a puzzled look.

Celia glanced sideways and lowered her voice. "*E.T.,* the movie, is an allegory for the story of Jesus."

"What? What are you *talking* about?" Char's face bent into a baffled question mark. *This girl is weird,* Char thought.

"Look at the picture on the poster. See the finger-touch thing?" Celia held up the index fingers of both hands and drew them together until they almost but didn't quite touch. Char stared at E.T.'s long skinny pointer finger reaching out to touch the boy Elliott's.

"That's just like the painting of God reaching out to Adam on the ceiling of the Sistine Chapel in the Vatican."

"What???" Char's eyes grew big.

"Except Adam is on the left and Elliott is on the right. But that doesn't matter. And the bike..."

"What about it?" Char said dubiously.

"That's part of the American collective unconscious. Doesn't it look familiar somehow?"

Char looked searchingly at the iconic image of Elliott's bike flying over the trees.

"That's part of the scene from *The Wizard of Oz* where Dorothy gets knocked out by the window frame and she sees Miss Gulch riding her bike in the tornado outside her window before she turns into the Wicked Witch of the West. Remember how her cape was flying in the wind? That's just like Elliott riding up in the sky with E.T. in his Halloween costume cape, only in *The Wizard of Oz,* she was bad, but in *E.T.,* Elliott was good. It's still scary, only good scary."

"What are you, crazy?"

"No, I'm telling you. I learned all this stuff in class."

"What class?"

"This Humanities class on Christian themes in movies. Okay. How is *E.T.* an allegory for Jesus Christ? One, at first nobody believes in him because they can't see him. Two, he can heal with a touch. Three, he has to hide his true identity from those who want to kill him. Four, he is taken away by the authorities without having committed any crime. Five, he says, 'I'll be right here,' and 'Be good,' and number six, at the end, when he goes home, he ascends into the sky and his spaceship makes a rainbow. A rainbow! And you know that scene at the end? Where it shows his big heart all glowing red like a furnace? If that isn't the Sacred Heart of Jesus, I don't know what is."

Char stared dumbly, her mouth hanging open. She had just made friends with a religious fanatic and a maniac on top of it.

"Oh and number seven, I almost forgot. The most important part. He dies, but he comes back to life. I rest my case."

Char tried to think of something, anything, to say, but her right-brain/left-brain connections were backfiring in weird flashes of cognitive lightning.

"That is why at the end of this movie, everybody—I don't care who you are, everybody—cries their eyeballs out."

"That's true," Char sighed.

"'Judeo-Christian Foundations of Cinematic Culture.' That was the best class ever. We got to sit and watch movies. Last day of class, he let us bring popcorn. Ha! But if my mother heard me compare Our Lord to a little green alien, she'd beat me with a belt!"

"If my mother heard me compare a little green alien movie to the life of Jesus, she'd send me to a shrink!"

"Yeah, well I'd rather get a whipping. It's over faster!" Celia snorted.

"So, how did they do it? I mean, Steven Spielberg is Jewish, isn't he?"

"The screenplay was written by Melissa Mathison. She was a fallen-away Catholic. She was also the associate producer."

"Wow, really? So she put all that stuff in there?"

"Not on purpose. She went to a Catholic high school in L.A. run by the Sisters of Providence, back before Vatican 2. She may not have realized it at the time, but the whole screenplay is just dripping Christianity! And get this—her dad, Richard? He was the religion editor for the *Los Angeles Times!* Of course, after she graduated high school, she got into Buddhism, like all the baby boomers. Then her parents divorced. And *then* she went to Berkeley and studied political science."

Char nodded, totally clueless.

"And that's what's *so great*!" Celia leaned in close, lowered her voice, and still gesticulating wildly, said, "She quit the Catholic Church and went to the most liberal university in the nation, and she STILL ended up spreading the Gospel. *How awesome is that!?*"

"Melissa Mathison," Char repeated.

"She was married to Harrison Ford, that guy in *Star Wars* and *Raiders of the Lost Ark* and *Apocalypse Now*. That's how she hooked up with Steven Spielberg."

"I've always wondered about that. What's an ark?"

"I don't know. That thing Noah and his family put the animals in?" Celia teased.

"No, not that! The thing in *Raiders of the Lost Ark*. They were carrying it around. Remember? The Nazis wanted it because it was so powerful."

"Yeah. That was the Ark of the Covenant. That's what the Lord told Moses to build to keep the Ten Commandments in. The Jews carried it around with them wherever they went into battle."

"How do you know so much?"

"Because I go to college!" Celia grinned and spun around in a pirouette.

Char laughed, but Celia suddenly looked away, twirling her hair in her fingers.

"No, not really. I'm not so smart."

"Yes, you are," Char reassured her. Celia *was* smart. And some of what she said actually sort of made sense, in a strange, new kind of way.

Miraculously, as if on cue the next group of filmgoers to walk in the Roxy was a group of elderly nuns.

"Look! I'll bet they're coming to see the *The Nun's Story*!" Char whispered dramatically.

"No duh!" Celia doubled over, belly-laughed, and punched Char in the arm.

"Ow!" Char shouted, wincing.

Overhearing their teenage antics, one of the nuns shot them a disapproving glance. Without thinking, Celia automatically stood up straight and wiped the smile from her face. Confused, Char did the same. Duly chastised, they walked to the snack bar and ordered sodas.

"Four ninety-five? For a Coke?" Celia cried indignantly, fishing around in her purse and coat pocket.

"That's okay. I've got this." Char said, whipping out her credit card. "You drove us here. I'm just paying you back."

"Thanks, Char!"

"And I'll have a Coke also, and a box of M&M's."

"Wait! We should get Reese's Pieces for *E.T.,*" Celia exclaimed.

"Ohhhh-kay," Char smiled. "Forget those M&M's. Reese's Pieces please!"

The coterie of nuns bypassed the snack bar and lined up at the velvet-roped entrance to the hallway leading to the movie screens.

"I wonder what order they're with?" Celia thought aloud.

"Don't ask me. I'm not even Catholic, remember?" Char joked.

"Oh well, we'll see about that! I'm gonna have to go to work on converting you," Celia retorted.

Char smiled good-naturedly, drinking her Coke and munching the Reese's Pieces.

"How can you eat that and still stay so skinny?" Celia marveled.

"Believe me, I've tried," Char said between bites. "I couldn't gain weight if my life depended on it."

"Lucky you!"

"Not really. Guys like girls with curves."

"Well, unless the curves are bigger than they are," Celia joked again.

The girls broke into loud laughter again, and this time, one of the nuns turned around and fixed them with a baleful eye.

Choking, Celia apologized. "Sorry, Sister."

Temporarily satisfied, the sister turned back to listen to the conversation going on in their group.

"Why did you do that?" Char whispered nervously.

"Do what? Apologize?"

Char nodded. "The movie hasn't even started yet. We don't have to be quiet in the lobby!"

Celia smoothed her shirt and looked over at the gray-haired octogenarian sisters, sporting identical short black veils and heavy beige support hose. "You didn't go to Catholic school, I take it."

Char shrugged and shook her head. "Nope."

"Well, it's a whole other world, let me tell you. They do not suffer fools gladly. They have God on their side. I could tell you stories..."

Char listened with interest, quite certain that some of the students she'd known in public school could have benefitted greatly from a Catholic education. For a split second, she envied Celia.

* * *

Two and a half hours later, they emerged from the dark theater.

"That was amazing!" Celia exclaimed.

"Totally! I can't believe how it ended!"

"I know. But war does that to people. It pushes them over the edge."

"Like after her dad died, and then she decided to join the underground?" Char asked.

"Yeah. I don't know. I think she was way too hard on herself. Like she couldn't accept anything less than complete perfection. She couldn't accept her sinfulness."

They watched for a break in the traffic and then sprinted across the street.

"Can you believe how they used to treat the mentally ill back then?" Char cried.

"I know. That part was so *awful*. Can you imagine?"

"And the Archangel? *That* was scary. I don't know about you, but I would NOT have unlocked that padded cell for anything!"

"Me neither. But that little monkey they gave her was so cute!" Celia laughed.

"I know. That was cool how they had her up in that treehouse."

"I loved the beginning where they showed all the nuns. That was awesome."

"Yeah, me too. I can't believe how many of them there were! They had like two hundred nuns or something."

"I know."

"Is that how the sisters were when you were growing up?" Char asked.

"No, but it's how they used to be in some communities—back before Vatican 2." Celia answered thoughtfully.

"What's Vatican 2?"

Celia frowned. "That's when they made all these changes, supposedly to bring the Church up to date. They changed the Mass, and a lot of the old rules. That's when most of the sisters stopped wearing the long habits and veils. Actually some sisters don't wear habits at all anymore. Kind of sad."

"I think they looked totally *beautiful!*" Char said emphatically.

"They did, didn't they?" Celia agreed.

* * *

Across the street, the elderly nuns they'd seen in the theater were making their way back to the convent car.

"Thank heavens we don't have to wear those heavy old wool habits anymore!" declared one.

"Remember all those hours we spent washing and starching and ironing those awful guimpes?" another agreed.

"I read some of the newer communities are going back to the full habit again," the third sister divulged in low tones.

"I cannot imagine why," replied the first. "All those yards of material cost money."

"After everything we went through to change with the times," grumbled the second, "and they want to turn back the clock again!"

"But why? Wearing a long dress and a veil doesn't make you holy," opined the third.

"No, but it makes you *look* holy!" chuckled the fourth.

"That's the trouble! We looked so holy that nobody wanted to treat us like human beings! We were some kind of exalted, saintly creatures everyone had to bow and scrape to. They put us on a pedestal."

"Yes. Remember they used to call us 'the Good Sisters'?"

"I don't know about you, but I knew a few who weren't so 'good!'" And they all laughed. All but the third sister. She alone reminisced.

"What about the ones who left? There were quite a few of us who couldn't adapt so easily to all the changes," she said sadly. For a few seconds, no one spoke.

"That's right," the first piped up. "They loved their habits more than their vocations."

By then, they had reached the convent car and hurried to get in out of the frigid night air as the youngest, who was driving, quickly unlocked the doors.

"I remember Sister Monica Barnes," the third sister said, ignoring the last comment as she eased carefully into the back seat. "She was so kind to me when I first entered. She was our novice mistress until 1971, I think it was."

"Yes! I remember Sister Monica," the second sister brightened. "I remember once, I was pouring the coffee, and the lid came off and went all over the tablecloth. I nearly died, I was so ashamed of myself! But she never scolded me. She even helped me clean up the mess I made. Whatever happened to her?"

"She left when they started remodeling the chapel. She detested the shorter habit and the new Mass in English. She thought getting our own apartments was a mistake, that it would destroy community life. But when they took out the Communion rail and moved the Tabernacle out of the chapel sanctuary, it was the last straw. *'They have taken away my Lord,'* she said, *'and I don't know where they have laid Him.'*"

"She told you this herself?"

"She wrote to me a few months after she'd received a dispensation. Remember, we weren't allowed to discuss personal matters with the other sisters back then. She said she tried to convince Mother Celeste to keep the chapel the way it always was, but apparently she had no choice. There was too much pressure from the diocese. And from Rome."

* * *

Char and Celia found the ice-cold Cordoba and jumped in, shivering. Celia quickly started the engine and turned on the defroster.

While they waited for the windshield to clear, Char admired the beaded cross hanging from the rearview mirror.

"That's really pretty."

"Oh, thanks. My great aunt, Sister Gabrielle, sent it to me. It's the Trisagion rosary. They make them there at the convent. Only the Trinitarians pray it. It's different from a regular rosary, see?"

Celia lifted the strand of beads off the mirror and handed it to Char.

"Tris-ag-ion?" Char looked politely, but she had never seen a rosary before, so she didn't know how a Trisagion rosary would be any different. She wasn't even sure what a Trinitarian was.

"It means 'thrice holy.' That's from the *Sanctus* at Mass."

Baffled but intrigued, Char decided not to reveal the depths of her ignorance by asking still more questions even though Celia had seemed happy to answer them all. There was so much to being Catholic; it was just more than she could take in all at once. Carefully Char handed the rosary back to Celia, who swiftly looped it over the rearview mirror, clicked on the radio, gunned the engine, and pulled out into the dark street for the sweetly poignant journey home.

* * *

At Celia's apartment, beads of all colors, sizes, and shapes filled a dozen containers, covering the dining room table. Multiple rolls of colored cord, scissors, and strange slender pencil-shaped pieces of metal lay scattered about, along with bowls full of black, white and gold crucifixes and centerpieces.

"Sorry about the mess," Celia announced. Striding into the kitchen, she turned on the weak fluorescent overhead light and started washing out a coffeemaker. "Want some coffee? I've got decaf."

"No, I'd better not. I've already had so much today, I've almost got the shakes. Thanks anyway."

Char surveyed the living room. Behind the long sofa, stacks of books lined planks of homemade wooden shelves. Char read some of the book titles, wondering that she'd never heard of most of them. In the corner, perched near a brown ottoman, was a silver tripod music stand.

"I've got some leftover pizza. You want some?"

"Sounds good. I'm starved!" Char replied, walking back towards the dining room. "So what's all this? Looks like you're working on a big project."

"I make rosaries. It's a hobby. And it helps people. I donate them to Our Lady's Rosary Makers. They send them to prisons and hospitals, Catholic schools, the missions."

"Oh, cool." Char got up and examined the half-finished rosaries. There was a dozen of every color neatly piled in one corner.

"Here you go. Careful, it's hot." Celia slowly handed Char a steaming mug of tea.

"Thanks!" Char blew on the hot liquid and took a tiny sip.

Reaching out, Celia lifted several rosaries from the pile of finished ones and held them out to Char.

"Pick one."

"Really?"

"Really," Celia beamed.

"Oh wow! Thanks!" Char carefully set her mug on the counter and smiled. The plastic colored beads swung gracefully from Celia's outstretched hand and glittered in the warm kitchen light. Char chose a purple one, strung on a white cord with six larger clear beads interspersed with the others.

"You're welcome! It hasn't been blessed yet. You'll have to get it blessed by a priest." Celia put the other rosaries back on the table, then balanced herself on the edge of the couch to pull off her leather boots. "Ahhh...that's better! So. Char! Tell me about yourself."

But I don't know any priests, Char thought.

"Do you have a boyfriend?"

"Up until about three hours ago!" Char laughed mischievously, and Celia grinned.

"Uh, oh. What happened?"

"Nothing. He just wasn't my type. You?"

"Nope. Guys think I'm weird or something. What's your major? Wait, you already told me. Architecture, right?"

"Um-hmm. What about you?"

"I'm quote-unquote, undecided."

"Oh," Char nodded, sipping her tea.

"I *was* majoring in music until I got here and heard some of these other kids play. They are *way* more talented than I'll ever be." Celia shook her head. "There's no way I'll ever make it into a professional orchestra with this kind of competition."

Char glanced at the music stand back in the corner. There was sheet music and a black case of some sort on the floor. "What instrument do you play?"

"Violin."

"Oh, duh." Char hit herself on the head. "I've heard you playing."

"Oh, I'm sorry. I hope it wasn't too annoying!"

"No, it wasn't annoying. It sounded nice. Would you play something?"

"Oh, no. I mean, I haven't been practicing very much lately. I'm pretty rusty."

"I don't care. I'd still love to hear you play."

"Well, okay. *If* you insist." Celia stood up and made her way past the table to the corner, flicked on a lamp, and took the violin and bow out of its case. She rosined the bow and drew it over the strings tentatively, then tightened a few strings. Intensely focused, she began playing something lilting and swirling and wonderful. Char was entranced. But after only a few minutes, Celia lost her place and stopped.

"I'm sorry. I'm just really out of practice." Somberly she lowered her violin and carefully put it back in the case.

"That was awesome! What was that?"

"A little bit of Mendelssohn's *Violin Concerto in E minor*. I learned that a really long time ago."

"Wow. That was great!"

"Thanks. But no, it really wasn't."

"I've never really listened to classical music very much," Char confessed.

"Oh? Well if you're interested, I have a few CDs you can borrow." Celia got up and started digging in a cabinet against the wall. "Here!" she exclaimed, pulling one out of its case. "Beethoven said, 'Music should strike fire from the heart of man and bring tears from the eyes of woman.' This is what that concerto is *supposed* to sound like."

She set it carefully in her CD player and turned it on. For the next twenty minutes, they basked in the brilliant sound. She didn't know why, but something about it made Char start to tear up. She fought to hide it, but Celia wouldn't have noticed anyway. She was so completely focused on the vibrant notes that she was totally oblivious.

It lifted them up to another place. They were no longer college students eating warmed-over pizza in a Pittsburgh apartment. They were immortal spirits, soaring through a secret, magical place, where the masters of fine art and music and literature can take us, if only we will let them, if only we believe and take that blessed chance.

Chapter 29: Bittersweet Symphony

There are the lilting trills of melody,
Sweet, happy sounds, that cadence joyously,
Fair, lovely dreams of songs, that seem a part
Of that true joy within the pure of heart.

– Sister Mary Louise, a Presentation Sister of San Francisco
"To a Nun Violinist"

The next day dawned unexpectedly warm and bright. Char awoke from a deep sleep, the most restful she'd had in weeks. Stretching, she rolled over and contemplated the shafts of sunlight streaming through her dusty bedroom window. Something in the light made even the dingy, unwashed windows beautiful to behold. It was going to be a glorious day.

Padding into the kitchen, Char poured herself a bowl of cereal and milk and put the teapot on to boil. There on the table was the pile of CDs Celia had lent her. Curious, Char studied the cases and the names of the composers. Vivaldi. Albinez. Listz. Mahler, Dvorak, Elgar. Who were these guys? Beethoven—okay. There at least was a name she had heard of. Mozart. Tchaikovsky. Shostakovich. Sibelius. Smetana. Debussy. Ravel. Bizet. It sounded like the grand itinerary for a lengthy vacation railway tour of exotic old cities in Europe and Russia. She was a reasonably well-educated person, wasn't she? Then why had she never heard of these composers?

Maybe she was too uncultured to be friends with Celia. Violin concertos? Celia was obviously much too sophisticated to be friends with someone like her. *But she didn't act sophisticated,* Char thought.

Sighing, Char poured herself a cup of Earl Grey and read the back of one of the CDs. It was labeled "Happy!" in big block letters. "Jazz Suite Number One by Shostakovich. Dvorak's Scherzo Capriccioso. Prokofiev's Classical Symphony. Sounds like a real party," Char muttered, stumbling over the foreign words. "More like a meeting of the Dead Russians Society."

But her curiosity got the better of her. She plunked it in the player and hit "play."

Amazingly, the jazz suite waltz was light and playful, and the scherzo was wild and fun. It sounded familiar in places, like maybe she'd heard it in the background of a movie once, but she wasn't sure. All she knew was, she enjoyed it. Prokofiev's Classical Symphony was simply joyful bordering on the ecstatic, and it wasn't long until she was dancing around the kitchen in her flannel pajamas, playing the air violin and waving an imaginary conductor's baton.

"Oh, Sergei!" she crooned dramatically. *"Where have you been all my life?!"*

By the time she sat down again, out of breath, the cereal in her bowl had gone mushy and her tea was cool. But it didn't matter. The whole world was opening up to her, and it was going to be a great day. She quickly shoved the cereal in her mouth, downed the tea, rinsed the dishes in the sink, and ran in her room to get dressed.

When she and Celia had parted company the night before, Celia had asked her if she wanted to go to Mass with her the next day. "It's Sunday. And, it's the feast of Saint Michael," Celia had said meaningfully.

"Sure!" Char had responded.

"I haven't really committed to a parish yet. I've been going to the Cathedral mostly since it's so close. But you know what's really cool? We have to go to Saint Anthony's Chapel on Troy Hill."

"Oh? Why? What's so great about it?"

"I can't tell you! It's a surprise!"

"Okay," Char had said, although she couldn't understand how Celia could get so excited over a little chapel. Probably had some pretty stained glass windows or something.

"I won't spoil it for you," Celia smiled enigmatically. "But we absolutely have to go there. And here's something else you're gonna need," she added, handing Char a little leaflet.

"'How to Pray the Rosary.' Thanks Celia!"

"Oh, and here. You don't have to, but I always say the Prayer to Saint Michael at the end."

"Saint Michael," Char repeated, examining the picture of the sword-wielding angel and the short prayer on the back.

"So tomorrow, then. I'll call you. What's your phone number?"

"I have to look. I just got this cell phone, and I can't remember the number. Oh, wait. Here it is."

"You've got a cell phone? Cool! I could never afford one of those things."

"Well I couldn't either. My dad got it for me."

And Char had given Celia the number, and Celia had scribbled it on a scrap of paper by the old black landline phone in the kitchen. Life was good.

"Great! See you tomorrow!" Celia had beamed.

"K. See ya tomorrow!"

* * *

It seemed very strange to Char that she had to come fifteen hundred miles to meet someone who would invite her to go to church. After the Fishers had returned home from their momentous Cleveland vacation, she'd often thought about the monastery. There was just something about it that was unlike anything she'd ever experienced before, and she wanted to experience it again. She had asked her parents if they could go to church, but even when Kayla chimed in wanting to go too, nothing ever came of it. Her parents always said they'd think about it, or start questioning her as to why she wanted to go to church all of a sudden. She'd caught the fragments of a few heated arguments between them, her father's supportive openness crushed by her mother's stubborn refusals. Somehow, her mother's views always prevailed, and Char's spiritual hunger remained unsatisfied. Besides, the only Catholic church in their neighborhood looked like a boxy brick elementary school with its flat roof, narrow windows, and acres of parking—so plain and uninspiring compared to the lofty Gothic towers and lovely ornate spires that adorned Holy Angels Monastery.

A couple of years later, she'd been at a soccer game after school and had spied a little red brick church across the street from the soccer field. A small, box-like convent constructed of the same red brick sat squarely on the opposite corner. Tired of waiting for her mother, she'd decided to walk over and investigate. "St. Gerard's Catholic Church" read the sign in front. A strange melancholy sweetness emanated from the place, and Char had longed to go inside. Excitedly she had tried the handle of the church door, but it was locked tight.

* * *

It was a couple of minutes before nine. Char brushed her teeth, wiped out the sink, and flicked off the bathroom light. Celia would be here soon, and they would be off on another adventure. She debated having another cup of tea, but decided not to. She wanted to be ready to go as soon as Celia called. Besides, she was too excited.

Stepping over to the window, she looked down at the street below. One solitary man was out walking his dog. Otherwise, the street was empty. Sunday morning—everyone was asleep. She cracked the window to let in a bit of fresh air, but the chill soon forced her to close it again. A few birds hopped about on the pavement, searching for bugs or crumbs, but the pickings were slim. On impulse, Char returned to the kitchen and rummaged around for an empty bread wrapper. Opening the window wide, she shook out the remaining crumbs on the cement sill. "Breakfast!" she called out cheerfully. But the little brown wrens and sparrows didn't seem to hear her and instead flew away at the threatening wrapper.

The man and his dog drew nearer. Ignoring him, Char pursed her lips and closed the window again, tossing the wrapper into the trash.

She checked her watch to make sure the time was right on her alarm clock. It was. Then she remembered her new cell phone. Digging in her purse, she saw the pretty purple rosary Celia had given her, and she lifted it out and set it on the side table. Finally she found the phone and immediately panicked. She'd forgotten to plug it in! The battery was probably dead. Maybe Celia had tried to call her and hadn't been able to get through. Maybe Celia had already left without her.

"I am such an idiot!" she fumed. But Celia wouldn't have left without knocking on her apartment door, she was sure of it. She finally got the charger plugged in, and within a few minutes, she was able to check her missed calls and voicemail. No calls.

Char exhaled and paced back into the kitchen. Maybe she should put that teapot on after all. Who knows what time the Mass was? *I should have asked her what time to be ready,* Char thought dismally. *Why am I such a social moron?*

Filling the teapot with water to heat and putting the teabag in her mug calmed her down. Dejectedly she sank down into the dinette chair to wait for it to boil. But after a few minutes, she jumped up again. She thumbed through the pile of CDs but put them down again just as quickly. After a few more minutes, she compulsively checked her watch again. The minute hand hadn't moved, or so it seemed. She thought of her family back in Great Falls, sound asleep. With two hours between them, it was too early to call Montana. She didn't know what to do with herself. But at last the whistling teapot sang out an encouraging note.

Cup in hand, Char went back to the window and peered out. Where once before had been the promise of a sunny day had nearly vanished behind gray and gloomy clouds. A few sterile flakes of snow darted around the window, covering the breadcrumbs she had put out earlier. The birds were nowhere in sight.

"I wish she would hurry up and call!" Char said aloud and retreated to her bedroom in search of a warmer sweater. Bundled up against the chilly morning, she threw herself down on the twin bed and hugged her pillow for what seemed like eons. Rolling over on her back, she stared up at the ceiling and resigned herself to wait. And wait. And...

An hour later she jerked awake and wondered why she was asleep with all her clothes on. Groggily she sat up and stared dumbly at the red digital numbers on her alarm clock: 11:20. *Eleven twenty!* Then she remembered. Surely Celia would have called by now. She checked her cell phone, now fully charged. No missed calls, no voicemail, no texts.

Char fought off the sinking feeling in the pit of her stomach and stumbled out into the common hallway down to Celia's door. Knocking softly at first, she waited. No answer. She tried to peer through the security peephole but saw nothing. She knocked again, harder. Still no answer. She listened for any sounds, but it was quiet as a morgue. The sinking feeling in her stomach was coiling itself into familiar twisting knots. *Why did I ever think I could have a real friend?* she mourned. And she slunk back to her empty room and glumly shut the door.

Chapter 30: Full of Grace

*My first knowledge of God came to me as a gratuitous
gift of mercy, granted to me at eleven years of age.
For the first time in my life, I heard the Hail Mary.*

– Carmelite nun, aged 53 years

Just about dusk, Char shuffled outside to haul out the trash. The wet streets were mostly empty except for a passing bus and a lone female figure shimmying down the street. At first, she didn't recognize her, wearing the strings of black and gold party beads, the oversized Steelers' football jersey and ski hat. Char blinked with disbelief, then looked away in disappointment. Icy fingers of resentment gripped her heart. Apparently Celia's Sunday plans had involved something other than going to Mass. Rushing angrily up the stairs, Char darted down the hall, through the door, and into her apartment before Celia had a chance to spot her.

After that, an invisible wall grew up between them. It was as if all the fun they'd had at the movie had never happened. For two weeks Char racked her brain, trying to figure out if she had done something wrong, but all she could remember was Celia taking down her phone number and smiling as she had left. Plus, she'd given her a rosary and lent her those CDs. It made no sense.

The fall semester dragged on, and soon she forgot all about it. Char was way too busy with school to worry about anything else. Mid-terms loomed on the horizon, and exams and research papers occupied her thoughts. Between spending long hours reading in the library and studying with student groups in the cafeteria, she barely had time to sleep. She was hardly ever home.

"This place is a wreck," Char said to herself one Saturday, looking around her apartment. She'd simply had no time to clean. Noticing the pile of Celia's CDs by the stereo, Char wondered why Celia had never asked for them back. *I guess she's really given up on playing the violin,* Char thought. *Just like she's given up on me.*

Morosely she slouched into the kitchen and dug around for an empty shopping bag, placed the CDs inside, and then quietly sneaked down the empty hallway. Rock music boomed from an apartment at the far end of the building, but as usual there was no sign of Celia. No violin music wafted through the colorless walls. Taking a deep breath, she slipped the bag of CDs over the doorknob of Celia's apartment and zipped back to her own without being seen.

There. I don't have time to listen to all that stuff anyway, she thought with relief.

Back in her apartment, Char looked around dejectedly at the mess. She hadn't thought to buy a vacuum. She hunted in the kitchen until she found an old broom and cracked dustpan and began sweeping. Soon she had a big pile of debris, which she carefully swept into the dustpan and poured into the trashcan. A few wadded up pieces of paper had fallen under the side table by the landline phone. As she reached down to get them, she spied something purple. *Celia's rosary!*

Carefully Char lifted it up off the floor and examined it. The colored beads were pretty, but the white plastic crucifix that hung from the bottom was plain—almost cheap looking. *This whole thing probably only cost ten cents,* she thought cynically. She stared at it, curious. Surprisingly, there was a certain delicacy, an elegance of form in the extended arms, the nailed hands, and the bowed head that hypnotized her. *Who was this Jesus?* she wondered. *And what is this rosary for?* Did people wear it like jewelry? She'd seen videos of Madonna wearing rosary necklaces. Remembering the little pamphlet and prayer card Celia had given her, she stepped into the bedroom and quickly dug them out of her purse.

"The Joyful Mysteries: the Annunciation, the Visitation, the Birth of Jesus, the Presentation, the Finding in the Temple," she slowly read out loud. "Begin with the Sign of the Cross: In the Name of the Father, and of the Son, and of the Holy Spirit. Amen."

* * *

"Do you believe in God?" Char had asked. Her mother was chopping carrots to put in a salad they were taking to the potluck for
Kayla's graduation party at Skyline Alternative High School. She
paused only long enough to look up at the recipe, glance sideways at
Char, and keep on chopping.

"Yes."

"So, how come we never go to church?"

"You don't have to go to church just because you believe in God."

"Well, what are we? I mean, what religion are we?"

Barbara stopped chopping. "Why all the questions?"

"I just want to know, that's all."

"Obviously." Mrs. Fisher brushed the carrot pieces into the salad
bowl and set the knife down by the cutting board. For a few
moments there was an uncomfortable silence. "I don't know how to
answer that," she said finally, wiping her hands on her apron. "I
was brought up Catholic. Your father was also. But that was a long
time ago, and things have changed. The Catholic Church your father
and I were raised in, for all intents and purposes, no longer exists.
And it's probably just as well."

Char bit her lip pensively. "So, what are we?"

Thoughtfully lifting an eyebrow, Mrs. Fisher slowly rinsed the
knife and the cutting board and set them in the dish drainer to dry.
Then she looked at Char. "We decided to let you girls make that
decision for yourselves, when you were older. Now, if you would
please go find the croutons in the pantry—the plain ones, not the
garlic—I can finish this salad and we can go."

* * *

Fingering the purple beads, and referring frequently to the booklet,
the sixty-five prayers took about twenty-five minutes. But at last,
Char finished saying her very first Rosary.

Chapter 31: When Did We See You?

I have loved, O Lord, the beauty of thy house,
and the place where thy glory dwells.

> – Lavabo Prayers before Mass
> 1962 Roman Missal

The Columbus Day Parade in Pittsburgh's Little Italy had drawn a good crowd the year before, so the organizers hoped to make it an annual event. Char had taken the bus over to Liberty Avenue and stood watching the blaring high school bands and the valiant Knights of Columbus in their dashing white-plumed hats process through Bloomfield as balding dignitaries in classic convertibles threw candy at the crowds and shrieking children raced after the brightly colored treats. It had truly been a fun way to spend the cool autumn afternoon.

On the corner of Liberty and Thirty-Fifth in the borough of Lawrenceville, just south and west of Little Italy, was a venerable old church with a strikingly elegant rose window. On impulse, Char decided to stop in for a visit. She was feeling more and more drawn to the Catholic Church, and she needed to find a quiet place to pray. A wheelchair-accessible ramp had been added to the front of the building where neatly trimmed shrubbery framed the hundred-year-old red brick, inscribed with "1902" on the corner. A bicycle rack stood at the ready, but no bikes were parked there. A large white sign on the corner in front of a smaller brick building bore the words "Church Brew Works" in Old-English-styled lettering, but nothing indicated what times Masses were held. But no matter. Happily Char skipped up the steps and opened the heavy church door, which swung open to reveal what lay inside. Instantly she froze in her tracks, mouth ajar, and did a double-take.

"Hi! Just one today?" A young woman in a tight tee shirt and jeans held out what appeared to be a menu.

Char squeezed her eyelids shut as though her eyes were failing, then opened them and refocused her eyes. Scanning the church, she took it all in—the bar, the tables, and the gigantic silver brewing tanks at the front of the...*sanctuary? Sitting atop the altar?* Overwhelmed by the incongruity, Char laughed nervously.

"I'm sorry," she began, not knowing how to act. "I thought..."

"You thought this was still a church? Don't feel bad. It *was* a church, until the owners bought it and turned it into a restaurant."

"Oh! I see." *Sure, why not. Why not?*

"At least they didn't turn it into a dance club like they did up in Millvale! So will you be dining with us? Can I get you something to drink?"

"No, that's okay." *Dance club?* She didn't want to order anything, not in here. It just didn't feel right.

But her stomach begged to differ. She hadn't eaten all day, except for that big pretzel at the parade.

"Well, maybe on second thought." She might as well get a sandwich or something and take home. Hopefully God wouldn't mind.

"Here's our menu. Let me know when you're ready to order," the waitress said cheerfully. "Everything's available to go except alcoholic beverages."

Char ordered a Reuben on rye with French fries and sat down at the bar, chewing her lip. Her thoughtful blue eyes swiveled up past the soaring, stately columns to the elegant hanging lights and beyond to the jewel-like, arching stained glass windows bearing the names of saints and the former parishioners who had donated them. What had happened to drive them away from their beautiful hundred-year-old church? It was truly bizarre.

"Here you go," the waitress efficiently handed her a white paper bag heavy with food. "It'll be $9.73."

Char handed her a ten and dropped the change into a tip jar full of dollar bills and assorted coins on the counter.

"So do you know of any Catholic churches around here? That are actually churches?"

"Our Lady of the Angels is just a few blocks from here, up Thirty-Seventh," the waitress said, slamming the cash drawer shut.

Char smiled her thanks and headed out the door just in time to hold it open for an elderly couple coming in to grab a quick bite to eat. She glanced at their faces to gauge their reaction, but they didn't seem the slightest bit disturbed by the church-turned-beer-garden.

Somberly she headed up Liberty Avenue towards Our Lady of the Angels, clutching her lunch. The carefree gaiety she had felt earlier at the parade had been drowned in a strange wave of confusion. Shaking it off, she stepped purposefully towards Thirty-Seventh Street and then headed left, grateful to be away from the constant whoosh of traffic. Already she could see the twin towers at Our Lady of the Angels inviting her closer, and her steps slowed to a thoughtful, even pace. Knowing that she would soon be able to pray in peace quickly calmed her nerves and banished her anxiety. Hungrily she reached into the white to-go bag, fished out a couple of steaming crinkle-cut fried potatoes, and quickly polished them off. She wished she had bought herself something to drink. The salty fries had made her thirsty.

She had just folded the bag down again when the wind began to blow from the north, slowing her progress. A shovelful of giant maple leaves whirled into her, brittle thugs hurling threats and warnings. *Who are you? What are you doing here? This is our territory!* But they quickly fell under her feet where they were crushed to the sidewalk, or blew out into the puddled street and were trapped under the tires of cars parked at the curb.

A boy on a bike raced past. She watched him pedaling farther and farther up the street until he had almost disappeared, and for a moment she caught herself weirdly wondering if he was about to fly away with a little green alien, heart all aglow, precariously clinging to the handlebars.

But now she was here. Our Lady of the Angels was majestic. Standing under the twin towers, three arched doorways welcomed her under a twelve-foot statue of Saint Somebody or other. She was just deciding which doorway to try first, when a man spoke to her. She couldn't hear him at first. He spoke in a low voice, almost mumbling to himself. He sat huddled far to the left on one of the steps, entombed in a soiled granite-colored coat and scuffed brown boots. A gray knit cap covered his head, neck, and ears. His hands were folded quietly in front of him as though deep in thought or prayer. Char looked at him, but his eyes were focused on the sidewalk. Had he been speaking to her?

"Have any spare change, miss?"

Char's heart jumped into her throat, and for a minute she couldn't speak. She wasn't used to being asked for money by homeless strangers on the street.

"I don't. I'm sorry," she murmured in a low voice. Racing up the stairs, she yanked on the handle of the great oak door and rushed inside. The door hadn't yet closed behind her when she reversed course and cautiously came outside again. The man on the steps hadn't moved.

"Are you hungry?" she asked, holding out the white to-go bag. "Would you like to have a Reuben on rye?"

And the man on the steps smiled.

Chapter 32: Treasure on Troy Hill

Send forth thy light and thy truth:
they have conducted me,
and brought me unto thy holy hill,
and into thy tabernacles.

– Preparatory Prayers from
the 1962 Roman Missal

She was nervous at first and more than a little rattled after her encounter with the man on the steps, but the brown-robed Capuchin priest at Our Lady of the Angels had been very kind and easy to talk to. He'd ushered her into a small conference room of sorts, and after talking for a while about school, and Montana, and trends in church architecture, he handed her a folded gray pamphlet entitled, "This We Believe: Prayers and Teachings of the Catholic Church." He also gave her an old copy of the *Catechism* and a Saint Joseph's Catholic Bible, New American version, plus a list of parishes in the area around Carnegie Mellon, their addresses and phone numbers. All she had to do was pick one.

The pamphlet was clear and concise. It listed, among other things, the precepts of the Church, the Ten Commandments, the four cardinal virtues (justice, prudence, temperance, and fortitude), the three theological virtues (faith, hope, and charity), the seven gifts of the Holy Spirit, the corporal works of mercy, and the spiritual works of mercy—the goals and obligations of every good Catholic and the essential foundations of spiritual growth. *There's so much to being a good Catholic,* she thought. *They actually tell you how to live a good life, not just a bunch of scientific theories.*

But where should she go for instruction? She would need to sign up for a special program for converts called the Rite of Christian Initiation for Adults—RCIA for short. In the old days when people went everywhere on foot, people joined the nearest church in their neighborhood. But nowadays, you could pretty much go wherever you wanted. She looked at the list of parishes the friar had given her. There was the Cathedral of Saint Paul, the Oratory of Saint Philip Neri, and several more. For a moment, she hesitated.

We have to go to Saint Anthony's Chapel.

The words kept echoing in Char's brain like a half-remembered song that wouldn't go away.

Saint Anthony's Chapel. It's a surprise!

She looked it up on her huge, wrinkled paper map of Pittsburgh. She finally found it, tucked away in the Troy Hill neighborhood on the North Side, about a mile from downtown. 1704 Harpster Street.

Harpster! Perfect street for a chapel, Char had laughed cynically. *The angels must be there, playing their harps.*

* * *

The trip took longer than she'd anticipated. As the crow flies, it was only five miles or so, but on the winding bus paths, making stops every few blocks, it took forty-five minutes just to get to the Thirty-First Street Bridge. As she rode along, earbuds plugged in, she looked out the filmy bus windows and marveled. The streets of Pittsburgh were so unlike Great Falls it was as though she was in another country—even on another continent. Gone were the miles of tacky pawn shops, garish casinos, and dingy tattoo parlors back home. Gone were the bars and the tiny box-like houses and the miles and miles of dry, yellow grass.

Pittsburgh was unique. To Char it was as she imagined parts of Europe might be. Emanating an aura of tradition, row upon row of hundred-year-old, three-story frame houses that had stood the test of time provided a comforting sense of stability. Gothic-spired churches with dignified steeples and stone bell towers anchored nearly every corner. The hills were thick with trees, and the promise of flowers lay sleeping just beneath the low shrubbery. The Allegheny River poured powerfully through, carving a broad niche between downtown and the Island, just before joining the historic

Monongahela and Ohio Rivers. There, at the Thirty-First Street Bridge, she hopped off the bus and began her trek north.

A half hour later, she was standing in front of Saint Anthony's Chapel. From the outside, it looked like any ordinary old stone church in a working-class neighborhood. But where was everyone? Char double checked the address. 1704 Harpster. This was the place.

But where was everyone? Char checked her watch. Eleven forty-five. Mass was supposed to start in fifteen minutes, but there were only two cars parked on the narrow street in front. Timidly she mounted the steps to the white wooden doors, pulled the handle, and walked inside.

A small stately vestibule contained tables with signs and pamphlets and holy cards. Just beyond it, a floor-to-ceiling black wrought iron grate separated the entrance from the main church. In all other respects, it looked like an ordinary chapel. Three young men knelt motionless in the dark wooden pews in front of her, facing the main altar. But there was something different here. Char could feel it, but she didn't know what it was. Something *more*. Slowly she advanced and tried to take it all in. Where to begin? The place was completely filled. But not with people.

All along the sides of the walls were heavy glassed-in display cases made of dark wood containing thousands upon thousands of little round gold and silver charms. Affixed to velvet backing, each charm was labeled with tiny strips of paper bearing abbreviated names written in Latin. Thousands more were enshrined in small gold stands encrusted with jewels and surrounded by small golden sunbursts. Hundreds of white candles in tall glass globes glowed brightly in front of smaller altars. A sparkling crystal chandelier hung from the ceiling. Char didn't know where to look first.

Prominently lining the aisles on both sides of the chapel were twelve colorful life-sized statue groupings in alcoves under ornate archways depicting the arrest and death of Jesus at the cruel hands of Roman soldiers. Spears, tears, blood, thorns, and the Cross. For a moment, Char felt strangely dizzy and had to look away. Then, looking up towards the front of the chapel, she felt her stomach lurch. There was an altar just like in a regular church, but beside it was a glass-walled coffin containing a human skeleton.

Weakly Char lowered herself into one of the pews and tried to get her bearings. The old, worn kneeler was in the down position. Gingerly she knelt on it and folded her hands together in front of her face as if trying to hide. She bit a nail half-heartedly, her thoughts a random jumble of images. Gradually her breathing slowed. Her mind quieted, and everything was still. She noticed an elderly nun in a short veil walking slowly down the right aisle and thought of her Aunt Mary. What had her life been like? Why had she become a nun? And why had she left religious life so many years ago? Why had her parents stopped going to church? She tried to imagine her parents going to Mass in a place like this, but somehow she just couldn't picture it.

What am I doing here? her anxious thoughts intruded once again. None of the kids she knew ever talked about religion. She supposed she should pray, but her mind was an empty blank. *Maybe God will see me kneeling here,* she thought finally.

When was Mass? There were no priests in sight. So she knelt. And knelt. And knelt.

A vacationing family with two teenage daughters slowly made their way up the left aisle, and Char felt the empty pang of home-sickness. She longed to see her parents and Kayla and Mikel. The father peered intently at one of the glass cases and pointed, quietly explaining something. Char strained to hear what he was saying, but she was too far away. She contemplated moving closer, but she didn't want to just wander around. She'd get herself in trouble for sure. She squeezed her eyelids together, determined to stop the hot tears that threatened to spill over her pale cheeks.

Why am I feeling so emotional?

She clenched her fists and wondered if maybe she ought to just leave. Right then, a middle-aged woman leading a small tour group walked in. A few moments later, Gregorian chant began playing softly from speakers mounted on the walls, and a man's voice bearing the distinctive Pittsburgh accent began to speak.

"Welcome to Saint Anthony's Chapel. During your visit here, we ask you to be aware that the Chapel is an active worship site and that the Blessed Sacrament is reposed in the Tabernacle. Holy Mass is celebrated here as well as other devotions, such as our weekly novenas to Saint Anthony of Padua."

Char exhaled, leaned back in the pew, and listened.

"The front part of this chapel was built in 1882 and 1883 as a private worship site for the first pastor of Most Holy Name Parish, Father Suitbert Gottfried Mollinger.[7] His mother was a baroness, a blood relative to the ruling family of the Netherlands. His father was a commissioned officer in the Belgian cavalry. He pursued his medical studies in Naples, Rome, and Genoa. Upon completion of these studies, he was now a practicing physician. He entered the seminary in Cleveland, Ohio, and was ordained there in 1857.

"Throughout the nineteenth century, revolution and war forced much of Europe into political and religious turmoil, famine, epidemics, and death. Church lands were confiscated and sold. Many churches and monasteries and convents were looted."

I don't remember hearing about this in school, Char thought.

"Because of the religious unrest that had spread throughout Italy and Germany, these countries began to systematically close down the great churches and cathedrals in the area, and they imprisoned bishops and expelled the priests and religious workers. Those churches and cathedrals that were closed down were known for the relics they had, and as a result a lot of those relics found their way into private hands or into pawn shops. Father Mollinger began to

---

[7] Pronounced "Sweetbert Gottfreed MO ling er"

ransom some of these relics and added them into his already growing collection."

Relics? What are relics? Char wondered.

"In 1868 he was named the first pastor of Most Holy Name of Jesus church here in Troy Hill. From 1868 until 1880, Father Mollinger added to his rapidly growing collection of relics. Father Mollinger proposed to the parishioners his idea of a chapel to house his relics. The cornerstone was laid on the Feast of Saint Anthony, June 13, 1882, and exactly one year later, the chapel was dedicated. At the time, Father Mollinger had about twenty-six hundred relics that he housed in the reliquaries throughout the chapel."

Twenty-six hundred relics of what?

"Over the ensuing years, Father Mollinger continued to travel back to Europe to take care of his holdings there and to continue to acquire relics. On one such trip in the late 1880s, he was visiting the royal ecclesiastical art studios of the C. Mayer Company in Munich, Germany, when he purchased the Stations of the Cross that are displayed in the back part of the chapel.

"Honoring his medical training, Father Mollinger saw patients every day of his life. When he was not attending to priestly duties, he would minister to the health needs of anyone who asked for his help.

"Father Mollinger collapsed mid-morning of June 13, 1892, and passed away on June 15. He was buried on June 18, 1892. To this day, the Chapel is maintained by the volunteers, patrons, and benefactors of Most Holy Name of Jesus parish."

Wow, Char thought. *This is some kind of a museum. A Catholic museum.*

The ethereal chant music started up again. Now a woman's voice came across the speakers.

"Directly above the Stations are the stained glass windows. They were created by the Royal Bavarian Art Institute for Stained Glass in Munich, Bavaria. They depict eleven of the twelve apostles, plus Saint Stephen, Saint Paul, and Saint Lawrence.

"The largest bell was christened Saint Anthony and is located near the window of Saint Anthony. There are two smaller bells in the adjacent bell tower. They were christened Saint Francis and Saint Clare."

Cool, the bells have names!

"Below the statue of Saint Anthony in the center of the altar in the reliquary is the tooth of Saint Anthony..."

Whoa. What?

"Please walk to the center of the chapel facing the high altar, and we will tell you a little bit about the original chapel architecture, the relic cases, the catalog of the chapel relics, how to locate the chapel relics, and the source of the relic collection.

"The relics are displayed individually or in groupings as a collage mainly within reliquaries, the size of which varies widely. Notice the full-wall reliquary cases built against the wall directly in back of the high altar and to either side of the altar. The many reliquary cases are arranged from floor to ceiling. More cabinet-like reliquary cases are along both walls of the nave within the right and left arms of the transept.

"All the relics in the windowed cases along the walls of the original chapel are those collected by Father Mollinger, including a molar of Saint Anthony, which is displayed at the Tabernacle below the statue of Saint Anthony near the Fourteenth Station of the Cross. To complete Father Mollinger's collection of relics in the chapel, the altar of the Blessed Virgin Mary near the first Station of the Cross contains twenty-six more relics.

"The beautiful statue to the right is that of Saint Elizabeth of Hungary, the girl queen. She became queen at the age of fourteen and died at age twenty-four. She was known for her charity and her good works.

"Since the early days of the Church, the remains of saints or holy persons were called relics. Relics are divided into three categories.

First class relics are parts of the bodies of saints and the instruments of Christ our Lord's Passion."

Parts of the bodies? Char gripped the bottom of the pew.

"Second class relics are objects sanctified by close contact with
the saints, such as articles of clothing, objects used in life, or in the
case of a martyr, the instruments of his torture."

Torture? Char bit the inside of her lip and tried not to look at the
skeleton encased by the altar.

"Now, if you continue on to the large reliquary case on the left
side of the chapel...."

Rapidly Char's heart began to flutter like a butterfly. She didn't
know what had possessed her to come here, but this mansion of the
dead was freaking her out. Teeth? Bones? Body parts? She was
starting to feel faint. In desperation she stood and carefully walked
as unobtrusively as possible up the main aisle until she reached the
vestibule, then skittered out the front door—right into the pouring
rain.

Chapter 33: Help Wanted

*Towards the age of eleven, in the course of a sermon,
one phrase struck me: 'The virgins follow the Lamb
wherever he goes.' Immediately I perceived an interior
wordless response: 'That is for me.' It was not a matter of
an explicit understanding, but of a certitude that God had
laid his hand on me, and that he wished to be my only love.*

– Carmelite nun, aged 64, in religion 41 years

"Oh, heck!" Char fumed and dodged back inside to escape the downpour. Annoyed, she flung the drops of rain from her face.

The recorded tour had ended. A few people were slowly making their way to the vestibule, picking up pamphlets, while others admired the ornately carved antique confessionals. The three young men kneeling in the front pews hadn't budged. The vacationing family strolled past, heading for the front doors. Char hugged herself tightly and tried to look nonchalant.

The vacationing father opened the door and stood looking out as if trying to decide whether to wait it out or make a run for it.

"Did you put your window up?" his wife asked anxiously. The girls beside her fidgeted and jumped in place. The man murmured something, but Char couldn't hear. Frustrated, she wandered over to the table and examined the brochures and holy cards. She recognized one of them. It was just like the one Celia had given her with the picture of Saint Michael.

Celia. The last thing she wanted to think about. Rain or no rain, she was getting out of there. Several people stood at the doorway, watching and waiting for the weather to clear. Char excused herself and was just about to walk out between them when a plump matronly woman with silvery white hair suddenly appeared out of nowhere.

"Are you going over to the gift shop? I have an umbrella, if you'd like to share," she asked kindly.

Anything to get out of here, Char thought, and mumbling her thanks ducked out with her into the soggy air. They quickly crossed the narrow street to the gift shop, where the woman produced a set of keys, which she deftly juggled with one hand while holding onto the umbrella with the other.

"There! That's more like it," she said cheerfully. Then she opened the door, and a little bell jingled merrily from its hook.

"Thanks," Char said and smiled uncertainly.

"Is this your first time here?"

"Yeah."

The woman looked at her sideways as she hung the dripping umbrella on a coat hook and wiped her feet on the mat before flicking on the lights.

"Well, make yourself at home. I'll be right back. I just have to turn off the security system, or the cops'll be here in ten minutes!" she exclaimed.

"Okay." She really didn't want to stay, but it was better than waiting inside that house of bones.

The woman hurried about methodically, turning on lights, opening blinds, and adjusting the thermostat. Then Char lost sight of her. The little bell above the front door jingled again, and a couple of elderly women entered.

"Did you know Saint Anthony was declared a saint less than one year after his death?"

"No, I did not know that."

"Nowadays, it can take decades. Even Padre Pio wasn't canonized until he'd been dead for thirty years."

Death, death, death! Why all this talk about death? Char rolled her eyes. *Maybe that's why old ladies go to church. They're all scared of dying!*

Soon the woman came bustling back up the hallway, smiling brightly. She was wearing a big flowery apron and a round campaign button that read, "Ask me about the Mass." Stopping in front of Char, the woman looked her up and down with razor-sharp eyes that were a bright, piercing blue. Char felt like she'd just been x-rayed by a powerful machine with scanners and sensors and a foolproof, state-of-the-art lie detector. Char swallowed hard.

"I'm Barbara Malley," the woman said.

"Hi."

"And who might you be?"

"I'm Char Fisher. Barbara—that's my mother's name," she added.

"Barbara. That's a good Catholic name!" Mrs. Malley observed. "Even if they did take her off the calendar!"

Char was about to say that her mother was anything but a good Catholic, and in fact wasn't Catholic at all, and what calendar was she talking about, when the door opened and closed again, and in came the vacationing family with their two antsy daughters. It must have finally stopped raining.

"Char. Sounds like Charlemagne. Are you going to Pitt?" Mrs. Malley asked.

"No. Carnegie Mellon." *Charla who?*

"Oh, a science major."

"Um, architecture, actually."

"Oh! So you were here doing research for a class? Most people don't come here to look at the architecture," the woman laughed a friendly, hearty laugh.

"Well, I ..." Char stammered. "My friend suggested that we, that I..."

"I hope you didn't come thinking there was Mass here today. Sunday Mass is at the parish church across the street."

Thankfully, the door opened and closed again, the little bell tinkling. Mrs. Malley's face lit up like a dozen fireworks.

"Oh! There you are! I wondered when you'd be coming." And she walked over and gave motherly hugs to the three young men Char had just seen praying in the chapel.

"Hello, Mrs. Malley," said one. The other two smiled, a trifle embarrassed.

"We were going to call you when we got to Canton, but the weather was so bad we couldn't get a signal."

"So how did it go? How was your trip to Clear Creek?"

"Oh, it was great. Kind of rustic," the second one said. The others laughed, sharing a private joke.

"They've converted a horse barn into a chapel. The postulants are living in sheds."

"Really! How incredible. How many monks are there?"

"There's twenty-four total. Eight priests and five brothers— the founders—plus eight novices and three postulants."

"And they've been there since when?"

"September 1999."

"Eight novices! That's a lot of vocations in only three years! Are you going to apply?" Mrs. Malley said.

"We're thinking about it," the first one responded solemnly, and then glancing sideways at the others, he cracked a conspiratorial grin.

"We brought you some CDs," he added, ceremoniously handing over a wrinkled grocery bag.

"From the monks?"

"From their motherhouse in Fontgombault. It is excellent. The chant is just...out of this world."

"Thank you! I can't wait to hear it! And who knows? Someday maybe you'll be making your own CD!"

Char looked away. She felt out of place, like she was intruding on a private conversation. She didn't want to be rude, so very casually she began walking around the gift shop. But part of her wanted to keep listening. Those guys were pretty cute, too.

"They've got the plans drawn up to start digging the foundation for the church and the gatehouse next year. They have a herd of sheep and a wood shop. And they're going to build a Roman-style arched stone bridge over the creek," the tallest of the three said.

"Sounds exciting! Are your parents in favor? I know yours are, Gregory, and yours," she added, looking at the other one happily.

"They're coming around."

"If they don't, you let me know and I'll make sure they do!" she chuckled forcefully. "The Church needs more priests! If we don't have priests, we won't have the Eucharist, and then where will we be!" It was a challenge issued, not a question raised; a simple, self-evident fact not open to debate.

Char stole another glance at the men. They didn't look anything like monks. They were all-American types: clean cut, boyish, and friendly. They seemed like ordinary guys, just like the guys back home, except for one thing—they were beaming with happiness.

"Well keep me in the loop, please! I want to know all about it." Mrs. Malley said emphatically.

"We will," they said together.

"I haven't been praying for you for seven years to lose track of you now!"

* * *

Mrs. Malley whooshed past on her way to the cash register. "Those boys are from my parish. I've known them since they were in middle school. I've got to wait on these ladies. Char, would you mind grabbing that mop in the corner and going over the floor there? It's wet, and someone might slip."

Char nodded, too surprised to speak.

The women waiting at the counter smiled. "Did they finally get someone to help you out, Barbara?"

Mrs. Malley trained her gaze on Char, who had obediently gone for the mop. "I don't know. Char? Would you like to be a volunteer and help me out here? I could sure use it."

Char was stunned. She was even more stunned to hear the sound of her spontaneous answer to Mrs. Malley's question.

"Sure!"

"Great! When can you start?"

Chapter 34: I'll Be Home for Christmas

I was asked—Why am I a Catholic?
I said that among other reasons was this—
that I had the strongest objections to going to hell.

– Fr. Bernard Vaughan, S.J.

The next morning, Char got out of bed and winced. Her left knee was stiff and swollen up like a basketball.

"That's what I get for praying on that hard kneeler," she moped, painfully limping to the bathroom.

She hobbled into the kitchen and started some tea, then dug around in the freezer, scrounging for ice cubes to make an icepack with a plastic bag. No way she'd make it to class today, not with her knee like this. So she picked up the phone and called Nadia, one of the girls in her economics class, to ask if she would let her copy her notes. Then she called Dr. Miller's office and left a voicemail. Most of the professors didn't care if you showed up or not, but Dr. Miller called roll, just like in high school.

The teapot whistled encouragingly, and Char hopped back to the kitchen and made herself Earl Grey tea and whole wheat toast with grape jelly. Then she inched her way back to the couch, carrying the ice bag in her teeth, balancing the toast, and trying not to spill the hot tea. Easing onto the sofa, she set down the mug, propped her leg up on the coffee table with a pillow, arranged the ice pack, and pressed the power button on the television remote. Success.

"Thirty-six confirmed fatalities have been reported from this weekend's outbreak of tornadoes impacting fourteen states in the south and Midwest, including twelve deaths in Alabama and seventeen deaths in Tennessee. Five fatalities occurred in the town of Van Wert, Ohio, 110 miles southwest of Toledo, after a tornado touched down there. With wind speeds of up to 260 miles per hour, that tornado has now been officially confirmed as an F-4. The Ohio

Emergency Management Agency and the Ohio National Guard will be coordinating cleanup and recovery.

"Here in Pennsylvania, one death has been reported in the town of Clark after an F-2 tornado packing winds of over 150 miles per hour destroyed over a dozen homes and businesses yesterday about sixty miles northwest of Pittsburgh."

Char's flip phone began vibrating on the lamp table, so she put down the tea and hit the mute button on the remote. The caller ID said "Kayla Fisher."

"Hey," she said mechanically, eyes glued to the television.

"Good morning! How's it going?" Kayla sang.

"Fine."

"You don't sound fine. Did I wake you?"

"No, I just got up," Char mumbled, shifting the ice bag on her knee. "How's the baby?"

"He's good," Kayla replied cheerfully.

"That's good," Char said, staring at the aerial photos of devastated homes in Ohio and Tennessee.

"Whatcha doin' today?"

"I'm not doing much of anything. I hurt my knee again."

"Oh, bummer. How?"

"I … don't really know," Char lied. "But it's the size of a grapefruit."

"Ouch! I'm sorry," Kayla sympathized. "We're going to get Mikel's booster shot at the Clinic."

"Fun stuff," Char said. "How's Mom and Dad?"

"They're okay. They're never here. You know—work, work, work!"

"Yeah. How's the weather out there?"

"It's good. Not too cold. How's it out there?"

The aerial shots of tornado destruction had been replaced by a picture of Iraqi dictator Saddam Hussein, a map of Iraq, and a quote from the United Nations Security Council about "serious consequences."

"It's okay. Heckuva lot better here than it is in Ohio. Did you see the tornadoes?"

"Oh, yeah I did see that. Were any near you?"

"Not too close. One about sixty miles from here, they said."

"Oh my gosh. Just like Cleveland!"

"Yeah. I don't like tornadoes. Those things make me nervous!"

"So have you heard from Tia lately?" Kayla asked.

"Nope. Not since last summer."

"I wonder if she's a nun now?"

"She said she was entering in September. Maybe I should give her a call." Char blew on her tea and took a sip.

"Tell her I said hi if you do. Hey, guess what?"

"What?"

"Eric's been coming around," she said excitedly.

"Oh really? That's good."

"He plays with Mikel, and we talk and stuff. I think he wants to try taking him over to his house to spend the night, but Mom said he's not old enough to be away from me yet. What do you think?"

"Well, I don't know, Kay. As long as Mrs. Mattson was there, it would probably be okay. Don't you think?"

"Well, maybe. Dad says we just need to take it slow and let Mikel get to know him first."

"That sounds about right."

"Melissa said she and Mercedes saw him out with Bethany Johnson last weekend when they went to see *Minority Report.*"

"Oh."

"You know, that new Tom Cruise movie? She said Bethany was wearing this really short tutu and pink leggings and...."

But Char was tuning out. She loved her sister, but they lived in different worlds now. It was hard to listen to the same old Great Falls gossip and act like she still cared what Bethany Johnson wore.

"Char!"

"Huh? I'm sorry. What did you say?"

"I said have you been to any good movies lately?"

"Um, yeah. I went to see *The Nun's Story* a few weeks ago."

"*The Nun's Story?* What's that about?"

Char snorted. "It's about nuns, duh! What did you think, silly?"

"I'm not silly! I just never heard of that movie before, that's all! Did you see *The Sopranos* last night?"

"I don't really watch TV much anymore."

"Oh." For a minute, Kayla didn't know what to say.

"Because Daddy said he would pay for cable or the internet, but not both."

"Oh! That would be a tough decision to make," Kayla said with relief. She couldn't imagine not watching television on purpose.

"Anyway, I don't have time to watch TV. You would not *believe* the amount of work they give you in college. It's totally unreal."

"Oh. So, what do you do for fun?"

Before Char could answer, Mikel wailed in the background.

"Hold on!" Kayla dropped the phone and ran to comfort Mikel, who had tripped and tumbled over his stuffed toy elephant and smacked face-down on the carpet.

Char glanced back to the TV again, now playing commercials. She finished off the toast, which had turned cold, and the tea as well.

"Okay sorry, I'm back! We had a little accident, didn't we baby?" Kayla soothed the little toddler, who was snuffling traumatically into the phone.

Char's heart melted. "Hi, Mikey! Did you fall down and go boom?"

"Oh, please don't call him that, Char! It sounds like that kid on the Life cereal commercials!"

"No, it doesn't! Besides, he'll outgrow it." Char grinned unapologetically.

"I'm not kidding, Char. Nicknames stick, you know that."

Char did know. "Yeah, you're right. I'm sorry. Hi Mikel!"

"Did you hear that sweetie?" Kayla sang to the toddler as she cuddled him on her hip and wiped his nose. "Auntie Char called you Mikel! So. Are you coming home for Thanksgiving?"

"I don't know yet. I'm thinking not. I'm so swamped with home-work, and…" *And I need a couple of days to myself so I can think.*

"Dad'll be disappointed."

"Yeah, I know. But I'll be home for Christmas."

"Hey! Just like that song. *I'll… be… home… for Christmas…,*" Kayla crooned.

"*You…can plan…on me…*" Char sang along. "*Please have snow…* Well, not too much snow!"

"Yeah, just a couple of inches, right?" Kayla agreed.

"Right," Char said solemnly. "Kay? Can I ask you something personal?"

"What?"

Char took a deep breath. "Do you ever think about—God?"

"Like how do you mean?"

"I mean like, do you ever think about what God is really like? Or what happens to us when we die?"

"I guess," Kayla said uncertainly.

"Well I've been thinking about it a lot lately. Kind of like, I don't know…"

"Char. You're not sick, are you?"

"No, nothing like that. I'm fine. It's just that, all my life it's felt like something was missing. A part of me that was looking for another part of me. Did you ever feel that way?"

"No. Not really. Well, maybe. Sometimes," Kayla finally admitted, thinking about Eric.

Char threw her fingers through her hair in frustration. She wanted to confide in her sister, but it was like they were living on different planets. Kayla simply had no interest in spiritual matters. But she wasn't going to give up.

"Once I even asked Daddy if I was adopted. I'll never forget the look on his face! I think he felt bad. But anyway, that's not the point. The point is, I've been thinking about this for a long time, and I think I'm gonna do it."

"Do what?"

"Become Catholic."

"*What?* Why? Mom and Dad'll freak out."

"No, they won't. Mom might, but Dad won't."

"How do you know?"

"For one thing, Aunt Mary was a nun. We come from a Catholic family, Kayla! I'll bet you didn't even know that."

Silence hung from the other end of the phone.

"What if Heaven is everything they say it is? What if it's this wonderful place where you can have everything you ever wanted and be happy forever? And nobody told us?"

The only reply was an awkward silence. Then, Char overhead their mother, murmuring in the background.

"Okay, I'm coming, Mom! I'm sorry, Char. I've gotta go. Mom's ready to take us to the Clinic."

"Oh. Okay. Bye, Mikel! Bye, Kayla. Tell Mom and Dad I said hi." Char forced herself to sound cheerful, but her heart wasn't in it. She was about to make one of the most important decisions of her life, and she was doing it alone.

"I will. I hope your knee feels better soon! Bye, Char!"

"Bye!" Char sighed and closed the flip phone. Pensively she turned off the TV, closed her eyes, and tried to imagine what it would be like spending Thanksgiving Day all by herself.

Chapter 35: Time to Think

My (private) First Communion at seven: the first sensible manifestation of the presence of Jesus in me. That was what gave me my faith. God made me understand that he wished me all for himself, and I was clearly conscious of the fact that it was he who chose me and wanted me. I myself had no hand in it; it was just because he loved me. I knew that I would never marry even before I knew what marriage was. I passed that whole day as if I were not on earth, I was there without being there.
(I have never spoken of this to anyone).

– Poor Clare nun, aged 39

Char removed the ice bag from her knee and gingerly tried to move her leg. It was a little less painful, but still very stiff and swollen. She swung around lengthwise on the couch and arranged a pillow underneath it to keep it elevated. Pensively she pressed her lips together. She had wanted to talk to Kayla about God, about her desire to become Catholic, but she just didn't seem to care. She just wouldn't understand.

After studying for about an hour and a half, she decided to take a break. Gingerly she limped over to her storage cube by her desk and started digging through piles of papers—letters from her parents, a birthday card from Kayla, reams of stapled handouts from her professors. Finally she found what she'd been looking for: her address book. And inside it, Tia's letter telling her she was entering, and the phone number at Holy Angels Monastery.

She picked up the phone, and then hesitated. Maybe she shouldn't bother her. Maybe she wasn't allowed to have phone calls. She'd only been in the monastery for a few months, after all. Char bit her lip. She needed to talk to someone who would understand, someone who could give her a little advice and maybe answer some of her questions. But could she trust Tia? She didn't really know her all that well. They'd exchanged a few cards and letters and talked on the phone a couple of times. Not exactly best friends. But what choice did she have? Not many girls became nuns. She dialed the number. After three rings, the answering machine kicked in.

"Hello. You have reached the Holy Angels Monastery. The sisters are at prayer or are otherwise occupied. Please leave your intentions after the tone, and we will bring them before the Lord. Thank you for calling, and may God bless you."

BEEP!

"Hi, this is Char Fisher. I'd like to leave a message for Tia—*Sister* Tia. If she could please give me a call, I would appreciate it. Thanks!" Her phone shut with a snap.

"Oh, heck!" she exclaimed. "I forgot to give them my number. Dang it!" Hitting the redial, she waited for the answering machine to kick in again.

"Holy Angels Monastery, Mother Bonaventure speaking."

For a split second, Char's breath caught in her throat like a frightened animal trying to hide.

"Hello, Mother Bonaventure! I was just—actually, I just left a message for Sister Tia," Char stammered.

"Yes, I heard your voice on the machine. I just happened to be in the office when you called."

"And then I realized, I hadn't left my number."

"Oh, I see. Would you like me to give her a message for you? Tia isn't able to make telephone calls right now."

Char pressed her lips together. "No, that's okay. I mean, maybe if you could just tell her that I called." *Who am I going to talk to now?*

"Yes, of course. And you can write to her, you know. New postulants aren't able to use the phone except to call family. I'm sure you understand."

No, I really don't, Char thought.

"May I have your name again, please?" Mother Bonaventure asked.

"Char Fisher," she said with a touch of gloom.

"Char Fisher. Char! I remember you now. You were here a few years ago with your family from somewhere in the northwest. Wyoming, wasn't it?"

"Montana. Yes, that was me—us. I can't believe you remember. That was three years ago!"

"Well, that was a day to remember, as I recall. But blessed be God for sending that thunderstorm. It was what brought Tia to us!" Mother Bonaventure exclaimed. "And how are you and your family doing, Char?"

"Oh, we're all doing really good, thanks."

"Wonderful. And how is life in Montana?"

"Well actually, I'm not in Montana right now. I'm going to college in Pittsburgh."

"Oh, college! How exciting. I drove through Pittsburgh with my family on the way to Cleveland once upon a time. Will you be traveling home for Thanksgiving?"

"I'm going to stay here. I've got so much homework to do, I really can't go."

"Oh, that's too bad. I always enjoyed spending Thanksgiving with my parents and grandparents," Mother said nostalgically.

"Yeah. I'll miss it, but I'll get to see everyone at Christmas."

"Yes, Christmas will be here before we know it! If all goes well, Sister Tia may be clothed on December 8."

"I'm sorry, did you say 'clothed'?"

"Yes. That just means she'll be accepted into our community— clothed in the habit of our order. She'll be a novice then," Mother explained.

"Oh wow! I didn't know that."

"Perhaps you can come and see! I'm sure she would be glad to have you. I'm not sure how many of her family members will be able to make it." Mother Bonaventure thought of Tia's family and wondered if Gloria would even attend. It was a sure bet that the father wouldn't.

"Oh yes, I would love to!"

"Unless you have too much homework, of course," Mother Bonaventure chided her gently.

"I will make a special effort to get all my homework done so I can come see Tia's clothing!" Char declared.

Mother Bonaventure chuckled softly. "Very good, Char. I hope we see you then. In the meantime, I'll give her the message that you called. I'm sure she'll be very pleased."

"Thank you."

"You're welcome. We'll be praying for you, Char. Good-bye."

"Bye!"

Char closed her phone and slowly set it down on the lamp table. How would she get to Cleveland without a car? It was definitely time to ask her parents to help her buy one. Taking the bus was okay for in the city, but sometimes a girl needed to travel. And waiting for a bus could be a major pain when the weather was frigid and icy.

Next to the lamp, a careless mound of purple beads spilled over a blue pamphlet. Having nothing better to do, Char began praying her second Rosary. When she was finished, she picked up the phone again and called Mrs. Malley. When her knee was better, she'd be volunteering at Saint Anthony's on Tuesday afternoons, helping out in the gift shop. She told Mrs. Malley about going to the Church Brew Works, and Our Lady of the Angels.

"So you're thinking about becoming Catholic?" Mrs. Malley had asked brightly.

"Yes."

"Have you been praying about it?"

"I've started praying the rosary."

"Oh, that is excellent! The rosary is the best prayer there is! Have you picked out a parish yet?"

"No, that's what I wanted to talk to you about. I'm not sure where to go. And honestly, I don't have time to go visit a different parish every weekend. I want to join *now*."

"You could always come to Holy Name parish. They're just right across the street here," Mrs. Malley suggested.

"Yeah, I thought about that." She wasn't sure why, but she just couldn't make up her mind where to go. It was like something was holding her back. It wasn't like she was even going to be staying in Pittsburgh forever. Once she graduated, she might end up anywhere.

"Where did you go to church growing up?" Mrs. Malley asked.

"That's the problem. We didn't go anywhere," Char admitted.

"How did you become interested in Catholicism?"

"I'm not really sure," Char replied. "I think..." She was about to tell Mrs. Malley about the monastery and meeting Tia in the thunderstorm, but there was something else. She tried to remember.

"I met this girl here, and we went to see the Audrey Hepburn Film festival."

"Oh, I love Audrey Hepburn. She was such a great actress!"

"And we saw *The Nun's Story*. Have you ever seen it?"

"No, I never did. But I read the novel many, many years ago! Was it a good movie?"

"It was so awesome. I loved the part where she became a surgical nurse in Africa. Her father was a surgeon, so she already knew a lot of medical stuff. And it showed this one priest who was living with lepers out in the jungle, and they would go check on him once a year, and they were like sailing up the Nile or something in a big canoe. And then in World War II, the Nazis were bombing around the hospital and she got mixed up with the underground."

"Sounds exciting!"

"But in the very beginning when she was learning how to be a nun, it was so hard! I never realized how hard it was. The new nuns didn't even have their own rooms!"

"Were you ever baptized?"

"I'm not sure. I don't know."

"Were there any Catholics in your family?"

Char paused, lost in thought. Her mother's words echoed in her brain: *Your father and I were raised Catholic.* What did that mean, exactly?

There had been that day long before, when her father had taken her up to the attic, the day she had asked him if she'd been adopted. Later, she'd gone back up there all by herself. How carefully she had examined all the treasures contained in the old big black steamer trunk. Old crocheted doilies and hand-embroidered pillowcases made by her Italian grandmother—her mother's mother— Constance D'Ambrosio. Letters to her father from his parents—her grandparents—Joseph and Elsabeth Fisher. Elsabeth, the one she called "Nana," but hardly ever saw. There had been photo albums and high school yearbooks. A few battered LP records and plastic, boxy eight-track tapes. Baby clothes she and Kayla had worn. Old black and white family photos in tarnished silver and wooden frames of people she'd never met. It was, all of it, priceless.

Down at the bottom of the trunk, underneath her father's college diploma and carefully folded letter sweater, there had been one box of old photos. They looked abandoned, as though they had once been carefully placed in a family photo album and hastily removed later on, tossed together in a jumble so that the timeline was unclear. Some had penciled in names and dates on the reverse side, but not all.

Photographs. The older ones in black and white, the newer ones in fuzzy, faded color. Pictures of mom pregnant. Mom in bangs and pigtails! Dad on the debate team. Dad graduating high school in a maroon cap and gown. Dad with longer hair, wearing a tux and a white boutonniere, escorting some nameless blonde in a flashy formal floor-length dress to the senior prom. And a young nun with serious eyes, wearing a long black habit and veil, hands hidden beneath her scapular, standing purposefully in front of a solid brick elementary school with the barest hint of a smile. *Your teeth are just like your Aunt Mary's,* her father had said. Somehow her slightly crooked teeth were comforting in that moment, a genetic trait that seemed to tie her to previous generations of Fishers and made her feel like she really did belong to them after all.

There was another picture, also in black and white, of a young religious sister. She was attired in a shorter veil and habit, awkwardly smiling at the camera. They looked so different, the two nuns, it was hard to tell if they were one and the same person. Char had compared the two, looking on the back. One said "Sister M. Genevieve, St. Francis Xavier, September 1962." The other simply said "Mary, 1969." Her father's sister, her Aunt Mary. Char had been shocked by the deep feeling of connection she felt to this woman she had never met.

Char stared into the distance. Her mind was a jumble of memories. Mrs. Malley waited patiently, phone up to her ear, eyes twinkling.

"My Aunt Mary!" Char finally blurted out.

"On your mother's side or your father's?"

"My father's. She was my father's sister."

"What about the rest of your father's family?" Mrs. Malley asked.

"I don't know!" Char's eyes darted around her apartment as though the answer was written somewhere on the walls. It was such a simple question. Why did it seem so difficult to answer?

"Well, then, how do you know your Aunt Mary was Catholic?"

"Because—the pictures I found of her—she's wearing a nun's habit."

"Oh, I see," Mrs. Malley's face grew serious. "Then your grandparents must have been Catholic. And your father, too, at some point."

Wonder, anger, and joy fluttered mutely across Char's face. She didn't know whether to be happy at this latest revelation or angry that no one in her family ever bothered to tell her the family history.

Mrs. Malley's face brightened into its characteristic beam. "This is really interesting! You're making all kinds of important connections. Who knows, maybe you're related to Saint John Fisher!"

"Who?"

"He was a martyr of the English Reformation. King Henry the Eighth had him executed. Did you ever watch *A Man for All Seasons?*"

"Uh-huh," Char shook her head.

"It's a great movie, you should watch it. It's all about Saint Thomas More and how he refused to go along with Henry when he wanted to have his marriage to Catherine of Aragon annulled so he could marry Anne Boleyn. Saint John Fisher was a bishop and theologian, and Saint Thomas More was Lord High Chancellor. The king put both of them in the Tower of London for months and months and finally cut off their heads."

Char grimaced. "I'm not so sure being a Catholic is all that safe," she observed half-jokingly.

"No, it wasn't. It still isn't, in some places. Freedom of religion is no laughing matter! Even now there are Catholics being martyred for their faith."

The other end of the phone was silent.

Mrs. Malley paused. "But that's okay! Because then you go straight to heaven, and everyone prays to you, and they put a statue of you somewhere in the Vatican!" Mrs. Malley laughed impishly, and the pained look left Char's face as she slowly broke into a wry smile. *Nothing dampens that woman's fiery spirit,* Char thought.

But then a troubling question popped into her head.

"Does it matter? I mean, do you have to come from a Catholic family to be Catholic?"

"Oh my, no. The Church is there for everyone. That's what the word "catholic" means. Universal!"

Char breathed a sigh of relief. The doors were opening, and Mrs. Malley had just put out the "welcome" mat.

"So how's that knee?" Mrs. Malley interrupted her thoughts.

"It's still pretty painful, actually."

"Well, while you're recuperating, I have a couple of books for you. I'll drop them in the mail, and you can bring them back when you're finished with them."

"Oh, you don't have to do that! I have tons of books for class," Char protested.

"These aren't college books! They're much more interesting. You'll see! I think you'll like them. And a very beautiful CD of Gregorian chant from the Benedictine Abbey at Fontgombault. You're gonna love it!"

"Sounds great!"

"I've got a customer, so I've got to hang up now. You stay off that leg and get better!"

"I will. Thanks, Mrs. Malley!"

* * *

The unexpectedly large package arrived just two days later. Eagerly Char sliced open the package tape with scissors and pulled the box open. Inside were a sturdy tin canister, two books, a CD, a couple of pamphlets, and an envelope with her name on it. Excitedly she examined the envelope and gently opened it. Inside was a colorful card with a cartoonish dragon on the front. Smiling, Char opened it. "Heard you've been *dragon* around. Get well soon! God bless you, Barbara Malley."

Laughing with delight, Char removed the first book. It was a hardcover volume, well-worn: *Song of Bernadette*. She couldn't remember if she'd seen the title on Celia's bookshelf or not, but it seemed familiar. Underneath it was the second book, *True Devotion to Mary* by Saint Louis de Montfort.

Below that, wrapped in bubble wrap, was the chant CD. Fontgombault? Where was that? Sounded French. The snapshot on the cover, revealing one lovely corner of the thick-walled medieval abbey, was magically enticing. Looked European. Char recognized the style—Romanesque—from her architecture class. These monasteries, her professor explained, had taken decades to build and changed hands numerous times, depending on whether the ruling elite of the day favored the Catholic Church or the reigning pope. During the Protestant Reformation, many had been sacked and burned or had gradually succumbed to the elements.

But her professor hadn't said anything about the monasteries of *today*. He had made it sound like it was all ancient history. Maybe Fontgombault wasn't a real monastery. Maybe the photo on the CD was just a picture of an old abandoned church. Mrs. Malley would know.

Char reached into the bottom of the box and lifted out the worn canister. Surprisingly, it was heavy. She gently shook it, but it didn't make a sound. Carefully she pried it open. It was packed to the brim. Soon the room was permeated with a powerful, tantalizing scent: homemade chocolate chip cookies. Char sank her teeth into one and took a delicious bite. Heavenly!

Chapter 36: Green Bean Casserole

Be very gentle and courteous toward your poor. You know that they are our masters and that we must love them tenderly and respect them deeply.

— Saint Louise de Marillac, D.C.

If you can't feed a hundred people, then feed just one.

— Saint Teresa of Kolkata, M.C.

It wasn't long before Char's knee returned to normal and she was back in the gift shop at Saint Anthony's.

"You can come to my place for Thanksgiving. I'm only about ten blocks from here," Mrs. Malley said.

"I appreciate that so much," Char replied, "but I've already got plans."

"Going to a friend's house?"

"No." Char glanced towards the glass enclosed display case housing a hundred rosaries of different sizes and colors.

"Well, where are you going? You can't spend Thanksgiving by yourself!" Mrs. Malley declared.

"I'm going to the Rescue Mission. They need volunteers," Char stated simply.

"Oh! That's wonderful. Do the volunteers get to eat for free?"

"Yup! Sure do," Char grinned.

"Well I hope they put on a good meal. If you want to, you could come over for dessert afterwards."

"Thanks, Mrs. Malley. But I'm probably just going to go home."

"Are you sure? I always have a big crowd on Thanksgiving! My kids will be there with their families, and my sister will be there, and her son, Robert, and my neighbor Sally across the street. Her husband died last spring and she's all by herself."

"Oh. It sounds really nice."

"Well, come if you can. You don't have to call or bring anything. Just come!"

"Thanks! I'll try."

Mrs. Malley pulled a pen out of her pocket and after fishing about for a few minutes, grabbed a small piece of scratch paper from behind the counter.

"Here's my address and phone number. It's just about a mile up on Mt. Troy Road. Big yellow house with green shutters. You can't miss it!"

Char smiled and nodded, folded the paper, and tucked it in her coat pocket.

* * *

Thanksgiving Day dawned cool and dry, a blessing for all the college kids heading home for the long holiday weekend. Even though she wasn't traveling, she was glad there was no rain in the forecast. She still didn't own an umbrella or a raincoat; she'd never needed one. It had hardly ever rained in Great Falls.

The bus down to the Rescue Mission was mostly empty. She arrived promptly at ten as instructed. After filling out a short volunteer application, followed by a quick orientation from the Volunteer Coordinator, Char was handed a heavy blue apron and a hair net and guided to the kitchen, where half a dozen people were rushing around putting together the final touches on a hot turkey dinner with all the fixings to feed the homeless members of the community.

Wielding a clunky yellow electric can opener and huge silver serving spoon, Char began opening five gigantic cans of cranberry sauce and emptying them into a large stainless-steel bowl. She'd never done much cooking at home, so it felt awkward at first. But she soon got the feel of pressing the turning, humming steel wheel as it churned into the top of the can and getting the sauce out of the can and into the bowl without making a gloppy, purple mess.

The first guests ("We always call the homeless our guests," the Volunteer Coordinator had stressed emphatically) began entering the facility at eleven, and by noon a long hungry line of people reached the back of the dining hall and circled around out the back into the parking lot facing the alley. There were whites, blacks, and Hispanics; men, women, and children. Some looked like they'd been living on the street for a while; others looked as ordinary as any middle-class family from Pennsylvania.

Standing at one of the tables laden with sumptuous holiday fare, Char gingerly ladled green bean casserole into their plates, wary of spilling any. At first, she was embarrassed to look at them, embarrassed by their poverty. Gradually, though, she began to look at their faces. Mostly they ignored her. They were too excited about the prospect of a big turkey dinner to pay much attention to the people serving it.

"Green bean casserole?" she asked. Everyone nodded.

"Thank you, young lady!" The man was older than her parents, but not elderly. Tufts of white hair stuck out from beneath a navy-blue ski cap.

"You're welcome!" Char relaxed a little.

"Green bean casserole?" she asked the next person, a woman just a few years older than Char with a young boy by her side.

"Yes, please!"

"That's my favorite," the boy said shyly.

"Well here's a little extra," Char said, heaping his plate high with the luscious dish.

The woman smiled gratefully, and Char began to feel as though a light were beaming out from inside of her.

At twelve-thirty, another volunteer, a young woman of about twenty-five, tapped her on the shoulder.

"My turn," she said. "You get to eat now."

Char smiled happily and handed over the ladle.

"Just go in the kitchen and help yourself to anything. You don't have to wait in line."

"Thanks! I'm starving!" Char scooted into the warm, spacious kitchen and quickly loaded a thick paper plate with turkey, dressing, mashed potatoes and gravy, and, of course, green bean casserole. A freshly baked roll and butter topped off the mountain of food. She balanced it all in her left hand and carefully picked up a cup of coffee with her right. Picking a table at the back, she sat down and quietly said grace.

As she ate, she watched the army of volunteers, a mix of students and retirees. There were ten servers at the tables where she had just been serving. Four more bussed the tables, pushing a huge gray trash can on wheels from table to table, throwing away trash and wiping up any spills. Still more rushed back and forth from the kitchen, carrying big tinfoil trays of hot food and carrying off the ones that had been emptied. It all worked like clockwork. A little boy rushed by carrying a piece of pumpkin pie and whipped cream like it was on fire, and she suddenly remembered Mrs. Malley's offer to come over for dessert after she'd served at the Mission. But after all that turkey, she couldn't imagine eating another bite.

What she really wanted was to go for a long walk. She needed time to think. The Thanksgiving break gave her the gift of unstructured time, a very precious commodity she never seemed to have enough of. She couldn't afford to waste it. Not when she had so many important things to consider. So she gathered up her things, threw away her trash, and after signing out with the Volunteer Coordinator, headed for the downtown bus that would take her to Point State Park.

Chapter 37: Converging

*In face of the mercy by which I have been chosen
for the service of the Lord, I can only think of the
words he spoke to Saint Catherine of Siena:
'I love you more than you love yourself.'*

– Dominican nun, aged 45, in religion 8 years

There is a large triangular park on the edge of downtown Pittsburgh where three great rivers meet. Just beyond the bustling downtown business district, a flat, grassy arrow of land with a majestic concrete-encircled fountain at the far corner points west like a baseball diamond surrounded on three sides by blue-gray ribbons, where the Allegheny and the Monongahela flow together to form the Ohio. At the Point, living history converges. Pennsylvania's past and present combine, creating the future for the proud people who live in that once-and-still-great state.

Built by European immigrants and their families, skilled craftsmen and laborers in Pittsburgh worked hard to create useful things—things that benefitted the daily lives of ordinary Americans—Heinz ketchup, Bayer aspirin, and American-made, best-in-the-world, U.S. Steel. But in the 1970s and 80s, good jobs once held by generations of Pittsburghers were deemed better invested in foreign countries where non-unionized workers would produce similar goods for lower wages, allowing American corporations and their shareholders to earn higher dividends. At the same time, the OPEC oil crisis gave the leading edge to Japanese carmakers and their fuel-efficient Datsuns, Hondas, and Toyotas. Detroit couldn't sell its gas-guzzling Cadillacs and Camaros anymore, so Pittsburgh couldn't market its most famous commodity: steel.

Within a short time, the steel mills closed. People lost their jobs, and in some cases, their homes; but they never lost their hope, their determination, or their Steelers pride. Eventually, the city once known for smoking steel mills would smartly reinvent itself as a

world-class medical provider and tech hub, and the tallest skyscraper in the city, the U.S. Steel Tower, would one day be known as
the UPMC Building—the University of Pittsburgh Medical Center.[8]

Char knew nothing of the history or the struggles of the people
of southwestern Pennsylvania. She knew nothing of their resource-
fulness, their resilience, and their tenacity. But it was there—in the
water, in the trees, in the buildings, and in the very air she
breathed. It was in the stately houses standing proudly on the edge
of Mt. Washington just above the quaintly venerable Duquesne
Incline tram. It was in the churches and the synagogues, in the
universities and the hospitals. It was in the crumbling bones buried
in the cemeteries dating from colonial times, and in the old abandoned coal tunnels winding underneath the neighborhoods. It was
there in four hundred steel bridges and fifteen miles of city streets
built of character-building stair steps. It was there now on the edge
of downtown at Point State Park, where Char was contemplating
her past, imagining her future, and wondering what it might hold.

From a far distance she spied the fountain. It had been turned
off at the end of October; cold weather was on the way. There were
few people out on Thanksgiving Day. Most people were with their
families—stuffing their faces, watching their televisions, and
putting up their Christmas trees. As she approached it, she wondered what her family was doing back home. They always ate late in
the day on Thanksgiving, which her father jokingly referred to as a
"holy day of gobbligation." At this her mother would always roll her

---

[8] Tragically, as of the date of this novel's publication, UPMC and the
University of Pittsburgh are engaged in grossly unethical research activity (e.g.,
"humanized mice"), using fetal tissue from elective abortions conducted in
their own facilities. "Human civilization is premised on respect for human
rights. We believe those rights begin at the first moment of conception to the
moment of natural death. Please pray with me for an end to these practices at
the University of Pittsburgh and its allied medical institutions." – Most
Reverend David A. Zubik, Bishop of Pittsburgh, October 12, 2021.

eyes, while she and Kayla would look at each other quizzically, not getting the reference to mandatory attendance at Mass.

Her mother had called a week ago, asking if she were coming home. Char had hesitated, not knowing how her mother would react. Inevitably, she'd pinned Char down, the expert lawyer cross-examining the witness. Char had no choice but to give in and tell her: The answer was no.

"Oh. Your father will be disappointed."

"That's what Kayla said."

"I'm sure she already told him. I wish she would have had the courtesy to inform *me*. I'm the one who is doing all the cooking," she sniffed icily.

"I'm sorry, mom," Char lied.

"Don't be. It's perfectly normal for college students to want to spend their Thanksgiving holiday alone in their apartments."

Char frowned angrily, but a pang of homesickness stabbed her heart. Why couldn't her mother just accept her for who she was? She wasn't a kid anymore.

"Well, I suppose you won't be home for Christmas, either."

"I'll be there. If you still want me," Char snapped.

"Oh, grow up, Char! I really don't have time for this right now."

"Okay, Mom. Mom, I've gotta go."

"I'm sure you do."

"Bye." Char snapped the cell phone shut and dropped it on the table with a loud whack.

* * *

The afternoon sun at Point State Park was just warm enough to stave off the damp and misty river chill. A few lone birds soared across the Ohio, rising up to the trees on the far shore by the Duquesne Incline. Only a few people were out: parents with strollers, solitary walkers like Char, young couples oblivious to everything but each other. Char thought of Aaron. He'd texted her the week before, but she hadn't answered. On she walked. She put in her earbuds and played her "walking" playlist—Satie's *Gnossienne #5;* Dvorak's *Romance for Piano and Violin.* Soon her steps became rhythmic and her breathing more even. Had she heard these mesmerizing pieces before, she might have become a musician like Celia. And on she walked.

She'd only been at Carnegie for a few months, but already it felt like college was making her into someone she didn't really want to be. It was like those cans of cranberry sauce. They filled her full of facts, then she opened the top of her head and dumped out the contents of her brain on multiple choice exams. This was education? For what? So she could get a job, earn money, and be a contributing member of society. Everyone did it. You played the game. But something was missing. School was great for learning facts, but there was something else out there, nagging at her. Something important.

The week before, at Mrs. Malley's prompting, she'd gone over to Holy Name Parish and made an appointment to see the pastor. He'd been very positive and encouraging, and asked her lots of questions. At the end of their meeting, he'd given her the number for the director of their RCIA program, Deacon Furmoile. She'd finally worked up the courage and called, and he'd invited her to start attending classes there once a week with other adults interested in learning about the Catholic faith. Then the following Easter, they would all be baptized, confirmed, and receive their first Holy Communion. It was all very easy and painless. All she had to do was show up. Then why did it seem so scary? Why did she feel like an adult one minute, and the next like a little kid needing her parents' approval?

When she finally reached the end of the Point, she stopped. There the three great rivers joined together, their deep waters invisibly blending into each other. Sitting on the edge of the concrete base of the fountain, she opened her book bag and took a drink from her water bottle. Then she dug around until she found one of the pamphlets she had picked up from the gift shop: a vocational brochure for the Little Sisters of the Poor. She carefully studied it once again, and then put it back in her book bag. They looked like a really good group, and she liked their apostolate of service to the elderly poor, but somehow it didn't feel right.

The air was turning colder now, and Char shivered. The sky had taken on a steel gray color, and the clouds were spitting sleet. Twilight was approaching; time to go. Looking up one last time at the big old homes on Mt. Washington, Char unexpectedly let out a little cry of pure delight. Magically and without warning, one of the houses had suddenly flashed into a magnificent display of brilliantly colorful strings of old-fashioned Christmas lights.

* * *

Later that afternoon, Char arrived home tired but happy. The walk had relaxed her. Strangely, when she reached the door of her apartment, there was a small folded note taped just below the peephole. She reached for it, hoping it wasn't from Aaron, and unfolded it to read.

"Dear Char,

I am sorry for being a total jerk. I wouldn't blame you if you didn't want to be my friend anymore.

I'm going home today, but if you want to go to Mass and breakfast on Sunday, call me.

Your friend (I hope),

Celia."

At that moment, the door to Celia's apartment opened a crack and quietly shut again. Char twisted her neck around to look. After a few seconds the door opened again, very slowly. Sheepishly Celia emerged. Her arms were folded protectively over her waist. She glanced at the far wall, then down at the gray hallway floor. Char's mouth opened slightly, waiting, but Celia remained silent.

Char spoke first. "Hi."

"Hi," Celia replied, still hugging herself, still staring at the floor.

"I got your note." Nervously Char waved the piece of paper as though Celia might not know which note she was talking about.

Hesitating, Char took a couple of steps. "How was your Thanksgiving?"

Celia shrugged and sighed. "Oh, you know. The usual. Turkey. Football. Chaos."

"Sounds like fun."

"How about yours?" Celia looked up.

"Oh, it was good."

"Did you go out?"

"Yeah, I went to the Rescue Mission."

Celia's eyes lit up. "You did? How was it? I used to want to do that, but I was afraid it'd be too depressing."

"It wasn't depressing at all. In fact, it was great, actually."

"Yeah? Cool."

"I think I'm going to go down there again in a couple of weeks if you want to come."

"Okay."

"So, you want to try for Mass again tomorrow?"

"Char, I'm so sorry about the other day. I really am."

"So, what happened?"

"I don't know. I just—I've had a lot of stuff going on lately, and...."

"That's okay."

Celia's face brightened like a sunlamp. "You forgive me?"

"Of course. Just this once."

Celia laughed. "Okay. I promise I will act like a responsible adult from now on."

Char snickered and shook her apartment keys, placing the key in the deadbolt. "Okay. I'll see you in the morning. Is ten okay?"

"Yeah! Great! Wanna go see *E.T.* after Mass?"

"I thought we were gonna eat first."

"Oh well, yeah. I meant after that."

"Sounds like a plan," Char agreed, letting herself into her apartment.

"Thanks Char." Celia grew serious. "See you tomorrow."

"Goodnight, Cece."

"'Night!"

Chapter 38: In the Churches

But as for me I have walked in mine innocence:
redeem me, and have mercy on me.
My foot hath stood in the direct way:
in the churches I will bless Thee, O Lord.

— Lavabo Prayers at Mass
1962 Roman Missal

This time, Celia was early. Char was in the bathroom, still in her long nightshirt and brushing her teeth when she heard three raps on the door. She rushed to rinse and then ran to let Celia in.

"Sorry, I'm kinda early. I wanted to make up for last time."

Char cast a sideways look at her before rushing back to the bathroom. "That's OK. I'm still getting ready," she replied over her shoulder.

"Where do you wanna go to Mass?" Celia called after her.

"Hold on." Char hurried to the bedroom, threw on a nice pullover sweater and her newest pair of jeans, pulled on her socks, and grabbed her phone off the charger. Putting on some lip gloss and a headband, she rushed back out to the living room where Celia was looking at the magazine Char had brought back from the gift shop.

"*Sacred Art & Architecture?* This is cool."

"Yeah, it's got some really beautiful photos in it. Check this out," Char riffled through the pages. "Isn't that just gorgeous?"

"'The Royal Monastery of Saint Mary of Pedralbes, founded by Queen Elisenda de Montcada in 1327.' Wow. Unreal!"

"So where are we going? I was thinking maybe the cathedral."

"Yeah, that sounds nice. But I was wondering if maybe..." Char hesitated.

Celia lifted her eyebrows. "Maybe what?"

"Well, I've never been to a Latin Mass, and I'd kind of like to go to one."

Celia's brows lifted even higher. "A Latin Mass? Where at?"

"Mrs. Malley said there's one at the old Saint Boniface Church on the North Side."

"Yeah, there is. Who's Mrs. Malley?"

"Mrs. Malley is the lady who runs the gift shop at Saint Anthony's. I've been volunteering there on the weekends."

"Oh! So you went without me."

Char's eyes darted around the room and back to Celia, who looked shocked and amused at the same time.

"That's okay," Celia smiled. "I'm glad you went. So what did you think? Isn't it great?"

"It's really amazing. I've never seen anything like it."

Celia nodded.

"It kind of freaked me out at first, all those bones and everything," Char added.

"Did you see Saint Anthony's tooth?" Celia mercilessly pressed for details.

"Yes," Char laughed.

"Brave girl!" Celia teased.

"Shut up!"

"Okay, okay," Celia said agreeably. "But if we're gonna get to Mass on time, we'd better get going." Then, under her breath she muttered, "Wish I would have known where we were going. I would've worn a dress."

* * *

A thin film of ice and snow covered the sidewalks. Celia hacked away at the rock-hard layer of ice obscuring the windshield of the sturdy Cordoba while the defroster blew full-bore. Char sat shivering in the passenger's seat, arms wrapped around her for warmth, rereading the rubrics of the Latin Mass. The windshield finally cleared, and soon they were smoothly cruising past miles of parallel parked cars whose owners were still sound asleep on a chilly Sunday morning. Minutes later they were speeding through the tunnel under the river and quickly emerged on to the nearly empty freeway heading north.

"Have you ever been to a Latin Mass?" Char asked.

"Yeah. I thought it was pretty antiquated at first, but then I kind of got into it," Celia replied. "It's so different than the regular Mass, the quote-unquote Novus Ordo. You have to really study the TLM to understand what's going on. But I like it way better now."

"TLM?"

"Traditional Latin Mass."

"Oh." Char thumbed through the Ecclesia Dei booklet again and frowned. "How do you remember all this?"

"You'll pick it up, don't worry. Just do whatever everybody else is doing."

"So where do you go to Mass now?" Char asked.

"Sometimes I go to the Oratory, sometimes I go to the Cathedral. It all depends."

"Do they have the Latin Mass at the Cathedral?"

"Nope."

"Why not?"

"No idea."

"Oh. Have you ever been to Saint Boniface's?"

"Unh-huh." Celia grunted.

"Well, that's the only Latin Mass around here, I thought."

"Yeah, you're right. It is." Celia answered.

Char paused. "Then where did you go when you went to the TLM?"

"I went to Immaculate Conception when I lived with my sister Nathalie and her husband in Cleveland last year."

"Oh. So why don't you go to Saint Boniface's?"

Celia threw a sideways look at Char and flexed her fingers on the steering wheel.

"I'm sorry," Char said apologetically. "I didn't mean to be nosy."

Celia scowled. "It's okay. I'm just lazy. I don't want to get up and drive all the way to the North Side to go to Church. I like to stay up late on Saturday nights, and it just doesn't work out. I mean, I could if I really wanted to, but it's the only day I get to sleep in. Three of my classes start at eight this year, and by Sunday I am totally wiped out."

"Yeah," Char agreed. "That's understandable."

"It's just a lot easier to drive a mile to the Oratory, you know?"

"Yeah."

"So thanks for getting my butt out of bed this morning, Char!" Celia joked sarcastically.

"Anytime," Char retorted.

* * *

St. Boniface's was spacious and lovely and full of people, mostly young families with children, a few elderly folks, and several serious-looking young adults. Most of the men wore suits and ties, and the women wore modest dresses or skirts and lacy veils over their hair. Char felt vaguely uncomfortable in jeans, even her nicest ones, but the man at the front entrance handing out bulletins and Ecclesia Dei booklets seemed not to notice. He just smiled and said, "Good morning," and motioned to a basket containing extra veils if they wanted to borrow one. It was entirely their choice. Celia grinned and grabbed a white one, lifted it up for inspection and then gleefully tossed it over her dark brown hair. Char followed suit, and as the old deep-toned bell began ringing the call to Mass, they chose a pew in the middle, genuflected, and knelt to pray.

Ten minutes later, a tinkling bell rang inside, and four altar boys in black cassocks and white surplices, bearing incense, a crucifix, and large candles, processed into the sanctuary, followed by two young adult servers and two priests in birettas wearing beautiful embroidered chasubles. They genuflected in unison before the Tabernacle, knelt briefly, and rose. As the choir sang a Latin hymn, the priest celebrant sprinkled holy water on the servers and all the people. Then they all went back to the altar, genuflected in unison once again, and with their backs to the people, with great reverence and concentration, the celebrant began offering the prayers of the Mass. There was more incense, more singing, and as the choir intoned the *Gloria in excelsis Deo*, the priest and everyone else sat down.

Celia pointed to the words in English in the Ecclesia Dei booklet, and Char tried to follow along as best she could. She couldn't understand a word of the Epistle read in Latin, but Celia showed her the text for that week in the bulletin, and later the priest read the Epistle, along with that week's Gospel, in English. The priest sat down again, and there was more singing—beautiful, otherworldly singing with organ accompaniment. Then there was more incense, and the servers came with their tall candles and stood behind the priest, who faced the altar and prayed quietly for what seemed to Char like ages.

Processing with the servers bearing sweet incense and candles, and facing the subdeacon holding open the large evangeliarium, the priest folded his hands to proclaim the Gospel in sung Gregorian chant. Then the other priest gave a homily. Then all the focus turned to the altar, most of which Char could not see. But she didn't mind because she was overwhelmed by a sense of rightness, a sense of mystery, of the hidden mystery of the Mass, which begged not so much to be understood as lived, revered, and humbly contemplated with profound, unending gratitude.

Then after the *Sanctus*, everyone knelt for the Consecration and kept kneeling for several minutes. One of the altar boys rang brass hand bells at the Consecration, at the Elevation, and again when the priest received Holy Communion. Then it was time to for everyone else to receive Holy Communion.

"You know you can't receive Communion, right?" Celia whispered. "Not until you're Catholic."

Char nodded and shifted on her knees. She knew that much. Only Catholics who were in a state of grace could receive Holy Communion. It was hard, though, watching the majority of the congregation go up to the altar rail and kneel to receive the Sacred Host when she had to stay behind in the pew. Was it her imagination, or was everybody looking at her? As she watched Celia slowly approach the Communion rail with the rest, one row of pews at a time, hands folded, she wondered what it was like. *How could one receive the Body of Christ,* she thought, *and not be changed* forever?

* * *

"Next weekend is Advent."

"What's that?" Char asked.

"That's the four weeks before Christmas. It's the beginning of the church year."

"I love Christmas! I can't wait to get back home." Char sighed.

"Yeah, Christmas is great. And then it'll be Easter before you know it. And then you can come into the Church, and we can have a huge party," Celia grinned.

Char leaned back on the headrest and smiled dreamily. "A party would be nice."

"Where do you want to go for breakfast?" Celia interjected.

"I don't care. Actually, on second thought, I'd rather have a hamburger. It's almost noon."

"Hmm," Celia pondered for a minute, then shouted. "I know! Primanti Brothers!"

"That sounds Italian."

"Really?" Celia snickered. "You're so observant, Char."

"Well, isn't it?"

"Yeah, but don't worry. It's not a pasta joint. They just have the best burgers on earth. Wait 'til you see them!"

"I know. It's a surprise, right?" Char teased.

"Let's just say, we make our burgers a little differently here." Celia imitated Groucho Marx holding a stubby cigar.

"I'll bet!"

"Pittsboigh-boigers!"

"I'm a Pittsburgher, you're a Pittsburgher, we're all Pitts-burghers! Even the burgers are Pitts-burgers!" And they cackled and guffawed.

On Smallman Street down in the Strip District, Celia parked the car. Originally the busy warehouse district by the Allegheny River in Pittsburgh's early years, many of the empty warehouses in the Strip District had recently been converted into modern urban condos commanding high prices, while the short, narrow side streets remained lined with imported food markets plus many newer eclectic shops and cafés. Nimbly Char got out of the car, slinging her purse over her shoulder and checking her phone.

"It's just a couple blocks," Celia said, pointing with her chin.

"That's good. I'm starving!"

Celia swiftly zipped up her jacket against the November cold, and they set out. A nearly empty bus groaned past, along with the occasional food delivery truck. Mass-goers at the iconic Saint Stanislaus's Church were on their way home. Tantalizing aromas of freshly ground coffee mingled with freshly baked Italian bread steamed up from the restaurants nearby. It was a family-friendly, safe spot to spend a Sunday afternoon.

After a short hike, they reached the corner of a narrow side street and stopped for the red light.

"And when we get done eating, we *have* to go to the Pennsylvania Macaroni Company." Celia jabbed the air with the flat of her right hand towards the iconic Italian market. "They have an authentic Italian deli with, like, a *hundred* different kinds of imported cheese and salami, I kid you not. They even have a self-serve olive oil station where you can bring your own container. They sell it by the *gallon!*"

Char smiled happily. "Oh wow! I'm gonna have to learn to cook Italian food, I guess!"

"Darn right. So. Char. Have you heard from Aaron lately?" Celia asked.

"No, and I hope I never do," Char responded passionately. She clicked her phone shut and reached for her purse to stow it away. Celia glanced at her to see if she was telling the truth.

"Maybe you should give the guy a chance, Char. Guys just sometimes don't have a clue, you know? Maybe you should just sit him down and..."

The light turned green, and the "walk" sign lit up.

"...and try to explain that..."

Char looked back at Celia and then down, shaking her head, and darted defiantly into the crosswalk.

And Celia lunged towards her, eyes bulging, muscles straining, throat convulsing into a stifled scream, vainly trying to reach her, trying to snatch her back out of harm's way. But it was too late, too late for anything except the screaming.

* * *

The world turned upside down. Or was she the one who had turned upside down? Char wondered vaguely, but in the end it wasn't important. She thought she heard Celia's voice calling to her from very, very far away, but she was flying, floating freely in mid-air now. And suddenly she was at Mass, and the priest was genuflecting, and holding up the Host, offering the Spotless Victim to God the Father, and a bright, silver-white light was shining out of the Host and into her eyes, so bright it hurt to look at it. And she heard voices, and she wondered whose voices they were. She had thought she was all alone.

But the light was too bright to look at, so she closed her eyes. And when she opened them again, a beautiful nurse wearing a blue cloak with a red cross on it was kneeling beside her. She was holding her hand and smiling sweetly. And the beautiful lady spoke.

"It's going to be all right, Char, I promise," the lady said kindly. "I'll be right here. Okay, Char? Everything is going to be all right. Everything is alright. And I'm right here."

Chapter 39: The Gates of Hell Shall Not Prevail

Yesterday is gone.
Tomorrow has not yet come.
We have only today.
Let us begin.

— Saint Teresa of Kolkata, M.C.

$\mathcal{B}$arbara Fisher stood at the nurse's station, pale and exhausted from the eight-hour journey from Great Falls. Gripping her Blackberry phone in one hand and a worn My Little Pony backpack in the other, she patiently waited for the nurse to answer her question.

"Four-oh-one. Yes, that's where she was yesterday. You're on the wrong floor, Mrs. Fisher. Char is down on the main floor now, Room 211."

"Thanks so much," Barbara Fisher muttered automatically and hurried back to the elevators from which she had just emerged, pushing the "down" button so hard her fingernails turned purple, and then white.

"Why can't these people get their act together?" she griped mechanically to no one and rubbed her eyes.

* * *

Char blinked blindly up at the ceiling. The lights were so bright! The long white fluorescent lamps looked just like the ones in the classrooms at CMR High School back home. But why was she lying flat on her back?

She was so sleepy. Then, she took a deeper breath and reached out with her right arm, only to panic when she felt the IV needle tubes taped securely to her thin wrist. Her puffy eyes widened as she looked down at her inert body lying flat in the hospital bed, covered in a spotless white sheet. A ghostly pale cast trapped her leg from her ankle halfway up to her pelvis, and her left arm and hand were completely covered in multiple layers of taped bandages, stained with her own blood. She gasped with a little cry of shock, then squeezed her eyes close again because it was too much to take in.

Maybe it wasn't real. Maybe she was hallucinating or something. She didn't want it to be real. *What happened? Where am I?*

"Hello, Miss Fisher!" A chipper young nurse whisked efficiently into her room. "'About time you woke up!" Gently she felt for Char's pulse. "How are you feeling, honey?"

Char swallowed. "I'm thirsty," she whispered hoarsely.

"Here, let me get you something. You want some water or some juice? I've got some nice apple juice."

"Juice, please." Her voice was scratchy and rough, the voice of a stranger she didn't know and didn't want to meet.

The nurse held a cup and straw up to Char's lips with one hand while supporting Char's head with the other. She took a long, slow sip before easing back on the pillow.

"Where am I?"

"You are at Presbyterian Hospital in Pittsburgh, P–A. And lucky to be alive, from what I've been told."

"What—what happened?"

"The lady you were with said you were hit by a delivery truck and almost thrown right into traffic. You could've been killed."

"Lady? What lady?"

"Char!!"

At the familiar sound, Char's eyes widened and swiveled towards the door. *"Mom!"*

"Oh, Char!" Barb Fisher made a beeline for the bed, and reaching it bent and kissed and caressed her daughter's tangled, matted hair over and over. "Oh, honey! Are you okay? I came as soon as I found out."

Char's hair smelled to her like sweet perfume, like a baby's soft fine hair, like summer sunlight after a hard, torrential rain; she inhaled it into her lungs like pure oxygen, drank it in like the sweetest, clearest water, as though her very life depended on her deeply imbibing it. And just like that, her fatigue vanished, just as it had twenty-one years before when she was a young mother with a new baby who insisted on waking her up every two hours to be fed, held, and changed.

"She just woke up a little while ago," the nurse said happily. "I was just about to get her some more juice. Would you like some, Mrs. Fisher? Some coffee? Water?"

Mrs. Fisher came to herself again and slowly stood up and stretched. "Some coffee would be divine, thank you. I haven't slept for two days."

"I'll be right back, Char!" And the efficient nurse bustled out of the room.

"Mom!" Char mumbled with tears in her eyes as she gazed into her mother's. "I'm so sorry! I don't know—what happened."

"That's okay, sweetheart. We'll figure it out. You just rest now. Look, I brought your old backpack, some notepads and pencils, some magazines, and some of your old CDs! And...ta-da! Mr. Peanut!"

"Mr. Peanut?" Char stared at her mother doubtfully. "The Planters Peanut man?"

"The one and only!" Barb lifted the tattered toy out of her backpack and presented it to Char like a gilded trophy.

Grinning, Char hugged it gently with her free arm. "Thanks, Mom!" she said weakly.

"You are most welcome! I have a feeling Mr. Peanut is very happy to be getting a hug from you again. It's been awhile."

Char chuckled, then grew quiet. She stared suspiciously, yet hungrily, at this new version of her mother. "Mom—I..." she began, then started to cough.

Protectively, Mrs. Fisher poured a cup of water from the pitcher on the bed stand and carefully put the straw up to her daughter's mouth so she could take a sip.

"Don't try to talk now, honey. We can talk later." Setting the cup down, she reached into the book bag and drew out a card. "Look! Here's a card from Daddy and Kayla."

Char's eyes glowed. As she opened it, the card played the theme from the TV show, *Wonder Woman*.

"I can't believe I used to like that show," Char groaned. Then she read the messages.

Hey, I'm the only one who gets to break bones in this family!

(Just kidding.) Get well soon Sis!

Love ya, Kayla and Mikel

The note from her father was more emotionally compelling.

Dear Peanut,

Please get well soon. I miss you and hope you feel better fast

so we can take this guy to court. See you at Christmas!

Love, Dad

At that moment, a middle-aged priest entered the room, carrying a small black suitcase. Seeing him, the motherly smile fell away from Barbara Fisher's face.

"Can I help you?" she asked coolly.

"Hello," the priest greeted them warmly and checked Char's name on the bed chart to be sure he had the right room. "Hi, Char. I'm Father Mitchell, one of the hospital chaplains. How are you feeling today?"

As he patiently waited for an answer, Mrs. Fisher looked quizzically first at Char, then back to the priest, and back to Char again.

A wan smile played across Char's face. Then she looked up apologetically at her mother and said, "Somebody must have told them I was Catholic."

Chapter 40: The Fire of His Love

May the Lord enkindle within us the fire of His love,
and the flame of everlasting charity.

– The Incensing of the Offerings at Solemn Mass
1962 Roman Missal

It was late afternoon the day before Christmas Eve, and the Fishers' home on North River Glen Drive was decorated to the hilt. Blue and white icicle lights dripped from the eaves, multi-colored nets of miniature lights covered every shrub, and an overinflated Santa in a flashing fiberglass sled pulled by inflatable reindeer glowed obesely in the front yard. Plastic candy canes, the kind Char and Kayla loved but their parents hated, lined the curving sidewalk. Pixie elves sat impishly on the mailbox, and a huge evergreen wreath with gold and silver ornamental balls lavishly adorned the front entrance where Paul, Kayla, Eric, and a woman Char did not recognize stood grinning and beaming as Barbara, assisted by the cab driver, helped Char slowly make her way on crutches up the snowy walkway.

"You made it!" Paul called out, walking out to welcome them and take Char's heavy suitcases from the cab driver. "Here you go, sir. Merry Christmas to you!" Handing the driver a twenty-dollar tip, Paul turned, first to kiss Barb and then to enfold his eldest daughter protectively in his waiting arms.

"I'm sorry, Daddy," Char said morosely, her head buried in her father's shoulder.

"None of that nonsense, now. We're just so glad you're okay," Paul said hugging her gently. "And you're home."

Kayla burst out the door with Mikel and ran to greet Char.

"Careful, Kay. No bear hugs! Your sister is pretty fragile at the moment," Mr. Fisher cautioned.

"Kayla Fisher! You take that child inside this very instant! He'll catch a chill!" Mrs. Fisher exclaimed.

"I know, Dad! Hey, Char! Say hi to Auntie Char, Mikel!" Kayla waved Mikel's hand in Char's direction. "Don't worry, Mom! He's warm as toast!"

"Hey, Mikel!" Char said weakly, grinning at the pudgy little toddler. "He looks just like you, Kay! What a cutie!"

"Please, Kayla. He doesn't have anything on except a t-shirt."

"Okay, mom. Geez!" Kayla rushed back inside, cupping the back of Mikel's head with her hand.

The woman Char did not recognize stood with her hands clasped in front of her, friendly yet rather formal, smiling as she observed the happy homecoming scene. As they all converged in the entry-way to return inside, she unobtrusively stepped back to make room for them. Eric Mattson had retreated to the dining room, trying to remain unnoticed. But Kayla quickly spotted him, and after handing Mikel to him, turned to help Char remove her winter coat and scarf and hat and hang them up in the closet.

"Can you give me a hand here, Eric?" Paul said. "Oh wait. I guess you've got your hands full there already. Kayla? Can I borrow Eric for a minute when you're done helping Char?"

"Sure, dad." Kayla beamed happily at Eric. "You can borrow him all you want. As long as you give him back."

Horrifically embarrassed, Eric gently handed Mikel back to Kayla and bent to pick up the suitcases Paul had indicated.

"Down the hall, fourth door on the right, if you would please. Thanks, Eric."

"No problem," Eric replied, glad to have something to do that didn't involve holding babies.

"So, can I get you girls anything? Hot spiced tea?" Paul asked. "I would have made glögg, but Char can't have any alcohol with her medication."

"Yeah, that sounds great," Char replied.

"So no more school for you for awhile, eh?" Paul said over his shoulder on his way towards the kitchen.

As Char eased down into the long leather couch, Kayla helped prop her leg up on the ottoman. "Nope, guess not."

"Kayla, can you help me with my bag, please?" Mrs. Fisher asked. "Just take this big one, and I'll get these others later. I've got to sit down."

"Sure, Mom. And then I've got to get Mikel a bath and ready for bed." Kayla replied and disappeared down the hall.

"Thanks so much." Barbara collapsed into a rocking recliner and pulled off her boots. "Paul, is there anything to eat? I've got to get something in my system. I can't eat those peanuts they serve on flights anymore."

Paul quickly returned carrying a huge tray with holiday paper plates and napkins, hot water for tea, honey, milk, cold cuts, cheese, veggies, dip, and Christmas cookies.

"Oh, thank God. I'm starved half to death."

"Anytime, milady," Paul replied gallantly. Then he offered the tray to Char, Eric, and the woman Char didn't recognize. "This is just to tide us over until dinner. Pizza should be done in about twenty minutes."

"Yum, pizza!" Char said.

"Char, your bed is ready whenever you are. Kayla will help you once Mikel's asleep."

"Thanks, Mom."

"Which is where I'm going, too," she announced after finishing off the tea. "It's been a long week. Hope you all sleep well."

"Goodnight, mom. And thanks for coming to get me," Char said, her eyes crinkling into an elfin smile.

"You're welcome, Char dear."

"No pizza?" Paul asked as his wife turned and gave him a peck on the cheek.

"Not for me, thanks. I'm sure it's delicious. Maybe save me a piece for tomorrow? Please?"

"I'm not making any promises with three hungry teenagers in the house, but I'll see what I can do," Paul grinned and kissed his wife on the cheek, momentarily embracing her.

Barbara laughed and headed down the hallway, and Paul followed. Char stared after them, wondering.

Sipping her tea and nibbling on a Christmas cookie, she gazed up at the big brick fireplace, roaring brightly with a crackling red fire. It looked like something out of a Charles Dickens novel. As her parents stood in the hallway talking in low voices, she looked around the familiar room. Christmas cards were lined up on the fireplace mantel like tombstones in a graveyard, bearing the names of all the people they once knew but would never see again. But it was all very festive. And there in the corner, across from the picture window with the drapes drawn back for all to see, was a breathtakingly lavish Christmas tree with dozens of colorfully wrapped gifts arranged beneath it. The sweet and spicy scent of balsam fir filled the room and mixed with cinnamon, nutmeg, and cloves emanating from the kitchen. It was impossible not to feel the holiday spirit.

It feels so good to be home, Char thought, and tears welled up briefly in her eyes. The force of her emotions surprised her. She had felt so very free, so very grown up in Pittsburgh, she just couldn't imagine wanting to be back in Great Falls again. But everything looked so comfortingly familiar—the people, the places, everything. Everything was where it was supposed to be, where she knew it should be. Tonight, the tree and the cards and the stockings all looked familiar, too, but there was something new. Something made this Christmas feel different, but Char wasn't sure what it was. *It must just be because I've been gone so long,* Char thought. *Or maybe it's these painkillers I'm taking... Or maybe...*

"Char?" The woman she didn't recognize was speaking to her in a gentle, slightly reticent voice. She was in her late sixties or early seventies, with gray hair cut very short. She looked like the bookish type but wore no glasses. And she was tall. Not as tall as her mother, but taller than her father by at least an inch. Her clothes were neat and clean but rather outdated, as though she had bought them new twenty years ago and taken excellent care of them.

Char turned her head towards her, wondering who she was. Something about her was vaguely familiar. Had she been a teacher at CMR High School? A relative of Eric's visiting from out of town? Then she noticed the small sterling silver cross pendant she wore around her neck.

"Hello, Char. It's so nice to finally meet you. I'm your Aunt Mary."

"Aunt Mary?" Char mouthed in response, half uncomprehending. Surely this wasn't... And then the woman smiled. The features looked strangely familiar, a face that was unmistakably like her father's and, oddly, like her own.

"Aunt Mary!" Char repeated, not knowing what else to say. Thankfully, she didn't have to say anything, because the woman she now recognized got up and very delicately put her arms around her niece. "It's so nice to finally meet you, Char."

Her father, who had just returned to the great room, came to the rescue. "And it's so nice to finally have you here. What took you so long?" he joked, knowing it hadn't been by deliberate choice.

"Well, it's a long story," she began gamely. "Why don't you tell it?"

"I'd love to, but I was just a little toddler at the time," Paul argued. "I think maybe you'd better be the one to explain."

The woman laughed, and dimples formed in her cheeks. "Oh, alright. I guess I can do that."

"But first, Char, I have to give you a message," Mr. Fisher interjected. "Your friend Tia called last month. That's how this all started, actually."

"Sister Tia called? What did she say?"

"She wanted to invite you to her clothing ceremony, but when you didn't answer her letter or return her calls, she got worried and called us."

"Oh, wow."

"I told her about the accident, and she was extremely concerned. I didn't know you two were such good friends."

"We aren't, really," Char replied. "I mean, we are kinda, sort of."

"She said she would have Masses said for you and for us, and that the nuns would be praying for us. And she made me promise to call them right away if you took a turn for the worse."

"Their prayers must have worked!" Mary said brightly.

"I'll say they did," Paul agreed. "The doctors said it was one of the fastest recoveries they'd ever seen. When your mother talked to Dr. Sanborn, he told her he didn't think you'd be able to walk for at least twelve weeks. Said there was no way you'd be home for Christmas."

"But here you are," Mary said.

"And here you are. So that's what got me to thinking. When she said "clothing ceremony," and talking about the nuns praying novenas for you, I started thinking about *you*," Paul said, looking at Mary. "You left when I was what, two? Three?"

"You turned three in August, and I left in September to join the sisters in Wisconsin. My clothing ceremony was in June, and you were there, Paul! I remember as clear as day."

"And I don't remember a thing."

"That's why we take pictures."

"And I still have a couple. I stole them out of Mom's photo album when I went to college," Paul confessed.

"Oh, so that's why they were all in a jumble," Char mused.

"That's right. I never took very good care of them, but somehow they survived."

"And I found them," Char added.

Mary's eyebrows rose. "You did?"

"Yup. After daddy took me up to the attic once, he showed me a picture of you, and I went back later and looked at all of them."

"Nosy creature, isn't she?" Paul said proudly.

"Be quiet, Paul."

"Yes, Sister."

"No, I'm not 'Sister' anymore. But I am still *your* big sister. So hush! Go on, Char."

Char giggled. It wasn't every day she heard an ex-nun telling her father to hush. "So anyway, I found two photos of you in your habit. One was older, and the other one was shorter."

"Yes, that was me in my modified habit. We went through many changes back then. Some good, some not so good."

Char was going to ask her to explain, but just then Eric emerged with Kayla.

"Mikel's asleep, finally! I think he picked up on all the excitement," Kayla said. "I didn't think he would ever fall asleep."

"Thanks for coming over to help out, Eric," Paul said.

"You're welcome. I'm gonna head home, I guess," Eric replied.

"Will you be able to join us tomorrow night? We're going to leave here about nine-thirty. Then a big feast after we get home, and open some presents," Paul said.

"Yeah, I'll be here. Sounds great! Well, goodnight everyone."

"Goodnight, Eric," Paul said.

"Bye, Eric," Char called out.

"See you, Char. Bye, Ms. Fisher," Eric said to Mary, who waved in reply.

As Kayla and Eric headed out the front door, Char caught a glimpse of the colorful lighted Christmas wreath adorning the doorway outside.

"So, what's tomorrow night?" Char asked as the front door clicked shut.

"Why Char! Don't you realize? It's Christmas Eve," Mary said incredulously.

"Yeah, I know. But besides that. Where are you guys all going?" Char looked from her aunt to her father and back again.

Paul smiled. "Well, we thought that since you've decided to become Catholic, you might like to go to Midnight Mass."

"Midnight Mass? Us?" Char gasped. "No way!" Not her parents. Not ever.

"Yes. Us," Paul replied.

"And who suggested this grand idea?" Mary chided.

"Well, it was *your* idea. But I'm the one who talked Barb into it," Paul retorted. "And that was no mean feat."

"I'm sure it wasn't," Mary replied dryly.

"Where are we going?" Char asked excitedly.

"St. Ann's Cathedral. I hear they have an excellent priest from Ireland and a superb choir."

Wow, wait 'til Celia hears about this, Char thought. She'd planned on going to Midnight Mass, but she'd assumed she'd be going by herself, not accompanied by her entire family. And here it was being handed to her, gift-wrapped, and she hadn't said a single word about it to anyone.

* * *

"You need anything tonight, just holler," Kayla said. "I'll be right next door!"

"Thanks, Kay. I'm sure I'll be fine." Char eased gingerly into the wonderfully familiar sheets and blankets of her very own bed.

"You took your pain pill?"

"Yes, thanks."

"There's only four or five left in the bottle. Do you need us to get you some more?"

"No, that's okay. I'll be fine. Thanks." Char smiled and sighed as she eased under the covers. "It's so great to be home again."

"And it's great having you here. I've missed you. Um, Char? Can we talk?" Kayla perched on the edge of Char's bed and clasped her hands between her knees. "I wanted to ask you something."

"What?"

"Remember that day a couple of months ago when you called, and you asked me if I ever thought about God?"

"Yeah." Char tried to conceal her excitement.

"I wanted you to know I thought about what you said. I wanted to talk about it, but Mom was right there, so I couldn't. But I thought about it."

"Oh?" Char gingerly propped herself up on one elbow.

"Yes. And, well... You've got to promise not to say anything to mom or dad!"

"Okay. I won't."

"You know how when I had my accident, when I fell?"

"Yeah."

"You weren't here, or I would have told you then, but..."

"But what?"

"I saw an angel, Char. I fell, and I blacked out, and it hurt so bad. But then I saw an angel."

Char struggled up to a sitting position. This was simply too good to listen to lying down.

"How do you know it was an angel?"

Kayla stood up and paced to the window and back again. "Because—I don't know, Char. I just do! He was like all shimmery and blurry and stuff. And he smiled at me, the sweetest, most wonderful smile I ever saw! He was standing right between Mrs. Kellogg and Brittney and all the kids. And they were all looking at me, laying on the ground, and they were scared and crying and worried. But not him! He was just smiling and smiling at me like he loved me more than anything, like it was the happiest day of his life. I'll never forget it, I swear, as long as I live!"

"Wow, Kayla!"

"And I couldn't tell mom and dad, because I knew they'd just say it was the accident, I hit my head or something, and I was seeing things. But I wasn't seeing things. I mean, I *did* see him. He was there. He was real!"

"That's so awesome, Kay. I'm glad you told me," Char said.

"And I was like, okay, if angels are real, that means that God is real too, right?"

"That kind of makes sense."

"Or at least, God *might* be real. Only, we don't find out until after we've died! So like, it's kind of stupid not to believe in God when you don't really know for sure, because if He is real, and you didn't go to church and live a good life, when you're dead it'll be too late!"

"Yup. You've got a point there."

"I got a second chance, Char. And I don't want to blow it. So, I talked it over with Eric, and he said it's okay if I get Mikel baptized. And I want you to be his godmother. Will you, Char?"

"Oh, Kayla," Char reached out and hugged her sister. "I would be honored to be Mikel's godmother!"

"I'm going to have him baptized Mikel Charles."

* * *

Christmas Eve dawned clear, cold, and windy. Char rested on the couch, watching Kayla play with Mikel, who talked non-stop and wanted to know what was the great big sock on her leg. While their parents slept in, Aunt Mary was up early and cooked eggs and oat-meal, watching Kayla feed Mikel, who managed to smear most of it all over his high chair and his face and toss the rest on the floor. But a goodly portion got into his stomach, so all was well.

"You need to get a dog," Aunt Mary said, "to clean up all this food!"

"That's a great idea!" Kayla said, scooping up bits of egg from the floor and throwing them into the garbage can. "You are a messy boy!" she teased as Mikel busily sucked oatmeal off his pudgy fingers.

"Either that or a compost pile."

"Yeah. We never did have a vegetable garden. Maybe next year."

Aunt Mary walked to the sink and rinsed the washcloth out, wringing it and hanging it up to dry.

"I'm so glad I got to meet Eric, Kayla. He seems like such a fine young man," Aunt Mary said.

Kayla beamed as she spooned the last of the oatmeal into Mikel's mouth. "Yeah, he's pretty great, alright!"

"Any wedding plans in the future?"

A slight shadow crossed Kayla's youthful features, but only for an instant. Smiling brightly, she shrugged and wiped the mess off Mikel's face and hands. "I don't know. I hope so!"

"Have you talked with him about it very much?"

Kayla's face grew thoughtful. "Not too much. Not lately anyways. We did at first, only he was really not into it."

"Oh."

"But that was a long time ago. Anyway, he *has* been coming over a lot lately, so..."

"Oh, that's good," Mary said encouragingly. "I hope he keeps coming over. A boy needs his father. Especially as they get older."

Kayla nodded. "Um-hmm. I agree completely. I would never want Mikel to grow up not knowing his dad. I just hope...I just hope that someday it works out for us to get back together. Even if we don't actually get married. You know, I think the whole idea of marriage just scares guys off. It might be easier to just live together a while, so he won't feel like I'm trying to force him into it or something."

"Well, Kayla," Mary began. "I don't really know you or Eric, but I have to say from my experience in the school system, the children that were happiest and healthiest were the ones whose parents were married and living in the same household. I can't say all of them were, but the majority were. If you just let Eric move in here, he won't legally be responsible for supporting you and Mikel. He can just come and go as he pleases. And that wouldn't be fair to you or Mikel."

"Yeah, I've talked to Mrs. Johansen about this a lot! My friend Annie's mom? And she just is like, 'Kayla Fisher, you make that Mattson boy marry you!'" Kayla laughed. "And I'm always like, 'I'm trying! I'm trying!' And she says Eric was too young, but he's a good guy, and as soon as he graduates he'll be going to work at his dad's company, and then he'll be more ready to settle down, I guess."

"Well, it sounds like you're getting some good advice."

"Yup! I think so." Kayla agreed, lifting Mikel out of his high chair. "It was really nice talking to you Aunt Mary!" And she leaned over and gave her a sweet, tight hug.

"Thank you Kayla! You too!"

And as Kayla carried Mikel down the hall, Mary Fisher took a deep breath and wiped her eyes with the back of her hand.

* * *

"Hey, Cece!" Char excitedly answered the call.

"Hey, Charlie!" Celia shouted into the phone. "How's it going? Where are you?"

"I'm back in Great Falls. Why are you shouting?"

"Oh, sorry. I thought, Montana and all. But how are you?"

"I'm pretty banged up," Char laughed. "I've got a big cast on my leg, but I'm getting around okay."

"Can you walk?"

"Yeah, I've got these crutches. Kind of a pain, but better than a wheelchair, I guess."

"So—your family all doing okay?"

"Yup. Everybody is fine."

"That's good."

Char lowered her voice to an operatic whisper. "You'll never guess who's here!"

"Who?" Celia whispered back.

"Aunt Mary! My aunt who was a nun! She's here!"

"No!"

"Yes! And she's like seventy or something, but she's really nice."

"Cool! She looked you guys up?"

"No, I think my dad found her. He said my friend Sister Tia called to invite me to her clothing, and when I didn't call back, she called here. And he said he started thinking about her. I guess he hadn't seen her since she left to go in the convent. And then—I'm not too sure about the rest. We haven't really had a chance to talk much."

"Oh, yeah. You'll probably get a chance to talk in a couple of days. Holidays are the worst times for trying to have a private conversation," Celia opined.

"Yeah. But hey, get this: my dad is taking us to Midnight Mass!"

"Get out!"

"For real, I kid you not. I about fell on the floor when he told me. I don't know what he did to my mother to get her to agree, but whatever it was…"

"He didn't do anything."

"Huh? What do you mean?"

"I mean, he didn't have to do anything to your mom. God did it all."

Oh, here we go, Char thought. *Another E.T.-is-Jesus story.*

Celia didn't miss a beat. "I talked to your mother on the phone after the accident. Do you . . . How much do you remember, Char?"

"From the accident?"

"Yeah."

"Not much. I remember—the last thing I remember is us driving in the car after Mass, and then," Char wrinkled her nose and frowned, "it's kind of fuzzy."

Celia cleared her throat audibly.

"So, what happened, exactly?" Char demanded. "You saw it all, right? I'm so sorry, Celia. I'm such a dork, I must have walked right into the street or something."

"It wasn't your fault, Char. We had a walk signal. We had the green light, and you were in the crosswalk. No. Not your fault at all."

Char sighed with relief.

"No, what happened was, we were walking to Primanti Brothers, and we were talking, and I asked you about Aaron, and right then the light changed. And you…" Celia's voice cracked and rose half an octave higher. "You kind of looked away and stepped into the crosswalk, and this *truck* barreled right into you."

"Oh." Char's voice grew childlike.

"I don't know if his brakes failed, or they locked up on the ice or what, but he hit you at like twenty miles an hour at least. At least." Celia's voice was venomous. "And you went flying through the air, and you land right in the middle of Smallman Street, and all these cars slamming their brakes and swerving around trying to not run over you. And your bag went flying, and your cell phone, and half the stuff in your bag. And I'm running out in the street, and this off-duty cop pulls over and calls 9-1-1 and parks right behind you so nobody can run you over. And while he's doing that, I run and pick up all your stuff out of the street and grab your cell phone and your missal. And the ambulance came really fast—I think cos that cop was the one who called—and they had you up in the back of that thing in like five minutes flat. And the cops came too. And they asked me questions for like fifteen minutes, and I was like 'Let me go to the hospital with her! She could die and I'll be here talking to you!' But the driver, God bless him, he confessed everything, standing there crying like a little kid. And so they let me go find you. The off-duty cop—Steve Sylvester, Sylvestri, was his name I believe—called around and told me where they'd taken you. And I went to Presby and you were in surgery for maybe two hours? And then you were in recovery, and then finally they took you to a room and I got to see you for like five minutes, and they made me leave."

Celia finally took a breath. Char swallowed hard.

"But then I got to see you the next day, and you sort of came to a little. They said you had a broken femur, a lacerated left elbow, a concussion and compound fractured right tibia, and a bunch of other stuff I can't remember at the moment." Celia took another deep breath. "And I called your mother on your cell phone."

"Oh, thanks Celia." Char whispered. "Thank you."

"You're welcome. I'm just sorry you're having to go through this. But it's all God. Your mother was beside herself. I mean, really beside herself. First thing she says was, '*Were you drinking?*' And I says, "No, Mrs. Fisher, we weren't drinking. We'd just gotten out of church and we were on our way to lunch.' And she goes, '*Church?*' and I says 'Yes, ma'am.' And she got really quiet. And then she goes, '*Well, so much for going to church.*'"

"She said that?"

"Yeah! And I was like, you know, lady, your daughter could have been killed, and if I were you, I'd be on my knees thanking almighty God for sparing her, not blaming Him for some accident some idiot driver caused that didn't know how to drive properly."

"You *said* that?"

"I did, yes. More or less."

Char groaned. "Oh, my gosh."

"But I was upset. I'm sorry."

"So then what did she say?"

"She didn't say anything at first. Like, I think it started to sink in how bad off you were. And she said something about needing to book a flight, and hung up. And that was it."

Char sighed and wiped the sweat off her hands onto her pants leg. Her stomach was doing flip-flops.

"But there's something I need to ask you, Miss Charlie."

"What's that? My blood type? It's AB."

"No, what I want to know is—if it isn't too personal—who was that lady you kept asking about?"

"Huh? What lady?"

"When you came to—well, you weren't really all there yet. You were like half awake, half dreaming or something. You looked at me and you kind of smiled, but you didn't really recognize me, I don't think. You kind of were in and out. But you opened your eyes, and you looked at me and said, 'Where is the beautiful lady? Where is she?' And I thought maybe you were talking about one of the nurses, but they all looked pretty ordinary to me."

Char looked over at the big picture window. The northern sun was shining weakly but clearly, illuminating the dust motes and turning them into sparkling fairies dancing in the air over the leather love seat and the brass plant stand with the big dracaena by the entryway. And below it the perfectly symmetrical red poinsettia plant with the wide red satin bow, the annual Christmas gift from the Fishers' law firm to all the partners, associates, and their families. Then she looked back at the cast sheltering her shattered leg, and once again she tried to remember what had happened that day. Celia's story had filled in the pieces, but there was still a big blank spot in her memory.

"And you kept asking, so I said, 'I don't know, Char, what lady?' I felt bad, cos you were like really worried about it. You kept asking me, 'Where is the beautiful lady?' It was weird."

Trying to remember, Char seemed to recall being in the back of the ambulance, lying flat on a hard gurney, an immobilization collar around her neck, the EMT sitting beside her, taking her pulse, asking her name over and over. She tried to recall getting out of Celia's car, walking together to the corner. But all she could remember was leaving Mass and saying she'd rather have lunch than breakfast because it was almost noon. She couldn't remember getting hit, and she couldn't remember any lady.

"I don't know. I have no idea." Char said weakly.

"Oh." Celia paused for a brief heartbeat. "Oh. You must have been wanting your mother."

"Yeah, that must have been it," Char mused.

"Yeah. Well, I'd better let you go. You probably need to rest," Celia said kindly.

"Thanks for everything, Celia. I mean that."

"You're welcome. And you hurry up and get back out here, okay?"

"Okay, Cece."

"Oh, and Mrs. Malley sends her love. She is having Mass said for you at Holy Name."

"Oh, that was sweet of her. Thanks, Celia!"

"I hope you guys have an awesome Christmas!"

"Thanks, you too!"

"Merry Christmas, Charlie!"

"Merry Christmas!"

"Bye."

As she slowly closed her phone, all of a sudden it hit her—the full force of the truth. Just as her mother had, she understood for the first time how perilously close she had come to dying.

Chapter 41: Yours and All for You

I find no renunciation but only a great joy in leaving the past to God and counting on him and his grace for tomorrow. Each day I begin anew, hoping to do better than the day before. But as I know my own weakness, I ask God for his grace, 'just for today'; and tomorrow will be another today, and so on until the day of the eternal wedding feast.

– Visitation nun, aged 70, in religion 44 years

Sister Anthony had spent the last two weeks in retreat, preparing for this most solemn event. She had to make absolutely sure that she was ready. After tomorrow, there was no turning back. It seemed like only a few months ago, not six challenging years, since she had entered the monastery. How afraid she had been when she first entered, but that had soon been replaced by a lasting peace. Her family had been so upset at first—especially Troy. He didn't seem to understand that she wasn't entering the monastery to get away from them. She wasn't running away from something, she was running *to* something—or rather, to someone. To Christ.

She read Char's last letter once again. It seemed impossible that nine years had passed since they'd first met. Char had changed so much. *I hope she'll be here tomorrow.* Sister Anthony mused. *I'll look for her after Mass.* She wanted Char to meet her family and for them to meet her. Strangely, even though they hadn't spent much time together, Sister Anthony felt a special bond with Char that went beyond simple friendship.

After six years, Gloria had finally accepted her daughter's vocation and came to visit as often as she could. Troy had changed, too. He lived in his own place now, a tiny apartment about four blocks from Willie Pearl's old house. He'd finally earned his GED and had just been accepted to an electronics trade school in San Antonio. Soon he'd be leaving Cleveland and moving in with their Uncle Ross while he studied to become a sound technician. She'd never seen him happier. Everyone in her life had changed. Had she changed, too? Sister Anthony felt just like the same person she'd always been. But after tomorrow, everything would be different.

Reflectively, Sister Anthony began to reminisce on her earliest days in the monastery. The headband on the postulant's veil had been too small, so she had asked for a larger one. That one, naturally, had been too big and kept slipping off. The plain dress she was given to wear by the nuns felt strange after years of wearing jeans. She had been terrified of making a mistake in choir, afraid that all the nuns were looking at her and judging whether or not she was fit for religious life. In actuality they were all very kind and helpful and tried to allay her fears, but she still worried that she wasn't good enough.

Eventually, she got into the daily rhythm of prayer, work, and rest. But when the nine months' postulancy ended and she was formally received into the community, wearing the habit with the white veil and being called by her new name, Sister Mary Anthony Therese—Sister Anthony for short—the anxiety began all over again.

The novices were formed and tested much more strictly than the young postulants were, so her canonical year had been painful at times. "The pain you are feeling, Sister Anthony, is the hammering and sawing of the angels building a beautiful cathedral inside of you," Mother Bonaventure had often said. Sometimes she even wondered if maybe she had been wrong about having a religious vocation. Then, as now, she poured out her heart to Father Ambrose, the Capuchin confessor who served as the nuns' chaplain.

Father Ambrose was a wise old friar. He had been in religious life for over forty years, and he knew the pitfalls and heartaches that lay in wait for every man or woman trying to achieve evangelical perfection. His gentle, friendly voice in the confessional booth was unfailingly positive and kind, and Sister Anthony always told him everything—how she worried about her family, how she struggled with making the sacrifice of her entire life to be spent in one place, never to see the world, never to know the joy of having children with a loving husband. She confessed to having doubts about her vocation, and even sometimes feeling angry at God for asking such a sacrifice of her. How could she spend the rest of her life praying every day for people she didn't even know?

"Remember Our Lady," Father Ambrose advised in grandfatherly tones. "She knows what it's like to make difficult sacrifices—impossible sacrifices for God. Ask her to help you, and I promise she won't let you down."

"But sometimes I just feel like I'm making a big mistake," she said quietly. "Sometimes when I smile at the older sisters, they don't even look at me! I feel like I'm all alone in this place."

"You must never feel alone, Sister. God is always with us. But remember, we aren't here to feel loved, but to love God and others," Father Ambrose said slowly. "It's never a mistake to give your life to God. He is the one who led you here, through the love of your grandmother and through the love you had—and still have—for your brother. Jesus will never abandon you, or him. Just keep letting Him lead you, every step of the way."

"But how do I know for sure?" she begged.

Father Ambrose shifted in his chair. "I've been in vows now for forty-three years. Some days, I am completely convinced that my becoming a Capuchin friar was the biggest mistake ever made in the two-thousand-year history of the Roman Catholic Church!"

She smiled at that. Father Ambrose was the holiest priest she'd ever known. It was inconceivable to her that his being a Capuchin could have ever been anything but the perfect grace and mercy and wisdom of God.

"But most of the time—not all of the time, but most of the time," he said thoughtfully, "I know I made the right choice. You can never be absolutely, one hundred percent sure all of the time, Sister. We humans are weak creatures. We second-guess ourselves and ask ourselves 'what if.' What if I made a mistake? What if God intended for me to be married, or to have a career? And of course, the devil doesn't want us to have any peace, either, and he tempts us with all kinds of doubts and worries. So we just have to take it one day at a time. That's all He ever asks of us, Sister. Just one day at a time. For your penance, please recite the Litany of Our Lady. And now, make an Act of Contrition."

"Oh my God, I am heartily sorry for having offended Thee...." Gratefully she recited once again the traditional prayer of sorrow for her sins before receiving sacramental absolution.

"Through the ministry of the Church, may God grant you pardon and peace, and I absolve you from your sins, in the name of the Father, and of the Son, and of the Holy Spirit."

"Amen."

"Your grandmother will be so proud of you, Sister," Father Ambrose whispered. "You know she'll be watching when you make your vows!"

"Yes! Thank you so much, Father!" And her heart soared with happiness.

* * *

Now, at last, it was here. In less than sixteen hours, she would finally be professing solemn vows in the presence of the bishop, Mother Bonaventure, and all the nuns. Alone in her cell after Compline, she wrote down the names of all the people and intentions she wanted to pray for. She would pin the piece of paper beneath her scapular over her heart, confident that her Heavenly Spouse would bless all of her family and friends as she made the total gift of herself in holy religion. She would carry them all in her heart as she gave herself to the Lord to be His alone. The last name she wrote was the name of her father, William Jackson, that God might bless him, wherever he was.

Earlier that day in Chapter, after a short prayer, Mother Bonaventure read some announcements in her clear, calm voice, including the reminder that Auxiliary Bishop Grimes would be coming tomorrow for Sister Anthony's solemn profession and reception and that Father Pio would be traveling from the provincial house to preach their annual retreat the following week. Then she cleared her throat and pulled out a thick sheet of paper—a letter from the Vicar General of the Diocese.

"I know we are all very happy about Sister Anthony's profession tomorrow. I wondered if I ought to postpone reading this to you, but I decided against it. I have an announcement from the diocese which I must read to you."

"'In accordance with the directives issued by His Excellency, Bishop Robert Leon last May, following implementation of the second phase of Bishop Joseph Shaw's Vibrant Parish Life initiative, and after careful review of the recommendations of the Vibrant Parish Life Committee in collaboration with the pastoral staff of those clusters identified below as well as the recommendations of the Presbyteral Council, and in order to preserve and reconfigure the presence of the Church to continue to meet the needs of the People of God in a prudent manner, taking into consideration the resources available to us at this time and for the foreseeable future, the Vicar General has been instructed to announce the names of the following parishes in the Cleveland diocese which have been identified as suitable for merger or closing.'"

The Chapter Room grew deathly still. There had been talk of parish closings ever since Bishop Shaw's Vibrant Parish Life committees were formed the year before, but no one knew if, when, or where the hatchet was going to fall. An icy chill descended on the nuns as Mother Bonaventure slowly read the very long list. A few minority parishes were named like Saint Cecelia's on the border of Shaker Heights, but mainly the list contained the names of venerable old ethnic parishes founded in the nineteenth or early twentieth centuries by immigrants to America from Eastern Europe, plus a few others. These were the iconic parishes of Italians, Hungarians, Lithuanians, Germans, Slovenians, and Poles where generations of Catholics had worshipped in the old neighborhoods in Slavic Village, Lakewood, and Brooklyn Center, and further out, even as far as Cleveland Heights and Brook Park and beyond: Sacred Heart, Saint Hedwig's, Saint Casimir's, Saint Hyacinth's, Saint Barbara's, Saint Emeric's, Saint Mary of the Annunciation, Corpus Christi, Saint Cecelia's, Saint Ann's, Saint Rose of Lima, and on and on and on and on. It was painful to read, and still more painful to hear. When she got towards the end, a few of the nuns gasped. Holy Angels Monastery was on the list.

Mother Bonaventure peered intently at the faces of her nuns, gauging their reactions. Sister Margaret Clare raised a small white hand, requesting permission to speak.

"Yes, Sister?"

"Will there be any way to appeal these closings?"

"It's possible. We won't know until next year which parishes will close and which ones will remain open."

"What will happen to us if we're no longer a parish?" Sister Bernadette asked, her voice quavering.

"We will pray that does not happen. Even so, we would still retain our monastery under the Capuchins. In that regard, nothing would really change."

Sister Agnes spoke bluntly. "My nephew lives in Boston. The archdiocese closed his parish down four years ago along with sixty-five others, but some of the people started a prayer vigil there to keep it open twenty-four hours a day while they appeal to Rome. There's been someone there in that church ever since."

"Yes. We must pray for those who are fighting to keep their parish homes," Mother Bonaventure said in a firm, unwavering voice, "and for those who have moved on to other parishes in their cluster. And we must pray very much for Bishop Leon, and for all the priests of the Diocese." Her arm swung wide, her iron finger irrevocably carving a semicircle in the air as she pointed to the crucifix on the wall behind her. "Whatever may or may not happen, and however long this process takes, we must stand with all of them there—with Mary at the foot of the Cross."

She paused and then continued, choosing her words carefully. "I don't need to tell you, dear sisters, that these are very hard times in the Church. Not only here in Cleveland, but throughout the world. Our own Bishop Leon came here from Boston just two years ago. Things were much worse there. Much worse. Bishop's own childhood parish was one of the ones closed in Boston."

The shocked nuns listened attentively, but without anxiety.

"No matter what you may hear from your families or friends, no matter what you may read in the newspaper, there should be no discussion of these matters among yourselves and certainly no criticism of the hierarchy. I will keep you up-to-date as I am able. And of course, if you wish, you may speak with me personally, or to Father Ambrose."

Her mouth set resolutely, Mother Bonaventure folded the letter from the Vicar and placed it back in its envelope. She directed a serious gaze at her daughters.

"These are days when our prayers and sacrifices are needed most desperately. These are days when we are called upon to be saints, saying with Mary, '*Ecce, fiat.* Be it done unto me according to Thy Word.'"

Mother Bonaventure paused only briefly before intoning the final prayer. "Our help is in the name of the Lord," she said, making the sign of the Cross.

"Who made Heaven and Earth," the nuns murmured.

"Hail Mary, full of grace, the Lord is with thee. Blessed art thou among women, and blessed is the fruit of thy womb, Jesus." Mother prayed, and the Sisters responded.

"Holy Mary, Mother of God, pray for us sinners, now and at the hour of our death. Amen."

* * *

The next day at Mass, as the nuns sang the Litany of the Saints, Sister Mary Anthony Therese lay prostrate on the floor of the Sisters' chapel. She was covered with a pall, the large white cloth used to cover caskets at funerals, because Tia Esperanza, the person she had once been, was now dead to the world and would never return to it. Offering herself to God before the bishop, the nuns, and all those present, she knelt before Mother Bonaventure, placed her hands in hers, and solemnly pronounced her vows:

"I, Sister Mary Anthony Therese, wish to follow the life and poverty of our most high Lord Jesus Christ, and to persevere to the end. And I vow to God, before the Blessed Virgin Mary, and I promise you, dear Mother, to observe for the whole time of my life the holy Gospel of our Lord Jesus Christ, by living in obedience, without property and in chastity, in the form of life which the blessed Francis gave to our Blessed Mother Clare and Pope Innocent IV confirmed. And I vow to observe enclosure."

Mother Bonaventure accepted them, saying, "I receive these vows on behalf of the Church and the Order. What you have vowed to God render to Him faithfully, and he shall reward you. Look up to Heaven, dear one, which beckons us on, and take up your cross and follow Christ who walks ahead of us. For whatever tribulations we may have here, we shall enter through Him into His glory."

Everyone watched while she signed her vows at the altar. Then the bishop prayed, "Lord, send the gift of the Holy Spirit upon your handmaid who has left all things for your sake. May her life reveal the face of Christ, your Son, so that all who see her may come to know that He is always present in your Church. We pray that in freedom of heart she may free from care the hearts of others; in helping the afflicted, may she bring comfort to Christ suffering in

His sisters and brothers; may she look upon this world and see it ruled by His wisdom. May the gift she makes of herself hasten the coming of His kingdom and make her one at last with your saints in Heaven. We ask this through Christ our Lord. Amen."

Bishop Grimes then placed a silver ring on her finger, and Mother Bonaventure placed a crown of thorns on her head in imitation of the one Christ, her beloved Spouse, had worn during his Passion and death. Joyfully she then embraced each of the nuns, one by one—her sisters in religious life. Then the bishop continued on with the Mass, offering the Spotless Victim upon the altar.

As Sister Mary Anthony Therese slowly approached to receive the Lord in Holy Communion, she was a bit surprised to feel as though nothing had changed. She was still herself; she was still a bride of Christ. Only now, those promises were written forever on the Heart of God, sealed with the eternal vows she had freely given and which the Church had accepted. No one could ever take that from her. She belonged entirely to Him, now and for all eternity!

In giving herself to God, she knew that in reality she was being given to others as well. She would spend the rest of her life offering prayers of praise, petition, and thanksgiving on behalf of the entire Catholic Church. And not only for the Church, but for all of those who had no one to pray for them, those who had never known Christ, those who could not or would not pray for themselves. She would offer herself for all of them just as Christ had done and continued to do each day at the Holy Sacrifice of the Mass in churches throughout the world.

Carefully carrying these intentions in her heart, Sister Mary Anthony Therese approached the white marble altar. The nuns had decorated it beautifully. Illuminated by tall candles and surrounded by vases of flowers, the Altar of Sacrifice was now the Holy Table of the Wedding Feast where she approached to receive her beloved Jesus in Holy Communion. As she received the small white Host on her tongue, all traces of doubt and anxiety left her. She gave thanks to God for this great gift, this confirmation of what she had felt so deeply for the past seven years—that she had been created for God alone. And the Lord in His sweet generosity filled her with Himself, an ethereal effusion of untold love, light, joy, and peace.

As the nuns sang, the angels and saints sang with them, unseen and unheard by merely mortal eyes and ears, worshipping the Mystery of Faith in union with the entire Church. And within the great invisible light that shines down into the sanctuary at every Mass, the prayers of the bishop, the nuns, and all the faithful rose up to the Altar of God. And the vows of Sister Mary Anthony Therese went up with them, into the Sacred Heart of Jesus Christ.

* * *

Deep in prayer, Char Fisher knelt in one of the long dark wooden pews in the middle of the Epistle side of the chapel. Sister Anthony's proud family and friends, along with many faithful supporters of the monastery, sat or knelt nearby. Having just received Holy Communion, Char leaned her head on her folded hands, eyes closed, elbows propped on the pew in front of her, making her thanksgiving.

All of a sudden, her head jerked up; her eyes flew open. *Who said that?* Her eyes darted around, looking for the source of the words she had just heard quite distinctly. But no one was paying any attention to her at all. Everyone was praying just like she was. Quickly squeezing her eyes shut again, the intimate question echoed in her brain over and over. Then, stunned, her heart began to pound hypnotically as she realized Who had just spoken to her so plainly, asking her the question that would change her life forever...

"Will you come to Me? I want you for Myself."

Meanwhile, Somewhere in Hell...

He looks like all the rest. ... We've shot him half a dozen times.

– Graham Greene, *The Power and the Glory*

Sidious Dimwitter, ancient demon of the Telemark Cult, his thick, moldy eyebrows lifted, his lipless, toothless mouth hanging open in bewilderment, stared disbelieving at the scene before him. He crouched—vulture-like—as near to Holy Angels Monastery as he dared, in total, dismal shock. Despite his best efforts, he'd been unable to stop the Esperanza girl's vocation. The Mattson boy had married the Fisher girl, and their son Mikel had been—how he hated the thought—*baptized*. In Cleveland, many of the parishes slated for closure had been reopened, and now, at this moment, Mikel's Auntie Char was racing like a woman in love towards the One True Love she could not resist, who, one delightful day, would transform her into a new creation no longer known simply as Char Fisher, but *Sister Charitas of the Holy Spirit*. It was disgusting! Like a falling line of dominoes, the ripple effects of these events would be unstoppable. Souls would be saved. Sinners would be converted! Where had he gone wrong?

Anger, fear, and confusion wiggled strangely across his wrinkled visage, while his demonian brain struggled to simultaneously accept his loss, determine its cause, and escape his certain fate. The rapidity with which the latter circumstance accosted him set him to shivering.

"Imbecile!" A nauseously familiar voice hissed behind him as the scene on Earth he had just witnessed dissolved and transformed into the bleak grayness of the Anteroom of the Archdemon Hagregious, that in-between place where demonic assignments began and ended and rewards and punishments were meted out in miserly, meticulous, malefic detail. Sidious' throat closed in a ghastly, painful swallow.

"Do you realize what you have done? Dungeness Crab Louie!" A leathery black elephantine hand swung around and cuffed him soundly.

"I have failed, Master," Sidious winced and whined from the cold, dirty floor.

"Dextro-meth-orfan! I told you when I gave you this assignment how important it was that the targets be destroyed, did I not?!"

"Yes, Master!"

Another ravaging blow knocked the miserable morb across the shadowy chamber.

"I warned you, when those ugly wenches escaped from your last miserable schemes—that bus ride you cooked up...the motorcycle date...the accident that only injured and failed to *eliminate..."*

"But the tornado, Master, that was good, wasn't it?" Sidious wrung his hands.

"Oxy-cotton, Sidious! The *tornado* was what made them run inside the nunnery, *you fool!"*

Sidious braced himself for another blow.

"I told you, Sss-idiot, did I not, that once she set foot in that annnnnn...annnnn..." GASP! *"an-Gelic place that only the most deceitful of devices could bring them down? And I warned you most carefully, did I not, that your failure to prevent their conversions would be highly cata-stroffic! I did! I did! Oh, yes I did, you phila-malomous vermin!"* the Archdemon began frothing at the mouth.

"I triiedd, Master, but...but..."

"How hard can it be, you oxymoron, to stop an American teenager in the twenty-first century? And silly little girls like that?"

"They weren't as silly as we thought, Master."

Crack! Another blow careened the foolish fiend off the farthest wall, where he fell moaning.

"You should have figured that out, beast!" the Archdemon cried shrieks of piercing anguish. *"You had them for twenty years! How stupid can you be?"* He growled and glowered menacingly.

"Very stupid, Master. Very stupid. *Oh, how stupid I am!"* Sidious knelt on the broken floor tiles and rocked back and forth, protuberant head cradled in his knobby calabash hands.

"Well..." Archdemon Hagregious, Supervisor of Cabalistic Dicalumnies, cracked his golf-ball knuckles and extended his twelve-inch-long fingers with the five-inch-long claws open wide. "They *did* have those *disgusting* creatures of light praying for them. I give you that. But you still could have stolen them away from their influence if only you had tempted them more *fervently!* What was their *fatal flaw,* Sidious? *Did you find it?"*

Sidious tried to recall what Char's and Tia's fatal flaws had been. Flaws they had, but none seemed great enough to overcome them. Their virtues always managed to rise to the top again, like blessed oil in a jar of muddy water. Guiltily the Telemark demon gasped as he struggled to his filthy feet.

"If only she had not met that *Ceeeeelia* wench," he wept, wringing his foul hands. "I *triiiiied,* Master, to keeeeeep them apaaarrrrrt! I *triiiiiied* to destroy their friennndshippp, buuttttt....." Sidious' hollow lifeless voice was elongating strangely so that he sounded like someone speaking at the bottom of a very deep and muddy hole. "Charrrr for-for-for-for..." Simultaneously he coughed and gagged. He simply could not bring himself to say the detestable verb, "forgave."

The Archdemon heaved out a fiery brimstone sigh and slowly paced the coffin-colored floor.

"Never mind that now, Sidious. I should never have given you that assignment. I should have realized it was far beyond your puny, pathetic capabilities. I was going to give you another, but it is far too important for you. I must deal with this myself." Hagregious stopped pacing and brooded morosely.

"What is that, Master?" Sidious' eyes sparkled darkly at the thought of new mischief.

Hagregious considered for a moment and then decided to confide in the lowly wretch.

"I happen to have it on very good authority, Sidious, that a Capuchin mission ppp....ppp...*priest,* who is particularly devoted to the Traditional L-L-L-Latin Mmmmaaa....mmmmaaa...*rite,* is coming to the monastery for an *entire week*! Who *knows* what *good* might come of it? He *must be prevented from doing so at all costs!!!"* The final sentence was punctuated by a piercing shriek of morbid rage that made Sidious cower and shudder even as it made him thrill with evil excitement.

"A car accident, perhaps?" Sidious drooled and rubbed his raw-bone hands with ragged glee.

"Oh can't you come up with anything more original? Fool! This is why, as I said, I will handle this myself." Hagregious carefully wiped the slimy sweat off his leathery Neanderthal forehead. "You may, if you wish, observe and learn, but *stay out of it*! I don't want your silly bumblings to interfere with my plans *this* time. Have I made myself clear, you impotent worm?"

"Yes, Master!" Sidious chewed his ragged nails in shame and disappointment.

The cloven-footed archdemon crawled forlornly across the room, then turned to face the cowering Sidious.

"The problem with Char Fisher and that *Ceeeeeelia* wench—It really wasn't your fault, Sidious. It was that *rosary* businessssss..." he said, hissing and spitting and cursing. *"It's always Her Highness who intercedes and interferes! Oh, how I wish she was..."*

But he never got the chance to finish. A megavolt flash of blue and red lightning knocked them both to the floor, and a painfully bright white light instantly filled the room to overflowing. A great and shining winged being, armored in shimmering silver and armed with a burning sword of golden fire, appeared above them.

Motionless, he read the situation at a micro-glance. The terrified demons painfully whimpered and wept sulfuric acid tears.

"You," the bright being's voice solemnly accused, pointing his powerful finger at the shaking, shivering archdemon. "You spoke *her* name."

The archdemon tried to remain silent, but was compelled and commanded to respond.

"Yes, I — I — she — we —" he stuttered helplessly.

"You said you wished something would *happen* to her."

"Oh! I didn't —"

"Might I ask what that something might be?" the bright being probed without mercy while piercing flames of light flashed blue and gold from his brilliant sword.

"But your Lordship—I mean, your Saintliness! I didn't actually say her name, as you surely must know."

Dead silence. They gazed aghast. Terror filled their empty little chests, and regret gushed from their filthy pores like worms from a subterranean corpse. Time froze in Hell as the leader of angelic armies awaited his command to execute the sentence of the Just One.

Finally addressing Hagregious, he proclaimed:

"Who is like unto GOD? He hereby commands you, vile drachenish: You will not be bound this day. But you will tell the others of your kind what will happen to them if they dare to speak ill of Our Lady. Perhaps their fate will not be so undeserved as yours."

Then Saint Michael the Archangel resheathed his gleaming sword and vanished, and the suffocating darkness enveloped them once again.

Acknowledgments

At the risk of sounding cliché, it takes a village to write a novel. Years ago I asked a young Katie Boutross (now Sister Katherine) and an even younger Kateri Lawless to read what was then a 180-page novel and grade it for teen appeal. Their insightful suggestions resulted in the greatly improved and expanded story you just finished. Kateri's grandma, Mrs. Maryanne Lawless, offered warm encouragement when I was struggling to weave the various plot threads together and figure out how to speak truthfully yet respectfully about the tumultuous changes in the Church over the past fifty years. Later, when the book was nearing completion, Danielle Zimmer stepped up to the plate when I desperately needed a cheerleader and sounding board and got me over the finish line with the first draft. My friend and co-worker Maria Gerber kindly offered to edit it, but was prevented by illness from completing the task. Eagle-eyed Cristina Borges providentially caught several major errors in what I thought was the final, FINAL draft. My deepest gratitude goes out to all of you, and to all the members of the Clear Creek community who have supported me in various ways, great and small, over the years.

Gracias muy especiales to my very dear friend, Robbie Madrid-Hansell, for assistance with the español and for all the fun times at The Caberet in Kerrville. I was always so proud to be seen with the cool and beautiful Madrid twins!

This novel was in the garage and up on jacks when I was hired as a copy editor by Andrew Pudewa, founder and director of the Institute for Excellence in Writing. IEW's writing techniques, which I learned quite inadvertently in the course of my employment there, fortuitously gave me the structural glue to organize and bind a thousand bits of loosely associated anecdotes into something more coherent and readable—a novel! May his personal motto be adopted by all: "Never grow weary in doing good." Thanks, Andrew.

In 2020, that most evil of years, I lost my beloved brother-in-law, Dr. Lawrence Randolph Weill. In 1971, he read the fourteen typewritten pages of what my 12-year-old self imagined to be the beginnings of a novel about a college kid named Perkins. He liked it and said if I enjoyed writing, I should capitalize on it. I had to ask him what "capitalize" meant, but that didn't matter. What mattered was that he believed in my ability to write, and he urged me to write more. No one else ever had. I wish he were still alive to read the result. (Never pass up the opportunity to encourage a child. You have no idea what it may lead to.)

Lastly, the person most directly responsible for helping me persevere with this protracted writing project would probably prefer his name not be associated with it, so in prudence and charity he shall remain nameless. But you know who you are. And so does Our Lord. *Deo gratias!*

For More Information

For more information on the stunning relic collection at Saint Anthony's Chapel in Pittsburgh, Pennsylvania, please visit saintanthonyschapel.org.

There are many websites with information about traditional religious vocations, including religiouslife.org and CMSWR.org. ReligiousMinistries.org has a listing of every single community in the United States! You can also check the website for your diocese for listings of religious communities in your area.

About the Author

Julie Ash is a graduate of Montana State University. A native of Southern California, Julie is a Benedictine oblate of Clear Creek Abbey and resides in Oklahoma within earshot of the Abbey bells. *In the Palace of the Great King* is her first, and most likely will be her last, novel. (Then again, one never knows.) Please visit her website at julieash.com.

Notes

1. Chapter 1 epigraph, Ernest Dowson, "Nuns of the Perpetual Adoration." *In Praise of Nuns, An Anthology of Verse*, James M. Hayes, ed., Books for Libraries Press by arrangement with E.P. Dutton & Co., Plainview, New York (1942, 1973), p. 43.

2. Chapter 2, "Profiles of a Cyrenean: Girl disappointed in love." *Collected Poems of Karol Wojtila* (Pope Saint John Paul II), translated from the Polish by Jerzy Peterkiewicz. Libreria Editrice Vaticana, Vatican City, and Random House (1979), p. 80.

3. Chapters 7 and 16, "Song of the Hidden God: Shores of Silence," *id.*, pp. 5, 15.

4. Chapters 3, 8, 13, 17, 25, 30, 33, 35, 37 and 41, *Contemplative Nuns Speak,* Bernard Bro, OP. Translated by Isabel and Florence McHugh. Helicon Press, 1964. pp. 42, 47, 51, 55, 152, 153, 167, 232.

5. Chapter 4, "Who Has Seen the Wind?" by Christina Rossetti. Public domain.

6. Chapter 5, Vita consecrata (The Consecrated Life). Apostolic Letter of Pope John Paul II, Vatican, March 25, 1996.

7. Chapter 6, Saint Teresa of Kolkata (Calcutta) quote, https://www.brainyquote.com/ quotes/mother_teresa_106501. Accessed July 1, 2021.

8. Chapter 9, "Famous last words: A martyr of the bloody Cristero War forgives his persecutors." Peterson, Larry, Aleteia, January 15, 2017. https://aleteia.org/2017/01/15/famous-last-words-a-martyr-of-the-bloody-cristero-war-forgives-his-persecutors. Accessed July 1, 2021.

9. Chapter 10, J.R.R. Tolkien, "On Fairy-Stories" in *Tree and Leaf*. Allen & Unwin, 1964.

10. Chapter 18, Parente, Pascal. *The Angels: In Catholic Teaching and Tradition*. TAN Books, 1994.

11. Chapter 19, "I Visit Carmel." Sister Mary Madaleva Wolff, C.S.C. *In Praise of Nuns, An Anthology of Verse, id.*, p. 199.

12. Chapter 21, Mother Mary Francis, P.C.C. *A Right to Be Merry*. Ignatius Press, 2001.

13. Chapter 22, Padre Pio's *Letters Vol. III*, "Correspondence with his Spiritual Daughters (1915-1923)"1st edition (English version), Fr. Alessio Parente, O.F.M. Cap., Editor; Edizioni Padre Pio da Pietrelcina, Our Lady of Grace Capuchin Friary, San Giovanni Rotondo, Italy, 1994, translated by Geraldine Nolan.

14. Chapter 23, *Autobiography of St. Margaret Mary.* Translated by the Sisters of the Visitation, Partridge Green, TAN Books, 2012.

15. Chapter 24, Audrey Hepburn quote. Brainyquote.com. https://www.brainyquote.com/ quotes/audrey_hepburn_394440. Accessed July 1, 2021.

16. Chapter 29, "To a Nun Violinist." Sister Mary Louise, a Presentation Nun of San Francisco. *In Praise of Nuns, An Anthology of Verse, id.,* p. 194.

17. Chapter 32, excerpts transcribed from the audio tour of St. Anthony's Chapel in Pittsburgh, Pennsylvania, used with permission. https://saintanthonyschapel.org, 2019.

18. Chapter 34, "Why Be a Catholic?" by Fr. Bernard Vaughan, S.J. in "The Truth About Catholics," 3rd edition. O'Donnell, Peter. Catholic Literature Society, Los Angeles, 1954, p. 5.

19. Chapter 36, Praying with Louise de Marillac, Gibson and Kneaves, 72, cited at https://www.catholiccharitiesusa.org/ prayers_reflections/feast-of-st-louise-de-marillac. Accessed July 1, 2021.

20. Chapter 36, Saint Teresa of Kolkata, https://www. goodreads.com/quotes/106242-if-you-can-t-feed-a-hundred-people-feed-just-one. Accessed July 1, 2021.

21. Chapter 39, Saint Teresa of Kolkata, https://www.ewtn.com/ motherteresa/vocationofservice.asp. Accessed July 1, 2021.

22. Postscript epigraph. Graham Greene, *The Power and the Glory,* William Heinemann Ltd., London, 1940.

"A Palace of Priceless Worth"

And now let us imagine that we have within us a palace of priceless worth, built entirely of gold and precious stones—a palace, in short, fit for so great a Lord. Imagine that it is partly your doing that this palace should be what it is—and this is really true, for there is no building so beautiful as a soul that is pure and full of virtues, and, the greater these virtues are, the more brilliantly do the stones shine. Imagine that within the palace dwells this great King, Who has vouchsafed to become your Father and Who is seated upon a throne of supreme price— namely, your heart.

Saint Teresa of Avila
The Way of Perfection